THE WAR ONGOING
—KNIGHTFALL—

Copyright © 2024 by Corey J Davis

All rights reserved.

No part of this publication may be reproduced, distributed, or transmitted in any form or by any means, including photocopying, recording, or other electronic or mechanical methods, without the prior written permission of the publisher, except as permitted by U.S. copyright law. For permission requests, contact [include publisher/author contact info].

The story, all names, characters, and incidents portrayed in this production are fictitious. No identification with actual persons (living or deceased), places, buildings, and products is intended or should be inferred.

Book Cover by Corey J Davis

Illustrations by Corey J Davis

First Edition 2024

First edit by Lauren M Davis

Second Edit by Peggy Jones

Final/Master Edit By Aly Eilers

Thank you to my family who has supported me every step along the way. Mom, Dad, Sami, Lauren, Abbi, Luna and Wynter I love you!
And another thank you to Everyone who helped fund this project via crowd funding. With out you this dream of mine would have been so much harder.

Contents

Content Warning		VIII
1.	Prologue:	3
2.	Chapter 1	9
3.	Chapter 2	13
4.	Chapter 3	21
5.	Chapter 4	29
6.	Chapter 5	41
7.	Chapter 6	51
8.	Chapter 7	57
9.	Chapter 8	67
10.	Chapter 9	75
11.	Chapter 10	85
12.	Chapter 11	91
13.	Chapter 12	101
14.	Chapter 13	109
15.	Chapter 14	121
16.	Chapter 15	129
17.	Chapter 16	137
18.	Chapter 17	143

19. Chapter 18   151
20. Chapter 19   159
21. Chapter 20   165
22. Chapter 21   175
23. Chapter 22   183
24. Chapter 23   191
25. Chapter 24   201
26. Chapter 25   207
27. Chapter 26   217
28. Chapter 27   225
29. Chapter 28   235
30. Chapter 29   241
31. Chapter 30   249
32. Chapter 31   263
33. Chapter 32   271
34. Chapter 33   279
35. Chapter 34   285
36. Chapter 35   293
37. Chapter 36   299
38. Chapter 37   305
39. Chapter 38   315
40. Chapter 39   323
41. Chapter 40   333
42. Chapter 41   341
43. Chapter 42   349
44. Chapter 43   355

45.	Chapter 44	361
46.	Chapter 45	369
47.	Chapter 46	377
48.	Chapter 47	383
49.	Chapter 48	393
50.	Epilogue:	403

Content Warning

You are about to enter the world of The War Ongoing Saga. In this first installment, you will experience a high octane science fiction and fantasy adventure designed for the modern age. A tale filled with relationships forged through tragedy and triumph that is intended for a **mature audience.** Within its pages, there are scenes depicting scenes of **violence, adult language, addiction, abuse, mental illness and manipulation**. Readers who may be sensitive to these subjects should proceed with caution. With that in consideration I, Corey J Davis, welcome you to the great land of Grandiose.

PROLOGUE
THE
MAN IN THE BAR

Prologue:
The Man in the Bar

Rain falls across the kingdom of Grandhaven. The streets are quiet, uncommon for this time of year. A young Dargone woman stumbles and falls to the cold, damp ground, eyes wide, searching the night for help. Her clothes are tattered, and her cold, reptilian skin is so tightly wrapped around her bones that anyone could tell she hasn't eaten for days. Her tail is bruised from top to bottom, and her hands are worn and bloody. She is on her last leg.

Finally, she sees a bar in the distance. She can hear the bustling of men as they cheer and drink themselves into oblivion, not a care in the world. Walking closer, she finds a sign that reads, *"HUMANS ONLY."* She knows the consequences of going in but has no choice: here or nowhere.

She enters the bar, and all the fun and laughter stops. Every eye turns to look at her: many in anger, but others in confusion.

"Please help me," she pleads. "Somebody took my child. I fear it might be poachers." Despite her appeals, no one turns to help. Instead, they all continue to stare, and she notices the tension continuing to build in the room. She stumbles to the bar, begging anyone who will listen for help.

"Please...anyone...it has been days! What if he's dead?" she continues. The bartender turns away while three young knights approach her from behind. For the citizens of Grandhaven, these black-clad soldiers symbolize hope; however, for outsiders like herself, it's a different story. Their pristine armor illustrates their recent graduation from the Academy, and their stench hints that they have been celebrating for hours. More importantly, their eyes scare her most. One look, and she can sense that they have the worst intentions. But what choice did she have?

"Please...good men, as protectors of this land, please...I beg of you, help me!" The Dargone mother's request only leads to the knights snickering in her face.

"Ha! Aye mate, the rumors must be true," one of the knights sneers at the other. "These overgrown lizards must have brains the size of peanuts."

"They are as dumb as they are ugly! Can't even read the damn sign outside," the other replies back. A third knight steps up to put his arms around his comrades.

"C'mon, lads, aren't we the great knights of Grandiose? We're here to assist this fine young lady," he mocks before gripping her by the shoulder tightly. Then, he pulls her back off the bar. Stumbling down, she realizes that this was a mistake. She catches herself right before hitting the cold stone floor, just to be pushed to the ground forcefully by another knight. The bar erupts in laughter, all except one man.

The young knights pull and shove the young Dargone woman back toward the front of the bar until she is kicked through the door fiercely. Bruised and even more bloody than before, she tries to escape back into the cover of the night, but one of the knights stops her.

"You know, it's bad enough your kind live on our streets unwelcomed...but then you have the nerve to come into our bar...and beg us to find your little mutt," he drunkenly slurs.

His comrade steps up, continuing, "To be honest with ya, I hope the damned thing is dead...roasted up good in someone's belly."

The third knight comes forward, unsheathing his sword. "I think we should do the world a favor and make sure she doesn't make another one anytime soon," he says, laughing.

They surround her with their blades drawn. The first knight pulls back, preparing to swing his sword, when the blade is suddenly yanked from his hand. The knights turn to see who dared to interfere with their business, and there stands the man from the bar – the only one who chose not to find pleasure in the Dargone woman's misfortune.

She could see now that he, too, is a knight. However, he is much unlike the others: his armor is worn with a single cape draped from his shoulder, his blade stained with battle, and his hands scarred from years of service. Yet even with his hard exterior, he glistens in the night, standing heroically before them. Looking upon him, she finally recognizes him as Sir Nolan of Riverhaven, a legend among knights.

"I may be mistaken but I don't remember the knight's oath saying anything about executing those in need," Sir Nolan says with a smile. The three young knights turn toward him, enraged.

Two knights immediately recognize the champion, but their belligerent comrade yells, "Who the hell do you think you are?" His friends grip their swords cowardly, not wanting to abandon the third.

"From the look of your gear," Nolan jokes as he moves closer to the men, "I'd guess that I am your superior." Playing with the sword he'd taken, he smiles, adding, "But if an introduction is necessary, I'll gladly oblige. I am Sir Nolan, the Steel Fist knight of Riverhaven, first of my name, and Squad leader of the one thousand and ninety-sixth platoon," he declares with such passion that – just for a moment – the rain stopped to take notice.

Nolan's showmanship does nothing to defuse the now-disarmed man; instead, his drunken rage rises to another level. He steps toward Nolan, making his intention clear.

"I don't give shit if you're the fucking King! Give me my damn sword back!" the young man erupts as he swings his fist towards Sir Nolan's head. Without hesitation, Nolan dodges the attack. The young knight continues swinging wildly while Nolan evades each one.

The Dargone woman watches on, amazed, knowing she should take this moment to flee; however, she is mesmerized by Nolan's heroism. Her heart races as he moves through the rain like a fish gliding through the ocean. The grace of his movement is only outdone by his rugged beauty. This man is the hero she envisioned encountering when she entered that bar, instead of the three hate-filled knights before her now.

The young knight finally steps back from his attack, winded. His anger has boiled over, and he knows he is outmatched, but his pride won't allow him to retreat.

"What the hell are you two doing?" he cries over his shoulder towards the other knights. "Get off your asses and attack him!"

The two hesitate, knees shaking, and the sweat from their palms running down their blades. As they inch closer, they understand their mistake, but whether it be drunken pride or youthful ignorance, they attack anyway. Nolan releases the confiscated weapon from his grasp, and, for the first time since arriving, the smile on his face disappears.

"And here, I had hoped you wouldn't need my fists to teach you this lesson in humility," Nolan says, switching to a fighting stance. With lightning speed, his fist makes contact with the disarmed knight. In the same motion, he sweeps the legs of the second. Before his body can even hit the ground, Nolan knocks the third knight's weapon from his grasp. The first knight stumbles to the ground, blood flowing from his nose. He watches on as Nolan makes fools of his friends. Taking both knights by the hand, Nolan simultaneously breaks a finger on each of the two men's hands with a loud snap before tossing them to the side of their bloodied comrade.

Standing over the young men, Nolan rebukes, "Allow your broken bones to be a reminder of the oath you took to protect the inhabitants of this world, not just the ones you deem fit!".

"You're a bloody monster.... just like that lizard whore!" the bloodied, instigating knight bellows, grimacing from the pain of his broken nose. "You're gonna regret taking the side of that immigrant over your own kind." He gathers the other two and starts to retreat, but before running into the cover of the night, he turns and exclaims, *"It's bastards like you that are ruining Grandiose!"*

Nolan walks over to the Dargone woman, a smile returning to his face. He helps her to her feet, wiping the mud from her face, and says serenely, "Do not let the ignorance of those young men allow you to lose faith in humanity."

"Please sir...my son...he's missing. Please help..." the Dargone woman breathed, each word followed by a cough. As Sir Nolan walks alongside her down the road, her legs give out, but he quickly catches her before she hits the ground.

"Easy now, you're hurt. Let's not make things worse," he says again, helping her to her feet. "My squad and I apprehended a group of poachers earlier this morning, and among their captives is a young Dargone boy. Please, let me take you to him," Nolan reassures her. Knowing her son is safe and waiting, she lays her head on Nolan's chest. Her tears begin to fall as the rain clears, the night sky shining brightly as they continue down the streets of Grandhaven.

"I can not thank you enough! But...won't there be repercussions for helping someone like me?" she asks.

Nolan looks her in the eyes, his smile growing wider as he explains,

"I am a knight of the great land Grandiose, and I took an oath to serve all of its kind equally. Trust me, fair lady: I'll be fine."

CHAPTER 1
THE
HANGING

Chapter 1

The Hanging

It is mid-spring in the Kingdom of Grandhaven, the largest human-inhabited city on the continent of Grandiose. The streets are full of hustle and bustle. The historical architecture is now complemented by its sister city's Quartz Applied Science Technologies, Q.A.S Tech for the common tongue. This recent hybrid of magic-infused gemstones and modern science has ushered in a new age of man: now, mechanical steeds pull carts across the land, the streets are filled with light during twilight, and the houses never grow cold, no matter the season. The citizens have never felt more secure, for its armies now wield weapons that rival even the oldest of magic. The city is at peace – or it would be, but today, a knight hangs.

"On this day, we put down a dishonored knight!" the executioner exclaims, the crowd of citizens growing larger. "Once an outstanding member of this city, Nolan of Riverhaven chose an outsider over his own kind!"

Nolan lifts his head slightly, the chain around his neck tightening. Looking out across the masses, he sees many cursing angrily and others weeping in sadness. He bears the pain just long enough to scan over the crowd again, hoping to lay eyes on the squad members he'll leave behind.

"Three young knights were left crippled due to his insistence to help the animals that live on our street illegally," rallies the executioner. "Let his liberal ways die with him on this podium! The rattling of his chains echoing through our streets will be a reminder to those not welcome here that they should stay in the shadows!" The executioner continues, and Nolan finally finds his comrades amidst the sea of chaos.

He locks eyes with Liam, "The Lightning Spear," a grizzled knight late in his years and Nolan's oldest ally. While his physique is that of a man a third his age, his silver beard and battle-worn eyes tell a different tale. He proudly wears an older style knight's armor, one passed down by his former commander, with silver metals contrasting beautifully off his warm, bronze skin. Nolan easily spots him in the crowd, smirking as he remembers their countless arguments over Liam refusing to update his ratty armor to the current model. Finally, they had come to the compromise that Liam would update his steed, spear, and one ceremonial shoulder plate instead.

Nolan's squad deputy, Marcus Lee, stands next to Liam. His tan skin pulled taut over his chiseled jaw, and his brow lowered in anger. Although the mastery of his sword led to his high ranking, his ostentatious nature made him a black sheep amongst his peers. Watching, Nolan can tell that he is holding his tongue – wanting to burst at the audacity before him – but he doesn't. Almost as if a final thank you to his squad commander, Marcus stays calm, not wanting to tarnish Nolan's legacy further.

Lastly, his eyes rest on Helena Blank, a fair-skinned, violet-eyed wonder. A mystery to others, she is Nolan's pride and joy. The first time they met, he was a stubborn young knight with no future ahead of him, and she was a young girl with nowhere to go. Without the responsibility of raising her, he would have never matured into the man who once garnered such praise. He would like to think that, without him, she would have never made it into the knight's Academy, but her bowmanship far outclasses anyone he has ever seen: a prodigy in her own right.

"Nolan of Riverhaven, traitor to the kingdom of Grandiose," the executioner belts out into the crowd, waking Nolan from his reminiscence. "Dare you have any words before we send you to Hell?"

Nolan stays quiet, putting his head down, as the executioner pulls a level. Before he can drop to the gallows, Nolan lifts his head one last time, smiling as he glances at his squadron and whispers,

"We will be alright."

CHAPTER 2
THE
LEFT BEHIND

Chapter 2

The Left Behind

As the streets clear underneath the amber sunset, Nolan's comrades settle in by the fire outside the place he used to call home. This space has always been a safe haven for the three: small yet comfortable. Memorabilia from past adventures hangs along the wood walls, a constant reminder of how close they all had been. Once filled with livestock, the stables now only house Hornet, a sizable mechanical hound that Liam proudly rides into battle. This place that once enveloped them in immense joy now pierces their aching hearts.

"It is all bullshit, you know," Marcus says, staring out into the night sky. "Nolan is – was – far from the first person to get into a scuffle with another knight."

"You're living proof of that," Helena interjects.

"Exactly! Yet I'm still here with my neck in one piece," Marcus vents before sitting down by the fire, the *unlike Nolan* strangled in his throat. Angrily, he continues, "And before long, he's gonna be fucking Crow food. How disgraceful is that? The man puts his life on the line for years and saves countless others. Now, this."

He puts his head down and finally empties the tears he's held back, choking out in a barely audible whisper, "Why the hell him, out of all of us? Why him?" Liam and Helena are taken aback at his brokenness, as Marcus has always displayed an audacious, though somewhat reckless, persona.

Liam gets up, sitting beside his sniffling friend. "Wipe those tears away, boy," he says gruffly while comforting Marcus. "Nolan prepared us for this. Even before that bastardization of a trial, he taught us that no knight's journey lasts forever. 'One day we'll all wake not to sleep again' and all that shit. Now, it's up to us to apply all we have learned from him in the next chapter of our lives."

"Chapters that don't include each other…" Helena whispers.

Marcus wipes the tears from his face, looking over at Helena. While he's always thought her beautiful, the moonlight highlights her features further, and he stares at her in awe. Suddenly, he is struck with guilt: while he and Liam may have lost a friend, Helena just lost her only family – and before long, she'll lose them too.

This time, Marcus breaks the silence. "Liam's right: the time for mourning is over! While the world may not want to honor his greatness, we can – the only way Nolan would want us to. Celebrate!"

Helena and Liam roll their eyes at each other, but Marcus grabs the jug of beer, pouring everyone a drink. His overenthusiastic mask was back in place, but tonight, that energy is welcomed – if only to distract from such a gloomy day. Raising his glass, he exclaims, "Let's raise a glass to the greatest knight Grandiose has ever seen, a man who could split a stone with a single punch, a man who turned a smart ass into a deputy–"

"A man who gave this old fart an ass whooping every time we sparred," Liam interjects, smiling, and then downs his beer.

"A man so gorgeous the Academy deemed him a distraction for both the women's dormitory and the men's," Marcus jests, filling Liam's glass once more. Attempting to break Helena from her sadness, he jumps to her side, pulling her close. Continuing his elaborate toast, he exaggerates, "A man who once dined with a bearturtle to claim it as his steed," finally earning a smile from Helena.

"A man they say captured the fiercest Dargone, only to let it free in exchange for an apple," Helena snarks, reluctantly joining Marcus' antics.

"Attagirl!" Marcus proclaims, clinking his glass with hers. He lifts his drink to the sky, pausing momentarily and hoping Nolan can hear them, wherever he may be. "To the man I'm happy to call friend," Marcus says calmly, and a tear once again rolls down his cheek.

"To the man I'd join on any battlefield, here or in the afterlife," Liam proudly claims, raising his glass as well.

"To the man I'll always call brother," Helena says solemnly, finishing the trifecta of drinks.

"To Nolan of Riverhaven!" they all cry into the night. Together, they drink the evening away, sharing stories of the past and honoring their fallen friend.

Before long, the sun rises. As usual, Liam awakens before the others, beginning the day as he has every other before. Methodically, he cleans his armor; with its origins from a different era, it requires a delicate hand to keep all the antique ridges and nooks clean. Next, he sharpens his spear. Unlike his armor, the spear is modern, built with contemporary tech, donning a slick and tactical design more similar to Helena's and Marcus' armor. The Q.A.S. Tech glints in the light like the lifeblood of the weapon, coursing up and down its edges. Once his armor and spear are in prime condition, Liam works with Hornet. His morning maintenance has become a highlight of Hornet's day, as it often culminates in a wrestling match with Liam.

With his morning tasks behind him, Liam realizes Marcus and Helena are still fast asleep, spread out on the floor where they passed out the night before. He or Nolan would typically wake them – only to scold them for wasting the morning away – but not today. Liam instead takes this independent time to reflect, deciding that he and Hornet would enjoy a bath at the nearby hot spring, a pastime he would often enjoy with Nolan on their scarce days off.

Arriving at the springs, Liam notices that a handful of others have the same idea. Yet he knows that his company will not last long; whether Hornet's menacing size or the gruesome scars revealed upon removing his robe dissuades the crowd, everyone has left by the time Liam enters the water. Washing the dirt away in the hot water of the springs, Liam is reminded of Dakuhm, the desert kingdom home to the mighty Dargone people and where he and Nolan first met.

Nolan was only a rookie then, and his squadron had been called in to assist with a group of bandits harassing the locals. Immediately, their chemistry, both on and off the battlefield, meant that he and Liam spent just as much time enjoying the exotic cuisine as they did putting an end to the hordes of thieves. During their many nights at the bars, Nolan would joke that Liam would be the first person he'd have by his side the moment he was promoted. At the time, Liam brushed off Nolan's claims. Then, almost a decade later, Liam would indeed be transferred to Nolan's squadron.

Shaking himself out of the memories, Liam sighs, continuing to bathe while Hornet watches over from the bank. Before long, he realizes it is time to move on, both from the spring and with life itself.

Liam packs up and readies himself to return to the house. As they travel, he tells Hornet, "If those two aren't up by now, you have permission to eat them for breakfast." Understanding Liam's antics, Hornet rubs her head on Liam's shoulder playfully. Liam has always marveled at how Hornet is both mechanical and lifelike simultaneously. The relationship he developed with her results in a comfort and kindness that he reserves for few others.

Suddenly, Hornet's demeanor changes: her playfulness is gone, and she snarls into the distance. Liam grabs his spears from Hornet's side, anticipating a threat. Reassuringly, he pets her head and whispers, "Steady, girl."

Over the horizon, a prominent figure appears, and as it grows closer, Liam recognizes Isaac Callahan, "The Bone Butcher." Callahan leads the First Squad, King Whitelion's private guard. Unlike the standard black armor, Callahan's is bone white. The Q.A.S Tech illuminates the trim of his armor, and the red glow that emanates from it is meant to intimidate his enemies before they even come face-to-face with him. While his silhouette is fearsome in its own right, his steed, Moses, inspires fear with every explosive roar. The massive mechanical battlecat is known for his fierceness, often taking out enemies with or without Callahan on his back.

Callahan approaches Liam, a notable tension filling the air. Liam grips his spear, internally questioning why Callahan would leave the castle walls to speak to him. Finally, Callahan stops and dismounts as both Hornet and Moses growl at each other. Before moving closer, Callahan makes a show of sporting his shield, a legendary weapon dubbed "The Iron Guillotine." This massive metal slab has often removed a head with brute force, even without a blade. The shield is elegant in its simplicity and flawless in every way except for a single slash across its face.

"Still haven't scrapped that dirty mutt, thief?" Callahan questions calmly, his mouth quirking to the side. Liam notices and ignores his baiting.

"Still haven't repaired the Guillotine, I see," Liam responds, casually pointing his spear at the shield. Callahan's nostrils flare as he is enraged by the callous reminder that Liam had managed to mar the face of his weapon.

Callahan surges forward, his breath hot on Liam's face as he grunts, "It's a reminder of debts yet to be paid." The knight is one of the few men who match Liam in size so that he can glare straight into Liam's eyes. Ethnically different, they are otherwise identical, save for Callahan's large, golden beard: a stark contrast to Liam's silver. Still, both are grizzled war veterans who are respected - if not feared - among their peers. Yet their immensely different upbringings divided them, developing a bitter rivalry rather than a fierce friendship.

"Are you here to collect?" Liam rebuts.

Taking a deep breath, Callahan retreats, removing his shield and forcefully impaling the ground with it, a thud echoing around them. Then, he pulls a document from his armor, the royal seal glinting in the sunlight.

"Not today, thief. I bring words from your King," Callahan gripes, handing the paper to Liam.

"Our reassignments, I presume," Liam says, spiking his spear into the earth, and a thunderous crack rolls across the field. Callahan picks up his shield as he opens the seal and mounts Moses.

"Your foolishness never fails to impress me," Callahan laughs. Circling them, he laughs as he continues, "You honestly think I'd personally deliver something so trivial?"

Slowly, he unfolds and reads over the letter but is struck by confusion as he takes in its contents. "A summoning...for a private audience with King Uther?" Liam calls out, failing to hide his surprise.

"Precisely, and if you or either of those insects you call comrades don't show up," Callahan shouts, "I will be back to settle our debt, thief." Before Liam can argue, the knight's shape fades back into the horizon.

Liam scans over the letter again before the gravity of the situation slaps him in the face. He folds it up, then plucks the spear from the ground and loads it onto Hornet before he mounts her. As he rides back to the house, he lifts his head to the sky and says:

"Nolan, I hope you're watching over us. I fear our darkest days are still ahead."

CHAPTER 3
THE
THE LION'S CASTLE

Chapter 3

The Lion's Castle

"Hmm, I thought it would be bigger," Marcus says as he, Helena, and Liam look up at the massive castle walls a few hours after Callahan had delivered the summons. The irony of his statement is not lost on them, though neither laugh. Together, they approach the castle gates, presenting the King's letter to the guards. After reviewing the document, the guard regards Marcus' blade with glee but sternly proclaims, "No weapons beyond the castle gates."

Assuming he's being singled out due to his reputation, Marcus rolls his eyes and complies. Forcefully, he hands his sword to the guard. Delighted, the guard takes the weapon, eyes gleaming, then unsheathes it. The sword is stunning in design, with its razor-thin blade and hilt infused with Q.A.S Tech, allowing it to fire swiftly across the battlefield and be called back to Marcus' hand.

"I'd put her away if I were you. She has a habit of removing the hands of the inexperienced," Marcus teases the guard.

His mesmerized gaze breaks, and he looks back at the comrades. "Yours too," the guard says to Liam and Helena. Marcus stifles a laugh while the guard fumbles to sheathe his sword.

Liam stabs his spear into the ground directly in front of the guard's feet, and he quickly leaps back, but awe resurfaces in his features.: Liam's spear is legendary. Its handle is wrapped in fine leather, and the spearhead is amplified with a Q.A.S Tech motor that allows Liam to electrify the blade.

Helena follows, removing her collapsible bow from her back. She snaps it open, the sound startling the guard from his unbroken stare at Liam's spear. Compared to the other weapons, the bow is unimpressive and plain. As the guard inspects it, though, his eyes widen. Unlike the others, this bow is a product entirely of science, formed of the same black steel as a knight's armor. At its center rests a blue gemstone with an attached pull string that, when released, emits a piercing funnel of arctic air that crystallizes its target upon impact.

She gently hands her bow to the guard. Smiling sweetly, she says, "Please excuse my comrades' brutish ways, but we are running late."

"Understood, my lady," he responds, then calls for the gates to be opened. Formally, he explains, "Commander Callahan will be waiting at the castle door to escort you to King Uther's chambers."

As the three knights enter through the opened gate, they take in the largest manufactured building in all of Grandiose. Watching over the kingdom, Castle Whitelion is a towering citadel constructed entirely of ivory. This castle alone houses a third of Grandhaven's population, all working as the King's caretakers or personal guards. Although the streets of Grandhaven are far from despicable, they pale in comparison to the near utopia within the castle walls. Pathways are paved in marble, trees all bear luscious fruit, and multiple fountains glisten while children play in the perfectly maintained meadows.

"Must be nice to live in paradise," Marcus muttered, glancing at the children.

"Paradise? Looks more like a cage to me," Helena scoffs.

Incredulous, Marcus questions, "Cage? If this is a cage, feel free to lock me up!" He continues, "Look around, Helena. These children will grow up never knowing the pains of the world; never will they have to wonder whether their father will make it home tonight or if their mother made enough at the brothel to put bread on the table. Hell, even the crumbs of a king here are better than what many others have out there."

"Maybe they won't know the pain," Helena replies, "Yet they will never know the beauty of the world, either. They will be raised within these walls, told they can never leave, and, when their parents pass on, they will take their place. It's a circle, an endless cycle." She sighs, and the weight of the words hangs heavy between them. Marcus doesn't know why, but he senses they hold more meaning to her.

"Just imagine a life where we never got to see the Academy cherry blossoms in Springhaven," she explains, and her face lights up at the memory, "Or even the dirt and grime within the mines of New Haven, never smelling the ocean off the shores of Riverhaven. Besides, what about the wonder of the Nest or the golden sand of Dakuhm? This world has so much more to offer than just pain."

She looks up to the sky in wonder before saying, "You're right, Marcus: these childrens' bellies will never go empty, but they will be starving for a world they will never know."

She hasn't met their gazes, but Marcus and Liam still see her eyes fill with tears, and she blinks quickly to try and hide them. Their group had been together for years, but neither she nor Nolan had ever shared anything about her childhood. Her mysteriousness had always been matched only by her beauty. Liam gently places his hand on her shoulder and smiles once her eyes find his. Helena wipes the wetness from her eyes before returning the gesture.

They approach the castle where Callahan stands, arms crossed and waiting, silhouetted against a huge stone doorway. Upon closer look, they could see the legends of the Whitelion family engraved into its exterior, from the founding of Grandhaven to the battle of Springhaven.

Callahan's eyes survey Liam and Marcus with apparent disdain, only recognizing them with a grunt. Then, though, he offers, "Good evening, Ms. Helena, a pleasure as always."

"The pleasure is ours, Commander Callahan," Helena replies, a proper greeting. To her side, Marcus rolls his eyes and begins a snide retort, but Callahan is already opening the door.

As he escorts them through the castle foyer, the comrades take in the luxuriousness of the palace. From top to bottom, the walls are filled with the most ornate tapestries; the marble floors are polished so brightly they can nearly see their reflections; lifesize busts flank the entrance. Beyond, the royal marketplace sits at the end of the hallway. Servants, lords, and elite merchants litter the castle's chancery, fine eateries, and various regal establishments. This illustrious foyer has become known as the Lion's Den, a section exclusively accessible to the privileged of Grandhaven. Once, a massive spiral staircase that led to the royal family's living quarters commanded the center of the space, but with the rise of Q.A.S Tech, a motorized lift stands in its place.

Nearly every socialite they pass stops and stares. Honestly, the comrades don't blame them; for these people to see any knights other than royal guards enter the Lion's Den is almost unheard of. Even more so, their affiliation with Nolan has made Marcus, Helena, and Liam somewhat famous. Marcus clenches his fist as he hears them whisper amongst themselves,

"Aren't they the knights who's leader went rogue?"

"They must be criminals too, if we're lucky King Uther will take them out as well."

"How dare they let such vermin in the Den!"

"Oh how joyous, it seems as if we will be enjoying another hanging soon."

Before Marcus can grind out a retort to the crowd, Callahan looks back, saying, "Hold your tongue, boy. They are assholes – every one of them – but they answer to no one except the King. So, for once, holster your temper before they shut that mouth for you." His tone is anything but pleasant, yet Callahan's words manage to calm Marcus, mainly because he realizes that Callahan is right. This foyer hosts the heads of many of Grandhaven's underbelly; without hesitation, they could make anyone disappear – even a knight.

They reach the lift, where two Royal knights stand guard. Seeing Callahan, they open the doors immediately, then stand in salute. Liam scoffs under his breath at the gesture. The guards close the doors once everyone is inside the lift, and at the press of a button, it begins to rise.

"Once we arrive at the top floor, I will seat you in the hall where you will wait for King Uther," Callahan orders. "Unfortunately, another cargo shipment has been attacked, thus promoting an emergency Council meeting."

"The Terra King?" Helena asks.

"We believe so, but no confirmation at this time," Callahan replies.

Liam inquires, "By any chance, would that be the purpose of our summoning?"

"I am not at liberty to say. Yet I seriously doubt the King would send one thief after another," Callahan counters with contempt. Marcus places a hand on Liam's shoulder, silently stopping him before he can respond.

When the lift finally stops and the doors open, the comrades gaze wondrously at the most beautiful view of Grandhaven imaginable. The royal chamber's hall is plated in glass – something the first King Whitelion took great pride in, saying it allowed him to watch over the people of Grandhaven without obstruction. The chamber also held strategic value, allowing the royal family to see far past the kingdom's gates into the horizon of Grandiose so that a surprise attack would be near impossible.

Callahan breaks them from their gaze, leading them to where they would wait for the King until after the emergency Council meeting Callahan had mentioned in the lift. "Once we are finished, I will come back and escort you to the King's office. However, if you move from this spot, I have ordered my men to remove you," Callahan barks before smiling crudely and adding, "By force if necessary."

Marcus, Liam, and Helena glare as he strides down the hall, approaching a marble door trimmed with gold. Again, two knights stand guard, and again, they salute Callahan before kneeling. A small, Elderly man answers Callahan's knock on the door. Large bifocals obstruct the man's face from the sitting knights, but his ivory lab coat gives away his identity. He is Red Regalia: head adviser to the King and eldest son of the Regalia family. Red is one of Grandiose's lead scientists, second only to his younger brother, Black Regalia, King of New Haven. Together, they single-handedly invented the Q.A.S system that now powers most of the country.

Callahan and Red exchange a few words before Callahan enters the room, the door closing behind them. More quickly than expected, they emerge from the room a few minutes later, this time followed by a tall woman shrouded in a gold-hooded robe that covers her from head to toe. Finally, King Uther Whitelion IV – the King of Kings – enters the hall.

The King's presence demands attention. He towers over the average man – and while no one would call Liam or Sir Callahan "average," the King stands almost eye-to-eye with both of them, and he is still as intimidating as either. For a man who has never seen battle, he is undoubtedly built like a warrior; his royal garments cannot hide his physique, a perfect mix of strength and agility. His midnight skin is flawless, radiating as the sun bounces off it, and his braided mohawk, decorated with embedded golden clips, drapes down his back. A near perfectly trimmed beard defines his chiseled jaw, but Uther's full lips, accentuated by his pristine mustache, are what women fantasize about most.

As the knights and nobility walk together towards the Council meeting, King Uther looks over to the group, his dark brown eyes piercing yet hauntingly inviting. For many, gazing upon him is like seeing a god.

"Is that them, Sir Callahan?" Uther asks in a deep baritone voice. Callahan looks to where he had just seated the three comrades, then lowers his head and whispers,

"Indeed, your sheep for slaughter."

CHAPTER 4
THE
COUNCIL

Chapter 4

The Council

"As usual, the meeting will begin with each royal or lord declaring any updates on current projects or concerns…" Red informs King Uther as they approach the Council gathering room. "Followed by you addressing the recent attacks before opening for questions."

Uther rolls his eyes and sighs, "God, do I hate these tedious affairs – don't you agree, my dear?" The hooded woman just nods, while Red is struck by confusion.

Hesitating, he says, "But, my lord, you are the one who called for this meeting," his voice lilting up at the end, questioning.

"One of my stature must keep up with current appearances even when knowing how meaningless they will be," Uther replies with a devilish grin. Red shifts uncomfortably at the response, knowing he cannot question it further. Though his family name led to his status within Grandhaven, his willingness to stay quiet ensures he keeps his head.

Finally, they arrive at a large stone door engraved with a map of Grandiose: the entrance to the Council Chamber. On either side of the door, several levers operate a lock mechanism leading to the Chambers. In times of war, the Chamber may be used as a safe room.

Callahan moves to the opposite as Red walks to the right of the door. Simultaneously, they pull the levers, and rather than opening from the side as expected, the door rises into the ceiling moments later. Once opened, the hooded woman enters, Red following behind. Before Uther can step inside, Callahan stops him.

Bowing his head, he declares, "My King, I understand your time is limited, but something haunts me…"

Uther pauses. "Isaac, you have been by my side since I was an infant. Those glorified peasants can wait; let me ease your mind. What bothers you?" he responds, taking Callahan's chin in his hand and lifting his head until their gazes meet.

"It's the mission you're sending those fools on! Why will you not allow me to handle it? They are average at best – and that was before chains shattered Nolan's neck. So why them?" Callahan's voice rises passionately as he blurts this out to his King.

Uther pats his hand against the knight's cheek, his voice easing into an air of condescension as he says, "Old friend, you're one hell of a force on the battlefield, but you do so lack the mind of a scholar. Why would I send my finest brute on a suicide mission? Not to mention the questions your absence would bring up." He laughs. "One would swear you're trying to get yourself killed," he says, walking into the Chamber, leaving Callahan to guard the door without another word.

Callahan sighs as the door closes behind the King, and a small tear escapes his cheek. With no one left to hear, he whispers, "If you only knew."

Inside the Chamber, Uther signals the hooded woman to sit in a chair left near the entrance. The Council Chamber is one of the smaller rooms in the castle, but one of its greatest treasures lies at the center of the space: the Table of Kings. This stone table was once used by the first King Whitelion nearly three hundred years ago during the Great War. Like the door to the Chamber, the table's surface is engraved with a map of Grandiose, with each major city and kingdom embossed by a gold sigil.

Above the table, a moving stone model of the city Lunagal – now commonly referred to as the Nest – hangs. Like the model, Lunagal is a floating city that slowly moves across Grandhaven, and many scientists use its location to determine the season. Summer is marked as it appears over Grandhaven; autumn as it moves over New Haven; winter as it roams over Riverhaven; and spring as it shifts across the appropriately named Springhaven before returning to Grandhaven, completing one cycle.

Six thrones surround the table: one for each member of the Council. Of these six, five thrones house life-size golems, their leader's mirror image in every minute detail. Uther's throne rests at the head of the table, and to its right sits King Black Regalia's. Regalia, the youngest Council member, is Grandiose's most extraordinary mind. As ruler of New Haven, he has made the kingdom the pinnacle of modern science using Q.A.S Tech. Regalia himself is thin, and his jet-black hair always gelled back as if never to hide his youthful emerald eyes. Unlike other royals, he never wears a crown or jewelry of any kind, vocal that it only hinders his work. Even more than being a king, he prides himself in being a man of science.

On Regalia's right, King Baron Grayscale, the Dargone king who hails over his native kingdom of Dakuhm, sits. Like most male Dargones, King Grayscale towers over any human, intensifying his already intimidating presence. Contrary to his name, his scales reflect warm reds, yellows, and oranges. While his stature, snout full of teeth, and massive tail are distinctive, his wings are his most impressive feature. His royal blood gifted Grayscale with flight, a trait shared amongst all his ancestors and one he will pass down to all his kin. Though he was once an outgoing and prideful ruler, he has spent much of the last decade an introvert, making decisions from behind the castle walls, haunted by tragedy.

To his side, the lovable island king, Chief Ramon Masina, is situated. This husky man oversees the city of Riverhaven, the kingdom's fishing capital. Known for a smile that could melt stone, Ramon exudes joy to all around him, even going as far as to live among his people instead of in a castle. His ever-tanned skin is covered in native art, which he displays proudly, rarely wearing anything more than his lavalava. Among his peers, Ramon is both love and light, often the life of any gathering, the antithesis of Uther. And since Riverhaven is only a day's travel from the only Oren city, Ramon has adopted a more liberal opinion of the race, seeing them as allies for the future rather than enemies of the past. This progressive outlook on the world is at the forefront of his and Uther's ever-growing animosity, something bound to be present during this afternoon's meeting.

The only woman on the Council, the mighty Queen Rosemary Bladestorm, waits. All rulers of Springhaven are required to defeat the previous ruler in battle, and until Queen Rosemary's reign, all former rulers had been men. Not only did she defeat a king, but she managed to do so at only nineteen years of age. Now in her fifties, she is one of the longest-sitting Council members, observing as others talk, preferring the classroom to Council; however, her ferocity as a warrior makes her the perfect ruler for a city home to the knight's Academy.

The final throne belongs to Dr. Simon Newson, the current Crow president of Lunagal. The Crow, a race of anthropomorphic, black feather-clad birds, call this city home, giving it its more recognizable name, the Nest. Like many Crows, President Newson's breath always smells of rotting flesh, while his claws are always covered in dried blood. Even at Council meetings, his royal garments are torn and stained. Since the end of the Great War, the Crow have served as treasurer to the other kingdoms.

While the other members often question whether a Crow should sit amongst them, Dr. Newson has earned the King's approval only halfway into his first ten-cycle term since Uther finds him obedient. What the doctor lacks in hygiene, he makes up for in loyalty, knowing that if he stays by Uther's side, he will avoid expulsion. The King has found that paying a few extra credits to the president ensures his will always wins when it comes to Council matters.

Arriving at his throne, Uther removes his crown, replacing it with one attached to the table. Inside this new headpiece is a fair-sized, white Q.A.S-infused gemstone. A large gemstone of similar style is embedded in the back of the other thrones. When Uther nods for Red to begin the meeting, he hobbles over to a panel of switches and levers positioned at the back of the room. The massive Q.A.S engine next to the panel starts to rev at Red's tinkering. As the sizable yellow gemstone within the engine spins faster and faster, the many tubes that protrude from it fill with light, illuminating the room as it pushes towards its destination, the Table of Kings.

Once the table is powered, the stones upon the thrones begin to pulse, matching the heartbeat of its corresponding leader. Lastly, the gem on Uther's crown glows before releasing a shockwave of energy through his body. Uther cringes in pain before succumbing to the pleasure the rush of power gives him, his eyes beginning to glow white. Each golem twitches, fingers loosening and jaws cracking before their eyes open, sharing the same glow as Uther's. While the leaders sit in the comfort of their homes across the country, their golems perfectly mimic their actions. The marvel of the Table of Kings is complete.

Stretching, Chief Ramon jests, "Damn, you'd think that after fifteen years, I'd get used to that awful sting."

"Maybe it would hurt less if the shockwave didn't have to travel over such a great mass," King Black mocks to the rest of the rulers.

Queen Rosemary smirks at the bickering before President Newson rudely interrupts with a belch. Unabashed, he interjects, "Apologies, I was just finishing my midday meal, and it seems these children's hearts are leaving me quite gassy." The rest of the Council sighs in disgust.

"On that note, I hope we can begin this meeting. King Whitelion?" King Grayscale shifts the conversation. Uther nods, leaning over the table.

"We will start with roll call. Please take this time to make any declarations before we move onto the purpose of this meeting," he declares, then points to Black to begin.

He nods. "King Black Regalia present. I'm happy to report New Haven is running as efficiently as ever. Thanks to a tip from President Newson, we were able to acquire a handful of goblins, allowing us to increase the workload in our gem mines and put down some of the older ones before they mature into orcs."

"Older goblin corpses are such a delectable treat. My Crows are happy to keep an eye out for the rogue goblins...as long as you're willing to make the trade," Newson interjects, licking his lips.

"Absolutely," Black continues. "As we continue to arm our city and knights with Q.A.S Tech, New Haven will need more hands to work the mines, and I think we can all agree it should be theirs instead of ours." While most of the Council nods in accordance, Chief Ramon remains still, marking him as the only outlier. Undeterred, Black closes by saying, "Lastly, my team of scientists hopes to use the recently discovered orange gemstones to produce new Q.A.S Tech weapons within the next Nest cycle. No guarantees, but by using the same infusion methods as other gemstones, we believe these will allow us to combat stone-based magic." Uther and the other rulers clap while Black motions for Grayscale to begin.

"King Baron Grayscale reporting. I'd like to begin by thanking King Whitelion for deploying more troops to Dakuhm. With Queen Grayscale finally laying a healthy egg, the extra security will help while she takes the next few cycles to incubate it."

"My pleasure, Grayscale. After what happened to your daughter, I feel it is my duty to ensure the safety of Dakuhm's future," Uther replies with a devilish smile.

"Again, it's very appreciated. We know we can never replace Krimson. A youngling in the castle will be a welcome sight..." he trails off momentarily. Blinking a few times, he clears his throat. "That reminds me: after so many stillbirths, the Queen and I have chosen not go public with the birth until after it hatches. I am formally requesting all of you to respect our privacy as well." The Council all agree, and Grayscale thanks them before they move on.

"High Chief Ramon Masina accounted for. As many of you know, even after a very promising fishing season, the numerous attacks on our convoys have led to either a delay or complete cancellation of many of your orders... I do hope that the abrupt nature of today's meeting reflects that Uther has come up with plans to address this matter."

"King Uther. It's King Uther, Ramon," the Grandhaven monarch corrects, glaring. While the rulers of each kingdom are equal in many ways, Uther is Council head, and he ensures now that the others remember he holds more power than they do, demanding their respect.

"So sorry for that, Uther. I'll try to remember that next time," Ramon replies. While his response is spoken lightly, his haughtiness heightens the tension in the room, its weight felt even through the stone golems.

Rosemary's voice demands the attention of her fellow Council members. "Before this gets out of control, I'll interject. Queen Rosemary Bladestorm accounted for. I have nothing to declare. The Academy continues to produce Grandiose's finest knights, and, to be frank, I'd like to return to it before nightfall. Can we please move on?" Without words, the maturity of the only woman at the table checks the two men's egos. Their gazes shift from glaring at each other to looking at the Queen; however, while Ramon stares sheepishly, Uther's eyes are shining. This no-nonsense approach to leadership often intimidates others, but to Uther, it's intoxicating. Behind her back, he frequently jokes that if not for her age, he'd claim her as his own.

"As much as I do enjoy the Council's company, I must agree with Queen Rosemary," Newson speaks up, then licks his fingers – taking his time to savor every speck of his most recent meal. "I, President Simon Newson, am here...obviously," he chuckles to himself. "The Nest runs as normal, keeping your pockets plentiful and your lands corpse-free. As a matter of fact, we are looking forward to our next stop in the cycle. Grandhaven does have the most delectable cemetery, after all." Newson slides his tongue over his pronounced beak, and the other Council members look away in disgust.

"I'll take that as a compliment." Uther replies slowly, shifting closer to King Regalia.

"As you should, my King. If not for you humans, us Crows would go hungry, after all. If only others on the Council were so generous." At that, Newson turns his attention to King Grayscale, pointedly licking his lips with each word.

Growling, Grayscale responds, "Again, the answer is no. Dakuhm will continue to control its own finances, and we will bury our dead. Besides," he adds, "I have my doubts your beak could get through our scales anyway."

"We will see about that soon enough." Newson whispers menacingly.

"That's enough!" Uther interrupts, sensing the tension and hostility from earlier rising back up in the room. "I, King Uther Whitelion IV, demanded this meeting. With my presence, all Council members are accounted for. Let's get to the heart of the matter." The

Council members straighten in their chairs, intrigued to finally understand why Uther called the meeting.

"This morning, another supply cart was attacked–"

"Again! That makes four in the last month! He has never attacked this many times in such a short span," Grayscale cuts in.

"That's true," Ramon agrees. "What's changed to prompt such increased activity?"

"Must feel like we aren't taking him seriously enough," Newson supplies.

Uther refuses to reduce himself to speaking over anyone else; he demands the attention due to him. He slightly raises his hand, an indication and command for silence. He continues, "The attack itself is not the reason for this meeting, but its aftermath. This is the first time all humans on the scene were found dead." At this statement, the rulers' eyes shift between each other, recognizing the severity of the situation. "Two of their bodies impaled multiple times with large stone spikes and one with the head removed completely. As I've feared, this self proclaimed 'Terra King' has drawn first blood," Uther concludes.

"Do you plan to take action, King Uther?" Regalia asks, leaning into the table, expecting to hear the answer he already anticipates.

"I do," Uther quickly confirms. "I wish to declare war on the Oren city of Goldleaf."

"WHAT?" Grayscale and Ramon exclaim in unison, slamming their fists into the great table.

Uther sharply raises his hand: another command. The other leaders slowly sit, still furious at his declaration. "Take a moment to examine the facts," Uther urges. "At every attack, this assailant has left large, unnatural stone installations. Previous attack survivors describe him as slim, amazingly quick, and agile. Unless King Regalia is lying about what progress our Q.A.S Tech is making, or unless Queen Rosemary is hiding an elite knight none of us are aware of – all signs point to this 'Terra King' being Oren."

"Well..." Grayscale concedes, "I'd be lying if I didn't say we here in Dakuhm have had similar thoughts." He sighs and continues, "At first, we thought it may just be bandits and thieves, but reports make it clear: this attacker has amazing control of the earth. Undoubtedly, that's a magic only an Oren could wield."

Ramon speaks up next. "Understandable, but war on an entire race over the action of one man? That seems unnecessary."

"I expected you'd be the one to defend them," Uther replies disappointedly. "All reports state that the man wears high-quality garments; the few daggers left behind display craftsmanship that rivals our royal blacksmith's. Clearly, this isn't a solo mission; this man must have quite the backing. I find it hard to believe the Oren Elder or his Disciples are not somehow involved."

"Your ignorance is showing, Uther. The Oren race isn't like us humans," Ramon interjects, stating facts without a hint of emotion interrupting his argument. "They don't have a class system that separates what clothes or tools one has. Wealth comes from knowledge, not credits. A commoner could easily share the same lifestyle as a king."

Dr. Newson chimes in, "If what you are saying is correct, Chief Ramon, reports would indicate this man is 'rich' in knowledge. Would his not apparent mastery of stone magic put him among the elite inside Oren walls?"

"Not necessarily, President Newson. They aren't monarchies; magic is a birthright, and any Oren with a willingness to learn could potentially display this level of mastery," Ramon informs the Council.

As the others chat amongst themselves, Uther sits back to listen, calculating the best moment to act to ensure his will wins out. Each ruler mentions 'what ifs,' questioning other possibilities and searching for more explanations. Finally, he cuts in, "Enough. It's clear we are divided on my request, so, like any other matter, we will take this to a vote. All in favor, say 'aye.'"

While Uther, King Regalia, and President Newson agree, only King Grayscale and Chief Ramon oppose. Surprised and frustrated, Uther turns to the only queen, demanding, "Queen Rosemary, you stayed silent on both accounts. I am afraid we do need your answer."

Rosemary sits back, crosses her arms, and closes her eyes. Letting out a sigh, she says, "I smell bullshit in the air, Uther."

That air feels thick as soup in the Council Chamber, each ruler holding their breath, waiting and watching for what would come next. Even Uther's frowns with worry.

"This 'Terra King' has attacked fourteen times in the last cycle yet has never taken life. He never steals the supplies – only destroys them," she continues, unbothered by the tension in the room. "Today, that changed. You all argue amongst yourselves about the nature of another race, voting for or against a war for the entire continent, but not one man in this room has taken the time to ask *why* the attack changed."

Though her voice has risen in anger, she stops to steady it. Speaking slowly, she says, "Well, I'll be damned if I let time take my beauty without getting some wisdom in return. Until someone can answer that 'why' for me, I will not vote. I will not send our children to die in a meaningless war."

Uther's infatuation with the queen does not overcome his irritation at her decision not to decide. Leaning back, he grits his teeth and addresses the rulers. "Per Council rules, no one can declare war without a majority vote. For now, we will close the book on this matter." Grayscale and Ramon drop their shoulders with a sigh, visibly relieved, while Rosemary's eyes stay locked on King Whitelion, refusing to back down.

Meeting her eyes, he continues, "I will personally work with those who were on my side today to investigate the attack further. Hopefully, by our next meeting, I can present more compelling evidence to sway those in disagreement." Pausing, he grimaces before snarling, " I only hope that doesn't include the loss of more innocent lives. With that, this meeting is adjourned."

One by one, the golems power down, the ruler's energy draining from the stone. Finally, each returns to the lifeless statute they were before the meeting began – all but Ramon, who waited to intentionally speak independently with Uther.

Once he believes they are alone, Ramon barks, "What the hell was that all about, Uther?"

"It's King Uther," Whitelion echoes from earlier. "And I have no idea what you're talking about," he snarks.

Ramon slams both fists on the table hard enough that the thud echoes throughout the room. "Cut the damn act! For months, you and I have been working to facilitate a meeting between you and the Oren Elder," he reveals. "Today, you called this meeting without warning. Just when I finally think you'll reveal our work to the rest of the Council, you instead call for war!"

"When I asked you to set up that meeting, I told you it would be for the safety of our people. It must continue to stay secret between us until it is successful," Uther refutes. "That statement still stands true. For three hundred years, no human has set foot inside Goldleaf. Should that suddenly change, it will only cause panic in our people – even more so in light of these attacks."

Ramon sighs in defeat; few ever argue with Uther and win. "So that's it? Every string I pulled in hopes of a better future goes to waste."

"Quite the contrary, River King. As we speak, a small band of knights sit outside my office. Unbeknownst to them, they have been personally selected to escort my confidant to you. Once they deliver, you will proceed to inform them of the true nature of our plan," Uther informs his conspirator. "If all goes well, the Elder can prove their innocence in these attacks. Hopefully, the first act of our new union will be bringing this 'Terra King' to justice."

At first, Ramon is taken aback by Uther's comment. After processing more, he, somewhat relieved, responds, "You and I have never seen eye to eye – something I regret after being so close with your father. But, if your plan works, you're gonna change the world." He sighs slowly, offering, " I'd be a fool if that doesn't earn you at least a little more of my respect...King Uther." With that, Ramon's golem finally powers down.

With the meeting officially over, Uther, too, removes his headpiece. Red tinkers with the buttons and levers for a moment before the engine powers down, and the room darkens.

Uther puts his crown back on and, grinning devilishly, laughs,

"And oh what a world it will be."

CHAPTER 5
THE
KING'S REQUEST

Chapter 5

The King's Request

"No wonder they think so little of us..." Helena sighs, looking out over Grandhaven from the castle tower's window.

"With a view like this, do you blame them?" Marcus replies. "Up here, they don't hear our voices or see our faces. Look: we're just shadows on the street," he continues, pacing back and forth with this hallway as his cell, his personal hell, waiting to be summoned by the King. "We're just gears in their machine, working our lives away for their comfort. They can invite knights to their perfect little castle only to have us spend hours sitting in the damn waiting room!"

Helena rolls her eyes. "Patience has never been your strong suit," she says, but he can hear the smile in her voice and stops pacing. Moving to be next to her, he places his forehead on the window glass before letting out a sigh.

"Once... Once we are transferred, it might be a while before we see this place again," Marcus speaks solemnly, and the others hear his unspoken *or each other*. "Other than my time at the Academy, I've never been outside Grandhaven. Grew up on its streets; took up the sword hoping to defend it." Marcus turns, leaning against the window in place of his forehead. "Maybe I'll get lucky and get one of those new assignments in Dakuhm."

"You're lucky to get anything but the gallows with all the people you've pissed off over the years," Helena replies, attempting to lighten the mood. "Plus, Dakuhm is no different from Grandhaven – or any other kingdom out there."

Marcus brightens up. "Have you been before?" he asks, his curiosity piqued.

"When I was younger – but that was before Nolan found me." With that, it's Helena's turn to look out the window. Again, the room is filled with sadness and words unsaid.

"Ms. Blank, you are an ever-growing mystery, one that – regrettably – I may never get the chance to solve," Marcus flirts, lowering his head once more.

A voice interrupts the unbearable silence. "Calm yourself, lover boy. We aren't being reassigned," Liam says, sitting quietly, his eyes closed and arms crossed, adjacent to the others. He's had time to think about their situation. He stares intently at his friends and continues, "You don't get summoned in front of the King just to be moved to a new squad. This is something bigger."

Marcus sighs, his boredom turning into frustration. Rubbing his eyes, he asks, "Like what? We were all deemed innocent during the trial, and I'd be surprised if any of your old sins are actually coming back to haunt us." His anxiety, masked by impatience, gets the best of him, and he returns to pacing. "Why can't it be that after Nolan's death, King Uther is so stricken with guilt that he feels it's his royal duty to put us on a better path?" he questions in vain. "Maybe he'll even overrule his father and give you the promotion you and I both know you deserve."

Liam stands and places his hand on his friend's shoulders, easing his angst. Gruffly, he reminds Marcus, "Optimism is poison for the minds of fools. Boy, your list of flaws is varied – but foolishness is not one of them."

Recognizing the truth and love in these words, every ounce of tension in Marcus' body dissipates, and his head falls against Liam's chest, at rest for the first time. It's rare for any of them to see Marcus so vulnerable: his pride forces his physical strength forward to shield his emotions. Liam embodies safety, allowing Marcus to let down his shield, allowing him to just *be*.

"These last few weeks have been treacherous, but we must prepare for more," Liam continues, his hand still resting on Marcus' shoulder, shielding his friend's brokenness from the world, elongating the seconds of vulnerability they have left.

Helena clears her throat. "Well, whatever is about to happen is happening soon," she says, nodding over to the end of the hall. Liam removes his hand from his friend's shoulder, watching Marcus straighten, pushing his chest forward. His eyes are guarded, the tension back in his muscles, as they watch King Uther and his consort return from their meeting.

Callahan moves forward to retrieve them, but the King stops him. Though the space between them makes it impossible to hear what is said, Helena can read Callahan's lips as he says, *"Now, are you sure?"* The King's answer must have been affirmative because Callahan walks off, and both the King and the hooded woman enter his office. Red continues forward, replacing Callahan, to get the squad. The knights bow respectfully, and Red smiles as signals for them to stand.

"No need to be so formal," he reassures them. "In fact, let me take this time to apologize for your wait. Once those royals are together in a room, they tend not to stop talking: who's making what, who's killing who... but I digress." He laughs softly, putting them a little more at ease. "Allow me to formally introduce myself: my name is Red Regalia, head advisor to the King. I will be taking over in place of Sir Callahan, as something of *great* importance requires his attention."

Red escorts the knights down the hall, continuing to ramble the entire time. Red morphs into a completely different person when the King is not around. Life and personality exude out of him, replacing the meekness and quietness of the older man standing at the King's side. As they arrive at the office door, Red says, "When you enter the office, bow, of course, and wait for King Uther to command you otherwise. You are all fine knights, and I am certain that Queen Rosemary beat all these tedious rules and formalities into your memory. But in case you have taken a few too many knocks on the head out there protecting this great kingdom of ours–" Red stops suddenly. As he turns to the knights, his vivaciousness disappears, his solemnity back in place. As seriously as if the King stood there, he advises, "Make sure to show King Uther the utmost respect. If you don't, it might just cost you your head."

When they enter the office, the knights are immediately aware of the enormity of the room. From top to bottom, the marble-walled office is filled with books and artifacts, accented by the room's trim outlined in gold. While Marcus stares at the space in awe, Helena looks at the office in disgust. Her vulnerability has been even more guarded than Marcus' over the past years, and while there's so much her friends do not know about her, it's easy for them to recognize how much Helena cares for the people. In Grandhaven, hundreds are poor, barely able to bring home food while living in the slums. This one room offered more space than two slum houses could hope to have. To Helena, the riches are a waste when the people the palace is meant to protect live in poverty. The city would thrive if only some of this wealth were shared with the people.

In the center of the room, King Uther sits at his desk, watching everyone come closer. The hooded woman, head down, waits quietly to the side, and Red bows before standing opposite her. As instructed, Liam, Marcus, and Helena all take a knee and wait to be addressed. Uther stands up, putting his hands behind his back, and begins to circle the group.

"I can only imagine you are questioning why you were summoned. Is it your inevitable reassignment? Or maybe, somewhere down the line, one of you has angered the wrong person, and it's finally reached my ear," Uther delights in how his words stab into their insecurities, smiling ruefully down at Marcus before taking his seat again. "Let me ease your minds: this is a simple request." At this, Uther signals for the group to stand. "Since the Great War, our race has lived in peace with both the Dargones and Crows here in Grandiose, but the Orens have always been an outlier. I believe it's time for us to change that."

Uther's words are shocking. In the three hundred years since the end of the Great War, there has never been any public contact between the humans and Orens.

"My family founded Grandhaven to bring man together in times of war, and over the last three centuries, we have opened our doors to the rest of Grandiose's inhabitants. Yet, due to the actions of those same founders, the Orens continue to live in exile." Waving the hooded woman over, the King continues, "I don't see a need for it to be that way going forward.

My many years of research are displayed throughout this office, and through that scholarship, I've found that our actions in the Great War may not have been for the best. Q.A.S Tech has helped bring us into a new age, but there are still several magic arts we can not harness. But imagine a world where we could? We could escalate man's progress exponentially overnight. The Orens are the key to that." Uther pauses for the first time, looking for the surprise and confusion he had expected to find written on their faces. He continues regarding them as he reveals, "With that in mind, Riverhaven's Chief Ramon and I have secretly been working over the last few cycles to acquire an audience with the Oren Elder – and have finally succeeded."

The hooded woman now stands behind the desk close to Uther's side. "My request is simple: escort my associate to Riverhaven, where Chief Ramon will help you cross the swamp bridge so that she can meet with the Elder and bestow a generous gift on my behalf," he finishes, smugly content as he watches awe wash over their faces.

Marcus, Liam, and Helena quiet the questions racing through their minds as they adhere to protocol, still standing quietly under the gaze of their ruler. Uther allows a few more moments to pass before permitting them to speak, and Liam is the first to step forward.

Bowing low, he says, "King Whitelion, please allow me to be first to thank you for inviting us to your home." Uther slightly inclines his head, accepting the acknowledgment, and Liam continues, "But I must ask: why us?"

Uther smiles. "Predictable, but understandable. The answer, though, is quite straightforward. Yes, your skills are far from average – especially yours, my dear," he explains, pointing at Helena. "But my studies have found that a job is done more efficiently when it's personal." His voice deepens as he says, "I can make this personal for all of you."

The knights glance at each other, intrigued. Marcus steps up to speak, bowing just as Liam had. "My King–"

"Allow me to elaborate," Uther interjects. "I understand unfortunate events have led to the hanging of your former squad leader...Sir Nolan, I believe was his name? Of course, you're all aware that, upon death, a criminal's body is given to the Crow for harvest, regardless of their past record. If you fulfill my request, I'm willing to make a deal and change that for your deceased colleague."

The knights light up, the gravity of the offer washing over them: they could give their friend a somewhat honorable burial and finally have some closure. It feels unreal, and Helena struggles to contain her emotions as the nightmare of Nolan becoming Crow food that has haunted her begins to release its hold on her mind.

Uther notices the undercurrent of emotions surging in the room and stands up again, tapping the hooded woman on her head, before walking to the back of his office. For a moment, he searches the shelves before taking down a book, returning to his desk, and opening it to a map of Grandiose.

"Now, I can't offer a knight's burial for him – no, that would raise too many questions," he says, "but I can allow the three of you to let his body drift into the Void." Uther points to an island far off the coast of Riverhaven, a large ring of ancient text surrounding it on the weathered map. "Entering the Void may be a one way trip, but it's certainly better than the belly of a Crow, wouldn't you agree?"

The knights nod, and the King takes his seat once more, looking each knight over one at a time. "So, how do you feel about my proposal?" he asks. Without pausing, he says, "Now, before you answer, consider for a moment that I could just as easily order you to do this without any compensation."

Though they take a moment to look at each other, the knights don't need to say anything – to each other or King Whitelion. The answer is clear. They know the journey to

Riverhaven is perilous, especially when charged with protecting someone untrained. Each of them would willingly put their life on the line for Nolan when he was alive, and none of them doubted they would do the same for the chance to honor him in death. It was an unspoken, resounding yes.

"Excellent," Uther remarked. "Now that we are all in agreement, let me introduce you to my associate, Elizabeth," he says, gesturing to the hooded woman. "But before I do, you need to understand that Elizabeth is amazingly unique. To be blunt, she is my most prized possession– so her safety is key to your success." As the knights process what he's said, Uther nods towards her permissively.

The hooded woman – Elizabeth – hesitates, then unclips her hood and lets her robe fall from her shoulders. The knights' eyes widen as they take in something – someone – unlike anyone they'd seen before. She is breathtakingly beautiful beyond belief, her Crow aspects accented by what could only be Oren features. Through the office window, sunlight glistens off her bronze skin. As with any other Oren, each of her ears split into two points. The bridge of her nose comes to a point, hard like a bird's beak, yet elegant. Out of her defined collarbone sprout pearl white feathers that cascade down her shoulder blades and under her arms to create her magnificent wings. Her copper eyes hypnotize the room until she's the only thing anyone can perceive, but she shifts uncomfortably under the attention, quietly fiddling with her jet-black hair.

Uther allows the knights a few moments to admire Elizabeth before he places her robe back in her hands. Graciously, she covers herself before returning to her seat at the side of the room. Her beauty is matched by her obedience, something only Helena seems to notice.

"I warned you she was unique," Uther reminds the knights, breaking them from the trance. "Now, I believe that's all the information you need. I would like to move towards this new future as soon as possible, so I will have Red prepare a travel cart so that your journey can begin tomorrow at sunrise. Remember," he warns, "this task requires the utmost discretion. Not a word to anyone along the way. Once you leave Grandhaven's walls, the only person you are permitted to discuss any of this with is Chief Ramon in Riverhaven. Is that understood?" Once witnessing their nods, he states, "Go, prepare for tomorrow's journey. You are dismissed."

Liam, Marcus, and Helena exit the office, finding a guard waiting to walk them out. Only once they are out of sight does another guard come to take Elizabeth to her room.

"Things seem to be going as planned, my King," Red says. He had stayed behind to consult with King Uther after the others had departed. "I am always impressed by how well you can convince people to believe in your mission – even when you don't believe a word of it," he quipped.

"A good king knows how to turn bullshit into gold. I'm sure your brother would agree," Uther replies, pulling a folded piece of paper from his desk drawer before getting up. "At the end of day, they will all die thinking they changed the world for the better. What does it matter if the details are a little murky?"

Uther walks out, Red following closely and closing the door behind them. Pausing, the King hands the folded document to his advisor. "We're officially on the clock now, old man. Have this finished before week's end." As Uther walks away, Red opens the document, marveling at the detailed blueprints for a somewhat staff-like weapon. He's too engrossed in dissecting the information given to him to see his King stop and turn, but he looks up as Uther adds, "I'll rectify the state of Grandiose if it's the death of me."

Red watches the King stride away in disgust. He folds the blueprint before placing it in a coat pocket, his fingers brushing against a small, hidden knife. Red quickly glances at the blade before glaring back up at Uther and whispering,

"Who am I to disagree, my King."

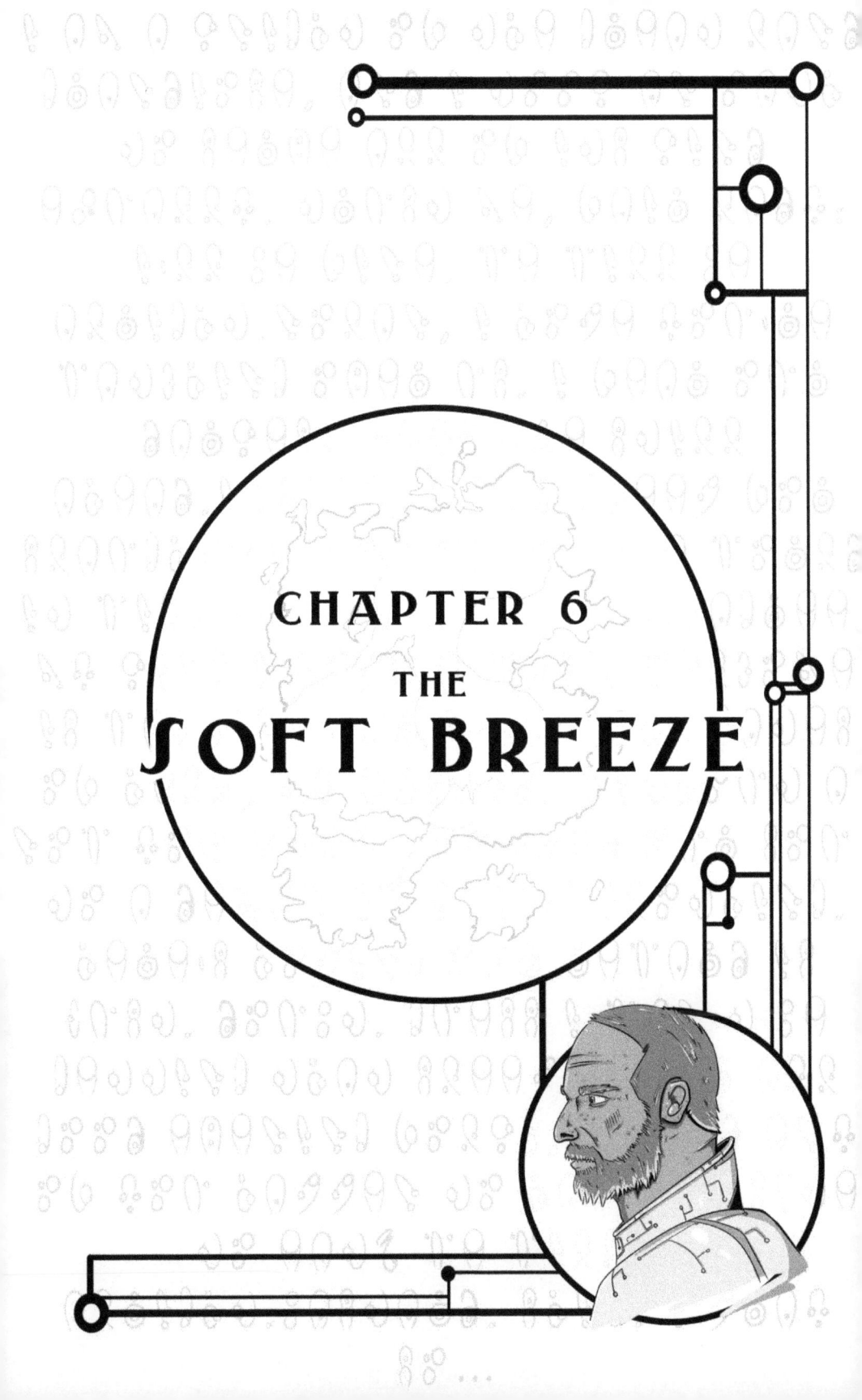

CHAPTER 6
THE
SOFT BREEZE

Chapter 6

The Soft Breeze

The midnight moon has reached its height in the pitch-black sky, shining brightly over a dirty road along the outskirts of the east side of Grandhaven. A local farmer follows the pathway home after a long day of work at the market; many locals must make their living selling goods in Grandhaven, which is a surprisingly cutthroat life. Arriving before sunrise, merchants work through the entire day and most of the night to only manage to make ends meet.

The noise of the day has quieted under the stars, a welcome change for the farmer, who looks back at his son sleeping in their cart. He smiles with pride, considering all the hard work his boy has done today. A soft breeze hits his face, and he takes it all in. He knows his life won't be recounted in any history book, but he's happy.

Continuing down the path a bit further, their striped horse suddenly comes to a stop, tossing its head from side to side. While the farmer attempts to soothe the horse, its frenzied neighing wakes his son. Rubbing the sleep from his eyes, the boy questions what's going on. Before his father can respond, a low growling from the side of the cart answers for him. They look over and see a towering man's figure approaching with a giant beast to its left, claws gripping into the dirt, prepared to attack. With a shaking voice, the farmer calls out, hoping for a positive response.

None comes.

When the man finally enters the moonlight, the farmer recognizes Sir Callahan and his beast, Moses. Before he can even greet the knight, Moses attacks his horse. Immediately, the farmer freezes in fear for his boy, watching with horror as the battlecat tears into the horse, viciously ripping out its organs. The farmer and his boy are frozen in fear as Callahan comes closer, throwing the farmer from his cart. The knight easily traps the farmer under his boot and maliciously presses down slowly on his windpipe. Choking out his last breath, the father tells his son to run just before Callahan crushes his neck under his weight. Terrified, the boy trips over his feet as tears sting his eyes, and he tries to follow his father's final direction. Callahan, indifferent, tosses his shield into the young man's back, gritting his teeth as he hears the cracking of his spine and the labored breathing of the broken boy.

Callahan roughly picks up the farmer's dead body like a sack of potatoes and slams it against the cart. He fishes in a side pocket with his free hand and removes a round, palm-sized Q.A.S Tech device. While it's a bit rudimentary in its initial appearance, when Callahan pushes the button in its center, it emits an orange glow. As he pushes it into the corpse's chest, a row of small metal teeth bite into the flesh. Stepping to the side and putting as much space as possible between him and the body, Callahan holds the shell of the farmer upright until the ground begins to shake, and, like a magnet, a large pillar of earth impales into the body through the device. Blood sprays everywhere, and Callahan wipes some off his face as he walks away from the body, now lanced into the cart.

The boy, helplessly trying to crawl away despite his injuries, cries as the knight turns in his direction, anticipating the same fate as his father. Callahan picks up his shield and walks toward the child, pulling another device from his belt.

Gruffly, Callahan grabs the boy's hair and lifts him into the air, looking directly into the boy's tear-filled eyes as he says, "Don't take this personal, boy. I'm just following orders." The child's tears finally fall from his eyes, silently cascading down his cheeks, but Callahan's cold heartlessness remains. "Honestly, I'm doing you a favor. Trust me: this world is fucked. You should choose to die happy, knowing that you got out before shit hit the wall," he concludes.

Before dropping the boy to the ground, Callahan attaches the device to his face. Despite his cruelty today, the knight is kind enough to ensure that this son does not spend his final moments staring at his lifeless father. Turning his back, he closes his eyes and walks away purposefully, doing his best to ignore the boy's cries until he feels the ground quake once more and hears the splitting of flesh as the pillar spears a body for the second time.

Moses, now finished picking the horse's skeleton clean, bounds behind his master, the gruesome scene behind them. Aside from the breathing of both beasts and the pounding of blood in his ears, Callahan notices that the night is once again quiet. He stops to breathe in the soft breeze, heaving out a sigh. Surrounded by darkness, he lets tears fill his eyes for the first time that night, petting his battlecat and murmuring disdainfully,

"I hope a warm welcome is waiting for me at the gates of hell, my friend."

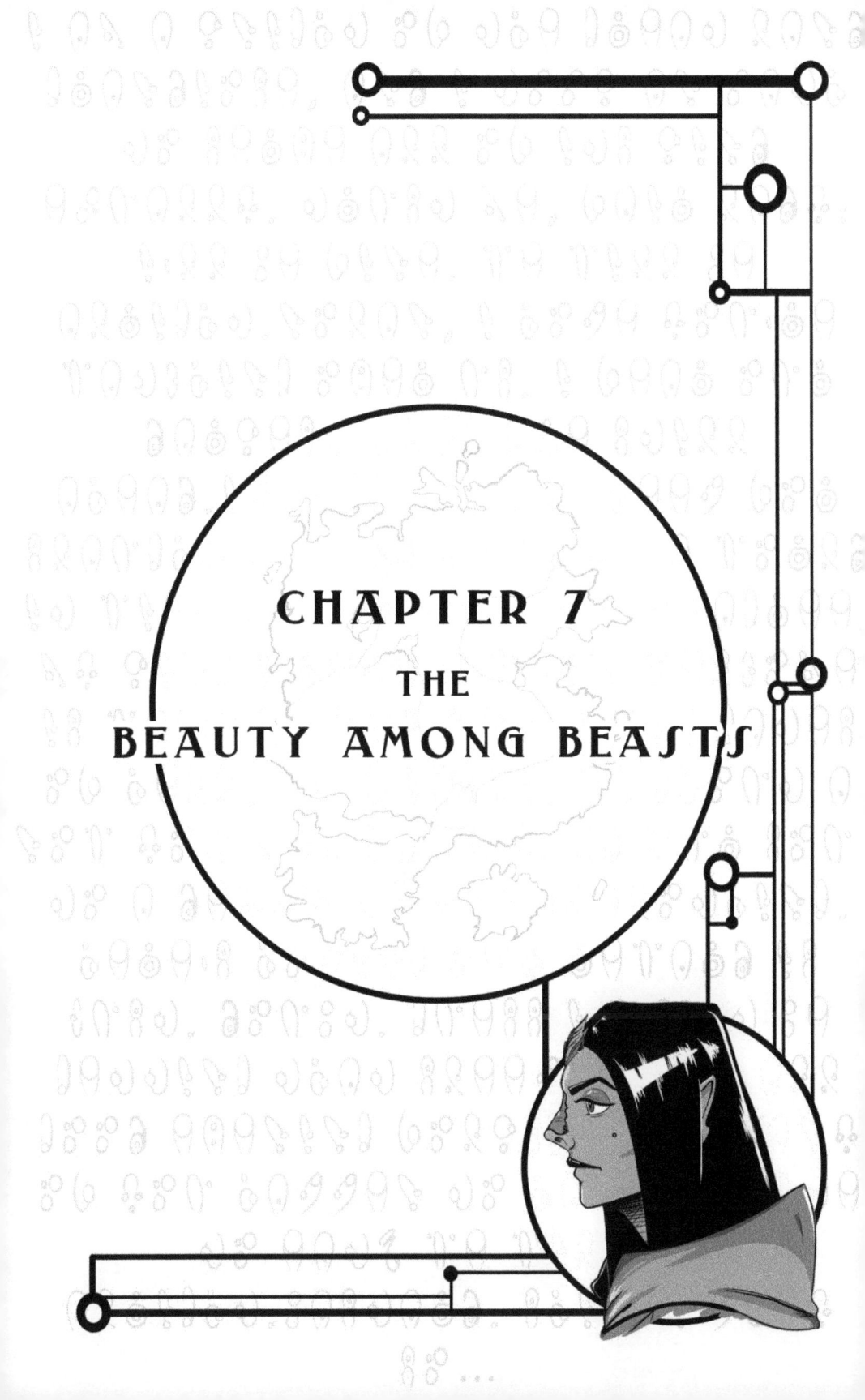

CHAPTER 7
THE
BEAUTY AMONG BEASTS

Chapter 7

The Beauty Among Beasts

As the sun rises, the market fills again, and Grandhaven returns to its usual bustling self. Helena and Marcus load supplies outside the castle walls into the escort carriage as Liam attaches Hornet to the front harness. As he latches the final buckle into place, Liam hears the monstrosity of Moses approaching and turns to see Callahan and his battlecat stopping a few yards from them. He notices the bags under Callahan's eyes, but his eyes widen as he takes in the dried blood on the knight and his steed.

After dismounting Moses, Callahan strides past them, his eyes slitting as he states, "Know that if any harm comes to Lady Elizabeth I will personally ensure you are reprimanded." He doesn't wait for a response, entering the castle gates and leaving them behind.

In his place, a large group of guards exit the gates, surrounding Elizabeth and Red's walk to the carriage. As they arrive, the guards form a barricade around the entire group, shielding them from prying eyes.

"Good morning knights," Red greets the group, "I hope you come to us well rested."

"No need for rest – we are some of Grandiose's finest, after all," Marcus jokes. As usual, his mask of strength and ego is in place, trying to impress the guards.

"Whether that's true or not is yet to be proven, but I have the utmost faith in you, young man," Red replies as he condescendingly taps his index finger against Marcus' chest, walking right past him to talk to Helena and Liam instead.

"I hope the supplies are adequate?" Red questions, but he cuts them off before they can answer. "What am I saying? Of course you do; King Uther has spared no expense ensuring the comfort of his prized possession," he continues. Turning to Elizabeth, he emphasizes, "Am I wrong, my dear?" She inclines her head softly.

Helena, disgusted by the verbalization that Elizabeth, or any woman, was only an objectifiable possession to powerful men, mumbles under her breath, *"She's not just an object."*

Hearing her, Red turns. His mouth smiles, but poison drips from his voice as he asks, "Is there something you'd like to say, Ms. Helena? I could, of course, summon King Uther if so–"

"My colleague was only thanking you for going above and beyond with the preparations," Liam quickly interjects, cutting the tension. "The road to Riverhaven isn't necessarily a rough journey, but riding any mount for several months can be grueling." Swiftly, he steps from Hornet's side at the front of the carriage to its door, smiling at Elizabeth as he bows, opening the door so that she can enter. He reassures the King's advisor, "A vessel like this will ease that pain exponentially."

For a moment, she smiles back.

Seemingly accepting Liam's explanation, Red finalizes the preparations, signaling the guards to move out. When he brushes past Marcus again, the young knight lets out a huff of annoyance at being swept to the side like dirt. "Allow me to apologize... My tone was inappropriate," Red offers to Liam and Helena. "You must understand how important your mission is to the King. If you fail, all of King Uther's work will go to waste." Marcus shoves his way between Liam and Red, ensuring that Red notices him as he speaks.

Shoving between Liam and Red, Marcus declares, "Oh, we understand completely. As knights, it is our duty to serve our King." His disrespect is apparent in his actions, but the glare in his eyes as he deadpans the words drives home his feelings towards the advisor – and he is confident the feeling is mutual.

As they continue to stare each other down, the silence seems to grow louder from the words unsaid hanging between them. Having only met Red twice, Marcus still caught onto his brown-nosing of the King, hating him for it on instinct alone. He also knows that Red believes him to be hot-headed and heading nowhere, much like the rest of Grandhaven. He knows his actions in the past few moments have only affirmed that perspective, but he cannot regret taking the stand against the advisor.

Red breaks their glare first, aware of the King's insistence on the schedule the knights keep. He knocks on the carriage window and waits until Elizabeth looks down at him through the glass to say his goodbyes. "Try to enjoy yourself Miss Elizabeth," he says, "but remember: the new world is in your hands."

With that, he and the guards re-enter the castle, the gates swinging shut behind them. Marcus, Liam, and Helena are left alone with Elizabeth for the first time, the mission's potential weighing heavy on each of their minds.

"That guy's a prick," Marcus mutters, climbing onto the driving bench at the front of the cart. His chest juts out like a proud peacock, and he defiantly crosses his arms over it as Liam follows him up, grabbing the reins.

Helena laughs at his childishness. "I have to agree with him this time," she teased, earning a dramatic eye roll from her friend. Moving to enter the carriage, she pauses with her hand on the door. "Liam," she says softly, "You know I'm a big girl now. You don't have to fight my battles anymore." Her gratitude is felt beneath the words.

Liam chuckles to himself. "You have it wrong, little lady," he countered, "it's Red I was protecting. Had he taken it any further – himself or the King – I have no doubts you would have ended the argument before it could even truly begin. Even if you didn't, Lord knows Nolan's ghost would have beat him to death in his sleep just for upsetting you." The smile on his face reaches his eyes, and Helena offers one back before climbing into the carriage with Elizabeth, settling in as they begin the journey to Riverhaven.

From the same window Marcus had stared so intently out of yesterday, high above in the castle's tower, the King watches the knights progress. Behind him, the lift doors open silently, and a bloodied knight enters the hallway.

Noticing Uther at the window, Callahan quickly takes a knee and apologizes. "I am sorry, my King, I did not expect you to be out of your chambers at this hour. Please excuse my appearance; I haven't yet had a chance to clean up after completing your request."

Without turning around, Uther commands, "Stand up, Isaac, and take pride in a job well done." Callahan obeys, and the King moves away from the window to walk with his knight. He proudly says, "I awoke to reports of the most gruesome scene outside the kingdom. Word is already spreading that the 'Terra King' has returned and is out for blood."

"It seems everything is falling into place, my King. Before long, your perfect Grandiose will be a reality," Callahan interjects. Uther halts, taking the knight's face between his hands in delight.

"Oh, Isaac, you have no idea how intoxicating this feeling is. Soon, my little present will reach the Orens; before long, this world will be engulfed in the most beautiful flames. From the ashes, a utopia will rise like a phoenix." Uther releases a haunting laugh as his hands drop from Callahan's face, leaving the knight in his wake as he enters his office alone.

Callahan looks down at the blood on his armor, then walks over to the giant glass window, taking Uther's place from moments before. His eyes search for the carriage, finding it just before it exits the castle's walls. He wishes his words would somehow transcend space and time to reach the knights' ears as he whispers, "Don't fuck this up, thief. Lord knows I can't do this anymore."

Inside the carriage, Helena keeps Elizabeth, who has remained silent the whole way, company. For the first few hours, she watches Elizabeth staring out the window in awe of the endless fields they pass, noticing how her fingers never leave the chain adorning her neck.

"A traveling gift?" Helena asks, hoping that this might be the question to finally break the ice.

The woman startles, shocked that anyone would talk to her. Gazing down at the necklace, it takes a long moment before she can find words to respond. "King Uther gave it to me before I left," she explains, "and said I have to look like royalty in order to represent him." She doesn't look at Helena as she speaks, only at the charm in her hand.

For the first time, Helena examines the necklace, her curiosity piqued. It is an objectively beautiful piece of jewelry: an ornate chain leading to a lion's head with a large pearl in its mouth. It is, without doubt, something that could only come from a royal treasury.

"You are beautiful in your own right. Even without the fancy jewelry, I must say, you look like royalty," she encourages the woman, trying to keep her anger at Uther's words in check. "I haven't experienced much of the world yet, but of the part I have seen…you truly stand out."

Elizabeth's head shoots up, looking at Helena for the first time. Instinctively, she wants to lash out at Helena for her boldness, but one look in the knight's eyes steals the words back into her throat. She isn't used to anyone speaking to her to begin with, so Helena's genuine compliment completely shocks her.

The quickness of Elizabeth's reaction tells Helena that she must have overstepped. "I am sorry to have offended you," she says quickly, adding, "I didn't mean any harm. You're just so unique."

Again, Elizabeth notices the easy way the knight offers her authenticity, and a tiny seed of trust takes root in her heart. "No need to apologize," she says softly. "Truthfully, I'm just not used to people saying kind things to me. When they do, it's usually followed by... well, the opposite." At this, her eyes shift away, staring back out the window.

"That's awful," Helena says, hoping to bring the real Elizabeth back out from the demure statue sitting before her now. "But I, too, understand how shitty this world can be."

"Do you?"

"I wasn't always a knight, you know," Helena laughs. She notices Elizabeth's body beginning to relax and continues, "When I was younger, I was lost – probably headed down the wrong path sooner rather than later. But then Nolan found me, gave me a home, and raised me right." Though she doesn't regret her vulnerability with the woman, her grief hits her chest. She stops speaking momentarily, joining Elizabeth in staring out the window as her reminiscences flash across her mind.

"I guess you could say the Whitelions did the same for me," Elizabeth says softly. Her openness draws Helena's attention back to the present, and she looks up to see Elizabeth looking at her again. "You said you haven't seen much of the world? My guess is you've never been to the Nest," she says, pausing to see Helena nod before continuing, "and few humans ever have. I mean, it is a floating city in the sky after all. But anyone who has seen it knows that Crows are... well. They feast on the dead, barely bathe, and obsess over money." Helena refrains from nodding, but she has heard and seen far too many humans express their disgust at the entire Crow race over the same points Elizabeth makes.

"Humans see Crows' behavior and think they understand the people," Elizabeth continues, anger underlying her words. As she pauses, Helena notices a single tear roll down her cheek. "What they fail to see," she reveals, "is how scared they are of the unknown."

"We don't have to talk about this. We can move on, if you'd like."

"No, no, it's alright," Elizabeth interjects, laughing breathlessly as she wipes the tear away. "Honestly, you're the first woman I've talked to in what seems like a lifetime. It's nice to be able to finally open up."

Reassuringly, Helena reaches across the space between them and places her hand on the woman's knee. "Well, in that case, I'm all ears."

Elizabeth smiles, and, for the first time, it actually reaches her eyes. Helena's unnatural warmth, authenticity, and willingness to listen after years of silence next to Uther have cocooned Elizabeth inside the carriage. An unknown feeling washes over her, and, for the first time in years, she remembers what safety feels like.

"I was left on the street mere moments after I was born. You find me beautiful and unique? Well, my fellow Crow thought I was disgusting. At first, they just tried pulling out my feathers, mocking their white coloring as they fell to the ground. They must have thought white wings were even worse than being wingless. But then, when my feathers grew back, they would throw dye and dirt at me. Realizing they couldn't get rid of my differences that easily, they found new ways to torture me as I grew older. The dirt eventually became rocks, and it was my blood that dyed the feathers red. They would spit on me, repeating their mocking refrain."

Elizabeth is too focused on finally being able to share her own trauma to notice how Helena's muscles tense and her fists clench in response to her words. Still, despite her anger at the injustices Elizabeth has had to face, she will not interrupt the woman's story.

"As if it wasn't obvious, I'm half Oren," Elizabeth continues, "so my stomach never could handle the trash they eat up there. Finally, I grew so sick of their mistreatment that I used all the strength in my wings to fly down to Grandhaven, believing that it would be a place where I would no longer be beaten and go hungry just for being different.

But, to my surprise, humans aren't much better. There I was, a young crossbreed being," she grits her teeth before spitting out, "passed around the streets of Grandhaven. Each night, a new monster. I guess the only silver lining was that they fed me occasionally."

Sighing, she looks back out of the window, staring at the fields once more as she regains her emotional strength. "I had all but given up, accepting this was my punishment for existing. This was the only life I began to believe I could deserve as an abomination to my kind."

At this admittance, Helena leans forward again, putting her hand back on Elizabeth's knee. As pissed as Helena was, she truly only wanted the woman to know that she heard her and would continue holding space for anything she wanted to share.

"Then one night, King Whitelion III entered the brothel I was staying at. Naturally, the madam wanted to give the King something he would never forget, so they dished me up for him on a silver platter. But he surprised me that night; for the first time since coming to Grandhaven, a man looked at me and didn't want to hurt me. Instead, he told the madam he would pay her a fortune to close her business, tell no one he had been there, and leave me in his care. And she did. He took me in and told me that I'd never want for anything – as long as I followed his one request."

Helena's voice fills the carriage for the first time since Elizabeth began her story. "And what was that?" she asks.

"To be forever loyal to his son, Prince Uther. So, for the last fifteen years, I have."

Speechless, Helena moves her hand from Elizabeth's knee, brushing it through her hair as she takes in the truths this woman trusted her enough to share. A mix of anger and sadness overwhelms her, and her calm exterior falters.

For years, Elizabeth has not known anyone who would listen to her story and actually care, and at Helena's silence, she begins to fear she has revealed too much. "Don't tell me I've scared you off, now have I?" Elizabeth awkwardly jokes.

Sensing Elizabeth's trepidation, Helena collects her own emotions and smiles gently. "What kind of knight would I be if I didn't want to give my life protecting you after a story like that?" she replies, and it's enough to put Elizabeth at ease again. If Helena was being honest with herself, tales like this are why Helena wanted to become a knight in the first place. Like a mosaic mirror, Elizabeth's story reflects parts of her own back to her.

"Can I tell you a secret, Helena?"

"Absolutely."

"When King Uther told me about this mission of his, I was so scared to go back into this world of pain and suffering. But he assured me that he had found the finest knights in his army to keep me safe. I didn't believe him – and when it comes to those two out there, I still don't." She laughs, reaching for Helena's hand and gently grasping it in her own. "But for what it's worth, I think he was telling the truth about you."

The two share a smile: a friendship being formed. They spend the rest of the day talking and trading stories, their laughter ringing so loudly and frequently that it catches the attention of the men driving the carriage.

"Seems Helena has won over another," Marcus says to Liam as the sun sets in the distance.

"She's the best of us, isn't she?" Liam replies, tugging on Hornet's reins.

Marcus closes his eyes, allowing Helena's voice to calm him. With a grin on his face, he answers,

"Without a doubt."

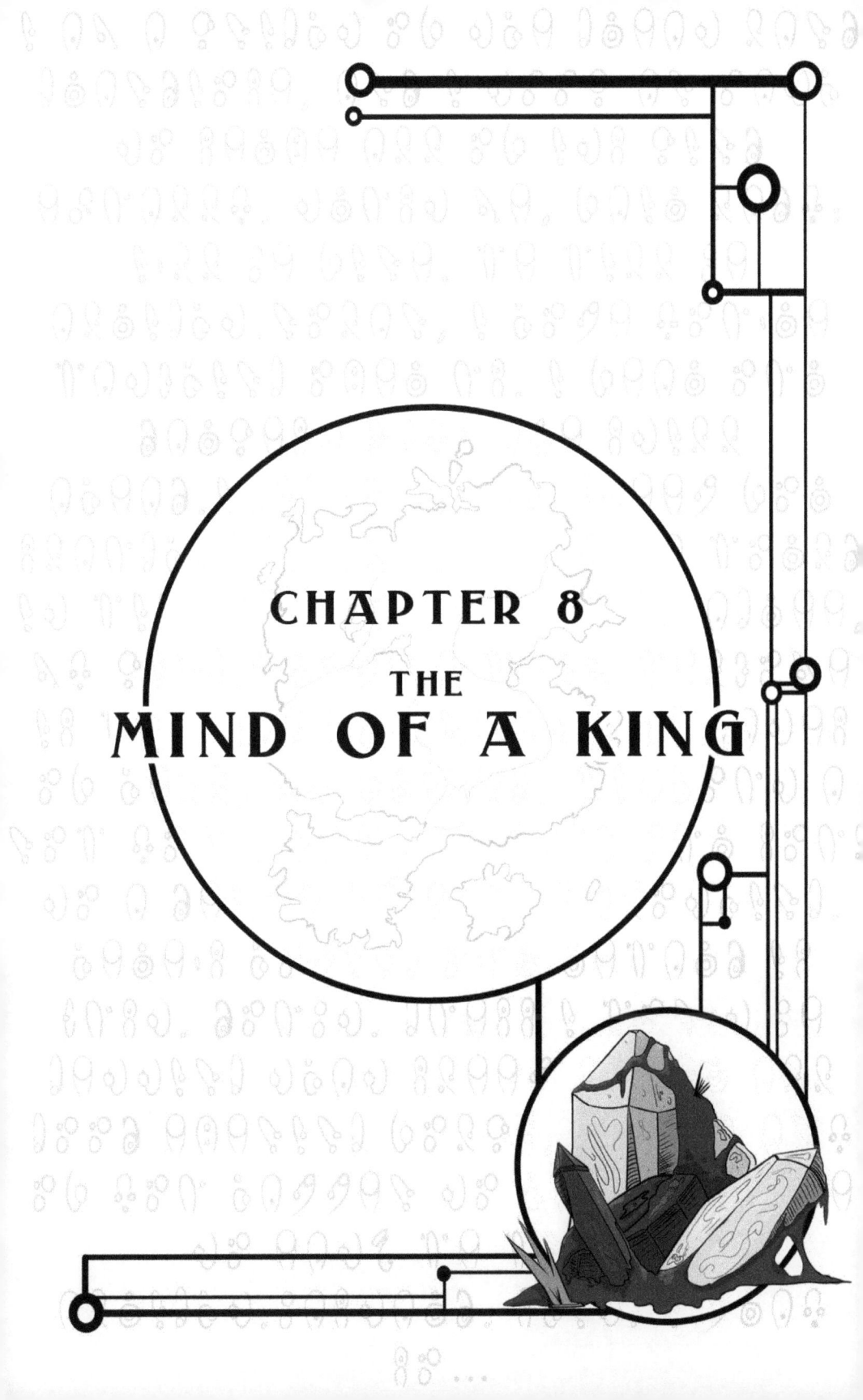

CHAPTER 8
THE
MIND OF A KING

Chapter 8

The Mind of a King

A few days pass, but back in Grandhaven, the Council reconvenes.

"Two more dead, yet you still wish to pussyfoot around as if people's lives aren't at stake!" Uther belts out, slamming his fist against the table.

"Uther, you're not talking about a simple retaliation, you're asking for a war! If it's people's lives you're truly worried about, how can you justify putting so many more on the line?" Ramon rebuts.

"*King* Uther–"

"Although your passion is captivating, Ramon," King Regalia interjects, "I, too, have to question you and Queen Rosemary's hesitance. This 'Terra King' is clearly making a statement against Grandhaven – arguably, against Grandiose itself, all of the Council's kingdoms. How many attacks should we allow before we do something about it?"

"I agree; it is time we do something about it," Queen Rosemary declares sternly. Her authority forces them to sit back and listen. "But this war of yours is not the answer. You still have yet to provide proof that this assailant has any ties to the Oren hierarchy; so, before we send our armies to burn down their front door, I say we shift our focus to capturing this 'King.' Force him to answer for his sins."

Uther rubs his eyes, aware that he is about to lose this argument. "And how would you go about doing that, Queen Rosemary?" he asks impatiently.

"Immediately following this meeting, I propose that we triple the number of knights who patrol after dark, adjusting their routes to ensure we are more vigilant of the roads that fit his attack patterns."

"And what happens if your delectable knights end up next on his list of victims?" President Newson speaks up, eyes darting to King Uther quickly to assess if he had earned his favor.

"The idea of one man having the power to take out one of our squadrons without the support of his nation is unlikely," she says, pausing to look at Ramon, her only support against an irrevocable war. "With that said, if any of our knights lose their lives to this 'Terra King,' then King Uther will have my full support to declare war."

King Grayscale and Chief Ramon second Queen Rosemary's notion, and Uther agrees to her terms before closing out the meeting. Though the others' golems power down, Uther remains in his chair, headpiece flung across the table, angrily mumbling profanities to himself.

"How do you plan to handle things now, King Uther?" Red has moved from operating the Q.A.S. Tech engine to being closer to the King. "Callahan is strong, my King, but even I question if he can take a whole squadron of knights out."

Slowly, Uther rises, placing his daily crown back atop his head. "I knew there would be pushback when I started. This is nothing more than a roadblock – one I will shatter through by any means necessary." With that, he strides out of the Council Chambers, nearly barreling over Callahan guarding the doors. Red follows close behind.

"My King, may I speak freely?" Callahan requests, noting Uther's demeanor and knowing it means the meeting could not have gone as the King had hoped.

"You may."

"You control the majority of the knights within Grandiose. Why go through the trouble of getting the Council on board? You can just order us to attack Goldleaf."

"Always the brute, Callahan," Uther responds, arriving at his office door. "Red, why don't you excuse yourself to your lab?" Bowing low, Red begrudgingly does as asked, watching as Callahan enters the King's office.

Uther motions for Callahan to sit as he approaches a chest lying behind his desk. He opens it slowly, revealing a Q.A.S Tech gauntlet resting on an ancient-looking book. Unlike the knights' standard armor design, which is clean-cut and solid black, this gauntlet is covered in ornate carvings designed to deceive any observer from recognizing any hidden weapons.

Uther puts the gauntlet onto his right hand, saying, "Callahan, you have always been loyal, so I know your question must come from a place of eagerness and curiosity. Am I correct?" As he speaks, he removes the book from the chest.

"My King, I would never doubt you," Callahan assures Uther, but he struggles to keep his voice steady as fear rolls through his body.

"Of course not, Isaac. Just as I thought. Allow me to enlighten you," Uther continues. He sits at his desk and places the book between himself and his knight. Wrapped in aged leather, the book's cover is embossed with symbols representing each of the world's magics. Callahan peers at it inquisitively, but he knows better than to touch it or say anything before Uther reveals what he wishes to share.

"You are not wrong when you say I could just order the attack myself, but to do so on my own would bring civil unrest. While the Nest and New Haven are already on board with my new world, the others are not so much. The Dargones historically stay neutral in the affairs of man. If, for any reason, they should take umbrage to our plan, their small army could easily lay waste to many of my men, making our assault quite tricky.

"Then, there is Queen Rosemary, who undoubtedly isn't going to approve of what I have planned for her men. Dealing with her after the attack, however, will be much easier than seeking her support before it. Lastly, there is Ramon, who I am absolutely certain is already planning some ungodly rebellion against me. Regardless of what he thinks of me personally, though, he is loyal to a fault. He will always do as the Council decides."

Uther places his gauntleted hand on the book, and the carvings on the gauntlet immediately begin to glow a dark violet hue—one Callahan has never seen. His frame twitches as he takes in its energy, then quickly removes his hand as if it were in pain. Throughout this process, he never stops his explanation.

"So, how do I avoid them getting in the way? I must make them think the attack is necessary. They give their blessing and the inevitable extinction will be nothing more than a casualty of war."

Callahan's face drains of color, but he fears Uther too much to stand anywhere but by his side. His head bowed low in both respect and fear, he affirms, "Your logic is untouchable, my King. But, forgive me, I still have a question."

Before he responds, Uther stands up, a devilish smile spreading across his face. He laughs under his breath as he works his way behind Callahan, placing his right hand on his knight's shoulder, the gauntlet weighing against him. Callahan freezes at the touch, yet he can't help but notice the King's hand still twitching.

"Your thirst for knowledge surprises me, Callahan. All these years, I thought you to be nothing more than an old man with a heavy hand and even denser head. I like this side of you," Uther says, chuckling, and lets go of Callahan's shoulder. "So ask away."

A sigh of relief escapes the knight's body before he asks, "What if the Orens are more powerful than we think? They are masters of magic, and our Q.A.S weapons can only match so much."

Sitting back down, Uther leans back in his chair, a smile spreading across his face once more. He points to the book. "Now, that is where this comes into play," he says, and the laugh that follows is maniacal. "I'd ask if you know the importance of this book, but I know you don't. Hell, it sat in the library for...who knows how long. Undoubtedly, I am the first to read it," he continues, stroking his own ego, "because if anyone else would have read any of its glorious pages, man would have already reached a higher plane of existence."

Uther opens the book, this time with his left hand. He leans over the desk, eyes wide. In a softly sickening voice, he says, "Callahan, this is the diary of the infamous War Shaman Sorro, and it holds the keys to powers we never dreamt of. Its pages contain countless secrets of the old world, truths about the forbidden arts, the origins of all Grandiose's creatures, and even the proof of myths like the Shadowbloods and sea walkers.

It will be the sword that cuts down the walls of my enemies and the shield that makes our skin impenetrable. With this, every knight on our battlefield will be immortal, and I will lead us to a new utopia."

Finished, Uther leans back and stares at the tome. Though Callahan looks up at him, the King is too fixated on the potential power before him to notice his knight or the intensifying twitching of his gauntleted hand. Callahan, though, is more observant than the monarch gives him credit for, noting the sweat on Uther's brow.

"That's enough questions for today. You are dismissed," Uther orders, gaze still transfixed on the diary. Callahan stands and bows low before exiting the room, closing the door behind him. As he turns to leave the hallway, a voice interrupts his thoughts.

"So, he showed you the diary?" Red asks.

Surprised, Callahan nods yes.

Red shakes his head, sure that Callahan knows the depths of madness awaiting them. For the first time, the knight quivers in fear, sweat dripping down his face as he realizes how dangerous Uther truly is.

"Now you know: we sold our soul to a demon in king's clothing. Here's hoping our reward is just."

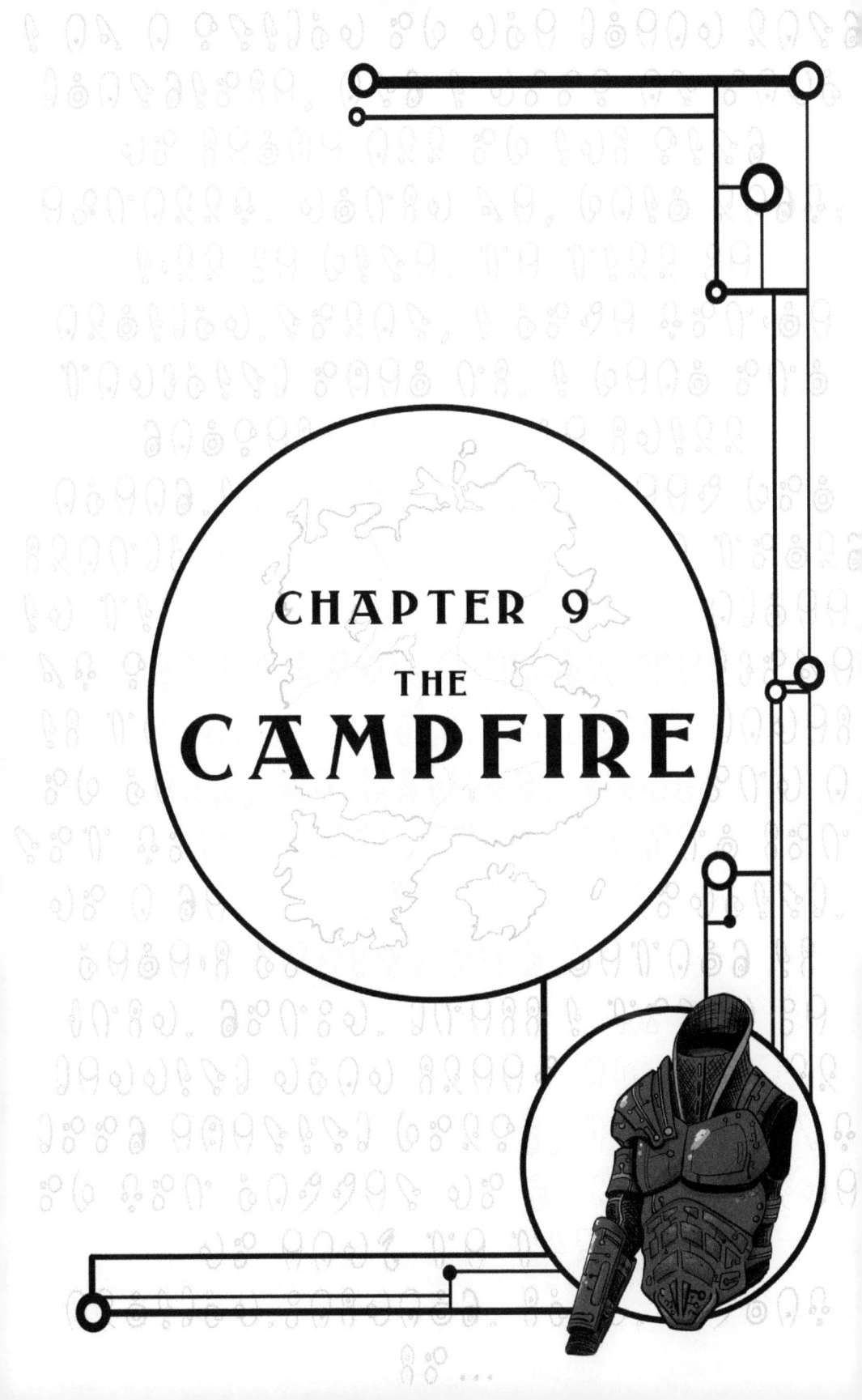

CHAPTER 9
THE
CAMPFIRE

Chapter 9

The Campfire

Night falls on the road to Riverhaven, and the company chooses to settle in for the evening. Liam takes Hornet out of her carriage harness, inspecting every inch of his friend before finally letting him rest for the night. The others gather around the campfire, and Helena and Elizabeth watch as Marcus endlessly fiddles with the flames. Marcus jumps back suddenly as a spark pops out at him, and Elizabeth laughs, a tinkling sound none of them had heard before.

"Oh, so she can smile?" Marcus teases, ego bruised and trying to deflect from his foolish response to the fire.

"Now, what is that supposed to mean, Mr. Marcus?" Elizabeth retorts, crossing her arms and pretending to pout.

"No harm, my dear, it's just that we have been on the road together for a week now, and you held that beautiful smile back this whole time," he flirts, eyebrows lifted as he cocks his head to the side.

"Don't you worry, Mr. Marcus," she replies slyly, "I've laughed at you behind your back many times on this lovely journey of ours."

Marcus grabs at his chest, stumbling backward, and slowly falls to his seat. Shaking his head, he continues his wounded act until a voice rings out behind him:

"Fair lady, you have broken his heart and hurt his pride all at once! I commend you," Liam laughs, clapping Marcus on the shoulder before sitting beside him. Throwing his head back, Marcus dramatizes how he could ever go on after such a fatal blow, causing the others to continue their teasing and joking with him while Liam shifts to preparing the group's meal for the evening.

Over the last few days, Helena has helped Elizabeth slowly open up to the team, learning more about each other each time. When Liam asks Marcus to get some food from the cart, Elizabeth offers to help. Together, they search the packs for the items Liam requested, and Marcus spots an unusual trunk among Elizabeth's things. Unsure of whether or not to bring it up, he continues hunting through the supplies with Elizabeth until they locate what Liam requested.

On the way back to the fire with the food, Marcus' curiosity gets the better of him. Deciding that Elizabeth's offer to help look through everything shows her blossoming trust, he allows his curiosity to get the best of him. "Forgive my ignorance, but was that a gift for the Oren Elder?" he asks.

"It was, something Uther personally picked out himself."

"Do you know what it is?"

"You clearly do not know the ways of royals, Mr. Marcus. It is customary for only kings to gaze at a gift presented to them."

"So you haven't looked? Not even just a little peek? I promise not to tell," Marcus asks sweetly, handing the food to Liam as Elizabeth sits down next to Helena.

"I would never do anything to dishonor Uther," Elizabeth answers, shifting uncomfortably away from Marcus. Helena notices and her body shifts towards her newfound friend, ready to intervene at any point should she become upset.

"King Uther is intimidating," Marcus says slowly, backing off a little as he realizes the shift in the atmosphere, "so I understand not wanting to upset him. But damn if I am not curious about what gifts kings give to each other." Pausing, he puts his hands behind his head, leaning back to look at the starry sky. As he daydreams about royalty's riches, he lists the many excessive, elaborate, and unrealistic ideas that race through his head.

Rolling her eyes at his delusion of grandeur, Helena interjects, "I doubt it's anything more than gold."

"Helena, you are always determined to ruin this farm boy's fun," Marcus fires back at her.

Elizabeth straightens her back and leans forward, setting aside her previous discomfort in favor of this new information. "Oh, so you were a farm boy before you became a knight?" she asks.

"Farmboy," Liam laughs, returning to the group while gesturing towards the food, letting them know their meal is ready. "He was barely on a farm long enough to piss on a pig."

"I was born in a barn, on a farm. By definition, that makes me a farm boy," Marcus insists.

"No," Liam dissents, "a farm boy grows up on a farm, works the field, feeds the livestock and picks up their shit. You may have been born in a barn, but took your ass to the city before you were even able to crawl."

Used to Liam's teasing, Marcus jokes back, "I reserve the right to declare myself whatever I like, old man."

Again, Elizabeth observes as they go back and forth, laughing at the bickering of true friends. While they squabble, Helena begins to serve dinner, giving each a bowl spooned full of a mix of vegetables and the day's hunt.

As they eat, Elizabeth silently examines each knight's armor. Unlike the knights who guard Uther, whose armor is polished and unvarying between knights, her new guards' are worn and dirty, each slightly different from the others. Liam's, a simple iron chest plate with matching leg and arm guard, is traditional and old-fashioned. Helena's is black and made of Q.A.S Tech, with glowing blue accent lines directed toward a gemstone on her back that charges her bow. Marcus's design is similar, glowing with faint red lines leading to his left side, where he houses his sword. While Helena and Liam sport a single shoulder plate with the Grandhaven crest, Marcus has one on each shoulder.

Her curiosity finally gets the best of her. She clears her throat between bites and asks, "Helena, I'm sorry, I just – why do you and Liam only protect one of your shoulders?"

"No reason to apologize. Our shoulder plates are a representation of our rank. When you leave the Academy, you're a rookie with no plates. After a cycle of service, you're promoted to officer – which is what me and Liam are – thus the one plate. After five cycles of service, a squad leader may promote you to squad deputy, which is where Marcus ranks, and you're awarded your second plate. From deputy, only the decree of a king or queen can promote you to squad leader. They are given a cape with that kingdom's colors to drape from their left shoulder." Helena pauses in her explanation, looking down at her bowl of food, now untouched. Quietly, she says, "That's what Nolan ranked before he passed."

Between spoonfuls of veggies and meat, Marcus adds, "Only someone ranked deputy or higher can protect the King, which is why you've never seen anyone with one plate."

"Sir Callahan has a cape on each shoulder. What rank is he?" Elizabeth questions.

"Well, technically, he is a squad leader," Helena answers, shaking herself from her reverie, "but unlike a normal leader, who only watches over a squad of knights, Sir Callahan commands every knight who guards the castle and King directly; easily a few hundred men and women."

"It's funny, but I've lived in that castle for cycles, yet Uther has kept me so close to his side that I've never gotten to see how things work or how the people around us really live," Elizabeth sighs. Then, thinking about it, she amends, "Actually, it's kind of sad... But who am I to complain? If I asked, Uther would give me anything, so maybe it's not that bad after all." She moves her spoon around the bowl, sorting each type of vegetable into families, lost in thought.

"No worries, dear," Liam interjects quickly, noticing how she's begun to disengage. "Life is filled with blind spots. Hell, Marcus over here will never know how to be a farm boy, no matter what he tells you."

"Ha," Marcus chokes out, rolling his eyes. "Go ahead, keep making fun of me. I'll remind you: while I may not be able to do much with a shovel, there isn't a man alive who can match me with a blade." He takes a small knife from his utensil set and feigns stabbing it through the air like a weapon. Spinning it through his fingers, he cocks an eyebrow towards Liam, grinning wolfishly.

Helena rolls her eyes before leaning over to Elizabeth and whispering, "There may not be a *'man'* who can match him, but I'd kick his ass anyday."

Helena's words put a smile back on Elizabeth's face, something she's beginning to appreciate more each time. As they eat, laugh, and tease each other, Elizabeth feels herself growing warm, watching them. More than the fire, the friendship surrounding her fills her heart. Once all strangers, these three feel like a family. She has no doubt they would die for each other, and even in their short time together, she feels they would do the same for her. She realizes she has never known love as they display.

Now, she understands why Uther picked them.

"Liam, Helena: you're both so incredibly talented and disciplined. How could Marcus have possibly become a deputy first?" Elizabeth asks, smiling sweetly at Marcus as she speaks.

"Because I am the best. Why is this even a question?" Marcus throws his hands up in defeat. "I truly am starting to think you just don't like me."

"Well, Marcus, you should be used to that! It's not like she'd be the first... or thousandth," Helena teases back. Marcus sticks his tongue out at her, scraping the bottom of his bowl as the meal ends, the conversation continuing.

"Elizabeth, the truth is: Marcus is an amazing swordsman, best I've ever seen, and Nolan thought the same. But you can't say that too often or too loudly," Helena whispers, loud enough for Marcus to hear. "Or else it'll go directly to his head. He knows that if I wasn't only a few cycles out of the Academy, that plate would be mine." At this, Marcus tosses the empty bowl at her head, which she aptly avoids. "Not to mention, if the law allowed it, Liam would have had Callahan's post ages ago."

Elizabeth's face scrunches quizzically at the last part of Helena's statement. "If the law allowed it?" she asks. Immediately, the undercurrent of laughter seizes, and the crackling of the fire is the only sound beneath the stars. Realizing that she overshared out of turn, Helena looks to Marcus for guidance, but her gaze passes him and rests solely on Liam. Her heart breaks as she sees his head lowered in shame.

"Maybe," Marcus breaks the silence, "that is a different story for another day." For all the times that Liam protected his vulnerability, Marcus would do anything to shield his friend at this moment.

Clearing his throat roughly, Liam says, "No. There's no reason for me to be ashamed of the truth; the young lady deserves to know the company she keeps." Standing up, he begins to collect the group's dinner dishes. Though he said there was no reason to be ashamed, he still isn't willing to make eye contact as he recounts his tale. "When I was young, I lost my parents and my home in a fire. I was out playing and came home to nothing but ash. I was only sixteen – still too young to join the Academy – and then I had nothing and no one. Not a coin to my name, not a thing to get through this life.

"So I started to steal. At first, it was just bread to fill my belly, but then it became the coin to fill my pockets. And, sure enough, it was that same coin that weighed me down when the knights finally came after me." He walks away briefly, setting the dishes down, and no one dares to interrupt his story. They know he's not finished; they each intimately know the need for a moment of separation in the most challenging conversations.

"And I'll tell you, the judges in Riverhaven didn't have time for a loud-mouth thief like myself, so they sentenced me to death by hanging and put me on the next transport to Grandhaven," he says, bitterness hanging at the end of his sentence. He returns to the group, sitting back down by the fire. "You see, to this day, Grandhaven is the only kingdom that will execute a prisoner. So, there is one transport that runs between every human kingdom, picking up every person on their death row roster."

Elizabeth's face goes gray at this moment: another piece of the world she knew nothing about. How many people, kind and caring like Liam, had been sentenced to death because they needed food to live? She pulls her arms around her middle, hugging herself close, trying to stay present for the rest of his story while her previously warmed heart aches.

"From Riverhaven, we headed to Springhaven. I kept my mouth shut the whole way; I was a petty thief, sitting beside murderers and rapists, a kid out of my bloody mind, thinking the only silver lining was at least I would get to see my mom and pa soon." Tears fill his eyes, and he looks away from the group as though it will hide the one that traitorously falls down his cheek. He wipes it away as quickly as it fell before continuing.

"So we get to Springhaven, and in the process of loading more criminals, the Crow attacks the Academy without warning. History will talk about that battle as the last victory of man: us overthrowing a corrupt president and bringing democracy back to the Nest. But those few days were nothing but a bloodbath." Liam shudders, remembering. "As evil as he was, President Falcone was smart. He attacked just after graduation, so most of the Academy's top knights had just been shipped off to new posts, and the halls were filled with young men just a few years older than myself. And Crow outnumber Springhaven's army three-to-one, so by the time King Whitelion showed up with his support, almost everyone was wiped out."

Liam leans into the fire now, more excited to tell this part of his tale, and the others begin to lean in, eager to hear. "But the King knew he needed more men, so he called to arm all the prisoners who were locked up, including us in the transport. The King isn't a dumb man, either, so he believes we would be nothing but a meat shield, just there to take hits and buy time for the real knights. So it came as a surprise to us both," he begins to grin, "I'm damn good with a spear. They threw me on that battlefield, and something clicked: I moved through those Crows like it was nothing. I'd throw my spear in one's chest, and before he hit the ground, I'd pull it out and cut another's throat with it. I fought for what seemed like days before the fighting just stopped.

"There I stood, surrounded by dead bodies, when the King approached me, covered in the same blood I was. And he said, 'Good work, boy, it's time to go home,' and they loaded me with the knights. They told me I was the only criminal who survived, so the King felt it necessary to reward me for my accomplishment.

"A few days after we arrived in Grandhaven, we were called to meet with the King. He was straightforward and said, 'Boy, you're too good in battle for me to claim your head, so I'll make you a deal. As of today, you will be a knight in my army. I will send you to the Academy, where you will study only the basics on an accelerated path, and then you'll report to a field squad.' I agreed to his terms without hesitating, but there was a catch. He told me he'd give me a better future, but it wouldn't erase my past. Although I would be a knight,

I could never rank higher than an officer. If I ever put my spear down, I would go back to being a thief sentenced to death, and the gallows would still await." For the first time, Liam meets their eyes, the fire glinting off his, the flames a smokescreen for the emotions under their surface.

Each person slowly leans away from the fire, processing all that Liam has shared – a rare story, indeed. Even though Marcus and Helena know his history, the weight of his words rests heavily on them. Besides, they know how protective he is of his past, so sharing it now with Elizabeth carries additional meaning.

"If what you say is true," Elizabeth begins, clearing her throat as she continues, "that means you've been a knight for over fifty years?" Liam nods, and she thinks back to their earlier conversations about the armor itself. His is so old compared to the others', and she thinks, just maybe, this is the armor that both saved and imprisoned him for the last fifty years.

"And I'm thankful for it. Because of this armor and this spear, I've gotten to see most of this land, and, more importantly, I've gotten to meet some amazing people along the way, like Nolan. Oh, and these two," Liam gestures to Marcus and Helena, smiling softly.

"You must have some more amazing stories then," Elizabeth smiles back, happy to see him in higher spirits.

"Just you wait – once he starts, he never shuts up!" Marcus laughs, getting up and grabbing his sword before turning towards the carriage. "But after such a rousing," he rolls his eyes, "night of being bullied by the three of you, I think I'll get some rest."

Laughing, the others begin to pack up, too, but before Marcus can get to the carriage, a second comes over the hill behind them. In their camaraderie, they had been so focused on each other that they had lost sense of their surroundings.

Though worse for wear, this carriage is larger than theirs, pulled by only one emaciated horse. Several brutes get out as it rolls to a stop, wielding clubs or rusty swords. Grabbing the mace attached to the front bench, the driver jumps to the ground, and Marcus notices that the guard's armor he wears is clearly stolen. Attaching his sword to his belt, Marcus readies himself. He puts one hand on the sheath, which has illuminated red like his armor, and the other on the blade's handle. His demeanor shifts with his stance as he says to himself,

"Guess I won't be getting that sleep after all."

CHAPTER 10
THE
HONOR AMONG THIEVES

Chapter 10

The Honor Among Thieves

"What do we got here?" The bandit's leader boasts, spit flying through the gaps in his teeth. "Looks like we found ourselves some lost little fireflies, boys."

Marcus scans the group, looking for their ranks' strongest and weakest links. Helena grabs her bow and strides confidently to Marcus' side; together, a wall between the bandits and their assignment from the King. Behind them, Liam puts his body between the rogues and Elizabeth. Unused to this kind of danger, Elizabeth pulls her hood back over her head, something she hadn't done since their first day in the carriage, and tucks her arms around her middle for comfort.

"Fireflies?" Marcus questions, looking over to Helena and cocking a smile. Addressing only the leader, he says, "That's a new one. You do realize that you are speaking to a squadron of knights, good sir."

"knights? I'm shaking in my boots," he mocks, and grimy comrades laugh. "You knights don't scare us; there's what, three of ya? Look around. We outnumber you four-to-one"

"Now, maybe I'm mistaken, but it sounds like you're looking for a fight," Marcus chided, "You must find your words threatening."

"Damn right they are threatening," the leader sneers, the other bandits pulling out their weapons. "If you couldn't tell by this nice little garment of mine, you ain't the first fireflies we've found lost out here in the dark," he boasts, flaunting his stolen armor. "But I aint no brute – I'll give ya a choice. We do this the easy way: you hand over your armor and your weapons," he says, tilting his head to the side and stroking his beard as if deep in thought. Grinning, he licks his lips and points toward Elizabeth, adding, "Maybe let us have a peek under the little miss' hood over there, and we'll be on our way."

Liam positions himself more defensively in front of Elizabeth's frame as she shudders with disgust. Helena glances back at her quickly, remembering the trauma she shared that first day in the carriage. She catches her gaze quickly from under her hood, and Helena gives her a reassuring look that says *we won't let anyone hurt you.*

"Huh, and what might the 'hard way' be, then?" Marcus inquires, condescension dripping from his voice.

"Well, that's simple: we get all those things, but this time, you lose your head!" the bandit leader declares, chuckling with his crew and gently beating his mace against his other palm.

Marcus glances at Helena, and she inclines her head ever so slightly. Their battle is about to begin. Gently yet firmly, Liam moves Elizabeth back towards the trees behind them, where they can better protect her. As soon as she is situated, he revs his spear, moving lightning fast to Marcus' left, Helena beginning to draw back on her bow from his right.

Behind them, Elizabeth watches, anticipation and awe washing over her, knowing that she is about to witness her escorts in action. She remembers her sentiments from earlier: they would die protecting her if it came to that. Despite her danger, Elizabeth suddenly feels safer and more confident in their chances.

"I can't lie," Marcus answers. "The first option sounds amazingly generous. Yet, we have no choice but to choose the second."

The bandit leader's playful grin turns malicious. Spitting on the ground, he steps forward, signaling his men to attack. Effortlessly, Marcus swiftly tosses forward the blade from his side, impaling the bandit before his foot can fall to finish his step. His lifeless body falls over, the sword firmly embedded in his skull. The other bandits, shocked, watch as the blade begins to glow red; Marcus' sheath also starts to illuminate. As they quiver in fear, two small Q.A.S engines on the blade's guard ignite, lifting the sword from the leader's skull, and Marcus uses the controls on his sheath to return the blade to his hand. With blade in hand, the edges of his armor now glow the same intimidating red, a telltale sign that the knight is ready for battle.

The bandits start to inch towards their cart when Liam, with surgical precision and lightning speed, decapitates a handful of them. His electrified spearhead leaves the headless bodies twitching where they stand before collapsing to the ground. As the rest panic and disperse, Helena raises her bow. She draws back the glowing blue cable, and each time she releases it, several small bursts of air crystalize midair, turning into ice arrows. Each one hits

its mark, causing their blood to freeze rapidly before death, if not killing them on impact. Within a few moves and moments, the knights have ended a dispute that barely began.

Elizabeth removes her hood and looks across the field of corpses, amazed and horrified by how quickly it all happened. Marcus wipes the blood from his blade before returning it to his holster. A cold, war-torn gaze replaces his usual playful demeanor. "At least the Crows won't go hungry tonight," he says, weakly attempting to justify the brutality. He takes a deep breath and motions for the team to survey the scene.

Liam investigates the battlefield, ensuring each body is indeed dead, and Helena feeds the bandits' horse before cutting it loose. Meanwhile, Marcus and Elizabeth approach the bandit leader's dead body. Looking down in disgust, Marcus shakes his head, then kneels and wipes the blood and dirt off the stolen armor's chestplate. Slowly, reverently, he removes it from the bandit leader and hands it to Elizabeth.

"Bring this with us," he says solemnly. "If we're lucky, someone will know who it belonged to. Might give a family a little closure."

"What happens if no one claims it?"

"Then it will be melted down and recycled into rookie armor. Either way, it's a better fate than staying on the corpse of a murderer." Marcus pauses for a moment, noticing how ashen Elizabeth's face has gone and how she wrings her hands, shaken, as she stares at the death and destruction surrounding her.

"I hope you don't think less of us now. I know it seems like we ended their lives quickly and without care, but believe me: they were planning to do the same," he says, and Elizabeth recognizes the strain in his voice. He doesn't like killing. She removes her eyes from the dead and looks at his living face as he continues, "No knight gives up their armor willingly. The fact that this thug had it means that there is a dead knight out there; worse, it's old guard, so there is likely a ransacked house with their dead family, too." As he stands, he cradles the armor in one arm and helps Elizabeth to her feet. "Grandiose is a dangerous place. I took up this sword thinking I'd be protecting the human race from it; yet, more and more, I see it needs to be protected from us."

Elizabeth shares the load of the armor as they return from the battlefield to their friends. As she looks down at the chest plate, her heart swells with a new respect for Marcus and it. The goofball persona she's seen the past few days still lies under the surface, laugh lines embossed into his cheeks and eyes. Still, she can now see him for who he really is: a warrior who hates to take life but is so good at it that he has to do it for a living, a man who hides his conflict behind a welcoming smile. He embodies everything she has ever imagined a perfect knight to be.

Regrouping, they confirm that all the bandits are dead. As Marcus and Elizabeth put the armor safely in their cart, a noise comes from the bandits' carriage. *"Did we miss one?"* Helena hisses, and they all grip weapons once more. Cautiously, they approach the carriage, Elizabeth lifting the hood back over her head protectively.

She stands back as Liam and Helena guard either side of the carriage door. They share a glance before Marcus nods, expertly cutting the door from its hinges, sword in hand to attack if needed, but the carriage is empty except for the overwhelming smell of shit. Slowly, Marcus enters, scanning the small space to ensure they haven't missed anything. His eyes fall on the layers of dirt and mud caking the floor, mugs heaved across it, and discarded food piled in its corners; however, he finds nothing of value and, more importantly, no one left to fight.

As he moves to the door to leave, they all hear a knocking again. Jumping back in surprise, Marcus cautiously taps the floor. Again, something knocks back. Each knight looks around the inside and outside of the vehicle but finds no explanation for the noise until Elizabeth notices a small latch on the bottom of the carriage. The knocking returns and the knights prepare for battle as Marcus pulls the latch down.

As Marcus lets go of the mechanism, the inside floor of the carriage opens up to reveal a man tied up, gagged, and in nothing but his trousers. The man sits up, smiling through the gag, and Marcus hesitantly removes the cover from his mouth. The disheveled man coughs, clearing his throat, and runs a parched tongue across his lips and around his mouth, attempting to remove the taste of the fabric. Smiling again, he greets the group,

"Good evening folks, would any of you happen to have to bite to eat?"

CHAPTER 11
THE
MAN IN THE BOX

Chapter 11

The Man in the Box

Elizabeth and the knights watch curiously as the now-freed hostage devours food like an animal, questioning how someone with such a small frame can eat so much. He cannot be older than his early thirties, and, through the layers of dirt, his hair seems to be blonde. His bright, xanthic eyes stand out most, shining through the darkness of the night.

"He's quite gross," Elizabeth whispers to Helena.

"In fairness, he's been locked in a box for who knows how long," she replies.

"Well, if we don't stop him, he's gonna eat all our food," Liam interjects. Though his heart goes out to anyone starving, his experiences in his youth have left him protective of resources, too. While he wants to help this man, he's hyper-aware of the needs of his group and the length of the trip they have left.

"Leave it to me," Marcus says as he stands up to confront the man. Goosebumps prickle his arms as the hair there stands up, unsettled by the man's questionable motives and appearance. As the man reaches for more food, Marcus sticks his sword between the hand and the nourishment, cutting him off. The man looks up at Marcus, cheeks still full of food, and smiles.

"Enough eating, it's question time," Marcus replies. "Who are you? What happened to you?"

Swallowing his food, he stands and reaches his hand out. "Name's Creed," he answers. "And who do I have the pleasure of thanking for saving me?"

Marcus looks down at Creed's hand, a mix of disgust and disdain painting his face, and refuses to shake it. Quickly, Helena moves to remedy the situation, grasping the man's hand firmly. "I am Helena, second officer of squad one thousand and ninety-sixth platoon." She gestures behind her, explaining, "This is first officer Liam, and *this* rude man by my side is our squad deputy, Marcus."

"My dear, it's a pleasure to meet you. Again, thank you – all of you," he adds pointedly, "for saving me. If only I was more presentable." He tries to wipe the mud from his face to no avail.

Graciously, Liam points over to a bucket sitting close to their carriage, nodding encouragingly. Offering his gratitude again, Creed stands, goes to the bucket, and begins to wash his face with the water inside. Never one for pleasantries, Marcus only gives the man a moment before following, interrupting this moment of humanity with more probing questions.

"I wasn't done. How did you end up tied up in the bottom of those bandits' carriage?"

Still cleaning his face and body, Creed seems unfazed as he grins, responding, "That's a simple answer: they put me in there."

"Don't be a smartass," Marcus growls. "Why did they put you in there?"

"Also a simple answer: they caught me stealing from them."

"So you're a thief?"

"Well, yes, but I only steal from other thieves. One must have morals after all." Creed shrugs, finished with both cleaning himself and the conversation.

He runs his hand through his hair, the final bits of dried dirt falling aside. Without the grime, Creed's body is revealed to be lean and defined rather than frail; his hair now glows as his eyes do; his face is handsome and chiseled. Suddenly, he becomes aware of his near-nakedness for the first time since being rescued. Turning to Marcus, he asks, "Do you mind if I borrow some clothes from one of our deceased friends?"

"Borrow? You mean steal?"

"They're dead. I don't think it would hold up in court." With that, Creed casually strolls through the dead bodies, piecemealing together an outfit not covered in dried blood and attempting to find shoes that fit.

While watching Creed, Marcus whispers to the others, "What should we do with him?"

"He seems harmless enough," Helena defends.

"Which means he is probably more dangerous than we think," Elizabeth challenges, watching over Creed, who is now attempting to spit clean a pair of pants.

Liam's voice joins the conversation. "Why do you think that?"

"He did come forward as a thief," Marcus answers before Elizabeth can explain her statement before he can even think about what he's said.

"I was a thief once, too," Liam's soft voice turns hard, arms folded over his chest, staring Marcus down. It's not the first time that evening that Liam has heard Marcus' apprehension towards thieves; while it was one thing for him to observe it directed only towards Creed, it was a different hurt to listen to the words spoken so callously to his face. "Would you be so quick to pass judgment on me?"

"Liam is right," Helena steps in, sensing the emotional iceberg buried under the surface of her old friend's question. "He hasn't done anything to harm us, and he doesn't seem intent to, either. If it were up to me, we would let him go. So, leader, tell us what exactly you have in mind for him?"

"Honestly," Marcus grits out between his teeth, "I'd think we should kill him before we give him the chance to do it to us."

"I'd like to request we don't go with Sir Marcus' idea," Creed calls out from across the field, "if I'm allowed a say." Struggling to get his head through the shirt he's settled on, he's unaware of the group's incredulity at his response.

Outraged, Marcus yells, "How the hell did you hear what I said? And, more importantly, how dare you listen in on our conversation!"

"I'm sorry," Creed answers, "it's just a little talent of mine. I can hear things from pretty far away. Got a pretty good sense of smell too. They're actually fairly handy tools being a thief and all." Finally fully clothed, he returns to the group, and Marcus is seething.

"You must not be a very good thief since you ended up in a box," he torments, pointing his sword towards Creed's chest, a wall between the man and them – a warning.

"See, now that's just not true. I intended to steal two things from those bandits: their gold and their beer. Problem was, I got to the beer first and indulged myself a little too much," Creed rambled. "In hindsight, I should have stolen their gold first, then the beer, and I wouldn't have ended up in said box."

"So you're not a bad thief, just a dumbass," Marcus taunts.

"Exactly," Creed grins. Not one of Marcus' questions or jabs has gotten under his skin. Putting his sword away, Marcus angrily rubs his eyes. "Fine, you're free to go," he relents.

Creed inclines his head in thanks as he readies himself to leave, but as he takes his first step toward freedom, he pauses. "Where are we exactly?" he asks, his head swiveling from side to side. "I've been in that box for probably a week, and I have no clue where we might be or which way to go."

"You have to be kidding me!" Marcus cries out, frustrated. "This would be a lot easier if you just let me kill him!"

"I understand you're tired, just like the rest of us," Liam responds firmly. "But our duty is to the people Grandiose even before our own needs. I know Nolan taught you that much. Did you forget your oath? We aid all those in need, even those who get on your nerves."

Marcus hangs his head. While he still disagrees with Liam and Helena's decision, he hasn't forgotten the question he'd left unanswered earlier: *would he have been so quick to judge Liam?* This was a man and friend who, in many ways, shielded Marcus from himself and, when his emotions finally got the best of him, from the world. Further, to bring Nolan into things? Whether he agreed with Liam or not, he respected his friend, and that was enough for him to shut up.

Liam shoves Marcus to the side, finished with his rebuke. Stepping closer to Creed, he points behind them and offers, "If you go back down this road, you're a few nights' journey away from Grandhaven. Go up it," he says, pointing ahead, "and you're a week away from Dakuhm. If you don't stop there, you're about another five days out from Riverhaven. Find a road west, and you're about ten days away from Springhaven; east, about two weeks to New Haven. Whichever direction you choose, there are a few settlements and inns along the way."

Creed stretches, pondering what Liam said. "Well, Grandhaven is no place for a man like me," he laughs, staring Marcus down. "And I'm not becoming a knight any time soon, so Springhaven is also a no." Unable to stop the grimace spreading across his face, Liam turns his head, not wanting to answer any more questions about his own past.

Creed starts to pace as he continues to think over his options. "I've already been to Dakuhm more times than I'd like, and New Haven is locked down since King Regalia is on holiday. That just leaves Riverhaven, which honestly sounds kinda nice, a few days by the sea, a couple of fine fish dinners," he rambles. He claps, approving his own idea. I think we have a winner." Creed claps as he approves his own idea, then asks, "Where are you all headed?"

"Riverhaven," Liam replies simply.

"Oh, we can be road buddies! What a joyous coincidence," Creed offers optimistically.

"Absolutely not," Marcus jumps in, finding his voice again.

"Why not?" Creed inquires. "We're going to run into each other constantly anyway."

"Because! You are a thief on the run, and we are on a mission from the King. Even if I did like you, our priorities don't exactly align."

"Well, that's where you're wrong," Creed counters. "I don't have any priorities. I just don't want to be right here anymore. Not to mention," he adds slyly, "maybe if you had someone with my skills around next time, a whole group of bandits wouldn't be able to sneak up on you."

As Creed and Marcus squabble, the others debate the merits of inviting Creed to travel with them. Surprisingly, Liam sides with Marcus – not because of animosity towards another thief, but due to the deal from King Whitelion that is seared in his mind. He isn't willing to risk the possibility of giving his longest friend an honorable ending for Creed, even while he empathizes with the story. Helena, always the humanitarian, wants to take him in.

Elizabeth observes both debates happening around her: Marcus and Creed, Liam and Helena. She doesn't intervene or interject at any point; however, once she feels she's heard enough, she stands up, gliding over to Marcus. Putting her hand on his shoulder, she says softly and firmly, "None of you can decide, so I will." Surprised at her boldness and willingness to take charge, he steps back.

Before Elizabeth can speak, Creed breaks the tension in the air. "Now, I had noticed they skipped you during the introductions," he says, grinning. "That means one of two things: either you're not worth knowing, or you are the most important person here. If you ask me, it's the latter."

"I have one question for you," Elizabeth says solemnly, "and I want you to answer honestly. No jokes, no bullshit." The graying sky above and the whipping wind between them punctuate her statement. "Creed, tell me: what is most wrong with this world?"

For the first time since they met, Creed's demeanor shifts from smiles and slyness. Soberly, he says, "That answer is simple, my dear: the world is upside down. It's a place full of hate yet also so much love. Where people are born in the wrong body, then get attacked for it as if..." Creed pauses as he looks down, "They have a choice in the matter. Then, we claim to be in a time of peace, but secretly, we all want war. Maybe not with swords and shields, but with words, cursing at each other for how we look or who we let in our beds. Hell, sometimes, just because we were born in different places.

"This is the part that gets me, though. I've traveled up and down these lands, and every time someone beats me down, there is someone like her–" Creed points to Helena, then to Liam, "or the big guy, or, even to an extent, the hothead over there," he says, jerking his head towards Marcus. "Someone who picks you back up. So just as you're ready to call it quits in this game the world plays, it gives you hope that makes you want to stay in just a little longer." A tear rolls down Creed's face, and Elizabeth, moved, reaches to wipe it off. He clears his throat, then says, "And maybe it's just me, but that's a little fucked up, don't you think?"

Acknowledging his answer, Elizabeth steps back and removes her hood. Eyes still wet, Creed's smile returns, and he says,

"So I was right; you are the most important person here."

*****

Restless, Marcus takes the first shift driving the carriage as the sun begins to rise. Looking out across the horizon, he's lost in his thoughts, Helena breathing softly next to him in her sleep. Elizabeth and Liam slumber inside the carriage, but the snores of their newest companion from atop the cart interrupt the peace and quiet Marcus is trying to find. As the lush green meadows change to golden desert sand, so does the wildlife. He no longer sees the howling deers or flighty sparrows; winged toads now rule the sky as hardened foxes swim the sands. When the warm air hits his face, Marcus is reminded of Nolan's war stories and days of traveling the world. Those stories are becoming his lived experience as each moment passes.

Marcus pulls over to replace Hornet's batteries, sitting beside her to take time for himself. The moment mistakenly becomes a few minutes as he drifts in and out of sleep until Helena flicks him on the nose.

"Sleeping on the job, I see," she jokes.

Blinking, he moans, "Ahh I'm sorry." He continues to tap his hands against both cheeks, fighting to stay awake.

"No, it's fine, you had a long night. I'll take it from here." Helena helps Marcus up, and they once again take to the road, trading places on the driving bench, where Helena takes the reins. Though she's given him the space to sleep, it's not long before Helena realizes Marcus can't seem to doze off again.

"What's wrong?" She asks, and he leans over, head tilting into his hands. "Seems like something is bothering you."

He sits back up and sighs, "I want to say I'm sorry..."

"For?"

"Last night. I lost my cool, let my emotions get the best of me, and I turned into an ass."

"Well, at least you know," she chuckles. "But, honestly, I don't understand why. Trust me, you're always a hothead, so picking a fight with a group of bandits isn't a surprise, but how you treated Creed was a little much."

"No...I know." Marcus pauses, gazing out across the horizon before looking over at Helena. "Can I be honest with you? Things haven't been the same since Nolan died, at least not for me. My head has been all over the place. One moment I feel like myself, then the next... I don't know, I'm just lost. Since I was a boy, all I've wanted is to be some kind of hero; a legendary knight that the world looked up to. But ever since the trial, I can't shake the feeling I'm on the wrong side."

"Then don't be," Helena shrugs, to Marcus' surprise. "Nolan recruited you because of your skills with a sword, but he promoted you based on your instincts. He knew one day you were going to be a great leader – you just have to get out of your own way. I know that, in your mind, this mission is all about giving Nolan some kind of honor in death. But we honor him by living up to his expectations."

"Easy enough for you to say," Marcus rebuts at the finality of her statement. "You're all but perfect in every way, Helena; your skills with a bow are unmatched. You showed Nolan more than enough for him to be proud."

"Not everything Nolan wanted for us involved a weapon, Marcus," she sighs, recognizing the naivety in his comment and the hurt in his heart. "The path we follow, we are responsible for leading, and that path should always allow us the privilege of accepting our death when that time comes. That's what Nolan wants for us, for you. That means taking your place as our leader, trusting your instincts, and coming out on the other side of all this a better person. Maybe even that legend you were talking about dreaming of becoming."

At her words, his shoulders drop, and he unclenches his jaw. He breathes in calmly for the first time since their conversation began, peace settling into his body. "You're so confident, Helena, and I admire that about you. But what happens when my instincts tell me to go against our orders? Will you still have my back then?" Though his body has relaxed with the peace she brings to him, the thoughts are unrelenting in his mind, convinced that she would leave at his leadership. She was worth more than a thousand men to him, and he couldn't dream of losing her in any capacity after losing Nolan.

"Trust me," she laughs, and he feels the breath he didn't know he was holding release from his lungs. "If I didn't have your back, you'd already have an arrow in it. But do you really think something's not right here?"

Marcus stretches, sitting back, and says, "I can't be sure, but from the dirty trial to the King's sudden willingness to break bylaws as long as we handle this 'little' mission of his, it's all just too odd for my liking." Despite the tense topic of conversation, Marcus has finally relaxed enough that his eyelids droop and he yawns."

"Liam and I agree. Everything just seems too convenient, like there's something bigger we aren't seeing; it even makes me question where Elizabeth stands in all this. I've been trying to get close to her, but she's...complex, to say the least."

"Honestly, I think she is as much of a pawn as we are. I can't help but want to protect her. Plus, why let Creed join us? If she is in on something it would just complicate things." Leaning his head into the palm of his hand, Marcus yawns again. "I'm not worried thoug h...the three of us will keep each other safe, just like Nolan would have wanted."

Helena watches as he finally falls asleep, sure that this man beside her will become the hero he's dreamt of becoming sooner rather than later. The slightest smile lights across her face at the thought, and, seeing his newfound peace flatten the crinkles in his forehead, a fierce protectiveness tightens around her heart.

A flock of winged toads flies overhead, croaking as they pass. She looks up as the desert sun warms her skin, a surprisingly familiar feeling. As she stretches under the blanket of heat, a gust of wind passes by, and she can't help but hear Nolan's voice simply say,

"We will be alright."

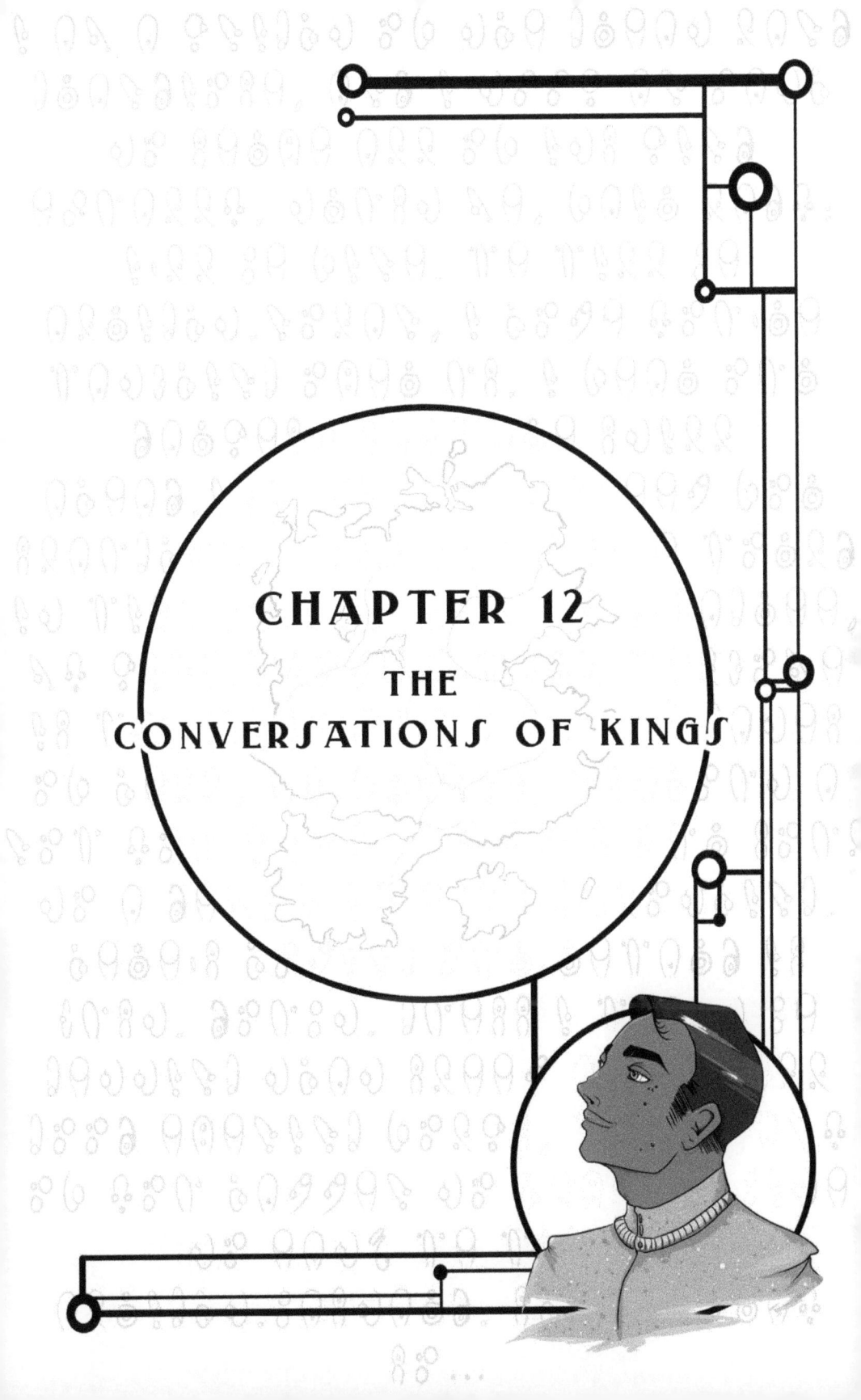

CHAPTER 12
THE
CONVERSATIONS OF KINGS

Chapter 12

The Conversations of Kings

"Get them back in line!" Callahan orders as the rowdy masses of Grandhaven pack the street, trying to catch a glimpse of the upcoming royal caravan. "Damn it, Regalia should have given us some more notice before just showing up at the front gate," Callahan bitches to himself as he continues to try to rally his knights to calm down the crowd.

"Well, we know the only thing greater than my brother's mind is his ego. Always lives like the world revolves around him," Red says, approaching Callahan from behind.

"Shouldn't you be at the castle to greet him?"

"My brother is here for King Uther; if he wants me, he'll find me afterwards."

Ordering his men to take over, Callahan observes, "You don't seem too excited to see him," and the lilt in his voice frames it as a question.

Red walks a step ahead of Callahan as they separate from the knights. "My brother and I have a complicated relationship. If it wasn't for us being mental equals, we'd likely never talk. Hell, I've lived his life three times over already. It's easy to understand why we don't have much common ground. Then, there's the fact that he's gorgeous and I'm, well, I wouldn't say I'm ugly, but I'm no prince."

While he had initially been interested in their dynamic, Callahan stops Red's ramble before it exceeds his limit for patience, directing him to the front entrance. The noise from the crowd rises to a blistering roar, and Callahan's eyes sweep his surroundings before landing on a carriage led by two large mechanical boars, flanked by knights on either side. Unlike other vehicles, this carriage is a modern work of art. Its slick, rounded edges and ornate carvings glow brightly, enhancing the white metal encasing it. The interior alone houses more amenities than many ordinary homes, including stoves to cook meals, heat, and lights so King Regalia can continue studying during the black of night.

Only once the caravan is safely within the kingdom walls does King Black Regalia order it to stop. He opens his quarters' doors, and a small platform extends from underneath the opening. Unlike his usual attire, Black does not don his typical lab coat; instead, he wears fine silk embroidered with golden details drapes from his shoulders. A bracelet embellished with small gemstones glows on each wrist, representing those used in his Q.A.S Tech. Each bracelet attaches to two small devices, one that covers his middle finger and another that covers the tip of his thumb. This gadget displays the capability of his Tech, and he often snaps his fingers to make a small flame or a tiny bolt of electricity.

Stepping onto the platform, he pushes a button. Suddenly, the platform rises into the air, a podium from which he can address the crowd as a whole – one that ensures every citizen can see him.

"People of Grandhaven, I thank you for the tremendous welcome. It means the world to me that you would allow me to disturb everyday life on such short notice, not to mention how much you have embraced my Q.A.S Tech. It's humbling." He continues to woo the crowd, snapping his fingers to impress them with his parlor tricks. The women of Grandhaven are particularly hooked on his every word, and he sends a wink their way, earning a handful of infatuated screams.

"For a man of science, he is impressively good at working a crowd," Callahan praises, watching from his place next to Red.

"People are machines to him: his words are just the tool he uses to bend them to his will," Red shoves off the comment, bitter, as he turns and heads back to the castle, Callahan joining him. Behind them, the crowd, entranced, continues to cheer at Black's every word.

"Well, if that's the case, he has truly mastered that tool. And he is all the more dangerous because of it."

Atop the castle tower, Uther studies, undeterred by the arrival of King Regalia or the cheers of the crowds below. Surrounded by books in his office, Sorro's diary lies directly in front of him. He reads through its pages, honing in on those involving now-forbidden magic. Closing the journal, Uther walks over to the case with his gauntlet and puts it on. Then, he moves over to a small table he has set up behind his desk, a dead bird and a small, violet, rod-shaped gemstone with its end sharpened to a point lying atop it. Uther examines the carcass before stabbing the gemstone into its back. As the gemstone goes deeper, it begins to glow, triggering the same reaction on Uther's gauntlet. As the glow intensifies, the bird's body starts to move. At first, there are only a few twitches, but before long, it moves as if it were living once more.

The gauntlet tightens around the King's hand as the bird hops around the table. Uther clenches his fist, and as he does, the bird's eyes glow the same violet as the gem wedged between its wings. He smirks, watching the creature move like a puppet attached to strings, following each move of his hand. He motions for the bird to take flight, and as it lifts its head, its body begins to smoke before bursting into violet flames. Uther now stares eye to eye with the hovering corpse, the translucent flames revealing the animal's skull underneath. Laughing like a child playing with a toy, he has the bird fly around the room, smiling devilishly. The bird soars through the air, and Uther's eyes begin to glow, his muscles tensing and veins bulging. The violet glow radiates through his skin, and before long, the magic starts to take a toll on him. His knees buckle, but he fights through the shaking of his muscles, slightly enjoying the pain. Sweat rolls down his face, and he calls the bird back to perch on his finger.

"You, my little friend, are the step towards a greater destiny," he breathes. The bird tilts his head as if curious about Uther's statement before suddenly exploding. Blood and organs splatter, dripping off Uther's face and chest as the glow dissipates from his body. Unfazed, he wipes his face off. Then, he hears a knocking on his chamber doors. Uther invites them to enter, and the guard announces his guest, *"King Black Regalia of New Haven."*

"Am I interrupting something?" Black asks mockingly as he walks into the room, a large briefcase in his hand.

"Unlike you, I can not put my life, or my kingdom's, on hold when you decide to show up unannounced," Uther responds, wiping the last of the blood from his body. "You should be thankful I even allowed you to get this far. Normally, when royalty approaches a kingdom uninvited, they tend to be followed by an army."

"Oh, Uther, you misunderstand my intention," Black laughs, placing the briefcase on Uther's desk and sitting down. "I only kept my visit a surprise to ensure my little gift made it here safely."

Uther shrugs. "Your fear is unwarranted. The actual *'Terra King'* hasn't attacked one of our *'shipments'* in nearly a cycle. Not to mention, since our feathered allies have gotten involved, our activity has been undisturbed." Uther returns to his desk and pulls the briefcase towards him.

"Well, with your bodyguard out there besmirching his name, I feared our *'friend'* might come out of retirement. That aside, I wanted to see your face when you saw my work. Some of my finest, if I do say so myself." Black crosses his legs and points to the case.

Uther clicks the case open, and his demeanor instantly shifts to excitement. Beneath its lid lies a custom forged morningstar. This perfectly crafted weapon sports a simpler design than Uther's gauntlet, with several markings carved into its black steel. The handle is wrapped in the finest leather, with a space for a small violet gemstone carved into the end. A sizable hollow sphere sits at the weapon's head with a second, much larger violet gem suspended within it. Several blades curve around the sphere with one final cone-shaped gemstone protruding from the top, its tip and sides encased in steel for support. Uther lifts the weapon from the case, and as he does, the morningstar and his gauntlet slightly begin to glow.

"You have outdone yourself, Black." Uther stands up, testing how the morningstar feels. At first, he ensures he has a good grip on it with a few mild swings before giving Black an extraordinary display of control. Uther moves around his office easily, spinning and swinging the weapon around as if it had been an extension of himself for years. After a few moments, he tosses the morningstar into the air only to jump off his chair to catch it midair, encouraged by the astonished look on Black's face. Before landing, he turns his body completely around and forcefully slashes across the air, a violet wave of energy firing from the tip of the morningstar. The wave slices through a giant statue sitting in the back of Uther's office, but the sculpture does not split. Instead, it bursts into a single violet flame almost identical to the one that engulfed the bird's head earlier. As his feet find the floor, the flame continues to cover the statue, yet it still does not burn.

Black claps, immensely enjoying Uther's display of acrobatics. His chest swells with pride: while Uther is undoubtedly talented, he knows that the other king's mastery of the morningstar is also attributed to his excellent workmanship. When Uther turns to return the weapon to its case, though, Black notices that his pupils now share the same violet glow.

"I must admit, when I gave your brother the blueprints for this, I never pictured it being so beautiful," Uther compliments. Once he closes the case, the glow softly fades from his eyes; not shortly after, the flame around the statue dissipates.

"You're too kind, Uther. Don't get me wrong, working a device of that magnitude into such a small casing was no easy task, but I am the smartest man alive," Black praises himself, "so if anyone could do it, it would be me." Pointing to the statue, unaltered by the flames, he continues, "Now, I only hope it yields better results against your enemies."

"The unliving tend to be immune to death," Uther says flatly.

"Says the man who would wish to control it," Black challenges, a shade of doubt in his voice.

Uther leans in. "Correct me if I am wrong, but your tone suggests you have lost faith in my plan." Staring down the other king, he cracks his neck and knuckles: a warning as Black prepares to respond.

"Not at all, Uther," Black says calmly, matching Uther's gaze. "I've been by your side since the start of all this, and I plan to see it through. But I've always been upfront with you, Uther. You're a man chasing the moon and, as happy as I am to help you reach it, I will not be there to catch you if you fall."

"Understood. I promised you long ago that you'd reap all the benefits of my success and none of the burdens of my defeat. Unlikely, though, as I do not foresee defeat in our future."

"Well, I continue to provide aid where I can to ensure this glorious future of yours."

Black and Uther take a moment, just staring at one another. Their allyship does nothing to attenuate the tension between them. While neither would admit it, this tension runs deeper than the rise or fall of Uther's glorious future: it's one that's been passed down for generations. The Regalias and the Whitelions always had very different approaches to ruling, which often led to conflict between them, which was generally only resolved when the two houses were forced to unite. Most recently, Black's aunt was married off to Uther's father.

"Well," Regalia sighs, standing, "I must be going. It would be rude for me to leave my wife and kingdom alone much longer. If you don't mind, though, I'd like to speak with my brother before I take my leave." When Uther nods his approval, Black bows, turning to the door.

As his hand turns the knob, Uther's voice breaks the tension between them. "Black, I understand having doubts. What I am attempting to accomplish is unheard of, and a man as wise as you would be a fool if you weren't somewhat concerned. But let me be clear: if you think you would benefit from my failure, then you are far from the smartest man alive. Is that understood?"

"Absolutely," Black answers before exiting the room. He momentarily stands outside the office door, his muscles trembling from anger at Uther's words. No one can outsmart King

Black Regalia, and he huffs under his breath, "Not even you." The flimsy foundation of his confidence in Uther is shaken at the implication.

Inside his study, Uther Whitelion can't shake his uncertainty about Regalia's support. Unbeknownst to him, the other king stands on the opposite side, questioning the trust between them as well.

Simultaneously, they both take a deep breath, uttering the same insult at the door to the other:

"Bastard."

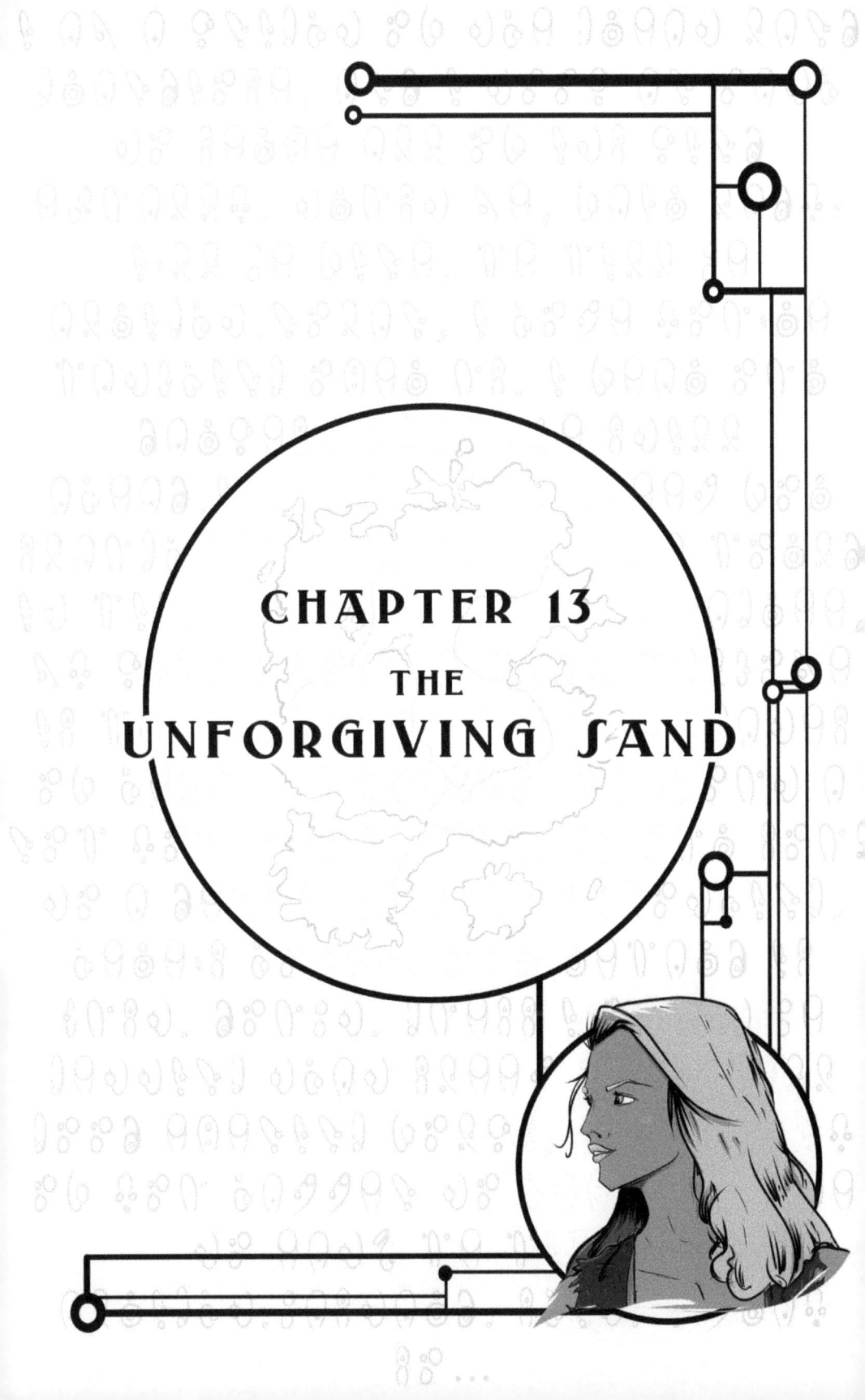

CHAPTER 13
THE
UNFORGIVING SAND

Chapter 13

The Unforgiving Sand

The sun beats down on the desert sands as the winged toads search for food. As one pulls a giant beetle from the ground, an ice arrow flies into the flock, just missing all the birds. Scared, the toads fly off.

"Not bad for your first shot. A little practice, and you may just put me out of a job," Helena compliments Elizabeth, using her armor to recharge the bow. From the cart, Creed watches the lesson. Helena says, "Now, this time, try to aim at where your target will be, not where it already is."

Stepping behind Elizabeth, Helena helps move her arm into place before she fires the bow. The arrow soars through the air, finding its target with ease. The fleeing toad hits the ground, and the arrow melts away. Elizabeth cheers, proud of herself, and Helena smiles.

Creed claps slowly, less than impressed. "Not that I could do much better, but I can't help but question whether that little toad is going to be able to feed us all," he mocks, rubbing his belly. Both Helena and Elizbeth roll their eyes before Helena takes back her bow.

"You're right, Creed, it won't – but like I said, you need to aim where your prey will be, not where it is." Just as Helena finishes, a hardened fox leaps out of the sand to snatch the fallen toad. Her reflexes are quicker than the fox's; Helena quickly turns around and shoots off an arrow, striking the fox in the chest in midair. Turning back to Creed, she winks. She and Elizbeth head out to collect the hunt while Creed stands, mouth agape, before rushing to catch up.

"Alright, then, color me impressed. Your little band of knights continues to blow my mind. No wonder the King trusted you with something so...important." His eyes scan over Elizabeth. "In fact, I can't help but feel like you're all doing a lot of work for very little reward.

Laying your friend to rest and all is commendable, but, if you ask me, a few extra gold pieces could go a long way."

"Knights are paid a salary, plus housing and rations in an amount dictated by the Council. It's illegal to pay them any less or tip them any more," Elizabeth informs Creed. They stop, standing in front of the fox.

"The King could offer us a fortune, and we would give it all back if it meant Nolan wouldn't end up in the belly of a bird," Helena tells them. Without pausing, she throws the fox over her shoulders, turning to head back to the cart.

"This Nolan must have been one hell of a man," Creed questions, quickening his pace to keep up.

"He was the best man I have ever known. He took me in when the world told me there was nowhere else for me, helped me be a better woman, gave me purpose...and I'm neither the first, nor the last, he did that for," Helena answers Creed, happy to honor her friend.

"Even before this little quest of ours, I had heard of the *'Steel Fist knight.'* His accomplishments on the battlefield are matched by very few other men," Elizabeth adds before Creed can interject again.

"He actually hated that name," Helena laughs. "He always said he was only able to break through that stone because it was cracked on the back side and no one noticed. He always joked that *'The Luckiest Knight Alive'* would have been more fitting."

"Seems like he lived up to the hype. So, how did he end up on the short list of next meals for the Crows?" While his question was sincere, Helena grimaces. She and Elizabeth stop immediately; unaware, Creed knocks into their backs. Eyes slit, Elizabeth looks back, silently asking, *"What the hell?"* Dumbfounded, Creed mouths back, *"What?"*

"Good question." Helena's voice is firm as she says, "Maybe when all this is over I'll have an answer." She doesn't look over at Elizabeth or back at Creed. Quickly, she walks forward, silent the rest of the way.

*****

Back at camp, Marcus and Liam watch and wait for the others to return with their afternoon meal. Removing a few logs out of the carriage, Liam throws them into a pile for Marcus to light with the end of his sword, building the fire.

In the distance, Hornet playfully chases passing tumbleweeds. Liam whistles to get her attention and calls out, "Hornet, calm down! Go rest before you wear down your batteries."

"I second that, old girl. It would be nice if you're awake the next time a group of bandits attack," the other's voice rings out. Marcus stares down at Liam, his eyes hard despite the light joke.

"Get over it, boy. It all worked out in the end. Not to mention, we got an extra set of helping hands out of the whole ordeal," Liam fires back. Hornet bounds up by his side, and they both take a seat.

"'Helping hands?'" Marcus argues, "Not sure I'd agree. Creed's been with us almost a week, and I don't think he's done more than sleep and shit."

"Give the man a break. If I remember correctly, it took Nolan a good half cycle to get your lazy ass straight." Liam reminds Marcus. His hand rubs the metal behind Hornet's ears, lulling her to sleep.

"That's true. But I'm sure as hell no Nolan." Marcus laughs as he takes a seat on Liam's other side. They watch the fire from afar, the late afternoon sun beating down on them.

"Nolan used to love this desert, said it was his favorite part about the trip to Dakuhm. That and trying to find evidence that Shadowbloods were real," Liam reminisces.

Quietly, Marcus asks, "Do you think we are making him proud?" His voice is soft, and Liam looks over at him as he continues, "You knew Nolan longer than any of us, if I trust anyone to speak for him it's you."

Liam smiles back gently and pats his friend's shoulder, giving him yet another chance to be vulnerable. "You two made him proud long before all this. From the moment you were promoted and the second the Academy handed Helena her bow, he knew his legacy was safe. He would tell me all the time how we were the family he thought he'd never have, how if he had a son he'd like it to be a lot like you. Still, that son would not be good enough for Helena." They both laugh. Removing his hand, Liam leans in the other direction, resting against the sleeping Hornet. "Marcus, I know how much this means to you, and I, too, would give my life to ensure my best friend rests easily. But know that Nolan would not want you to give up your future for a dead man. There is no doubt in my mind that someone had it out for him way before he even stepped foot in that courtroom – but let me worry about finding out who. You go back become a squad leader, give others the opportunities Nolan gave you. Honor him that way; that's what he would want."

Liam's words lay heavy on Marcus, but before he can continue the conversation, he notices the others' silhouettes across the horizon. Even though their faces are slightly out of view, Creed's voice rings out over the distance. Marcus rolls his eyes at the neverending talking.

"So, that's when I say to the bartender, 'If the drinks are this strong, just wait till you see your tip!'"

Marcus rises to greet the others, ignoring how Helena laughs at Creed's crude joke. "What took so long? Me and the old man are starving."

Handing the sandfox to him, Helena explains, "Figured I would take the opportunity to show Elizabeth how to use the bow." Her voice takes on an air of pride as she boasts, "A few more mornings of practice and we might be able to send her out there on her own."

"Almost brought back a flock of toads today, but Creed scared most of them off," Elizabeth teases.

"That's not how I remember it," Creed fires back. "But then again, it's early so I may still be sleep deprived." He laughs, walking past the fire to the carriage. Everyone sits around the fire except Liam, who stands off to the side, skinning the animals and preparing them to roast.

Instead of conversing with his friends, Marcus watches Creed intently, noticing how he fumbles around in the back of the carriage. "Looking for something to steal?" He asks facetiously across the distance, drawing the others' attention.

"Not at all," Creed replies, "I'm just making room."

"Room for what?"

"Me, of course. Like I said, it's early. Seems like a perfect time to catch up on my beauty sleep."

"Sleep! We're well into the afternoon. Get your lazy ass over here and help with this meal!" Marcus yells. Liam and Helena both laugh: though Marcus may not hear it in his own voice, he echoes the same rebukes Nolan once gave him.

"And how might you like me to do that, good sir? I don't know how to cook or skin an animal. To be quite honest, I'd just make a mess of things. You have to know your strengths, and those aren't mine. This is actually the most helpful thing I can do," Creed cheekily responds. Without waiting for a response, he disappears into the cabin of the carriage.

Marcus shakes his head. "Please remind me why we are letting him stay with us?"

"It's our duty as knights to help all those in need," Helena and Liam speak at the same time. Crossing his arms, he mockingly mouths the same answer, his nose wrinkled in agitation.

"One day, you'll be squad leader – and if karma has her way, most of your rookies will be twice the pain in the ass he is. This is good for your growth. Plus," Liam quips, "the girls seem to like him." He places the skinned fox over the fire to roast, a mischievous smile spreading across his face as he turns to see Marcus glaring at him.

"Creed's a good guy, he's just a little...different," Helena chimes in as she and Elizabeth slice a few vegetables.

"I have to agree: he's an oddity, but I like having him around. Maybe it's because I've been surrounded by knights and royalty for–" Hornet shoots up from her slumber in a panic, interrupting Elizabeth.

Liam tries to ask her what's wrong, but the ground begins to rumble. They all notice and reach for their weapons, Elizabeth instinctively putting her hood up. Before any of them can puzzle out what is going on, a large stone monolith erupts from underneath the carriage, sending it flying into the air. The moment the carriage hits the ground, several more monoliths erupt around it. As quickly as they rise, they close in on themselves, crushing the cart as they cave in on top of it.

"*Creed!*" they scream, staring at the rubble in shock. No one will say it, but they all know no one could survive the attack.

With no time to mourn, Liam, Marcus, and Helena form a protective barrier around Elizabeth as a shadowy figure approaches over the horizon. The figure begins to dash towards the group, creating a smaller monolith underneath his feet to launch himself closer. While midair, he pulls the stone structure from the ground behind him and fires it towards the group. Liam jumps in front of it, using his spear to slice the stone in two, each half falling to the side of the group. The assailant lands, and the knights can quickly identify him as the dust settles.

"Who the hell is this guy?" Elizabeth whispers, cowering behind Helena, to which she simply answers, *"The Terra King."*

In front of them stands Grandhaven's most wanted adversary. He's thin, but every muscle is perfectly defined and taut against his skin. Fine leather wraps around his arms and legs, and lightweight metal plates shield his chest and vital organs. The stone mask covering most of his head leaves his emerald eyes and double-pointed ears showing. While the top forms a crown of spikes, its face is covered in war paint, intimidating even to the knights. They recognize his apparent Oren descent between the exposed eyes, pointed ears, and dramatic display of magic.

"I would have thought my earlier warnings were enough, but I'm not surprised you humans are a stubborn lot," he says menacingly. Though his voice is muffled through the stone, his intentions are clear. As he comes closer, he summons a dozen fist-size rocks from the ground, commanding them to spiral around him.

Understanding the threat before them, Marcus motions for Helena to protect Elizabeth and then signals Liam to make the first move. Liam nods his head and whistles for Hornet, jumping to her back with ease, and they both charge towards the Terra King. As they get closer, the Terra King molds the stone into spikes before firing them directly at Liam. Liam directs Hornet from side to side, avoiding the spikes they can and using his spear to deflect the others. The Terra King's attack works: it slows them down just long enough for him to make his next move. As Liam clears the final spike, the Terra King disrupts the ground in front of Hornet, and she loses her footing, tossing Liam from her back. While Liam is agile enough to land on his feet, Hornet falters. Before she can get her footing, the Terra King forms a stone cage around her, trapping her inside. He allows it to completely encase her, drawing slow whimpers and eventual howls to escape from the animal as he makes it impossible for her to move.

"You son of a bitch!" Liam cries out, listening to Hornet's pained cries. He lunges forward, rapidly thrusting his spear at the Terra King. None have ever escaped from Liam's enraged attacks, but to the surprise of everyone, the Terra King can deflect each stab. Throughout the attack, Liam analyzes his opponent's skills: quick footwork and the instant creation of small stone shields when the Terra King cannot move away fast enough. Pausing, Liam takes a step back and resets his stance.

"Your reputation precedes you," he says, calming his breathing and preparing for his next attack. "I see why so many of my fellow knights have fallen to you."

"Your compliment isn't lost on me, so allow me to return it. You're the first of your kind to stand your ground against me." As the Terra King speaks, he again pulls several stones from the earth, morphing them into daggers. His ego shines through, choosing again to have his weapons rotate around him. "They tend to run the moment I crush their oh-so-precious cargo."

"Well, thank you for recognizing how I am not like my peers. It will help your death to not wear heavy on my soul." As the last word leaves, Liam again charges in for the attack. This time, he drags his spear against the ground and revs it up, causing sparks to fly off its tip. In response, the Terra King fires off a handful of stone daggers, but instead of slowing down, Liam pushes through, not stopping even as one lodges into his shoulder. As he gains ground against his adversary, he swings his spear upwards, tossing sand into the Terra King's face. His opponent falls back, shielding his eyes, and Liam takes the opportunity to swing his spear once more, this time cutting across his chest plate and leaving a fair-sized metal scar.

Shocked that Liam was able to get so close to him, the Terra King panics, building a large stone wall in front of himself. As the wall pushes the knight away from him, Liam pushes back on the wall, slowing down his backward movement to sidestep it, slamming to the ground. Liam, though, has no time to breathe. Just as he avoids one disaster, the Terra King is back on the attack, launching an onslaught of stones at Liam as he rushes in.

While Marcus had initially stayed with Helena to protect Elizabeth, he's observed the Terra King's strategy as well, and sees him beginning to wear Liam down. Refusing to lose another friend, Marcus orders Helena to get Elizabeth to safety before he, too, enters the battle. Yet unnoticed by the Terra King, who is still intent on his battle against Liam, Marcus fires his sword toward their opponent's head. At the last moment, the Terra King realizes the danger he is in and is forced to stop his assault on Liam so that he can duck out of the way. Freed from the onslaught, Liam rushes in, again attempting to take down the Terra King, but to no avail as the King narrowly manages to evade his spear. Marcus quickly recovers his sword and joins in on the assault. Together, they finally begin to overwhelm the Terra King's defense.

Recognizing that he cannot survive the frantic attacks of both knights, the Terra King raises a monolith to launch himself into the air and out of danger. Having spent the entire battle analyzing his opponent's strategy, Liam quickly launches his spear at the Terra King. Though it fails to land fatally, the spear bounces off his chest plate, forcefully knocking him back to the ground. The moment the Terra King lands, Marcus swiftly strikes, aiming for the King's neck. Simultaneously, Liam uses the monolith to his advantage, leaps into the air, catches his spear in its descent, and fires it back at the Terra King. Unused to fighting multiple worthy opponents, King is able to avoid Marcus's sword but is not quick enough to completely dodge the spear. It slices across his right bicep, drawing a guttural roar from deep within him, partly pained and mostly enraged. The Terra King grips his arm, but the wound does not slow him down.

Marcus and Liam immediately notice this change in demeanor. The Terra King pulls a metal shortsword from within the leather wrapped around his leg and dashes forward at a phantom-like speed, easily double what he was moving at before. Their teamwork moments before had given Liam hope for defeat, but with this new level of attack, Liam realizes they may now be outmatched. He moves to avoid the next round, but Marcus brutishly charges in for another attack. Usually attuned to Liam's moves, he is too focused on bringing down their opponent, and this uncharacteristic tactic opens Marcus up to an array of attacks. Quickly, the Terra King catches him off-guard and stabs him in the chest, just below his shoulder plate. With Marcus wounded, the Terra King confidently removes and launches the dagger at Liam. Though he can deflect it, he quickly realizes that, without his partner, he, too, is now open to the Terra King's next attack.

Immediately, their enemy encases both knights' feet in stone, trapping them where they stand. Laughing menacingly, he unleashes a fury of kicks and punches on both knights, his anger at being wounded taking over his body. Once finished, the Terra King steps back and swings towards Liam's face with the shortsword. Before the blade makes contact, an ice arrow comes out of nowhere, sending the shortsword falling from the Terra King's hand. Stunned, he looks over and sees Helena preparing for another attack. While he knew three knights were present, the battle with Marcus and Liam had distracted him from the third. Seeing a new threat on his battlefield, the Terra King pulls two stone pillars from the earth, sending them to strike both Liam and Marcus in the gut, falling across the desert in opposite directions. With both men incapacitated, he turns his attention to Helena.

Helena and the Terra King stare each down intensely, strategizing, as a gust of wind passes. For a moment, the world goes quiet. Then, the Terra King rapidly fires hundreds of small stone pellets at Helena; to his amazement, she deflects each one with equivalent arrows. The Terra King follows up his previous attack by catapulting himself towards Helena, firing off a fury of larger stones at her as he soars through the air. Again, Helena avoids the barrage, ultimately using one of the stones to propel herself into the air as well, landing a forceful kick to the side of the Terra King's head. Landing, Helena immediately goes back on the attack, firing numerous arrows with pinpoint accuracy to where her foot had contacted his skull. The Terra King can only stop the assault by once again erecting a large stone wall in front of himself and pushing it toward his opponent. She quickly moves out of the way, but before she attacks again, she notices that her previous shots are not in vain: a portion of his mask glints off the ground a few meters away. Seeing where her eyes fell, the Terra King quickly picks some of the earth from the ground and repairs what remains on his face.

Beginning to laugh, he compliments her, a distraction as he gains his bearings back. "You are impressive to say the least. Why in the eight kingdoms did you not lead the assault?"

"For a 'king,' you seem to lack the mind for battle. No army ever opens its assault with its greatest assets." Helena mocks, readying for her next attack.

"Oh, is that the case? Forgive me; I thought you were holding back your 'greatest asset' to protect your most important one this whole time." The Terra King points to a group of rocks near where they stand. A drop of sweat rolls down Helena's face as she realizes he knows where Elizabeth is hiding.

"I will never let you lay a hand on her," Helena threatens, gritting her teeth as she points her bow directly at his head.

"You are undoubtedly formidable, but you unfortunately don't have a choice in the matter," he finishes, slamming his fist against the ground. Immediately, the ground shakes before dozens of stone statues shoot up from the earth, each mirroring the Terra King's appearance. Helena is almost instantly surrounded by a sea of stone sculptures, and it becomes impossible to locate the true Terra King. Disoriented, Helna begins to fire arrows at the decoys, each crumbling upon contact. She destroys many of them, but she, too, has fallen prey to his distractions. Before she notices, the Terra King rushes in, forcing a stone pillar into her stomach and knocking the wind out of her. As Helena drops to her knees, the Terra King shoves another pillar at her, sending her falling across the desert, just as Liam and Marcus had.

He waves his hand, and his stone doppelgangers dissipate into dust as he turns his attention to Elizabeth. He lifts the rocks that hide her into the air before tossing them to the side and approaching the woman.

"Don't you dare come any closer!" Elizabeth cries in fear, breathing heavily.

"I do not wish to hurt you, but I do want answers. I can't help but feel you have them." As he speaks, he reaches his hand toward her.

Elizabeth's voice quakes in anger as she calls out, "I said stay the hell back!" She stands up, and as she does, her nails begin to extend from her fingers, blackening as they grow to a point. The Terra King stops, staring. He shakes himself out of his astonishment, thoroughly taking in the woman before him. After a moment, he realizes her true identity and his demeanor instantly shifts.

"You're half breed, aren't you? Do you understand how import—"

His words are interrupted in shock as the carriage flies towards him. Panicked, he creates a large stone blade, slicing the carriage in two to protect himself. Elizabeth and the Terra King both look over at the rubble where the carriage once lay. There, bloody and bruised, stands Creed. His eyes are pure white, and an unknown intensity radiates off him, his body trembling.

"I don't know who the hell you are, but I am going to rip your bloody head off!" Creed growls with a beastly undertone, and he begins to transform. His muscles triple in size as they tear through his skin, his face morphing into a snout and his teeth becoming an endless row of fangs. The sound of bones breaking echoes through the desert as his spine becomes a row of spikes protruding from his back, and a massive golden-scaled tail extends from his backside. In moments, the man they knew as Creed instead stands as a ferocious golden Dargone that stands ready to attack. Intimidatingly, Creed lets out a roar so fierce it pushes the Terra King back and wakes the knights out of unconsciousness. The Terra King looks over as Creed hones his gaze on him. He clenches his fist, cracking his knuckles, and utters the only statement fitting of the situation:

"Shit."

CHAPTER 14
THE
BEAST WITHIN

Chapter 14

The Beast Within

"He's a damn Shadowblood!" Liam cries out over Creed's monstrous roar as he, Marcus, and Helena struggle to their feet.

"Well, that's one thing I managed to see before Nolan did," Marcus quips, grasping at his side and coughing. Creed lets out another roar as he climbs out of the rubble, his eyes firmly locked on the Terra King.

"We can ask questions later. For now, let's take the opportunity to get Elizabeth to safety, then get our asses back in the fight," Helena rallies. They ready their weapons and charge into battle, but before he can pick up any speed, Marcus again starts to cough, immediately stopping him in his tracks. He covers his mouth as the cough worsens, removing it to find his palm filled with blood. His vision blurs as he watches the others fade from view, and before he can call for help, he passes out, crashing to the ground.

Back on the battlefield, Creed and the Terra King stare each other down. Like an arrow fired from a bow, Creed charges forward with unbelievable speed. Attempting to slow him, the Terra King creates several stone walls within the path between them, to no avail. As fast as the walls can rise from the earth, Creed smashes them back into dust. Before the Terra King can make another move, Creed is face-to-face with him. Creed smiles at the shock in the Terra King's eyes before unleashing a punch, their opponent flying across the battlefield.

The Terra King barely lands on his feet before Creed is back on the attack, landing a fury of punches and tail whips. The Terra King is only able to break free of the attacks by encasing himself in stone, allowing him to dive underneath the sand. Tearing away the rocks, Creed finds that the Terra King is no longer there. As he searches for his newfound enemy, a myriad of stone blades launch out of the ground and race towards him. Moving quickly, he uses his tail to deflect those he cannot evade, but the distraction allows the Terra King to launch himself from underneath the ground. Now, he has encased his hand within a mass of rock, forming a stone fist, which he uses to land his first hit against Creed. The Terra King follows up his attack with a series of high kicks, each time covering his foot in stone before striking it across Creed's face.

With each blow, he becomes more prideful, assured that he has the advantage, and the Terra King goes in for an uppercut with the large stone. Creed surprises him, quickly placing him in a vice-like bear hug. This stance quickly becomes a suplex, and the Terra King lands thunderously against the ground. He has no time to process this attack because, in an instant, Creed is on top of him, pounding away with dozens of tail slams before taking him by the neck and tossing him into the sky.

The Terra King attempts to reorient himself midair and keep his eyes on Creed, waiting for his next attack. To his surprise, an ice arrow strikes him across the chest. Distracted by Creed's onslaught, he hadn't noticed that the knights had escaped and were joining forces to defeat him. Wincing in pain, he has no time to identify where the attack came from before Liam leaps into the air, hammering the Terra King to the ground with both fists. Creed rushes in once more and grabs the Terra King by one leg before swinging him around and tossing him across the desert. As he soars across the battlefield, Helena fires off arrows, many making contact before the Terra King manages to surround himself in a stone coffin of protection. The coffin crashes to the ground and crumbles away, leaving the Terra King lying on the ground in pain.

"Here's our chance! Let's end this!" Liam encourages the others, going for one final blow. Helena and Creed follow suit, surrounding the Terra King. In pain and breathing heavily, the Terra King watches as everyone draws closer. The moment they reach attack range, he launches onto his feet, slams his hand against the ground, and cries, *"Enough!"* Instantly, the earth wraps itself around everyone's feet, stopping them immediately. As they struggle to get free, the Terra King pushes large spikes from the ground, stopping them inches from his attackers' necks. They stand rigidly, no longer able to struggle against their stone-covered holds without risking impalement. Frozen, they warily observe the Terra King, each observing how he is draining the last of his strength to keep them at bay.

"You're surrounded. Give up and turn yourself in!" Liam demands as he raves his spear in an intimidating fashion, ignoring his predicament.

"I think I'd rather not, old man," The Terra King replies, struggling to catch his breath.

"Then die!" Creed roars before biting down on the spike in front of him, crushing it. The Terra King quickly responds, extending what remains into a makeshift collar, which he uses to pull Creed to the ground. It noticeably takes more energy out of him.

Mockingly, he says, "Well, if I die today, at least I won't be alone." Then, he falls to one knee, struggling even more to keep them tangled up.

"For someone at the end of their rope, you sure are cocky," Helena tells him as she pulls back on her bow, readying her kill shot.

"Not cocky, just prepared. You see, that blade I used earlier may not have been legendary, but it was highly poisonous. Something your friend over there is finding out firsthand." The Terra King informs them, waving over at the unconscious Marcus with blood running from his mouth. The knights look over in panic, finally realizing he had not been fighting beside them.

"You son of a…I'll kill you!" Helena goes to fire her bow in anger, but the Terra King pushes the spike closer, forcing her to stand back.

"Listen: no one has to die today!" The Terra King yells out as he manages to stand up. "The poison I used disables my opponent quickly and, if not treated within a few hours, is deadly. But it is curable. Get your friend to a doctor, and he'll just need a good night's rest before he is back to normal."

Liam and Helena look at each other, conflicted. As knights, they should follow their duty and end the threat of the Terra King at any cost; as friends, if not family, the idea of losing another one of their own is unbearable.

"Hear me out!" The Terra King pleads, "You are clearly not what I thought you were, and I have a feeling we both have other missions to attend to. Let's agree to this draw so we all can leave this day with our lives intact." Liam and Helena look at each other before glancing over at Creed, who nods in approval after failing to free himself. Helena lowers her bow, and Liam follows with his spear. The Terra King sighs in relief, then lowers the spikes. "I commend your commitment to one another. Maybe if the rest of your kind could learn such compassion, someone like me would not exist." Finished, the Terra King again surrounds himself in a stone structure that quickly sinks beneath the ground.

After a few moments, the stone housing keeping the knights and Creed in place dissolves, freeing them. They rush to Marcus, Helena quickly pulling him into her arms. Elizabeth, who had gone to hide behind the remaining wreckage of the carriage when Creed emerged, soon joins them.

"We have to get him help," Helena pleads, checking for his pulse. "He's fading."

"Hornet, quickly!" Liam cries out to his now free companion. While Hornet wants to obey, she can barely stand. The battlecat attempts to move, but with every step, her limbs spark, and small parts fall off. She looks over at the group and cries as she falls to the ground. Liam reaches out to her, realizing that she cannot go on for now.

"There's no way we could make it to Riverhaven in time without her." Liam shakes his head in defeat, convinced he is about to lose another friend.

"How about Dakuhm?' Creed questions to the surprise of the others. "If you'll trust me, I can carry him there. At my top speeds, I should be able to get him there by tomorrow morning at the latest."

"Dakuhm?" Elizabeth questions with an odd amount of concern. "Making that detour could drastically alter the timeframe in which we get to Riverhaven."

'That's something we have to risk." Helena speaks up while wiping the blood from Marcus's mouth."Riverhaven will be there no matter what we choose to do. Marcus doesn't have that luxury."

"Then that decides it, we will tie Marcus to Creed's back and he will take our friend to Dakuhm. Meanwhile," Liam orders, "I'll repair Hornet, and we'll salvage everything we can from the carriage."

"But..." Elizabeth again questions. "I'm sorry. How can you trust him with someone so close to you?" Elizabeth takes a step back as Creed stares at her. "Hear me out: we just met Creed, and it's clear he's been hiding things. How do we know he won't just run off and we'll never see him again?"

Under his breath, Creed growls, then pleads his case. "I may not be what you thought, but I am not a monster. I can't promise I won't run off and hide once again, but before I do, nothing will stop me from getting him to safety." Approaching Elizabeth slowly, he puts his massive hand on her shoulder. "You all have treated me better than anyone I can remember in some time. Let me return that kindness. Not to mention, after seeing those two fight, I'd rather not be on their bad side."

Elizabeth puts her hand on Creed's; she can tell he is being genuine. She nods to the others and now, with all of them in agreement, helps load Marcus onto Creed's back.

"If I remember correctly, there's a doctor in front of the marketplace. Take him there and this should be enough to assure them we will have the rest once we arrive," Liam informs Creed as he hands him a bag full of credits. Creed says a quick goodbye before taking off with breathtaking speed, leaving a massive cloud of sand behind him. Liam and Helena watch as Creed fades into the distance. Elizabeth notices something glistening by her side and discreetly pushes away the sand. To her surprise, she finds the dagger the Terra King used to poison Marcus. Intrigued, she places it in her pocket before joining the others once more.

"Are we doing the right thing?" she questions. Liam and Elizabeth turn to her, both with tears in their eyes, and simultaneously say to her,

"I pray so..."

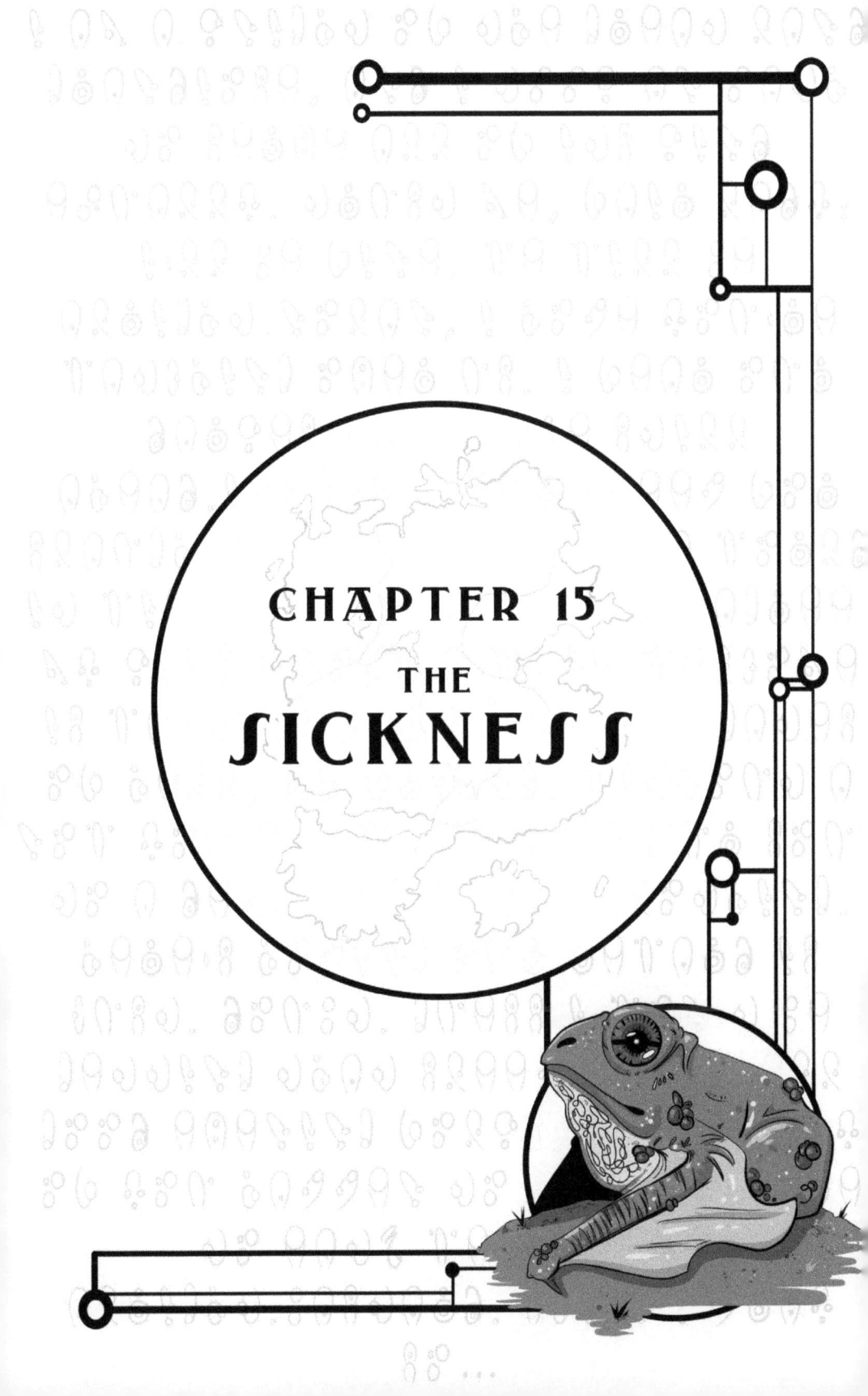

CHAPTER 15
THE SICKNESS

Chapter 15

The Sickness

KNOCK
KNOCK
KNOCK

Callahan awoke to knocking on his chamber doors, followed by the voice of a sweet Elderly woman.

"Time to awake, Sir Callahan, the rise is on its way."

"Go away," Callahan replies, but he begrudgingly climbs out of bed. His room is just inside the castle walls, at the end of the servants' quarters. A simple design with only a curtain separating the living area from the restroom, the room barely highlights the life of the one inside. Aside from a weathered painting of his father, the former leader of the first squad, his walls are barren. As he stands, he cracks his neck and looks out his sole window. As he heads towards the room's curtain, the sun slowly breaks through the darkness.

"I'm coming in. I can hear you pissing, so I know you're up," the Elderly woman calls out before she opens his door. Her warm smile seems out of place in a kingdom like this, radiating a kindness few know anymore. Her hands carry a tray topped with various morning foods and, more curiously, a scroll. The Elderly woman places the tray on a small table in the corner, turning toward a Q.A.S-powered ice box. She pulls out a jug of milk and pours Callahan a glass before he emerges from behind the curtain. Like a waltz, they effortlessly change places: he sits at the table and starts to eat while the Elderly woman goes to clean out his chamber pot. As she lifts the pot, she notices a large amount of blood mixed in with the urine.

"Are you eating the ginger root and drinking the carrot juice like the doctor said, sir?" she inquires, emptying the pot out the window.

"I don't have time for that shit," Callahan grumbles, a few bits of food flying from his mouth as he eats.

"You're just as hard headed as your father was. It would have been the death of him, too, if the sword hadn't gotten to him first." She scolds him while making up his bed.

"Leave my father out of your mouth, old hag," Callahan insults her, but she pays him no mind, continuing to clean up his quarters. "What the hell are you doing here anyway? Nothing better you could be doing with your time?"

"Not really, to be honest with you." With Callahan's bed done, she is now rummaging through his pantry, keeping up the conversation all the while. "Not much work for us handmaidens in a castle with no queen."

"Why complain? You're getting paid to sit on your ass most days." Callahan finishes the last part of his meal and then down the milk. As he does, the Elderly woman moves from the pantry back to his ice box.

"Not complaining one bit. Just like you, I'd give my life for this castle; but since Queen Whitelion's unfortunate passing, and with Lady Elizabeth gone, there's not much for me to do. So, I have to keep myself busy taking care of fools like you." She cleans up what's left of Callahan's meal as he leaves the table, beginning to get dressed.

"Trust me, you'll die in this castle waiting for another queen. So, do yourself a favor, ask for your release, and go enjoy the rest of your life outside these castle walls," Callahan warns the Elderly lady, uncharacteristically sincere, while he fastens his armor.

"Appreciate the warning, dear, but I'm happy just where I am." She places the scroll on his table before picking up the tray and leaving. Callahan finally notices the scroll and walks back toward the table. As he reaches for it, he notices that she has also left a bit of ginger root and a glass of carrot juice on the table. Sighing, Callahan sits down once more, opening the scroll. As he reads, he slowly finishes the glass of juice. With a disgusted expression, he swallows the ginger root before he leaves for the day.

Before long, Callahan is in the castle lift, waiting to start his typical workday. When the doors open, he steps back in surprise as two guards swarm his vision.

"Sir, it's the King," the first says hurriedly.

"Is he safe?!" Callahan cries, rushing through the lift doors and grabbing the guard who had spoken.

Trembling, he replies, "We aren't sure, sir. He locked himself in his bath chamber late last night and hasn't come out yet." To his side, the second guard breathes slowly, trying to calm himself. Both fear potential repercussions. "We knocked upon the door several times...but each time, he demanded we leave him be."

Callahan loosens his grip on the guard. "If he is answering you, then he is safe and only wants privacy – something we should honor," Callahan tells them, patting off dirt from the guard's shoulder.

"That's just it, sir," the second guard begins hesitantly. "A few hours ago, we heard terrible moans. He... he hasn't answered since." As he finishes, he takes a step back, bracing for backlash from Callahan. The guard's fears are realized when Callahan's demeanor quickly changes, grabbing both by their necks and slamming them against the wall behind them.

"Why in hell am I just now hearing this!" Callahan roars out in anger. He pulls them off the wall only to slam them back into it a second time. "I don't give a damn whether the King sneezes or loses an arm. I should be informed immediately!"

Their breath fades quickly, his grip crushing their airway. "Yes, sir," they pant out. It does nothing to appease his anger, but they're quickly tossed across the room, clutching their throats and catching their breath, as Callahan storms off in the opposite direction.

He arrives at the King's bath chambers and demands the guard there to move, then violently knocks on the door.

"My lord, it's Callahan. Please answer me. Let me know you're safe, or I will have no choice but to tear down this door." Callahan waits for an answer, but one never comes. As promised, he rams himself into the door, quickly knocking it off its hinges. He peers into the nearly pitch-black room, squinting in the dim light of a handful of candles surrounding the massive tub in the center. Seeing Uther sitting at its edge, Callahan slowly enters the room, equipping his shield in preparation – for what, he is unsure. As he approaches the tub, he notices a knife glinting in the candlelight on the floor near the King. With his next step, his eyes adjust, widening in shock as he realizes the swirls in the water are streaked red. Fearing the worst, he sweeps quickly toward his King. But Uther lifts his hand before Callahan reaches him, a wordless command. The knight follows his order.

"History tells us that humans cannot use magic because our bodies cannot handle it, yet, when we think about it, we have more in common with Orens than we do not." His tone is calm, as if he has ascended into a new realm of enlightenment, and it haunts Callahan. "We both bleed and breathe air; we have skin and eyes that all work the same. So why is it that when we try to play with fire, we get burnt?" Uther's fingers drip a mix of blood and water as he rises from the edge of the tub, but he seems unfazed. "Our forefathers chalk it up to divine intervention, that we are just lesser beings, untouched by Sorro's grace, but I believe there's more to it." Slowly, Uther raises his arms, and as he does, the flames of each candle shift from red to deep violet. "As I read more into it, I found that we never truly tried, did we? We failed and got scared of it, so we replaced it."

Uther turns around, and Callahan's breathing hitches, shocked. Even in the dim candlelight, he can see hundreds of Oren ruins crudely carved into his King's chest and arms, some so fresh blood is still dripping from them. His eyes glance at the knife on the ground before fixing back on Uther.

"But I am not scared that I will fail. Do you know why?" Uther asks. Knowing his knight well enough to know he would answer in whatever way would please the King, he continues, "Because I am willing to do whatever it takes to transcend this meaningless existence!" Uther's calm tone fades away with each word, and the flames intensify. His eyes glow a piercing violet, and each rune does the same. Now, Uther stands before Callahan, a new man giving off an undeniably powerful energy.

Noticing Callahan's hesitation towards him, Uther picks up the knife and comes closer, saying, "No need to fear me, old man. This is the start for everyone to get what they want." As he approaches the knight, the violet of the candles' flames fade back to normal, as does Uther's glow. He hands the knife to Callahan, then grabs a towel and covers himself. Trembling, Callahan looks down at the knife, blood still dripping down its blade. He knew the King wanted something greater but never thought he would go so far in his pursuit of power.

When Uther moves to leave, Callahan snaps out of his trance. "My King, before you go, there is something you must see," he says, pulling the scroll from his side as Uther turns back toward him. "Lady Elizabeth's carriage was attacked. Reports believe it was the Terra King." Callahan hands the scroll to Uther.

"Were there any casualties? Word on if the cargo survived?" Uther questions as he skims over the report.

"We don't believe so. Witnesses say that a male Dargone has rushed one of the knights to a medical facility within the walls of Dakuhm. Others say two knights are escorting a hooded figure in the same direction."

"Interesting," Uther says, which surprises the knight. He rolls up the scroll and hands it back to Callahan. "I do not want any of my belongings being housed in the slums of Dakuhm, so contact King Grayscale and ask for a favor. I will reach out to Ramon to ensure this delay does not affect our arrangements." Callahan complacently nods, and then Uther walks off. Shortly after, Callahan leaves the bathhouse, and Red awaits outside.

"The guards informed me of some disturbing noises coming from this room. Figured I should investigate," Red offers Callahan.

"Did you see the King on your way here?" Callahan asks.

"How could I miss him?" Red replies smugly.

"Then you should get ready," Callahan replies while walking away. Callahan never stops walking, even when he hears Red's inevitable questioning response. The whole time, the knight's eyes are transfixed upon the bloodied blade. His answer is simple:

"The new world."

CHAPTER 16
THE
KINGDOM OF DAKUHM

Chapter 16

The Kingdom of Dakuhm

Timidly, barely functional, Hornet trudges through the desert sand, Liam and Helena dragging what remains of their carriage beside her. Elizabeth, though, sits on the battlecat's back, examining the poisonous dagger left behind by the Terra King.

"No denying it now, our friend the Terra King is undoubtedly of Oren descent," Elizabeth declares, breaking the silence that has proceeded throughout the detour to Dakhum.

"Was it the pillars of rock he threw at us or the army of golems that gave it away?" Liam grunts sarcastically, the sun beating down on them. The weight of the carriage weighs down every step, and the weight of worry for his friend weighs down his mind.

"I'll chalk up your tone to fatigue," Elizabeth replies, uncharacteristically sassy. "You'd be surprised what can be done with Q.A.S Tech as of late, so neither. What actually cements it is this dagger and, more importantly, the poison."

"Didn't know you were so proficient in the study of poisons," Helena groans, enduring the pain of dragging their supplies.

"Well, I am no expert, but with the little free time I had in the castle, Master Red would help me study the particulars of my two species. In our time together, we came across an interesting tidbit: an Oren's blood is poisonous." The quick reflection on her time in the castle reminds her that she is no longer just a lady being transported by knights; now, she is capable of warfare, and these are her friends. Realizing they need help, she puts away the dagger, jumps off Hornet, and joins them in pulling the wreckage. "It's not deadly on its own, but mixed with the right ingredients, it could give someone an upset stomach…or even kill them in a few heartbeats."

"Interesting," Helena indulges Elizabeth. Though she knows their job is to protect her, she is relieved to have the help.

"We thought so as well, but at the time, neither of us could figure out how it could be used discreetly. Seems like our Terra King has beaten us to it."

"If what you're saying is true, that means he wasn't trying to kill us," Liam intervenes. "If he is capable of weaponizing it in that dagger, he knows how deadly it can be. That means he is intentionally using a survivable dose."

"Hmm...I didn't think about it that way. You're saying our assailant has a heart," Elizabeth jokes, but she, too, is intrigued by this train of thought.

"Anyone who forces me to carry this shit across a desert is a soulless asshole!" Liam yells out with a welcoming smile.

"Well, you're in luck, old friend, 'cause we are here," Helena informs them. They stop at a massive crater in the middle of the desert, and Elizabeth gazes across the horizon in confusion.

"The heat may be getting to you, Helena. There is nothing here but an empty canyon."

Liam and Helena smile at each other, amused by Elizabeth's naïve ignorance, then point downward into the canyon. Still bewildered, Elizabeth walks cautiously to the edge of the opening. Her eyes widen with wonder as her gaze reaches over the rim of the crater. Hidden deep within the canyon and its walls is the large stone city of Dakuhm. Together, they make their way down the side of the canyon, choosing one of the many stone-paved roads leading to the city. After declaring their purpose to the guard at the gate, they enter the city.

Elizabeth is left speechless.

Dakuhm is a sight to behold, with thousands of hand-built stone huts lying on top of one another. Ornate carvings cover each structure, depicting the city's and its people's history. Its streets are wider than Grandhaven, filled with hundreds of Dargones and only a handful of humans, almost all either knights or traveling merchants. Elizabeth watches in awe as Dargones leap from the street to the higher huts and vice versa. One landed right in front of her, apologizing with a smile for scaring her.

While Elizabeth watches in amazement, Helena and Liam check their cargo and Hornet into a local maintenance stable. Once everything is signed in, they begin asking the locals if anyone has seen a Dargone carrying a wounded knight. Before long, they are directed to a doctor's office within Dakuhm's Nourishment Circle, a large district within the city known worldwide as the home of Grandiose's finest cuisine. It lies in the city's center, and all roads lead to the circle, making it easy to find. As they approach, the air fills with the most enticing smells.

Liam's nose perks up as he reminisces. "Oh, this brings back memories. Nolan and I loved it here. We'd lose a few weeks' pay everytime we visited on food and drink alone."

"The food has to be the one thing I miss most about this place as well," Helena says, also losing herself in the smells of the city.

"You have been here before, my dear? Why have you waited 'til now to tell us?" Liam questions, breaking Helena of her trance.

She lowers her eyes, refusing to look back at Liam, upset by the slip of her tongue. "Sorry," she mutters, "I guess it never came up. It was a long time ago, and I was just a child. I don't remember much." Deflecting, she continues, "Maybe you can show us some of you and Nolan's favorite places?"

Liam's forehead creases as he wonders whether Helena is being entirely forthcoming, but he respects his friend too much to cross her obvious boundary. He nods but continues in silence, giving her the space he thinks she may need.

Not long after, they reach the circle. Elizabeth's awe is new, but even Liam and Helena still take a sharp breath at the sight before them. The Nourishment Circle is packed with Dargones surrounding numerous street chefs. Elizabeth exudes childlike joy, attempting to look over the crowds for a glimpse of these master cooks. Liam and Helena notice her excitement, handing her some credits, and she hurries off, giddy to try some of the renowned cuisine.

She snakes around the crowds of Dargones, easily spotting openings between their tails that she can squeeze through to continue down the street. Not far behind, her friends continue to question Marcus' whereabouts. Finally, she stops at a station whose scents make her stomach leap, purchasing a large bowl of local noodles and fried meats. Elizabeth is instantly lost in the flavors, distracted, and she doesn't notice a small group of Dargone soldiers surrounding her.

Each soldier sports leather armor, equipped with stone hammers and lances. As Elizabeth attempts to back away, she steps directly into the chest of a royal-looking female Dargone. Unlike the others, this Dargone is covered head-to-tail in beautiful tattoos, and her pierced nose houses a large diamond. She grabs Elizabeth by the arm, looks her in the eyes, and fiercely declares,

"Lady Elizabeth, by order of King Grayscale you are to come with us."

CHAPTER 17
THE
NIGHTMARES WE LIVE

Chapter 17

The Nightmares We Live

Unaware of the others' arrival, Creed waits in a room above the Nourishment Circle as his old family doctor tends to Marcus' poison. The doctor is an old Dargone, large in size but lacking the muscle mass of his younger counterparts. His blue scales have faded over the years; though he shakes when he walks, his hands are perfectly still as he sews up Marcus' stab wound. Once the wound is closed, the doctor gingerly walks over to a side table housing his equipment and begins to mix an antidote.

"Last time you were here, it was you in that bed," the doctor says, pouring the concoction into a syringe. "Been so long since then, I figured you for dead."

"You're not that lucky, Doc," Creed chuckles. "Plus, you know me; I'm pretty good at disappearing when things get out of hand." He rises, looking out the window. Sadness washes over him as he stands in awe of Dakuhm despite it once being his home.

"Not this time, it seems." The doctor's words break Creed of his trance. "The poison ailing him may not be the strongest, but it took a skilled chemist to make. Not to mention, both of you are wounded. In this old doctor's opinion, things most certainly got out of hand. Yet, here you are."

"Don't look too much into it, Doc, just keeping my end of the bargain." Creed sits back, his head down, embarrassed by the doctor's faith in him. "Once you get him back up and running, I'll sink right back into the shadows."

With the syringe full, the doctor makes his way back to Marcus and injects him with the antidote. "If that's truly your plan, then you'll be happy to know that this man will make a full recovery. He'll have a rough time as this antidote washes the toxin out of his blood, but once he wakes, all will be back to normal."

The doctor cleans up his equipment, but before he leaves the room, he sits next to Creed. "Boy, I understand that this kingdom's laws have made life for someone with your abilities unpleasant–"

"Unpleasant!? They'd lock me up and skin me alive if they found out I was a Shadowblood!" Creed explodes, struggling to keep his anger in hushed tones. He immediately interprets the doctor as downplaying the injustices he has lived with.

The doctor smacks Creed across his snoot with his tail, replying, "Hush, boy. Let me finish. Was I not there to bandage your cuts when the other hatchlings beat you in the streets? Was it not me who helped you bury the bodies of those who caught you prancing around in the human skin of yours? Or, maybe you forget, it was I who helped fill your bag with food as you ran from the only home you ever had."

Eyes low, Creed rubs his snoot and apologizes before allowing the doctor to go on. "What I was trying to get at is simple, Creed: I know life has not been easy for you, and the ignorance of others has led you down a life of crime and misery, but it brings me just the slightest joy to see you accompanied by a knight rather than your normal thieves and thugs. Even under these circumstances, it gives me hope you might actually outlive me." As he struggles to rise, Creed stands and helps the doctor do the same. Roughly, the doctor pulls Creed in close to him and gently touches his forehead to the other. "I care about you, boy, so maybe for once, if only for me, stick with this one just a little longer."

Creed nods, hugging the doctor goodbye, then watches protectively as the doctor heads into the streets. The moment the doctor fades out of view, though, he begins to gather his things to leave. For the first time he's ever left his home, he hesitates. Whether it be the doctor's words or the bond he's already made with Elizabeth and Helena, he just can't help but feel bad about trying to run off.

He contemplates his decision when Marcus starts to shake and moan in his sleep, just as the doctor foretold. Creed looks over in concern and finally makes his decision. Creed puts his bag down next to Marcus' armor, then pulls his chair over to his bed. He sits, leans back, folds his arms, and watches over the knight as he shivers and shakes. Then, Creed whispers to him:

"I may not like you, but it would be rude to leave you alone in this condition. After all, I owe it to the old doc to at least see where this all ends up."

*****

Creed watches over Marcus for a few hours when, suddenly, sweat begins to pour down Marcus' forehead as he sleeps. Without warning, Marcus starts to shake violently. Creed jumps into action, quickly holding the knight down against the cot while trying to hold down his concern as well. As the shaking ceases, Marcus breaks into chants and mumbles. Running his hands over the top of his head, Creed questions whether or not to search for the doctor; finally, he decides to sit, hoping to make sense of what Marcus is saying. At first, the words are nonsensical, but it quickly becomes clear. As the poison leaves his body, it awakens many of the demons that lay deep in Marcus' past.

Within Marcus' dreamscape, images of his past collide, forcing him to relive his darkest days. Like a ghost walking the streets of Grandhaven, he sees his younger self. This younger Marcus plays with sticks and rocks in the dirt as other children run past, only acknowledging him long enough to point and laugh. He doesn't let their ridicule phase him, allowing them all to pass by as he continues to play – something that seems foreign to his older self. The dream rapidly changes from day to night, but as the world around him moves, the young Marcus stays in place. With the moon shining down, a disheveled man stumbles out of the bar across from where young Marcus plays. He walks over to the boy, an intimidating shadow falling over the child as the man taps a bottle against his leg.

"Get the fuck...up, boy..." the man slurs, kicking away the stick and stones. "No son of mine...plays like a pig!" He pulls the boy up by his collar, then slaps him across his ass with the bottle before downing the rest, tossing it in the road.

Anger rushes over the older Marcus as he watches the abuse he once endured, and he takes a swing at the back of his father's head. He never makes contact. Just as his fist would connect with the man's skull, the world around Marcus shatters, leaving him in the darkness once more. His father's voice fills the void with endless insults belittling him and his mother:

"Useless boy, you're gonna be a nothing – just like your mother! But at least she opens her legs long enough to make me some fucking credits!"

"Fuck you and that garbage child; he's probaly not even mine! So, why the fuck is he eating my food?"

"How many times do I have to beat you before you shut the hell up?"

"Be happy I drink, because if I didn't, I would have strangled your whore ass long ago!"

The noise is crippling, forcing the older Marcus to drop to his knees. Tears run down his face before he finally lets out a cry into the void, screaming to nothing and no one, "SHUT UP!" His words melt away the darkness, leaving him standing in his old home, and the familiar scenery calms his nerves as memories of his mother's cooking fill the air.

Marcus' old home is tragically small. The house is dark, with only a few candles for light. He walks past their old dinner table, nestled beside a rickety stove. With almost every credit his parents made invested back into his father's favorite pub, they couldn't even afford a Q.A.S Tech stove, instead opting for a traditional coal-powered one. He turns away from the stove, his fingers lightly drumming against the tabletop. It is beaten down and worn, but it still holds memories: when he and his mother dragged it home from a neighbor's trash bin; the many times she sat there bandaging up his father after one of his many drunken brawls. Just behind the table rests the only other furniture in the house: two small beds, also in poor shape. The smaller of the beds was his; it wasn't much, but it kept him warm during the winter so that he couldn't complain. Though he can't remember a time when they ever shared it, his parent's bed sits next to his. They had never seemed to enjoy each other's company, and Marcus wonders whether it was due to his mother's employment or his father's focus on the bottle.

Marcus sits on the bed, reminiscing when the candles and stove suddenly ignite. Marcus jumps to his feet, reaches for his blade, and calls out, "Who's there?"

Right before his eyes, his mother materializes in the kitchen, just as mesmerizing as he remembers. She is a stunning woman: velvet black hair flowing past her shoulders and golden-brown eyes that would attract any man from across a room. She was notorious among the community for her seductive curves and promiscuous career. Still, Marcus only knew her as a loving mother with shadows under her eyes from lack of sleep, one who covered up her bruises just before every hug or kiss. He lets his guard down, standing in awe as she prepares his favorite soup. He walks over to her and tries to reach for her, but his hand passes right through her. His heart aches, and he is reminded that none of this is real.

Marcus misses her greatly, tormenting his adult self for never noticing the pain she was in. So many times, he's questioned if he could have done more to prevent her fate. The more he thinks of her life, the more his tears hit the floor. As he begins to wipe them away, the front door opens. A prepubescent Marcus walks in, his head down, and he aggressively pulls out a chair and sits at the table before burying into the crook of his arm. His mother walks over and sits next to him, rubbing the back of his head to comfort him.

"You know, you don't have to punch every little boy who says something nasty about me," she admonishes, seeing the bloodied gashes across his knuckles.

"It wasn't about you this time," he replies, quickly hiding his hand and turning his head away from his mother.

"Oh, really? Then what was this fight about?" his mother asks with a smile, already knowing the answer.

Hesitating, he mumbles, "I don't want to talk about..." She laughs, standing up and moving back to the stove. He buries his head back into his arms.

"Well, when you are, I'll be here. Just making soup." She begins stirring the meal again before jokingly asking, "Does the boy at least regret it?"

Marcus lifts his head and says, "Damn right he does."

The older Marcus watches as his mother and young self eat and enjoy each other's company, a sad reminder of what he has lost. Just as Marcus begins to find comfort in the memory, the door is kicked open. He watches as his father fills the frame, complete with a black eye and a jug of rum in his hand. Now, Marcus realizes what this nightmare truly wants to show him. He starts to tremble, his eyes widening and his throat stiffening. With the utmost fear, he says to himself,

"No...please...not this..."

CHAPTER 18
THE
NIGHTMARES WE LIVE
PART II

Chapter 18

The Nightmares We Live Part II

Marcus' father storms into the house, chugging from his jug, and approaches the young boy. His mother attempts to get between the two of them, faking as though she is greeting her husband, but she is pushed to the ground before any words can leave her lips. Marcus cowers as his father slams his drink on the table and lashes out at him.

"You know how fucking sick I am of getting into fights at the bar because of your punk ass?" He punctuates his statement by slamming the boy's head into the table. "I can barely get a few dozen drinks in before someone bothers me because you got in a fight with their stupid kid, and over what? Her dirty ass," he points at his mother, then picks up his jug and takes another drink. He finally lets go of the boy's head, but not his drink, and stumbles into the kitchen.

"Calm down," his mother intervenes. "How was he supposed to know someone would confront you over a little street fight?" His father quickly backhands her to the ground again. Even though he knows this is nothing but a dream, adult Marcus tries to catch his mother again, only for her to pass through his arms.

"I think it's time I finally teach you that there are consequences for your actions, you little pain in the ass," the father warns, grabbing a large carving knife from the stove. Frozen in fear, young Marcus watches as his father returns to him. The man angrily slams his jug down, grabbing the boy's wrist and slamming it to the table. "You won't be throwing any more fucking fists when I'm done with you!" A sinister smile takes over the father's face as he raises the knife in the air, preparing to remove the young boy's hand. Taking advantage of the small opening, his mother lunges for the jug, smashing it across the back of his father's head to protect her son.

Unfortunately, it does nothing to stop the man. Now covered in blood and alcohol, the father turns his anger towards his wife.

"You fucking bitch! I give you everything, and you have the nerve–" He trembles in unbridled rage. He drops the knife and grips her by the neck, lifting her off the ground as she struggles for air. The young Marcus watches helplessly as his father tosses his mother onto the kitchen floor and starts a violent barrage of stomps and kicks. He is relentless in his beating, seemingly getting enjoyment out of the pain he causes, even going as far as to start laughing as her blood begins to cover the floor. Neither can see her face, but they hear the sickening crack of her ribs and watch as her body falls slack. Her moans stop, and silence fills the room.

Both versions of Marcus freeze as their father ends their mother's life: his younger self is stricken with fear while the older is haunted by grief.

With the woman dead, the father stops his assault and, like a demon, cracks his neck as his gaze returns to the boy.

"Well, no reason to stop the fun now, is there?" His father licks his lips before charging at the boy. As the man lunges forward, the young Marcus gets his first glimpse of his mother's face. Though her skin is now stained red by blood and some of her features broken and bruised, she is still beautiful to him. A rush of memories fills his mind, and his fear suddenly turns to rage. The young Marcus grabs the knife his father dropped to beat his mother to death, and just as the man reaches him, he slashes open his father's throat.

The man reaches for his neck in shock as blood starts to run down his chest. Just as he realizes what has happened, young Marcus tackles his father into the kitchen stove, stabbing him several more times. The stove crashes over as the men make contact, and the kitchen erupts in flames as coals fall to the floor. Before long, both his parents' bodies are engulfed in fire, and most of the house follows.

Knowing what he has done, his childhood self flees to the backyard, hiding in the outhouse as the rest of the home burns. As the boy runs away, modern Marcus walks through the flames to see his mother one last time. He tries to touch her, but, as before, he is reminded he is nothing but a ghost in this memory, passing right through her. Tears roll down his face as he speaks to her.

"I'm so, so sorry, Mother. I promise, I am stronger now. I know we'll see each other again one day, but not today. There are still men like him out there, and I can't rest knowing that."

Marcus stands up, and flames burn away the world around him. Marcus is again surrounded by darkness, but before long, he notices a single snowflake as a cold breeze blows away the shadows. He stands outside his home as it continues to burn, a crowd forming around the house, questioning what has happened. Gossip fills the air as the roof starts to crumble, only to be silent when a grizzled voice shouts, "Move!" The crowd parts and a squad of knights storm through. Marcus turns to look and, for the first time in this nightmare, he feels relief. He smirks before whispering:

"About time you showed up, Master Tiberius."

*****

A legend among knights, Tiberius Lee's presence is unforgettable. Once he enters the area, all eyes are on him, from his silver mohawk to his rudimentary Q.A.S Tech armor that leaves his tattoo-covered chest showing. The crowd is silent, hanging on Tiberius' every movement as he approaches the burning building. He motions for his colleagues to step back and reaches for his blade, which looks identical to the sword the knight Marcus utilizes. Intense blue lights illuminate Tiberius' armor as the air around him chills. As snow starts to fall, Tiberius unleashes his blade, slashing through the air and towards the flames. The blade emits an arctic gust of wind that extinguishes some flames and freezes others in their place.

The crowd cheers in excitement as Tiberius sheaths his blade, but he calls out, "Silence!" The onlookers follow his order as the other knights stand at Tiberius' side. Together, they enter the wreckage of the home. Eager to see his former master at work again, Marcus follows. Once inside, Tiberius orders the others to look around. While they investigate the rest of the house, Tiberius immediately investigates the two charcoaled bodies in the kitchen. His face grimaces in disgust when he realizes that the woman, whose bones still stick out from her body at inhuman angles, was beaten to death before the flame even touched her. Moving over to the man's body, he smells boiled blood and burnt flesh. Tiberius uses two fingers to push the man's head back, reopening the slice across his neck and causing fresh blood to seep out of the crisped corpse.

"Looks like a domestic dispute at its worst," one knight says, returning to Tiberius.

"Not that simple," Tiberius replies, pointing out the man's bloodied knuckles. "There's no way she was able to slice his throat after being beaten to death, and it's just as impossible for him to kill her the way he did with his neck in two pieces." Before turning to his colleagues, Tiberius stands and chants a simple prayer for the deceased. "There is a third party involved. We need to find out who."

Tiberius looks around and notices the back door swinging open with the wind. He orders the knights to stay behind but stay on guard while he investigates further. The older Marcus follows Tiberius into the backyard, where he knows his younger self is hiding. Tiberius, masterful at his work, quickly notices the drops of blood on the ground and follows them to the outhouse.

He circles the outhouse, determining any level of threat that may be contained in the small building. Returning to the door, he raises his sword and slices the door from its hinges, revealing the young Marcus, still shivering in fear, who cowers in the corner. As Tiberius puts away his sword, young Marcus tries to run past him, but the knight quickly grabs him by the collar and throws him back to the ground.

"I wouldn't try that again if I were you, son," Tiberius threatens as he towers over the young man. Having been through enough abuse for the day, Marcus stays put, trembling even harder. Tiberius recognizes the terror radiating off the young boy in front of him. His eyes scan over the boy's body, assessing the blood and bruises on his body compared to the scrapes across his knuckles.

He lowers his voice slightly and asks, "Was this your home?" Young Marcus dips his chin, and Tiberius continues, "Did your father kill her?" Again, the boy nods. "So, you took his life in return?" This time, though he avoids answering, Marcus has given Tiberius all the confirmation he needs. The knight puts his hands out and helps young Marcus to his feet, patting ash off the boy's clothes. He tells him to clean his face off.

"The law doesn't favor murders no matter their age or motive," Tiberius informs the young man before turning his back. He lowers his voice once more – this time, not out of sympathy but secrecy. "So you're going to run." Young Marcus looks at Tiberius, rather his back, in shock. "And you will keep running and fighting 'til you are of age to join the knights. When that day comes, you make your way to the Academy, join, and then find me."

Young Marcus stands still as Tiberius walks back to the house. Before re-entering the ashen remains of the building, he breaks the boy out of his paralysis by shouting back, "Did you not understand me?" At that, the young man stumbles forward, hopping over the stone fence surrounding the yard, and runs off into the horizon. Only after ensuring the boy is gone does Tiberius enter the house, informing the others that they are done here.

Marcus now stands alone in the memory of his old home. Yet, after reliving his life's greatest tragedy, he is surprisingly calm. He takes a deep breath and closes his eyes. The world around him shatters once more, but this time, there is a light that shines through the darkness.

Marcus opens his eyes and starts to walk toward the light; as he does, more memories of his youth pass by him. Some depict his struggles while living on the street, while others remind him of those who helped him along the way. As he approaches the light, a figure walks out of it. At first, Marcus can't tell who it is, so he approaches cautiously before rejoicing as he recognizes Nolan standing before him.

"Tapping out so soon?" Nolan questions, a soft smile spreading across his face.

"I wasn't planning on it," Marcus replies, his guard dropping. "But things haven't been the same since you left."

"No one said it would be easy, but from the looks of it, you've been through worse," Nolan jests.

"Won't disagree with you there," Marcus, too, smiles as Nolan's presence brings him back to a happy place.

"Well, then it's time to wake up. There is still a fight out there, and you're not going to be any help laying in bed." Nolan playfully punches Marcus on the shoulder. Though he laughs the punch off, Marcus feels his eyes fill with tears, and he tries to blink them away before his friend can notice, to no avail. Nolan quickly envelops Marcus in his arms, holding him tightly in a hug.

"We miss you, and I pray we're doing you proud," Marcus mumbles into Nolan's chest, his shoulders quaking with the emotions he rarely lets show.

Nolan pushes Marcus back, shaking him slightly. He looks him in the eyes with his heroic smile and tells Marcus, "You are, so keep going." Marcus nods in agreement before the light behind Nolan overtakes everything.

Blinded by the light, it takes Marcus a few moments before he opens his eyes again, now lying in an unfamiliar bed. Turning his head, he is shocked to see Creed resting in a chair nearby, watching over him. Marcus sits up slowly, rubbing his eyes to ensure he isn't still dreaming. As he does, Creed stretches, too, snarling at the ache in his muscles. Once they both settle in, Creed looks over at Marcus and jokingly says,

"Welcome back to the land of the living, tough guy."

CHAPTER 19
THE TRUTH ABOUT DAKUHM

Chapter 19

The Truth about Dakuhm

Marcus shifts himself to the edge of the bed before removing the covers. He looks down at his near-naked body, bewildered by the number of bruises now covering it.

Creed notices Marcus's baffled expression and updates him on their current situation. "That Terra asshole did a number on you. Even before the poison, he really beat the shit out of you guys."

Creed gets up from his seat and brings Marcus' armor over to him, dropping it on the bed beside him so he can dress. Marcus first slips on the mesh protection that goes under his armor. Next, he puts on his boots and his wrist and waist guards. Marcus removes a small, hidden wrench from his wrist guard, which he uses to equip his chest and back plates before tightening the rest of the armor. Finally, he locks his shoulder plates into place. Now, with all his armor completely secure, the red-lighted trimmings glow faintly before fading away, signaling that the armor has entered passive mode. Creed finds the whole process oddly satisfying to watch. It's rare to see a knight without armor since many even sleep in it, so it's nearly impossible for a civilian to witness a knight putting it on.

"Where are we, and how long was I out for?" Marcus questions as he points to his blade, a silent request for Creed to hand it to him.

"Welcome to Dakuhm... and a little over two days." Creed replies as he hands it over to him. "Just so you know, you spent the whole time talking in your sleep." Though their travels together didn't create a brotherly bond, Creed feels that hiding what he heard would be morally wrong.

"How much did I say?" Macurs asks as he examines his blade for damage.

"Enough for me to know you're not as big of an asshole as I assumed," Creed says with a devious grin. As he puts his sword away, Marcus momentarily freezes, concerned about how much this outside may now know about him.

Shaking off his fear, he rolls his eyes. "Well, you're not exactly what I assumed, either."

"This world's full of secrets, isn't it?"

"Well, yours may be a little bigger than others'," Marcus jokes, tapping Creed in the middle of his massive Dargone chest.

Slapping Marcus' hand away, he responds, "Can you blame me for hiding? Creatures like me are not too welcomed around these parts." He walks over to the window, his own memories replaying in his mind.

"Didn't mean to offend you, big guy," Marcus apologizes, rubbing his hand. "I just find it hard to believe a Dargone would want to hide all their glory behind something as normal as a human."

"Glory? Is that what you think these scales and fangs are?" Creed's incredulity rings out across the room. "Well, not me. Even as a child, I felt like a rainbow in a world full of black and white. What I am may be beautiful, but it's different. It doesn't fit in with their master plan for our kind, so they hate it." Creed continues to watch over Dakuhm through the window, trying to silence the words from the past that reverberate in his mind. With the nightmares of his childhood exile fresh in his mind, Marcus sympathizes with Creed's pain.

"Excuse my earlier comment, Creed. I know very little about Dargones and even less about the kingdom of Dakuhm." Marcus joins Creed by the window, continuing, "Books only tell us about Dargone pride, how you all love your strength and size more than anything. But you're proof that the stories just cover a darker truth."

Though Creed welcomes Marcus' compassion, he refuses to let him know that. Instead, he continues the conversation in his usual snarky manner.

"This kingdom is built on the back of religious hypocrites. When we were young, they preached how a legendary dragon used their flames to rip a hole in the earth to give us a home, then flew into the havens, ignited itself, and became the sun that heats all of Grandiose. So, to give back to the dragon, they worship the sun. They built a massive church for it, then built Dakuhm around it."

"A massive church? All the buildings around here look the same to me other than King's castle," Marcus ponders as he looks out the window.

"That's because the church and castle are one in the same," Creed informs him. "The Dargones lived equally at first, nothing being more important than the church. Then, after a few generations, *'the miracle'* happened, and a Dargone was hatched who bore wings. The people fought for most of the child's youth over what his arrival meant, and, ultimately, the Elder priest decided he was a gift from the sun, a Dargone who could fly to the havens just like legendary dragons once did. That hatchling would become the first king of Dakuhm. Afterwards, the Elder priest decided to protect him by housing him within the church walls and, over time, that church became the castle."

"Interesting history lesson, but that doesn't make them hypocrites," Marcus interrupts, assuming he's heard the whole story.

"You didn't let me finish. You see, ages passed, and Dakuhm prospered under the first king. When his heirs also bore wings, the Elders declared that it was not just the king that was gifted from the sun but his whole bloodline, so, from that day forth, only those with his bloodline would lead the Dargone people, even going as far as to promised that one day this bloodline would give birth to a new legendary dragon. This would take the form of a Dargone, which bore both wings and a sacred flame that would bring us into a new age of euphoria."

"And people believed them?" Marcus interrupts again.

"Of course they did, why wouldn't they? The king brought them prosperity, and the Elders had only ever taught them the words of their faith; for them, this was gospel. Over the next generations, Dakuhm continued on under these beliefs. It had become so entangled with their everyday life that, over time, even the priests were phased out and the gospel just became law – an unquestioned law until a few hundred years ago, when the first Shadowblood was born."

Marcus and Creed move away from the window, sitting together at the table. Now entirely enthralled in Creed's tale, Marcus urges him to continue.

"The Great War hadn't ended that long ago and, though humans had won, the Dargone king's neutrality meant that Dakuhm came out of it fairly untouched. Yet the Dargone people were still fearful of mankind. While we could easily beat them in battle, they reproduce and reach maturity so much faster than us. Who's to say they couldn't overwhelm us just like they did the Orens and Orcs? So, when a Dargone was born with the ability to shapeshift into one, it's understandable that the people were equally scared and intrigued. How the royal family handled the situation, though, is despicable. They saw this new breed of Dargone, now commonly referred to as Shadowblood, as a threat to their claim to the throne. Instead of welcoming or worshiping him as the people once did their winged bloodline, they damned it. The royal family deemed the Shadowblood a curse, convincing the people he couldn't be a gift from the sun because the legendary dragon could not shapeshift. Instead, this must be a tainted bloodline: the first step on the road to their extinction."

"Am I correct in saying that's when they exiled the Shadowblood?" Marcus questions, finally feeling he was caught up with the story.

"Exiled would have at least left him with his life, but that wasn't good enough. On that day, the royal family declared being born a Shadowblood was against the law and the sole punishment was death. They publicly beheaded the Shadowblood Dargone the following day, and they have continued to do so to every Shadowblood child they have discovered since."

Face wrinkled in disgust, Marcus exclaims, "That's awful! No wonder you hate it here. A whole kingdom built around praising something unique, now publicly cutting heads off children for the same thing." For the first time, he has gained a new respect for Creed. Not only did Creed reveal his secret to save them from the Terra King, but he also returned to a place that wants him dead just to keep Marcus alive. Marcus, who had been nothing but suspicious and rude to Creed since they'd first met.

"Hypocrites, like I said, but storytime is over. The others should be here by now. Let's find them and get the hell out of here. Honestly, I'd rather not have to look like this longer than I have to." With that, Creed gets up and gathers the few rations the doctor left behind for them and his bag. Once Marcus stands, they both head for the door.

Before leaving the room, Marcus extends his hand to the Shadowblood. "Creed, I know we aren't going to see eye to eye very often, but you're welcome to accompany us as long as needed." Creed looks down at Marcus' hand and, for a few moments, hesitates to shake it before remembering the promise he made to the doctor. He grips it tightly. He and Marcus may not be friends, but they are respected allies from now on. Creed laughs as they walk out together and, with another devious smile, makes his plan clear:

"Glad you feel that way, because to be frank, I wasn't planning on leaving anytime soon."

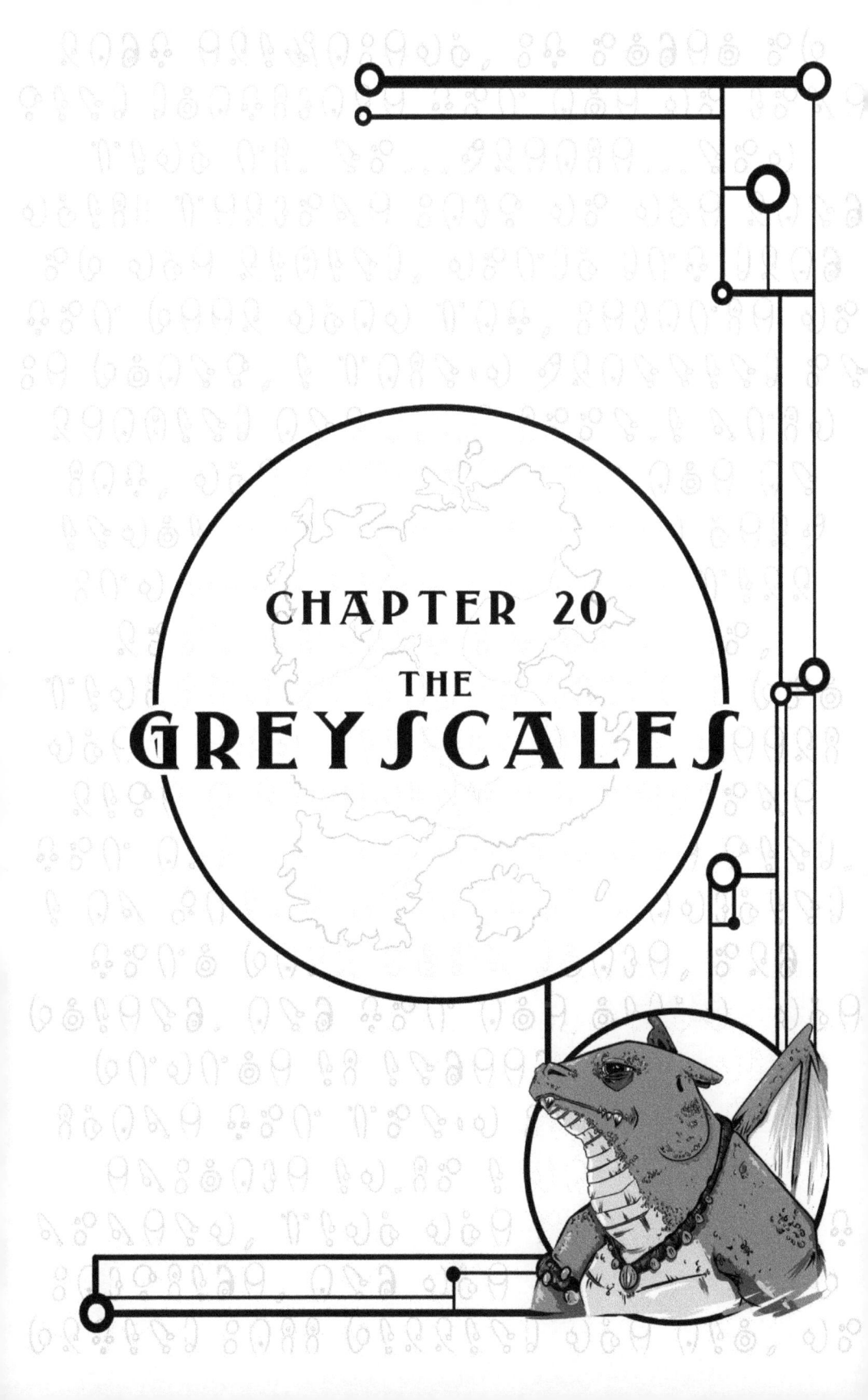

CHAPTER 20
THE
GREYSCALES

Chapter 20

The Greyscales

The blinding Dakuhm sun hits Marcus' eyes, and he immediately begins to complain as he and Creed search the city for Liam, Elizabeth, and Helena.

"How the hell am I going to find anything when I can't even see my nose in front of my face?"

Creed ignores his whining and continues the search when he notices an abnormally large crowd forming within the Nourishment Circle. To their surprise, they make their way towards it and see a handful of Dargone soldiers surrounding Elizabeth, who hangs, intimidated, in the grasp of a glamorous Dargone female. Marcus quickly shoves through the crowd, knocking the Dargone female's hand away as he comes to Elizabeth's aid. This prompts the soldiers to adjust their stance quickly, and they are now ready to attack him instead when the female Dargone tells them to stand down.

"Am I right in assuming that you are the knight Marcus Lee?" The female Dargone asks as she moves closer to him.

"Damn right! Who the hell are you and what business do you have with my associate?" Marcus shouts fiercely, reaching for his sword. Having observed long enough, Creed finally makes his way to Marcus and Elizabeth, where he quickly grabs Marcus' hand, motioning for him not to engage.

"Forgive me, eagerness to please my king has led to this confrontation. I am Lady Juniper, lead liaison to King Greyscale. At his request, I am to find the stray knights and their associates and bring them to the castle at once."

Now understanding her importance, Marcus drops his guard, pulling Elizabeth to him and reassuring her that she is safe.

"Next time lead with that instead of trying to pull someone off the street," Elizabeth snaps, but immediately cowers behind Marcus when Juniper angrily stares back at her.

"Again, I apologize, but it is my understanding that your mission is somewhat time-sensitive. Am I mistaken?" Juniper inquires condescendingly.

The crowd begins to part as a familiar grizzled voice breaks through the mass of scales: "No, you are correct, my lady," revealing Liam and Helena. As soon as she sees Marcus whole and healthy, Helena's demeanor brightens, and she offers him a quick smile before her face turns to stone once more.

"Barely back from the dead, and you're already starting trouble, I see," Liam whispers as he joins Marcus, a soft chuckle under his breath.

"You know me, old man. Life's no fun if no one's mad at you," Marcus replies, a childish grin spreading across his face as he is reunited with his family once more.

"Is this the entirety of your band of comrades?" Juniper questions in an attempt to move on with her request. When the group affirms, she motions for them to follow her to the castle. Before she can begin to escort them, one of the guards whispers something to her.

"Before we continue, I have been informed that our orders only report a squad of three knights and a young hooded woman. So, who is this Dargone accompanying you?'

A feeling of panic washes over Creed, scared they know who and what he is, but Marcus speaks up before anything can come of his fear.

"His name is of no importance; he's nothing more than a hired blade. With that said, we are paying good money for him, so if it's of no quarrel with you, I'd like him to stay close to us at all times. Don't want him running off with our money, after all," Marcus says coldly, dismissing the issue. However, knowing the truth about Creed, the others realize how important his words were in protecting their new friend. Juniper accepts Marcus' explanation, continuing her escort to King Greyscale.

Following at a distance, Liam moves closer to Marcus and whispers, "Didn't expect you to stand up for him so quickly. Are you going soft on me, boy?"

Marcus glances his way, seeing the familiar glimmer in his friend's eyes. "He saved my life, Liam. Honestly, all of ours, when it comes to our exchange with that Terra asshole. We owe it to him to return the favor, to protect him from this place." Liam looks at Marcus like a proud father, slinging an arm around his shoulders as they walk.

"You're becoming more and more like Nolan each day, boy. When all this is over, you're gonna make a fine squad leader, if I say so myself."

Marcus feels his chest swell at Liam's words. He opens his mouth to respond, but no words come out. No words could accurately express what Liam's affirmation means to him. Instead, he leans into Liam's embrace, confident that if anyone could read his silence, it's the one person he's shared his most vulnerable emotions with.

"That's if he doesn't die on us first," Helena jests, sidling beside them. Seeing Marcus well again, her heart feels lighter, and that brightness exudes into their reunion.

"He's tougher than he looks – well, at least for a puny human," Creed cuts in, smirking.

"Well then, he's not the only one who is more than they seem, big guy." Elizabeth playfully bumps her shoulders against Creed, and he brushes the comment off quickly, hoping to evade unwanted attention from the guards. His attempt fails as they all shoot him a curious side eye, and he knows he'll have to explain everything to the other Dargones once their business in Dakuhm is finished. That is, if he ever returns.

Throughout their walk to the castle, Juniper keeps an inquisitive watch over the group as they laugh together, unbothered by their guards. *'They're an odd bunch, aren't they?'* she ponders as they approach Greyscale's castle.

After a short journey through the streets of Dakuhm, the group arrives at castle Greyscale. The castle is beautiful, yet simple, in its design: a three-story frustum-shaped tower wholly made of stone. On a flat balcony, a giant statue carved from fine stone depicts a serpent dragon wrapped around the sun rising out of a fountain of fires. Like Creed had explained to Marcus in the doctor's office, this religious iconography is typical within Dakuhm; many have miniature replicas of the statue within their homes.

The guards accompanying the group take formation in front of the castle door, standing in two equal lines to each side. Juniper welcomes the knights in, and all but Helena enters. Juniper motions a second time, and after another brief hesitation, Helena follows the others. Once within the castle, they quickly find themselves in awe of the artistry surrounding them. The castle's first floor is a public church whose walls are covered in breathtaking paintings retelling stories of their faith, and a soulful voice fills the room with music. They follow the tune deeper into the church, where they find a handful of Dargones meditating in front of a painting replica of the statue they'd seen before entering. The group identifies the source of the soulful voice: a Dargone pastor singing hymns over the meditators.

When the knights stop to listen to the heartwarming gospel music and look over the amazingly detailed artwork, Helena lowers her head. Inconspicuously, she substitutes tapping her fingers against her thigh for bouncing her leg anxiously. Every few moments, she glances upward, assessing whether the group might move on soon. Having already noticed Helena's hesitancy to enter, Juniper quickly observes her inquietude. Continuing to watch her from the corner of her eye, she wonders why this place of worship is so disconcerting for the knight. Then, she notices Creed gently resting his hand on her shoulder in an attempt to ease her discomfort. Pieces of the puzzle begin to form, though she has no idea how to place them together to see the bigger picture.

Once the pastor finishes his song, Juniper escorts them past the worship sanctuary to a door protected by a pair of guards, who immediately open it upon recognizing her. Beyond the door, a staircase leads them to the castle's second floor. Unlike the first floor, the second area is closed to the public, while guards protect every room. Even with all the guards on duty, every room seems empty.

"Why so many guards for a bunch of empty beds?" Marcus questions as they continue to pass rooms with no guests in sight.

"This floor is King Greyscale's personal guest area. Only those invited by him personally can stay here. And, as you have clearly noticed, it's been many cycles since he has blessed anyone with that honor." As lead liaison, Juniper was once in charge of caring for the needs of these guests, so, unsurprisingly, her answer comes with a hint of disappointment.

"Not since his daughter went missing, correct?" Helena inquiries as they pass by a near-empty cafeteria.

Juniper halts abruptly before answering. "Although the answer to your question is *yes*, do not take it as an invitation to openly discuss Lady Krimson while within these walls. It has been some time since the king lost his beloved daughter, but he is allowed to mourn as long as he wishes." Juniper is aware of the rumors and whispers about King Grayscale and is quick to defend him. "Before any of you dare pass judgment on him, ask yourself, how would you handle the loss of your beloved? Then followed by the mystery of a missing child who came from that love? I praise him for moving on in any form. Is it true he has become a recluse? Yes, but he still leads this kingdom; he pays guards to watch over rooms he has no intention to fill, pays chefs to prepare food for a mess hall no one eats in, and pays maids to keep the bathhouse waters warm, although no one uses them. And why do these things? Because he believes no one should suffer from his depression, and he will gladly pay for them to do nothing than to put them on the street."

"A king's gold is nice, but the people deserve a leader they can see with their own eyes once in a while, one who proves he actually cares about what ails them. If he stays locked up in the tower forever, they may forget why they listen to him at all," Helena states, the animosity in her tone uncharacteristic of her. Offended, Juniper pushes the other guards to the side, quickly standing over the knight intimidatingly.

The situation escalates without warning, and Liam immediately offers, "Forgive me; I do not believe Helena meant any harm or disrespect. She was merely curious and, unfortunately, quite opinionated." He pulls Helena behind him, away from the Dargone leader, and Juniper reluctantly accepts his notion of peace. She returns to directing the group towards the king. Marcus, Creed, and Elizabeth continue onward, but Liam raises his arm, preventing Helena from following.

"Helena, that outburst is so unlike you. What came over you?"

"Apologies. You're right: I should have held my tongue. There's just something about this place...I'd rather not be here." Her voice trails off, her body shaking, and he tries to reassure his friend through her anger.

"Then let's get this meeting over to move on to more important things." Liam raises his eyebrows toward Helena, a question in his countenance. She nods, and he turns, allowing her to follow the group again.

As they return, Marcus pauses, Helena passing by him wordlessly so he can speak with Liam. "There's still so much we don't know about her, Liam. What happened?"

"Nolan used to tell me that, when she's ready, she'll tell us a tale we'll never believe. Told me that, of all the things he'd seen in this world, nothing outweighed the sadness she carries," Liam whispers to Marcus, ensuring that Helena cannot hear their conversation. "I may not know what it is about this place that's upsetting her, but whatever it is, let's get this over with so we can get her out of here." In agreement, they quickly regroup at a second staircase, guarded by even more soldiers.

Unlike the first set of soldiers, this group does not open the door at Juniper's arrival. Instead, they require her to state her purpose and introduce each knight and guest behind her. She adheres to their request; approving her responses, they move away from the door, allowing everyone to pass. The group follows Juniper up the stairs until she abruptly stops to address them.

"Atop these stairs are the royal chambers, and I expect you to act accordingly. Speak only when given permission, kneel at all times, maintain eye contact with his majesty unless told otherwise, and, most importantly, do not approach the queen or her nest. Do not look at her at all. If you do," she says gravely, "you will be promptly executed. Is this understood?" The group nods, and she turns her back to them, continuing the ascent.

"This Grayscale guy sounds like a prick. Even Uther doesn't have such strict procedures," Elizabeth whispers to the others.

"It wasn't always this way," Creed informs her. "When I was a hatchling, the royal family roamed city streets just like any other Dargone, interacting with their subjects as equals, greeting us with kindness and warmth, interested in businesses, ensuring we as people rose up as one. Then Queen Merida died, and he locked himself and his daughter in this castle. It wasn't long after that before he lost her, too, and suddenly a king known for his compassion had no one to share it with."

Finally, they reach the entrance to the royal chamber: a large golden door with the familiar sun Dargone icon imprinted on it. Juniper knocks softly before opening the door and leading them inside. The chamber itself is modest compared to the rest of the castle, consisting only of an average-sized courtroom in front of a large stage. On the stage itself sits the king's throne. Surprising to the knights, it is a simple, large stone slab. Behind the throne, a handful of plain stone doors lead to the royal family's living quarters.

The only exception to the dull decor is a massive chandelier that hangs from the center of the ceiling. The knights notice how this work of art is made up of beautiful gemstones similar to, if not precisely the same as, the ones used in the humans' Q.A.S Tech. Among the gemstones hangs the skulls of every deceased member of the royal family throughout Dakuhm's history, each with its name and lifespan engraved within them. The skull of Princess Krimson, King Greyscale's lost daughter, is absent. The chandelier is jaw-dropping and arguably so impressive it makes up for the bore that is the rest of the room.

Juniper walks them into the courtroom and instructs everyone to kneel directly below the chandelier. Then, she leaves them and enters one of the doors behind the throne. Following her order, the knights, Creed, and Elizabeth all wait, kneeling for some time before Juniper returns, joined by a guard. They both take position behind the throne before the guard introduces the royal family.

"I proudly introduce to you Queen Mauve Greyscale, second wife of King Baron Greyscale."

Immediately following her introduction, one of the large doors opens, and a handful of Dargone guards carry out the queen and her egg. Both sit atop another large slab of stone; the only difference between hers and the king's is the handles the guards use to carry it.

Queen Mauve is an older Dargone, most of her once vibrant violet scales worn and faded. She is covered in battle wounds from her time as a war general, the most prevalent being her missing left eye. As the guards place her pedestal down, she curls her tail around the egg, lifting it into her arms to grip it tightly. With her one good eye, she examines the party, and after looking over them several times, she lets out an earth-shattering growl so mighty that it shakes the chandelier above them. Yet her test to get them to break formation is for naught: not even Elizabeth, who trembles in fear, makes eye contact with Her Majesty. The queen is impressed with their resolve, so she permits the king's introduction.

"Without haste, it is my honor to welcome the almighty patriarch of this great kingdom of Dakuhm. First of his name, the winged crown, King Baron Greyscale!" Finished, the guard steps back into position beside Juniper, and a roaring symphony of drums begins to echo through the courtroom. Anticipation fills the room with every beat of the drums, and just as it becomes unbearable, the doors immediately behind the throne crash open as King Greyscale comes flying through them. He soars around the room, letting out monstrous roars before finally landing forcefully on his throne. Greyscale's silhouette alone would cripple the majority of Grandhaven's knights, his presence dominating the space.

As instructed, the group keeps consistent eye contact with King Greyscale as he inspects them. Once content with them, he takes a deep breath and addresses them:

"I will make this meeting quick, for I clearly have more important matters to attend to," Greyscale states, pointing to his queen. "My scouts inform me that you were attacked by the 'Terra King.' Is that correct?"

"Yes, your majesty, you are correct," Marcus answers. Being the highest-ranked knight in the company, he will speak for them unless otherwise directed.

"And due to injuries that occurred in said attack, you sought refuge in my kingdom, correct?" Grayscale continues to interrogate.

"You are again correct, your majesty, but with my injury taken care of, we request permission to return to our mission," Marcus pleads. Instead of earning the request he desired, his response angers King Grayscale.

With a thunderous roar, the king scolds, "I need answers only to the questions I ask and nothing more. Is that understood?" Marcus apologizes profusely before the king continues. "Normally, I do not care for unwelcome guests in my kingdom, especially a squad of knights I did not request. Luckily for you, when I contacted King Uther, he informed me of your importance to him and asked me to return a favor. So, for tonight – and I repeat, only for tonight – you will all stay in the chambers below."

Juniper is taken aback by the King's hospitality, noticeably scowling, and Grayscale slaps his tail on the ground in disapproval. She quickly returns to proper posture under his glare.

Appeased, he turns his attention back to the knights, declaring, "I've had my men gather your belongings from the gate and my royal engineers will do what they can to get your steed operational by morning. King Uther insisted I get you back on the road with the utmost urgency, but Riverhaven is still a few nights away. I will also provide a new carriage and enough rations to get you there."

With the utmost respect, they each thank King Grayscale for his kindness. Then, he stands, his shadow covering them in darkness, and his tone matches. "My daughter was quite fond of you humans, but honestly, I have found little worth in your kind over the years. Uther's aid with my wife's nesting has helped me see a glimmer of what she saw. As you sleep comfortably in royal sheets, remember that the kindness protecting you is hers, not mine." Finished, King Grayscale spreads his wings, and the drums start again as he takes flight. He forcefully flies back through the doors from which he came, the air from his passing shutting them behind him. Soon after, the guards also return the queen to her chamber, leaving only Juniper with the knights.

She steps down from the stage, and as she passes them, she instructs everyone to stand. They follow her orders, but just before she opens the doors to take them back to the guest suites, she pauses to look at the group. With a timid smile, she says,

"I must say, the five of you are an intriguing lot. I can't help but feel like history will look fondly on you. So, without further ado. – for the first time in what feels like a lifetime – I welcome you all as guests of the king."

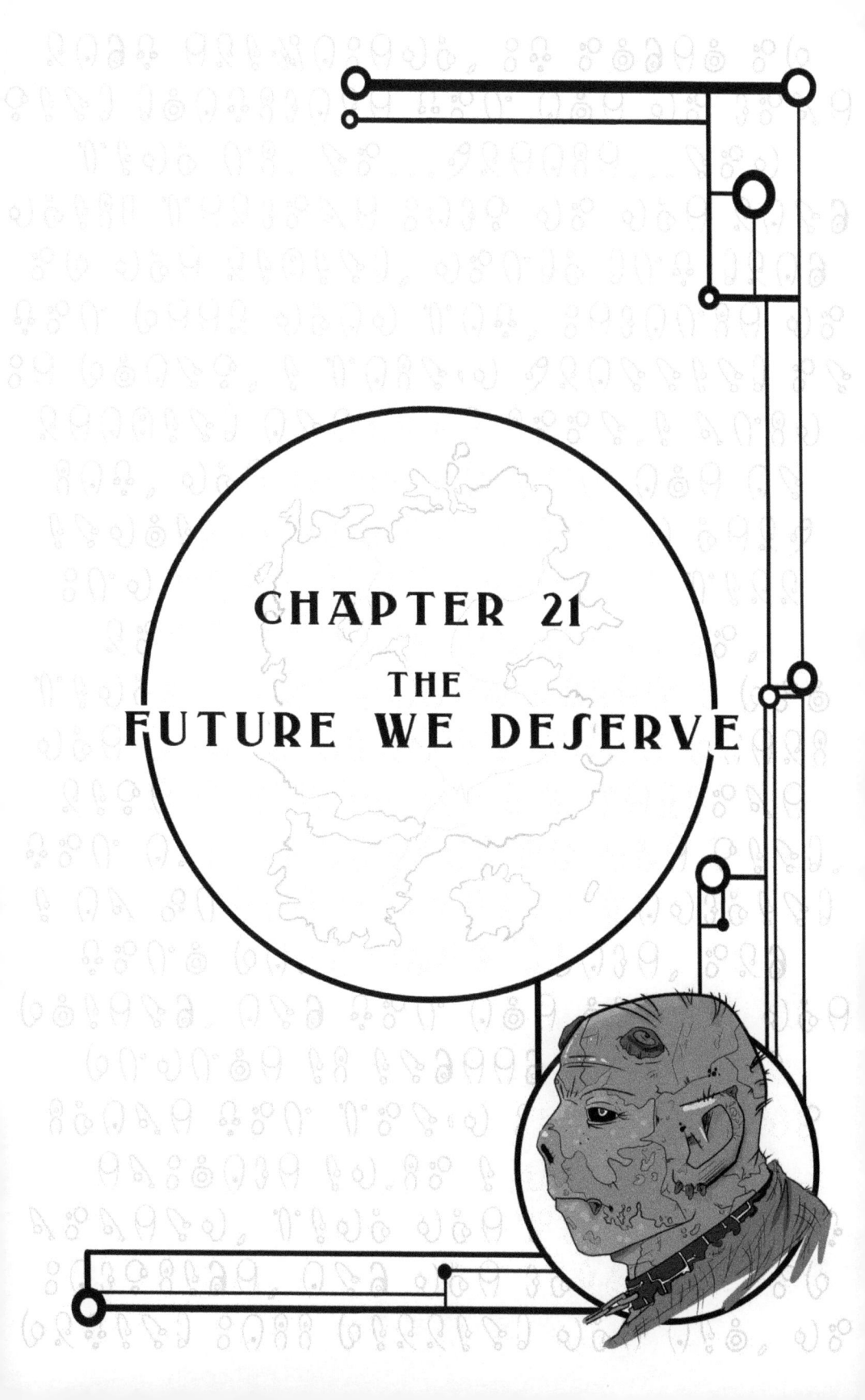

CHAPTER 21
THE
FUTURE WE DESERVE

Chapter 21

The Future We Deserve

Thunder echoes through the streets of Grandhaven as its citizens sleep under the patter of rain hitting the cobblestones. As the kingdom slumbers, Callahan watches over a mix of worker and enslaved goblins building a large platform atop the highest tower of Castle Whitelion. The working conditions are awful: many of the workers are barely clothed and near starving, now soaked to their bones. The weariness in their eyes and slowness in their mechanical movement make it clear that they have been working nonstop for some time now. Every enslaved goblin is chained by the neck to ensure they obey Callahan's commands. Unlike their mature form, goblins are small, only half the size of an average human. Despite that, goblins still have impressive strength, making them ideal for manual labor.

"Hurry the hell up! This should have been done days ago, worthless bastards." Callahan continues to bark orders, kicking the side of any worker who even slightly hesitates. As he goes to reprimand one worker, another caves over. In frustration, Callahan picks the passed-out man up and tosses him across the rooftop, crying out, "Useless!" as his body falls through the air.

The body hits the ground at the feet of a hooded man. Glancing over, Callahan notices Red, who is here to discuss the progress on the platform. Red's arrival causes a stir within the group of goblins, his scent similar to his brother Black's. The goblins cry and growl intensely until one starts foaming at the mouth and charges at Red. Callahan almost instantly grabs the chain around his neck and violently pulls the goblin back, catching it by the head in his right hand. Then, he forcefully slams the head into the ground, crushing it, and brains splatter across the other workers and goblins.

"Remember your fucking place or this will end up your fate! Now get back to fucking work!" Callahan demands, lifting the headless goblin's body before tossing it off the side of the building. The fear tactic clearly works, as every worker and goblin cowers and quickly returns to work.

"I have always been such a fan of your brutality, Callahan," Red drawls, stepping over the unconscious man to approach him.

"Don't tell me you came all the way up here to patronize me," Callahan grunts.

"No, you misinterpret my intent as disingenuous. Ever since my grandfather started using these vermin as mine workers, they have never been too fond of my family. If it wasn't for you, that beast may have ripped an old man like me to pieces." With that, he joins the knight, observing the work on the platform.

"Then why are you here, Red?" Callahan asks again, clearly annoyed.

"Uther is meeting with my brother and President Newson. Surprisingly, he doesn't want me there, so he told me to see how our little project is going," he answers, entranced by the raindrops that roll across his hand.

"Like shit. This should have been finished ages ago. It's not like Uther hasn't been planning these for over a decade," Callahan bitches before spitting on the ground in front of him.

"A giant landing platform on top of the castle is bound to make the people whisper. I'd like to think Uther's procrastination is him trying to keep those at bay," Red answers, now playing with the puddle below his feet.

"At bay? I'm pretty sure they are going to do more than whisper when you-know-what shows up here." Callahan laughs darkly.

"Once *that* is here, it won't really matter, will it? We will be in Uther's endgame, on the brink of a 'brand new world,' as he says." His nonchalant answer makes it evident to Callahan, for the first time, how emotionally detached Red has become, seemingly accepting this fate.

"A new world. One hell of a promise," Callahan sighs, then walks over to a worker and kicks him in the side to jumpstart his effort.

"Aren't you looking forward to his success? A man in your position is bound to make out quite well in the whole ordeal," Red pries.

"To be frank with you, I don't give a fuck about his success. I just need him to start the fire; whether or not it scorches the earth is of no importance to me." Callahan's tone is uncharacteristically depressing.

"You sound like my brother." Red rolls his eyes and then bends over to twirl his finger in the puddle.

"We need to be honest with ourselves, Red. Men our age have no need to care about the future. We have lived our lives, made our enemies..." Callahan pauses. "I care more about how my journey ends than whether or not Uther's fever dream of the future comes to be."

"Well, that's a shitty way to live, if you ask me. Unlike you, I don't plan on dying anytime soon. Age is nothing but a number after all, right?" Red stands back up, stretching. "You are boring me, and you've honestly become quite depressing, so back to my lab I go." Before he leaves, he offers the knight one threatening word of advice:

"Callahan do yourself a favor and try to enjoy the rain while you're out there. You never know, it might be the last time you get the chance to."

*****

TAP□□□ *TAP*□□□
TAP□□□*TAP*
TAP□□□*TAP*
TAP□□□*TAP*
TAP □□□*TAP*

□The incessant tapping of rain hitting the rooftop echoes throughout the castle as Uther hosts a meeting with King Regalia and President Newson inside the Council chamber.

"Uther, delaying the delivery any longer could lead to *it* being discovered," the stone golem of Newson scoffs, and he nervously twitches in his chair. "I'm in enough hot water as is. My people are starving under the false pretense of a recession. Can you imagine what they would do if they found out I've been hiding a giant warship for you? Let alone storing thousands of corpses in it!"

"If we're lucky, they would skin you alive and eat you," Regalia mocks, leaning back in his chair in annoyance.

"Fuck you, Black! You built the damn thing; you should be hiding it for him," the president rebuts in anger.

"Newson, I understand you're limited by your birdbrain, but let's think this over: your people's entire worth is based on the idea that you clean up our dead bodies for us. Don't you think everyone would notice if, suddenly, my kingdom started doing it? Logistically, the Nest was the only place we could house *it,* you idiot," Regalia aggressively reminds Newson. Uther rubs his eyes in an attempt to keep his annoyance at bay.

As the other two continue to argue, Uther's frustration grows, and as it does, the markings carved into his skin begin to glow. The illumination starts to shine through his clothing.

"Silence!" Uther slams his fist down upon the table, dissipating the glow from his body but causing all the Q.A.S Tech in the chamber to malfunction momentarily. "Newson, you will delay the delivery until I say so, and if I have to hear you bitch about it any longer, I'll personally come to the Nest, break your neck, stuff you, and hang you above my bed. Is that understood?" Despite the threat, his tone is melancholy. Still, the others cower in their chairs as he continues, "We cannot risk derailing my vision this close to the endgame."

"Although I do not share the same concern as our feathered comrade, the Terra King's attack on your little birdies' security party is another story," Regalia interjects.

"They survived, that's what's important. And although it has been a slight roadblock, thanks to Grayscale owing me more than a few favors they should still reach their objective in due time," Uther replies.

"It's not the timeframe that worries me, Uther," Regalia replies, "I have been keeping my own eyes on the group, and reports tell me that she has been getting quite friendly with those knights. I can't help wondering if she will be able to finish the job she was sent to do."

His implied interrogation reignites King Uther's dismay. "Are you questioning my decision making, Black? I've been planning this for decades. I put a hit on my own parents so I could get the throne while I was still young. I've put pieces in place so that every King and Queen respect and fear me. I've murdered countless innocents just to ensure my people know who the true enemy is. Now, you have the audacity to think I'd throw it all away by not putting my top player in one of the most important roles of my life's vision? Elizabeth was raised for this moment and she would give her life if told to." His intensity rises further as he says, "She will not fail me."

While Newson lowers his head in obedience, Regalia is unphased. "I'm glad you're confident, but I'm not as much. I left a prototype device with my brother on my last visit, and I believe this is the perfect time to test it," he suggests.

Irritated, Uther asks, "What device?" The idea that something happened in his castle without him knowing strikes quite a nerve, especially when it was connected to his advisor.

"It's a portable communication device that can temporarily connect to our chamber. Unfortunately, because it combines several different quartzes, the system fails shortly after being activated. With that said, I do think it presents the perfect opportunity to...reset Elizabeth, for lack of a better description."

"And how do you propose I do that, Black?" Uther asks, tapping his fingers angrily on the table.

"That part is simple. Newson will provide a Crow scout to fly the device to Riverhaven. It should arrive before she does as long as it's delivered by air. I'll have my brother attach instructions on how to activate it. Luckily, he has also been working on a companion beacon allowing her to contact you beforehand, giving you time to ready the chamber. Then, you can remind her of her purpose, to make sure she creates the distraction necessary for your vision to come to fruition." Regalia lays out his plan before Uther and Newson so that one would be ignorant not to follow through.

Uther thinks it over for a moment before acknowledging the two again. "I'll do this for you out of respect for you, Black, but let me be clear: from this moment forward, neither of you will ever question decisions again. And you, in particular, Black, will never come into my home and leave anything behind without my permission again. If you do, I will take it as a threat against my crown, leaving me no choice but to skin your dear older brother alive, send his flesh to your doorstep, and send my army to New Haven to burn it to the fucking ground!" With every word, Uther's anger becomes more apparent as he begins to illuminate again. Uther's fury is so intense that even his golem, kingdoms away inside Newson and Regalia's respective chambers, starts to crack, the same violet light shining through.

"I am the catalyst to the future we deserve! My vision will usher in the evolution of Grandiose, and both of you are merely pawns in my game! You need to remember you only reap the benefits of my success; you only feast if my table is full. History will remember me as a god among men, and it will act as if you never existed. I deem it so! Is that understood?" Uther's statement again causes the Q.A.S Tech to malfunction, causing sparks within the others' chambers, too.

Both Regalia and Newson nod submissively. Now, more than ever, they realize Uther has obtained a level of power only matched by his arrogance. Their display of obedience calms Uther down, and his glow fades.

"I'll send a scout immediately and ensure everything else is ready as well. I am sorry I ever questioned you, King Whitelion," Newson's voice quivers.

"I, too, apologize. I never meant to disrespect you, Uther. I only assumed you were above me and my brother's tinkering." Though his apology poorly masks his snarkiness, Black recognizes Uther's increased power and knows better than to get on Whitelion's bad side.

"We are on the precipice of greatness. Following me has gotten us this far, so we will continue on the path I have paved. We will not trip at the finish line. Now, go. We all have our roles to play, and I'll be in contact if needed."

The meeting is dismissed, and while Uther and Newson are quick to go on with their night, Regalia waits in his New Haven chamber. As one of his assistants powers down the device, he stares at Uther's now-cracked golem. Shortly after the chamber shuts down, a piece of the lifeless stone statue falls off, and Black breaks into menacing laughter. Finally, he rises from his chair and picks up the piece of the golem, still laughing to himself. He looks down at the decaying image of Uther and makes his intention clear:

"I am quite enjoying watching your fall from grace, old friend. And you are right, the future is indeed bright...a shame you won't be there to embrace it."

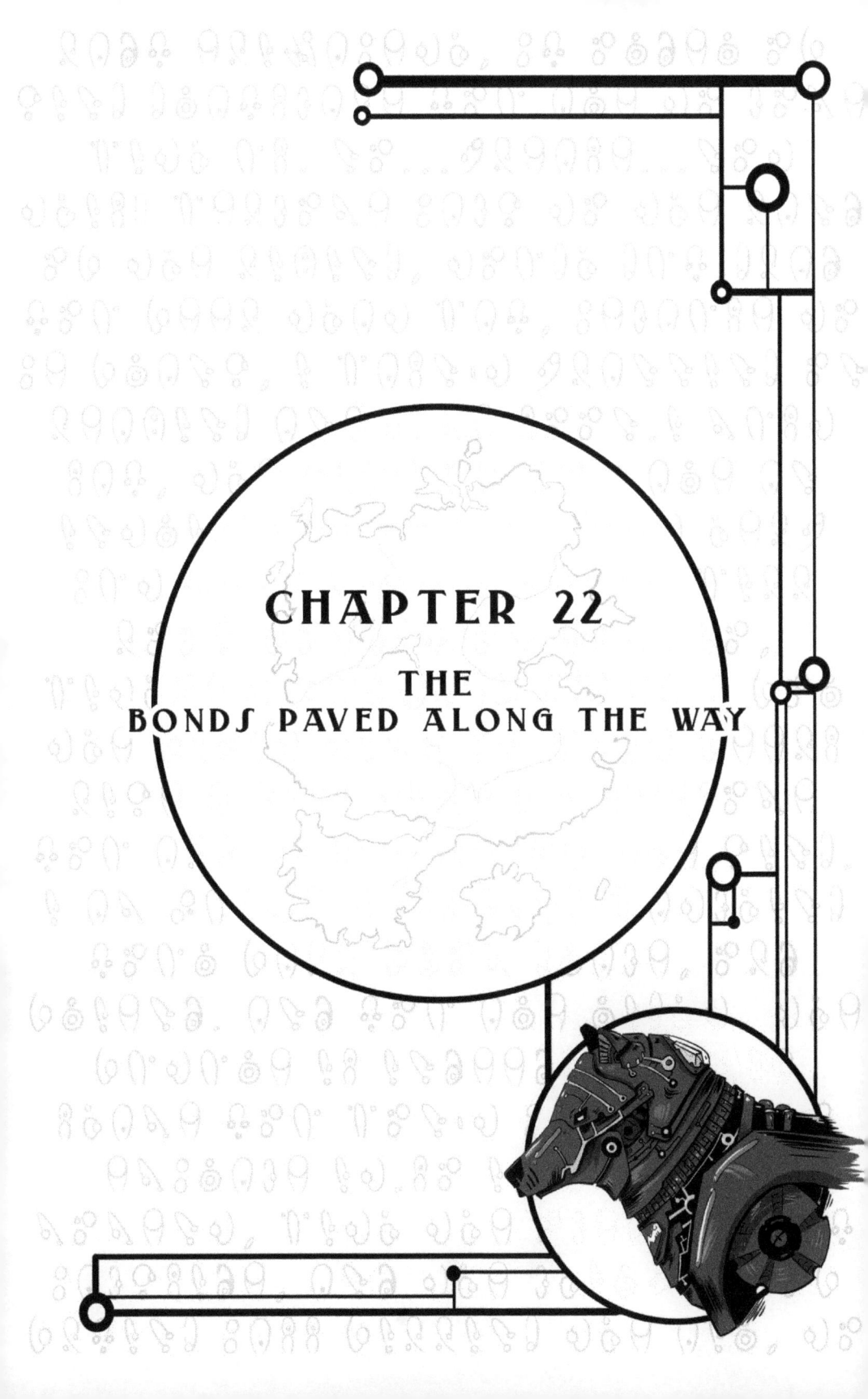

CHAPTER 22

THE
BONDS PAVED ALONG THE WAY

Chapter 22

The Bonds Paved Along the Way

The sun has barely risen above Dakuhm, but Liam is already awake, preparing the new carriage provided by King Greyscale. Unlike a regular morning, Liam is not alone at dawn; instead, both Creed and Helena accompany him.

"I appreciate the help," he thanks them, "and it's obvious neither of you enjoyed your stay here." He loads some of the gifted rations onto the carriage, wondering whether either will say more about their obvious discomfort.

"There isn't a warm bed in all of Grandiose that could thaw the chill this place gives me," Creed comments as he passes more rations to Liam. "Honestly, I can't wait to get back on the road so I can change into something more comfortable. How about you, Helena? Clearly you had a restless night as well."

Staring back at the castle, Helena doesn't answer him immediately. Waves of anger, sadness, and fear engulf her, and she stands there, frozen in her emotions, until a friendly hand rests upon her shoulder, rubbing light circles against the taut muscles there, soothing her. Broken of her trance, she turns to see Marcus, Elizabeth by his side.

"The last few days have been trying to say the least. One night in a castle won't release anyone from that feeling of unrest," Marcus softly consoles Helena. Though he doesn't know the half of her emotions, he knows he would do anything to lessen the weight she carries. "Why don't you and Elizebeth get comfortable inside of the carriage while me and others take the lead?"

"Not going to argue with that plan." Elizabeth grabs Helena's hand, playfully pulling her into the carriage. "Come on, Helena, let's give your mind and body some well-deserved rest." Elizabeth's whimsy is infectious, and Helena smiles for the first time in days.

As the men finish loading the carriage, Juniper approaches with a temporarily repaired Hornet following behind. Although lacking her usual enthusiasm, the moment Hornet sees Liam, she rushes to him, still managing to nearly knock him down.

"Our engineers aren't well-versed enough with such complex Q.A.S Technology to get her running at maximum capacity, but I do believe she'll make the trip to Riverhaven just fine now," Juniper addresses Liam, joining him in petting the large mechanical hound.

"Thank you, Juniper. The kingdom of Dakuhm has done a great deal to aid us, and we greatly appreciate it." Liam reaches out his hand in gratitude, and Juniper shakes it strongly.

"No, it's I who owes you thanks. I feared King Greyscale had lost all compassion, and, although brief, your time here has given me hope that one day we might see the return of the king I dedicated myself to serving so long ago." Juniper pulls Liam in, shifting their handshake into a hug before seeing them off.

Within the carriage, Elizabeth watches as Dakuhm fades from view. Once Helena notices they are no longer in Dargone territory, she lets out a sigh of relief. Internally, Elizabeth is conflicted by Helena's hatred of Dakuhm. On one hand, despite the kingdom's notable flaws, she immensely enjoyed her stay. However, a place that rattles someone as strong-willed as Helena must hide some darker secret.

"This look doesn't suit you," she says softly, seeking to defuse the tension she still senses in her friend. Helena murmurs to herself but otherwise stays silent. "Distress," Elizabeth continues, answering the murmur. "It looks bad on you. I much prefer it when you're the strong, confident one among us."

Helena quickly notices that Elizabeth is trying to uplift her spirit after a very stressful few days; she had been too wrapped up in her memories and emotions to consider how obvious her distress had been to her comrades. The gesture warms her heart: only a few weeks ago, they sat across each other as strangers, yet now, here they are, sharing genuine compassion for one another.

"Well, now that we are far away from that cesspool of lies and hypocrisy, I'll return to my more pleasant self," Helena replies.

"I never said you were pleasant before," Elizabeth teases, and they laugh. "Why do you have such dismay for Dakuhm, anyway?"

"I didn't always. In fact, some of my greatest childhood memories are there..."

"So, what happened?" Elizabeth inquires, hoping to finally gain some insight into the mystery of Helena.

"The same thing that happens to everyone eventually, the ignorance of innocence is taken away from us, and we see the world for what it is: a nightmare we are all just trying to survive." This vague response does little to quench Elizabeth's thirst for answers.

They both pause momentarily, reflecting on their troubled pasts before Elizabeth again attempts to pry into Helena's. "I can't disagree with you there. But, to be honest, I didn't even know humans lived in Dakuhm. That alone had to make your youth quite different."

"They rarely do; the summer heat can be deadly, and housing is far from cheap. Outside of the handful of knights and the wealthy, humans are a rare breed."

Elizabeth can't help but notice Helena knows an awful lot about a place she said she barely remembered, but before she can ask her any more questions, the carriage comes to a halt. The sudden stop confuses both of them, and Helena quickly reaches for her bow. A knock on the carriage door garners their attention.

"No need to get your guard up, ladies," Creed laughs, and both women relax. "We're finally far enough that I can get changed." He heads to the back of the carriage. Out of sheer curiosity, Helena and Elizabeth step out of the carriage, finding both Liam and Marcus, too, waiting to see Creed's shapeshift again.

"I see the concept of privacy has gone out the window," Creed jokes. "Who am I kidding? If I could see me in all my glory, I'd watch too." Creed then lets out a glorious roar, emanating pride rather than anger for the first time. His scales rapidly retract into his flesh as he shrinks in size, their golden color fading back into his human skin tone, the bones in his snout receding. As his human form becomes clearer, Creed's tail withdraws up his back, and other more human appendages return. The process seems immensely painful to the humans, but Creed never expresses any pain. The others are fascinated, and the transformation is complete after a few moments. Before them now stands the man they found hiding in the back of a thief's carriage, stretching and flexing as if nothing ever happened.

"Put some goddamned clothes on!" Marcus yells out, wishing his curiosity had not led him to see more of Creed than he ever wanted.

"What did you expect? Clothes to just magically appear as I change back? I'm Shadowblood, not a bloody Oren." Creed laughs as he continues to pose to rile up the knight. Marcus covers his eyes but continues to go back and forth with Creed like bickering brothers.

The levity of the situation is a welcome moment. For the first time in a while, Helena, Marcus, and Liam share a feeling they haven't had since before Nolan's death: as though their family was once again whole. A mix of laughter and playful banter echoes in the air before Liam finally admonishes Creed to make himself decent so they can all return to their posts.

"Come on, Elizabeth. I think I'll take this opportunity to make up for the sleep I lost," Helena says, opening the carriage door for her friend.

Marcus returns to the reins, and the caravan is on its way again, with Liam and Creed taking up the rear. Desert sand soon becomes paved roads surrounded by lush green fields, bluedeer galloping past, and giant woolboar lazily sunbathing. With the luck of clear roads on their side, they trot on, hours becoming days as they continue toward their destination.

Finally, the cliffside overlooking the Kingdom of Riverhaven is at the end of the road. This majestic domain sits directly against the ocean, with nearly every home facing the beachfront. There is no castle in sight. No home is bigger than its neighbor's, and the streets are filled with smiling families. Boats float just outside the ocean docks, and fishermen fish as their children swim closer to the beachside.

Though the pillars of The Void can be seen in the distance, not even they can cast a shadow over a kingdom that seems perfect compared to its counterparts. Here in Riverhaven, the sky shines bluer, the air feels clearer, and the people seem happier.

Liam steps forward, breathing in the ocean air, and the largest grin Marcus and Helena have ever seen engulfs his face. He stands in awe as a delivery Crow flies overhead, and a flock of flying bass, an enormous fish-like creature with wings, follows behind.

Liam implants his spear in the ground next to Hornet, once again taking a deep breath before turning to the others and proudly proclaiming, "I've finally returned home, and now, I get to share it with all of you. This, my comrades, has to be his final gift to me." Liam's typical stoic demeanor fades away as the others step to his side, letting the warmth of Riverhaven's ocean breeze overtake them. As they stand by each other's sides, the five of them all shed a tear; Liam's words moved some, and others were happy to have finally reached what seemed like an impossible goal. This moment alone feels like it was worth the journey, one that has brought strangers together and led them to this paradise, a light among the darkness of Grandiose.

Helena takes Marcus' hand as Elizabeth leans against Creed, and Liam finishes his decree:

"So I take this moment, with the ocean at my backside, and the chirping of flying bass filling the air, to say thank you, old friend. Truly, thank you, Nolan."

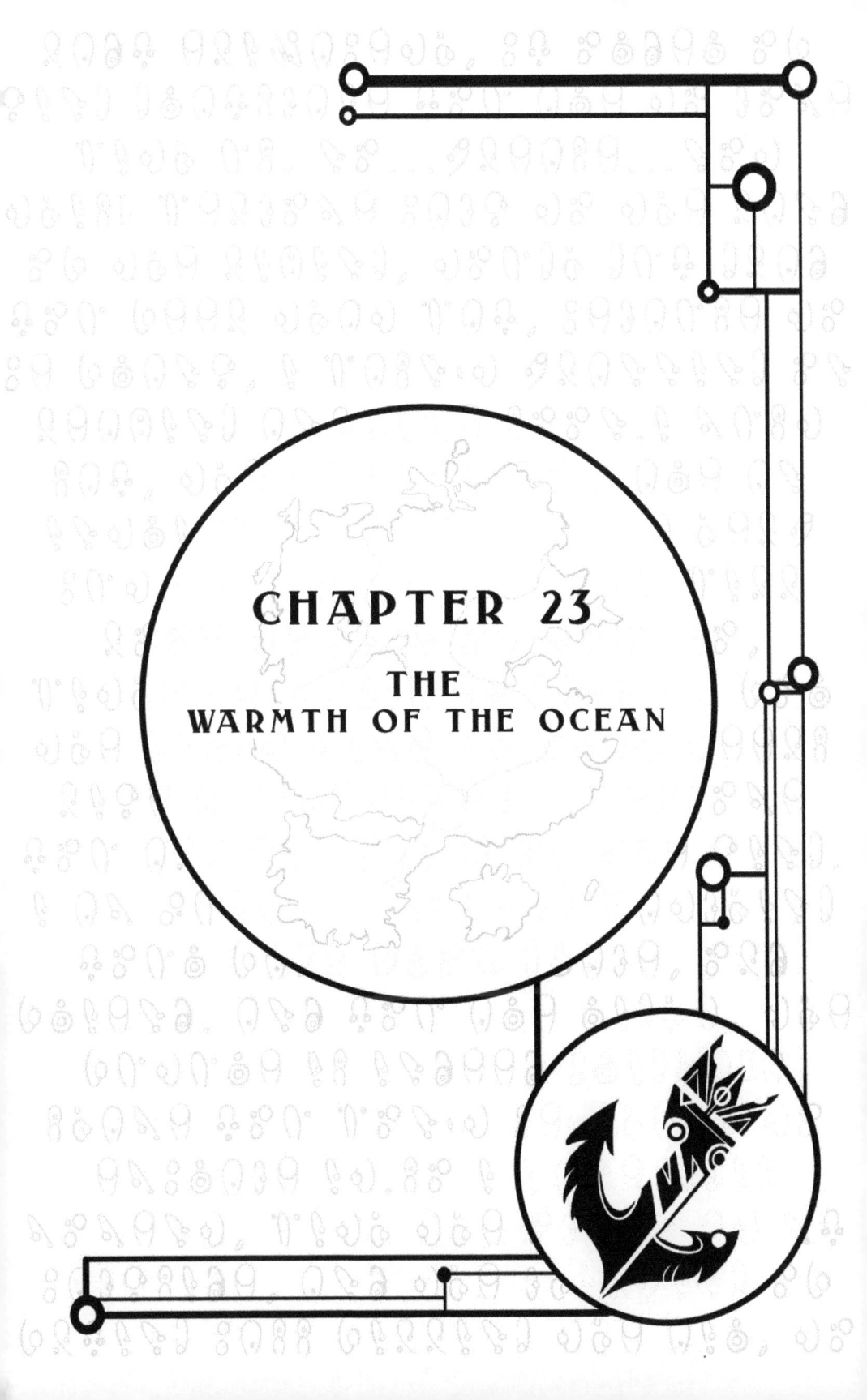

CHAPTER 23

THE WARMTH OF THE OCEAN

Chapter 23

The Warmth of the Ocean

Whimsy and jubilee are rare emotions to see radiating off the eldest knight, but with each new step into Riverhaven, more of Liam's stoic demeanor melts away. As surprising as Liam's bliss is, the others understand entirely. Riverhaven is a vision of perfection. From the white sand that leads into the glistening sapphire ocean to the inviting smiles on the faces of everyone they pass, the warmth of Riverhaven is infectious.

Liam insists everyone take a moment to visit the beach before meeting with Chief Ramon, and they agree without hesitation. As they reach the coastline, they notice it is filled with families enjoying the lovely weather. To everyone's surprise, the moment they step foot on the sand, several citizens get up to greet them. Many thank the knights for their service, while others go as far as to greet them with small gifts of fruit or handmade jewelry.

Their hospitality is daunting, but even more eye-opening is the diversity of races who call Riverhaven home. Here, humans walk side-by-side with a handful of Dargones while Crows fly in and out, carefree. Elizabeth quickly notices that these native Crows look immensely healthier than the few she had seen visit the castle in the past. Their black feathers are clean and shimmer in the sun, unlike the Crows native to the Nest, who are dirty and covered in wasted meals, whose odor would haunt the castle halls for days.

"This place is magical," Elizabeth states, wonderstruck, while a small group of children play with her hood and hide her gifts. "Uther talks as if Riverhaven is a disgrace on the face of Grandiose, but I wonder if he knows this place he's been dreaming of. Beings of every shape, size or color living peacefully and happily..." she trails off.

"All but one, at least." Creed nods to the horizon at the end of the coastline, where it hooks in on itself. There, a dense forest rests. Deep within that forest, past the infamous

Swamp Bridge, resides the mysterious Oren city of Goldleaf. This sea of trees is intimidating, even from afar, but nevertheless, there lies their final goal.

"Well, that's what we are going to change, right?" Liam breaks the tension with a smile as he taps Elizabeth on the back. "And just think: we will have this little lady to thank."

Elizabeth smiles back at Liam, only to abruptly lose herself in thought. She hangs her head in disappointment. Her quick change in demeanor doesn't go unnoticed, but before Liam can address it, they are interrupted by the jolliest of laughs.

"Liam, is that you, uso!?"

Turning to reply, Liam walks directly into an enormous hug from Chief Ramon. Ramon easily lifts Liam into the air, an impressive feat that leaves the others in awe.

"How long has it been? Seven? No, nine years. It was just after you resigned from Nolan's platoon," Ramon recounts, placing Liam back on the ground.

"Either way it's been too long, Ramon. But I see you have Riverhaven even more pristine than last time," Liam replies, his feet back on solid ground. "Where's Ethan? I'm not used to seeing you without him by your side."

"You know my husband: the only thing he loves more than me and Luna is his research." Ramon laughs, pointing out to the ocean and towards the Void. "He has a crew out there on our family fishing boat. They've been out there a few days, but he'll still likely miss out on your visit this time."

"That's a shame, I was looking forward to one of his elaborate history lessons. And speaking of Luna, how is she? She has to be at least thirteen now?"

"Fourteen, actually."

Helena and Marcus watch on as Liam goes back and forth with Ramon. Their banter and joy tug at the knights' hearts as their memories flood with the nights he would do the same with Nolan.

"This place brings the best out of him, doesn't it?" Marcus whispers to Helena.

"Nolan used to tell me Riverhaven's greatest asset wasn't the ocean or the fish, but the freedom that fills the air. I never understood what he meant 'til now." Helena once again looks around in awe at the countless smiling faces. So many of their experiences in such a short time have warmed her heart; the sight of children splashing water at Creed and him playfully returning the gesture being just one of the many.

"We have barely been here a few hours, and everyone is treating us as if this has been our home for cycles. Their welcoming kindness is magical. It's no wonder Nolan was such a great man."

"Well, when this is over and we have laid him to rest, let's promise to keep honoring him by visiting here as often as we can. We can use our status as knights to spread this kindness, just as he did," Marcus assures her as Helena looks out across the ocean.

"I'd like that, Marcus. I'll hold you to that promise," she says, smiling. Together, they continue to enjoy the beach until Ramon and Liam finally finish reminiscing.

"Liam, we can finish shooting the shit later. For now, why not introduce me to the others so that I can return to Luna and finish with tonight's preparations?" Ramon insists, and Liam calls the others over for a brief introduction.

"This is our squad deputy, Marcus Lee. Next to him is Creed. Beside him, one of the most promising young knights to ever come out of the Academy, Helena Blank..."

"Oh, I know that name Liam. This may be our first meeting, but there isn't a letter from Nolan in which you, Ms. Blank, weren't mentioned," Ramon interrupts Liam to greet Helena directly. "While my condolences extend to all three of you, I especially offer them to you. Nolan was so proud of you, and I take solace knowing such a large part of him lives on in you." Teary-eyed, Helena thanks Ramon

Clearing his throat, Liam finishes the introductions. "And lastly, this is Lady Elizabeth."

"The guest of honor herself." Ramon eagerly grabs and shakes Elizabeth's hand before looking down at it, noticing her uniqueness. Fearing his action, she quickly pulls it back, hiding it under her cloak.

Noticing her discomfort, Ramon flashes a giant smile and places his hands on her shoulders. "You do not have to worry here, little beauty. When I became Chief of this kingdom, I made a vow that no one would ever have to hide who they are as long as the sun warms the beaches of Riverhaven. So, please, honor us with beauty."

Elizabeth is hesitant to remove her hood, but after Liam's reassurance, she does. She braces for stares and ridicule but, to her surprise, gets neither. The people of Riverhaven simply go on with their day, and the few who do notice stop only to compliment her. As Elizabeth thanks the bystanders, Creed notices Riverhaven's unbelievably welcoming demeanor.

"You are truly a sight to behold, Ms. Elizabeth. In fact, after laying eyes on you, keeping you away from the world may now top the list of things I dislike Uther for." Ramon smiles, lilting a joke, but his seriousness shines through the facade. A moment later, he exclaims, "Now, with pleasantries out of the way, let's get down to real business: food!"

"Chief Ramon and his daughter Luna are preparing a feast in our honor this afternoon," Liam informs the others. "He has also readied personal huts so that we can properly rest this evening before heading out tomorrow."

"Speaking of huts, a delivery Crow arrived with something from Uther for Ms. Elizabeth not too long ago," Ramon interjects. "Said it was urgent but personal, so I had him leave it in the hut we were readying for you."

Unsure what could be waiting for Elizabeth, everyone agrees to escort her to her hut. Curious about why Uther would send a Crow to drop off a package, Ramon decides to join them. Once there, they find a chest similar to the one they have been transporting with them; atop it sits a royalty-sealed scroll. Written on it are the words " For Her Eyes Only." Elizabeth opens the scroll and quickly reads over it, then rolls it up, making it impossible for the others to see.

"No need to worry. The scroll says the chest is full of new clothes for me. Uther wants to make sure I look my best for Goldleaf," Elizabeth elaborates, but she continues to twist the scroll tighter and tighter.

"If they're clothes, why all the theatrics? It being urgent and all," Ramon questions immediately, dropping the jolly persona and allowing his suspicion to set in.

Elizabeth, aware of the intensity building, is too quick to defuse the situation. "If you must know, Chief Ramon, the letter is personal. One may say it's romantic in nature. Unlike the paradise you've built here in Riverhaven, the rest of Grandiose has never been too kind to me. Uther knows, and I believe he fears that if someone were to find out about me, let alone his possible affection towards me, it would be used against him or lead to my harm. His dramatic display was just to ensure that I was the first and only person to read this letter and look at the contents of this gift."

Ramon hesitantly accepts her explanation then excuses him to ensure things are ready for the feast. Shortly after his departure, Creed, Marcus, and Liam leave the hut to get prepared. Helena, though, stays back momentarily.

"Are you sure everything is okay? That letter seems to have made you nervous," she asks, noticing Elizabeth continuing to tighten up the scroll for what seems like the hundredth time.

"I am fine, just not used to him sending gifts. It makes me wonder what he expects from me in exchange. It's exceptionally difficult to get the King of Kings a thank you present, you know," Elizabeth answers solemnly.

"Well, my hut is next door if you need me," Helena offers and leaves her friend to rest alone.

Now alone, Elizabeth unrolls the scroll, revealing what it truly says.

"Elizabeth,

This chest contains replacement clothes; you should use that as a cover for its true purpose. Use the necklace just as I showed you before you left to open the front compartment. Inside, you will find a device and instructions on how to use it. If the steps I'm writing don't make it clear, only do this when you are alone and only when you are alone. I expect you to complete this task immediately.

King Uther Whitelion"

Elizabeth pulls the chest to her bed, opens it, and removes her clothes. This exposes a shallow false bottom. Before removing her necklace, she takes a moment to look over the garments. Even knowing they mask devious intentions, she can't help but admire their craftsmanship. Elizabeth rubs the new cloak against her cheek, finding odd satisfaction in recognizing that it smells like Uther. She lets herself imagine he packed them for her himself, even knowing it would never be so.

She shakes herself out of her daydream, removing her necklace and sliding it into the side of the chest. The slot the jewelry fits is hidden perfectly inside the chest's decorative design. Elizabeth listens intently for the click that notifies her that she has done it correctly; a moment later, the front of the chest falls open, revealing its secret compartment. Elizabeth pulls out a moderately sized cylindrical device and a second scroll. The device is forged from the same sleek metal as a knight's armor. Several smaller, yellow gemstones are powering the black machine, with a rare, large, orange one housed in its glass center. Elizabeth uses the handle on the device to place it upright and reads over the instructions:

"Step One: Push down on the handle to activate.
Step Two: Back away as the transmitter powers up.

Step Three: Once powered, the transmitter's top can be removed and placed on top of your head to send a signal to the host.
Step Four: Wait for the signal to be received.
Once communication begins, time is limited. Be wary of system failure."

Understanding the device's purpose, Elizabeth is hesitant to activate it. Just the thought of Uther going through so much to speak with her is both flattering and terrifying, yet ultimately, she knows that this can't be a good thing. For a moment, she contemplates just leaving for the feast, but making him wait would just escalate his frustration. With bated breath, Elizabeth pushes down the handle and steps back.

The bottom of the device starts to spin as its vertical lines fill with bright yellow light. Elizabeth then removes the crown-like top and places it on her head as instructed. The lights, now full, begin to pulse as they wait for an answer from the other end. Though it feels like an eternity for her, Uther makes contact only a few minutes later. Once the device is linked with Uther, the lights stop flashing and fold into three equal-sized parts. Each part is shaped like a spider leg, which immediately digs into the ground. Once implanted, a slight rumble sounds from deep in the earth below.

With everything now set, the orange gem starts to glow brightly as the machine summons the earth around it. Before her eyes, Elizabeth watches the small pillars of stones mold into a rudimentary yet unmistakable bust of Uther, similar to the statue found in the royal chamber. With the bust complete, its eyes open, startling Elizabeth as she now sits directly in front of Uther's gaze.

"About time you made it to Riverhaven," Uther talks down to her. "Red warns me that my time is limited, so I'll be blunt, Elizabeth. My allies are questioning your resolve. They fear you have grown too intimate with your escorts and you're unable to execute your part of my plan. Is there any truth to this?"

"I–I mean...it's not–" she mumbles, taken aback by his directness and unsure of how she should approach the accusation.

"Why the hesitation? Has this limited time away from me caused you to forget whose hand has been feeding you all these years? Or maybe you have forgotten whose bed you have been lying comfortably in all this time? Or is it that you just enjoy the life of a street pigeon over that of my royal company?" he belittles and berates her incessantly, knowing he will draw out the loyalty he believes he is owed.

"No, absolutely not!" Elizabeth interjects in panic. "I would never give up my life by your side. I just...I understand what must be done and I will not hesitate to complete my mission but – do the others have to die? They seem meaningless in the grand scheme of things."

"So, you have grown soft to them," he hisses. "Pathetic." Uther's words send a chill down Elizabeth's spine. "You're right, though: they are meaningless. Nothing more than pawns in the great game of change. You, on the other hand, are a principal part of it, one that history will see as a hero. But all that can change if I choose it to." Uther commands her attention, his voice soft and low. His firmness is what makes him even more menacing.

"Let me make this clear, Elizabeth: if they survive, they will be witnesses to your actions. Although the world in front of us is one of perfection, their words could rile up those who fear change. Then, they would no longer be meaningless. Then, their spark could become a flame. And if I have to take time away from reshaping Grandiose to stomp out said flame...then, mark my words, little bird, in exchange for my wasted time, I will pluck your feathers, skin you alive, roast you, and serve you at their funerals. Do you understand?"

Elizabeth stands frozen in fear by Uther's threat, yet she can't help her attraction to his resolve. It is the reason she is driven to him. Before her is a man willing to do anything for the cause he believes in, even throw away a relationship he has had since childhood. In this moment, she remembers the first time she saw this side of him, the day he chose to kill his father and take the throne. While this disturbing memory would haunt others, Elizabeth finds comfort in it, and her fear washes away.

"You're right, Uther. As always. I am a fool to even question you," Elizabeth humbly submits. "What's a handful of lives anyway, when compared to the countless ones born in your new world?"

The bust of Uther smiles as the transmitter starts to malfunction. Tiny sparks fly as Uther gets his last words in.

"Good girl, I was hoping I wouldn't have to replace my favorite plaything. Go forward, Elizabeth, act as my vessel and change the world..."

With those final words, the device loses power. Each yellow gemstone shatters individually as the stone bust crumbles on top of it. Folding the device back up, she places it with the scroll again in the chest's secret compartment. She removes her necklace, locks the compartment, and heads back to the bed where the new cloak and clothes still lay.

Elizabeth disrobes, exposing the countless wounds she acquired in her years before being taken in by the Whitelions. Her many whip lacerations are matched by scars left behind by men who got out of control during her time at the brothel. It's a disturbing sight that would even make Liam cringe, a permanent reminder of a world she will do anything to keep in her past. As she changes into her new clothes, she can't help but question, once again, if what she is about to do is right.

'I'm too deep to go back now,' she thinks. Now draped in luxury, she moves to leave. Before she does, she embraces herself in the cloak, once more breathing in the familiar aroma Uther left behind before the world washes it away. It brings her joy and anguish all at once, a combination she knows can be dangerous. So with tears in her eyes yet a smile on her face, she tells herself,

"Uther, what you are is toxic – but I'd rather sleep with the devil than on the streets."

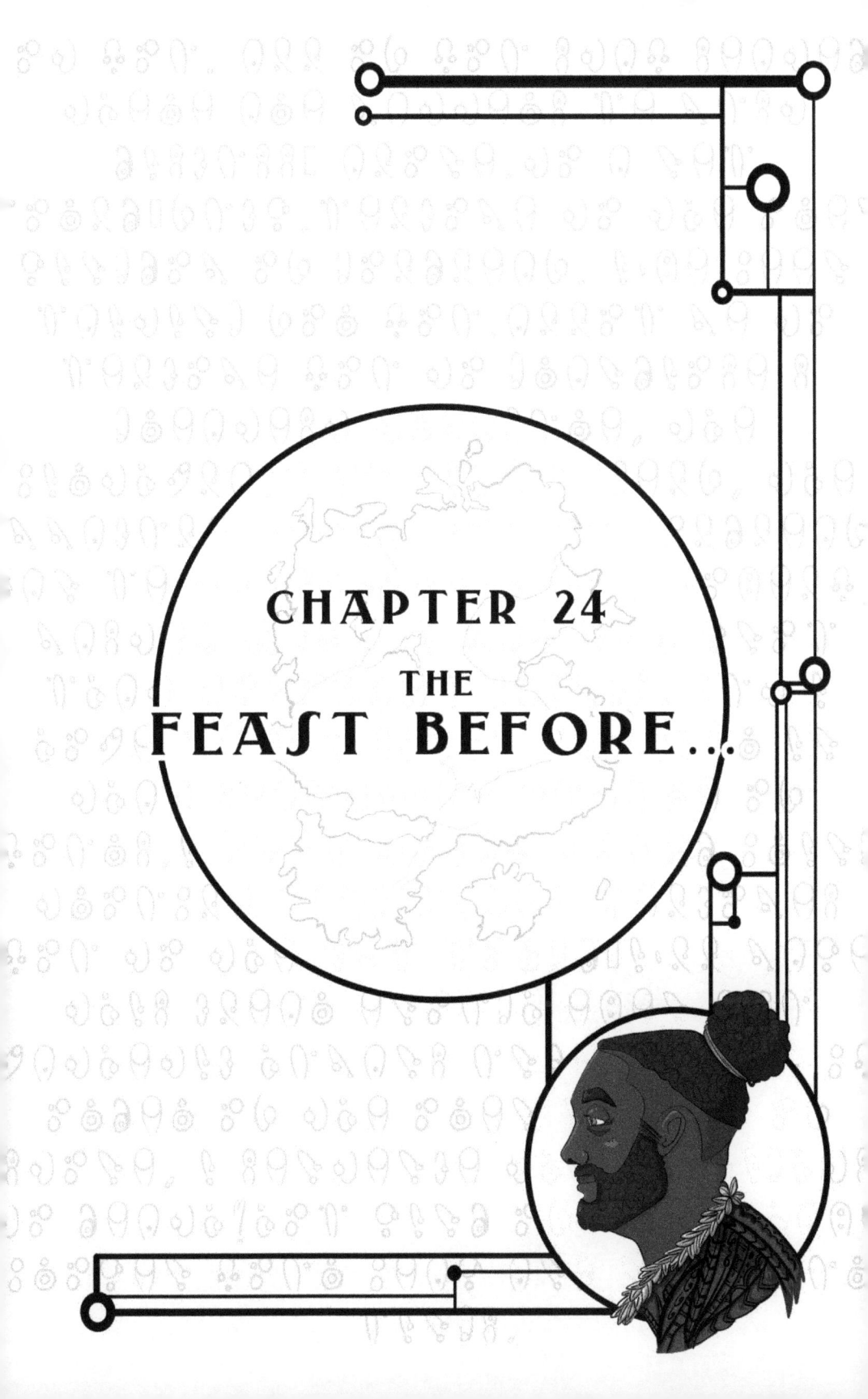

CHAPTER 24
THE
FEAST BEFORE...

Chapter 24

The Feast Before...

Elizabeth waits for the others outside her hut as the entirety of Riverhaven parties along down the streets on their way to the welcoming feast. The people's joyous shanties echo off the walls, songs so infectious that even the flying bass seems to chirp in unison. With a massive grin, Creed emerges from the crowd, his neck covered with leis, a drink in both hands.

"This place really knows how to welcome a man, doesn't it?" Creed laughs, handing one of his drinks to Elizabeth. She takes a sip of the fruity drink, her eyes fluttering immediately.

"They know how to make a girl feel special, that's for sure."

"Don't let it go to your head, little one. Riverhaven will take any opportunity to throw a party," Liam interjects with a smile as he, Marcus, and Helena join the group.

"You're telling me it's like this all the time? Why the hell didn't we come here sooner?" an enthusiastic Creed jokes as he downs his drink.

"Nolan used to boast about how this was the happiest place in all of Grandiose, promising he would take us whenever the squad was granted some time off," Helena reminisces. Quickly, she grabs a drink from one of the numerous street vendors, downing half of it.

Marcus laughs. "Joke's on us, though: we found out quickly there's no such thing as time off when you're a knight." As he talks, a handful of dancers shower him with leis before dancing away.

Everyone continues enjoying the festivities as they approach the large community hall where the feast is being held. With each hut they pass, they are greeted by locals, and the enormous amount of gifts, treats, and drinks they are given is almost overwhelming. Creed even quips that he has a full stomach long before they reach their destination. All jokes aside, the group finds Riverhaven's atmosphere infectious, a more than welcome break from the trials that have led them here and the ones that lie ahead.

Before long, they arrive at the large dining hall, which is surrounded by several areas full of outdoor activities. Some areas host families grilling flying bass as they play card games. Other areas are open sandpits where people can enjoy a round of rushball, a local sport in which players wrestle while trying to advance a ball into a large net using a basket on a player's back. The last of the areas houses wooden playgrounds, each filled with children playing and endlessly laughing.

Outside the hall stands a teenage girl with the most inviting smile waiting in a beautiful summer dress. The sun glistens off her curly, crystal-blonde hair held back by a sewn headband. Once she sees Liam, she charges towards him and jumps in his arms. He reciprocates her excitement with a giant hug, lifting her high in the air and spinning her once before setting her back on the ground.

"Master Liam, it's been so long...I only wish Master Nolan could join us." As she speaks, the young girl's eyes start to water, and Liam quickly takes a knee, grasping her face in his hands and meeting her gaze with softness and warmth.

Wiping a tear that falls down her cheek, he consoles her. "As do I, little moon, but we don't have to mourn our old friend alone." Liam stands up and introduces the young girl to the others. This, they learn, is none other than Luna Masina, Chief Ramon's daughter.

"What a pleasure to meet all of you. Let me be what I can only imagine is the hundredth person to welcome you to our humble abode. Master Liam and Nolan have been friends of my family since before I can remember."

Luna is a lovely young lady, amazingly polite and well-mannered. It takes mere moments for her charm to win over the group. After some idle conversation, she leads them into the hall, where they are instantly hit with the tantalizing smells of the feast. Inside are rows of tables covered in food, including multiple sandhogs, each stuffed with Riverhaven's finest fruits and vegetables. All the kingdom's citizens are welcome here, easily coming in and out of the hall, each time filling their plates or their drinks.

At the back of the building, Chief Ramon awaits the others at a much smaller table. Not only does the banner of Riverhaven fly above his table, but in a nontraditional fashion, the banner of every kingdom in Grandiose rests on either side of his own. The Oren city of Goldleaf is also included.

"Has Chief Ramon made contact with the Orens in the past?" Creed questions when he notices the banner.

"Unfortunately, no. Yet my father hangs their sigil in hopes to one day change that. He says that if we teach our people to treat them as equals when they are not here, once they are, it will be as if they always were." Luna's words strike a chord with Creed and Elizabeth, who are again in awe of Riverhaven's hospitality.

Ramon eagerly has the party sit with him, and Luna joins him. Plates of food and pitchers of drinks, each overflowing with riches, are delivered to their table, and Ramon insists on eating as he gushes over stories of the past. The feast continues into the night, everyone engrossed in Ramon's tales and the seemingly endless amount of drinks and food.

"Liam please tell me you remember the time you and Nolan visited, and Luna tried to tame a sharkswallow," Ramon drunkenly laughs.

"Dad, no! Not that story!" Embarrassed, Luna shakes her head.

"No, no, no, they have to hear this one. I don't know if any of you have encountered a sharkswallow, but they're nasty little bastards. Well, this one," he jerks his head toward his daughter, "finds one on the shore with a broken wing and wants to nurse it back to health. Mind you, she is maybe four cycles old and this thing is about the size of a carriage."

"Oh, I remember this," Liam laughs. "The whole time we were visiting we kept noticing her trying to sneak plates of food away from the table." Luna hides her head in her hands as Liam continues, "So, we finally follow her out to the beach, and we see she had built a little hut there for him. She had the beast eating out her hand like a baby!"

"Ethan nearly shit himself when he saw it," Ramon burst into tears as he laughed.

"Don't act so tough, Ramon, if it wasn't for little Luna's begging, you were ready to put your anchor between its eyes just to save yourself from being bitten," Liam mocks his friend.

"True, true. That thing scared the shit out of me, too." Ramon puts his drink down for the first time since the feast began. "You and Nolan always seemed to bring the good times with you." Once again, Ramon picks up his drink, lifting it high in the air. "To Nolan, the stone fist knight of Riverhaven! Let the stars above remember him as the greatest to ever come from these shores!" Without pause, the hall shouts in unison, *"For Nolan!"*

They all blink away their tears, feeling the love and warmth in the room for their fallen friend.

"Nolan talked about this place all the time, but I never knew how close you all were, or how many times you two visited. Why did that stop once me and Marcus joined?" Helena questions Liam. Now that they've discovered more of Nolan and Liam's past, Helena wants to know all they've missed.

"There's a lot me and Nolan hadn't told you." Liam pauses for a moment before downing his drink. He continues, "But it wasn't because we wanted to keep you in the dark or because we feared you knowing our secrets. We just thought we had more time. When you have been around as long as I have or when you gain the fame Nolan had, you see a side Grandiose many aren't privileged to. But, believe me, we had every intention of passing that knowledge down to you two."

"I guess the world fucked up those plans, didn't it?" Marcus disappointedly probes before taking a sip of his drink.

"It sure did, boy," Liam answers solemnly, staring into his empty glass.

"Answer me this, Liam: do you trust everyone at this table with your life? With your secrets?" Ramon asks, oddly restrained after hours of being the life of the party. Liam looks up from his glass and nods firmly.

Ramon then stands, and his irresistible smile returns. "My people, the night is young, but we will never see the stars while sitting inside this hall. So, let's move this celebration to the beaches of Riverhaven and get drunk to songs of the sea under the glorious night sky."

The hall roars in excitement, grabbing food and jugs while they make their way to the door. Ramon instructs his help and chefs to join the crowd, but as Elizabeth and the others begin to pack up, he turns to them and says,

"Not you. All of you stay seated, there are matters we must discuss... alone."

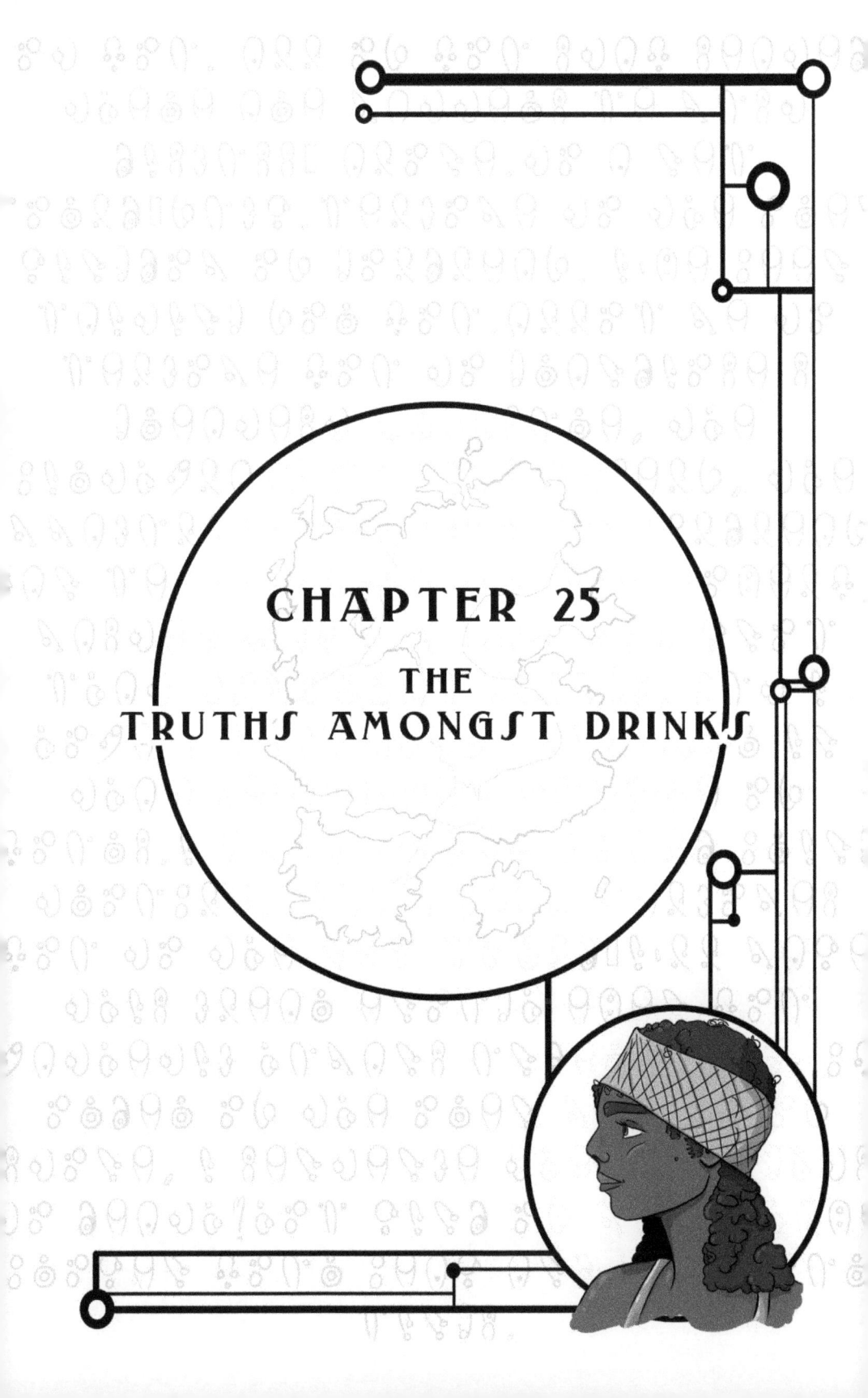

CHAPTER 25
THE
TRUTHS AMONGST DRINKS

Chapter 25

The Truths Amongst Drinks

As the hall clears, Ramon speaks with his daughter, Luna, in a corner near where Creed, Elizabeth, and the knights wait patiently. Only once the hall has completely emptied do Luna and her father return to the table. Liam quickly notes how she stands stiffly; her forehead has creased in concern.

They sit silently for some time before Ramon once again asks Liam, "Are you *certain* they are to be trusted?" When his friend nods, Ramon continues, "Before we go any further with this conversation, it needs to be known that what we are about to discuss is not to be spoken about outside my borders. And if I find out any of you breaks the trust we are about to bestow upon you, I'll personally hunt you down and ensure the last thing you see in this life is the end of my anchor."

Ramon's ominous warning reveals the capacity for intimidation that hides behind his joyous exterior. Though they had spent the night laughing by his side, they quickly understand how he earned the moniker *"Death Whale."* Everyone at the table acknowledges Ramon's threat with a shallow nod as they wait with bated breath for his following words.

"When I took charge of Riverhaven I had one mission: to build a safe haven where every and any citizen of Grandiose could come, and call it home. That started with removing an administration of oppression and hate so that a man like me could love his husband without fear of ending up at the end of a chain. I knew for these ideals to persist, though, I needed to instill them in whoever took salvation here – and hope that, if and when left, they would spread my message throughout this world. That message is simple: we all are one people, who should be treated as equals no matter who we are or who we love or who we want to be." As he speaks, passionate tears roll down his cheek, his voice gaining volume and resolve as he continues. "Riverhaven – no, all of Grandiose should be a place that celebrates life and individuality. And, for a moment, I thought I had succeeded. Riverhaven was seen as a paradise; meanwhile, men like Nolan and Liam were out there slowly but steadily spreading our gospel. Then, a woman, on her deathbed, with a baby in her arms, washed up on shore and changed my life."

As Ramon wipes the tears from his eyes with his rugged hands, Luna silently approaches and hugs him from behind. Taking a deep breath, he embraces her and pats her head before whispering to her, "It's okay…" Hesitantly, she lets go of her father.

He continues, "There is a side of Grandiose we have chosen to let our people forget, simply because it's easier to make them an afterthought than to look them in the eyes. I try to atone for our prior sins, but until we rectify that audacity, my gospel means nothing, and I need it to. I don't need it for me anymore but for her." Ramon points back to Luna, tears at the brim of his eyes again.

When the group turns to look at her, she hesitates, her hands trembling as she reaches for the headband, holding her hair back. After removing it, Luna slowly moves her back, exposing her pointed split ears to the party for the first time: Riverhaven's greatest secret. All but Liam are stunned by the reveal. Before them stands a full-blood Oren, a being believed not to have stepped foot in Grandiose since the Great War.

"Well…" Marcus pauses. Though he wouldn't usually expend the effort to think before he speaks, he heeds Ramon's earlier warning. After a moment, he says, "I think I speak for all of us when I say I have questions."

With that, he downs the rest of his drink, the others following suit. It's now clear that the time for celebration is over; the air is thicker with an expectation of the answers to come. Elizabeth, though, regards Luna with fascination and curiosity. Until this moment, she had always felt as though she was looking through a window at the lives of those who fit Grandiose's expectations. For the first time, she can look into a mirror, a side of her she assumed she would never have access to reflected.

Taking a deep breath, Luna steps forward. "I understand your reactions. It's unheard of for anyone outside of Goldleaf to understand anything about Oren culture. Allow me to enlighten you; hopefully, my presence here will become clearer." Luna retakes her seat, her eyes wide, eager to talk about herself in a way she rarely does. "Before the 'Great War,' the Orens had all of Grandiose to roam freely, so our near eternal lives were never an issue. Once we lost, human expansion thrust the entirety of our race into one city. Naturally, deprivation followed.

"To avoid starvation or, even worse, a second 'Dark Massacre,' our Elder and his Disciples made several primitive, yet effective, decisions. One of the more aggressive decrees was in relation to our expansion: a law was set in place banning any unauthorized reproduction until our rations reached more sustainable levels. Unfortunately, that day never came. As we speak, Orens live off an extremely regimented diet and lifestyle."

The more Luna speaks, the severity of the Oren way of life comes to light. Both Helena and Marcus sit stiffly, taking measured breaths as they process all she's shared. The unfortunate realization hits them: humanity's privilege, their privilege, is coming at a cost that they aren't paying. Elizabeth's hand rests over her heart, understanding how being a prisoner under the illusion of freedom must run in her blood. Reaching over, Helena grasps her other hand, a subtle act they both find comfort in. Liam's eyes rake over each person in the room, perceptive to the tonal shift, especially from Creed. His typically untroubled persona slowly fades away, and in its place, a haunting sense of loneliness creeps in.

"As the realization that our situation would likely never change became inevitable, the Elder amended the law, allowing a minimal amount to be born. Once, and only once, every fifty cycles, the Oren gather to hold what they call 'The Passing of Life Ritual,' in which the Elder and the Disciples hand-pick two couples to usher in a new life into Goldleaf. During the selection ceremony, they also ask if any Orens are willing to give themselves back to Grandiose; in exchange, the Elders select another couple to replace that life, and so on, and so on. In a good year, the ceremony leads to four or five Oren youth, but needless to say, in the many cycles since 'The Great War,' the number of legal new Orens has barely reached double digits."

Before Luna can continue, Marcus interrupts. "This is quite enlightening, but forgive me: I'm a little lost. At the Academy, they give us knights a brief course on Oren culture, and, admittedly, after listening to you, it was filled with propaganda bullshit. The one thing that seems accurate is that Orens are sticklers for law and order. So, correct me if I'm wrong, but doesn't one of your laws forbid Orens from exiting Goldleaf? And, if I understand what you're getting at, is this life ceremony quite important? You being here, let alone being his daughter, makes no sense to me."

"Well, if you'd shut your damn mouth and listen, she was getting there," Ramon barks, glaring. Under the chief's seething stare, Marcus quickly bows his head apologetically.

Luna quickly reassures the knight, then continues, "Marcus, I believe a lot of your confusion comes from your assumption that my existence has come as a result of 'The Passing of Life Ritual,' but you are mistaken. I am one of many illegal births that have happened over the years. You see, no matter how many laws are in place, love is inevitable – and love tends to lead to offspring. If the parents are caught, the punishment is isolation for several cycles; however, the offspring aren't as fortunate and, once discovered, are put down." An audible gasp fills the room as Luna reveals one of the Orens' dark secrets.

"Your reaction is understandable, but Orens defying the law is blasphemous among the majority. They truly believe following the law is what has kept them alive when the rest of Grandiose would see them dead. Yet there has been a growing faction of Orens who feel the laws are outdated and, quite frankly, represent a barbaric nature we pride ourselves in being above. My birth parents were part of this belief, so when I was born, they chose to run in hopes of finding a place where they could raise me away from the watchful eye of the Elders and, more importantly, far from the deadly reach of the Disciples. Although their allies helped them escape Goldleaf, they quickly discovered that the swampland between there and the Grandiose mainland is unforgiving." Luna takes a deep and shaky breath, but before she can speak again, Ramon takes her hand, indicating he'll take over from here. Being the father he is, Ramon would rather she not have to relive her earlier tragedies. She releases the breath she didn't realize she was holding, grateful for the reprieve.

"Details are scarce, but from what little Luna's birth mother told me in her final moments, my understanding is that they were attacked by wildlife during their escape. Her birth father stayed back, giving his life in the hope his wife and newborn could make it out of the swamps. Although her mother's wounds were already fatal, his sacrifice was not in vain: she was able to make it out alive before washing up on my shore. My husband and I found her bleeding out into the sea. We attempted to rush her to our medical facility, but she refused. She knew her time was coming to an end. As life faded from her eyes, she asked, no, begged us to take care of her daughter. Once I promised we would, she handed me Luna. Emotion instantly overwhelmed me: she was the most beautiful thing I had ever seen. In mere moments, I completely understood why these people would risk everything to keep her safe, and I've done the same ever since."

Ramon pulls in a teary-eyed Luna and embraces her, his eyes closing and face softening in love while his arms fiercely protect his daughter. This tale of loss emotionally strikes Creed and Elizabeth, tears silently rolling down their cheeks. Realizing the intense emotions running rampant through the group, Marcus insists they take a moment to replenish their drinks. After the short break, with everyone's drinks full and eyes now dry, Ramon continues.

"With an infant Oren in my care, I felt it was my duty to learn everything I could about her culture. It wasn't long before I discovered the same atrocities Luna described, and the truths about the Oren lifestyle haunted me. After weeks of sleepless nights and countless conversations with Ethan, I decided I had to do something to clear my guilt and hopefully leave Luna a world better than the one we're currently in. I began by reaching out to the rumored rebellion within Goldleaf, and, to my surprise, after only a few failed inquiries, I got a response from an Oren claiming to be their leader.

"Together in secret, the people of Riverhaven and I helped this anonymous Oren build a system in which he allows Orens who no longer want to live in Elder rule to escape, and we help foster them into a life here. But Riverhaven is only so big. We must find a way to hide them in plain sight among the rest of Grandiose. That's where knights like Nolan and Liam came into play. As Riverhaven natives, they welcomed our ideas of a world where all races would be equal, but their experience as warriors showed them it was not ready. Over cycles, the knights of Riverhaven helped find pockets of Grandiose whose eyes are blind to hatred; there, these orphans of a world trapped in time could live in peace. Along the way, these knights recruited others they felt could see our vision for the future, hoping that each new member would get a step closer to it.

"I often got letters from Nolan about how promising he thought the two of you were," Ramon continues, gesturing to Marcus and Helena. At his words, their breath catches. They lift their eyes from their drinks to meet the chief's softening gaze. "He mentioned his anticipation for your first visit here numerous times. He hoped to be the one to tell you all this."

Gently, Liam clears his throat and the chief quiets. "Nolan was extremely proud of our secret initiative, and – trust me – there wasn't a day that went by when he didn't want to tell the two of you about it. But he always concluded it would mean more if you were told here in Riverhaven after meeting our people. It was important to him that you met Luna first. He never contemplated that he wouldn't be around long enough to do so."

Helena has never doubted Nolan's resolve. Her chest swells with pride at what her friend has accomplished. He fostered a circle of safety in her life, and it warms her heart to know he has done the same for so many other displaced people. Nolan had always kept her secrets, even from Liam and Marcus; she could not muster any anger towards him for keeping this secret from her. She understood. Her respect for him, when she never imagined it could grow any greater, now skyrockets.

"The more I learn about Nolan, the more I admire the damn man. And at the same time, I can't help but be kinda pissed off at him," Marcus says gruffly, trembling with emotion. "This man saw something in me that I never thought was there. He helped me earn these plates on my shoulders, and the moment I did, he promised one day, my *'legend'* would even surpass his. And I am sitting here selfishly thinking to myself, how the hell do I surpass a man as great as him? Let alone match him? Especially," his voice cuts off for a moment, and the others notice tears streaking down his face as he continues, "when he's not here to guide me." The long journey and uncovered secrets strip away his valiant persona. As the reality of Nolan's death tightens around his heart, he feels as though he cannot breathe, choking on his sobs.

Helena wraps her arm around his shoulders, pulling him into her embrace and laying his head atop her breastplates. Everyone in the room watches as his tears roll down her armor, silently honoring a man who meant so much to many of them. Liam, always careful to give Marcus the space to acknowledge his feelings, waits until his tears dry up and his breathing stabilizes before continuing.

"Nolan wasn't wrong about you, boy. Greatness does lie in front of you. And I have a feeling that, by the mission's end, you and everyone else in this room will have a *'legend'* worthy of his promise." Sniffling, Marcus lifts his head and wipes the tear-stained tracks from his cheeks before downing a drink.

"Pardon my bluntness," Elizabeth says for the first time in a while. "But what is your *'mission?'* I can't help feeling like it's not the same one Uther believes he sent us on." Her words are soft but firm, and Ramon stares at her harshly, offended by her accusation of deceit.

Before the chief can lash out at her, Marcus quickly cuts in. "Elizabeth is right. Before all of–" he gestures around, "*that*, it was clear you had more to tell us, Chief Ramon. It seems that you've been working on one hell of a puzzle for some time. But I don't think we are the final piece, are we?"

"You're not, but you're damn close to it," Ramon says, blinking once more at Elizabeth before turning to address the knights. "For ages, my anonymous Oren and I have wished for a world where his people aren't locked behind a forest wall anymore, forced to slaughter their young. We want a Grandiose that embraces them, where they are free to live among us, where we share in each other's wealth, where we prosper together. I have casually hinted at the notion amidst the other leaders, but I either got no response or, more often than not, was laughed at as though I had told some hilarious joke. I had concluded that it was a dream I would not see in my lifetime.

"Seemingly out of the blue, Uther approached me one day. I am not sure if he has caught onto what I am doing behind his back, but he asked if knew a way to contact the Oren Elder. He went on and pitched this idea of a *'new world'* and his *'legacy.'* Although my gut tells me not to trust the man, I'd be a fool not to jump at the opportunity to jumpstart my own utopia. So with the help of my contact on the inside – and much, much pleading – I was able to set up the meeting that your group is now headed to."

Turning, Ramon glares at Elizabeth once more. " Contrary to your confusion, young lady, my 'mission' is the same as yours: build between here and Goldleaf. The question remains: once that bridge is built, what does Uther plan to use it for? I desire to help Orens across it, welcoming them into a warm future full of endless potential. Can you look into my eyes and say Uther wants the same?"

Elizbeth sits tall, squaring her shoulders, and channeling all of the power and control she has seen Uther use to command a room. She knows that what she is about to say could change the flow of history. She knows she must be clear, precise, and confident in every word, or Ramon will not take her seriously.

"Uther is many things, but for as long as I've known him, he has wanted to usher in a new age for Grandiose. And he knows the key to that is in Goldleaf: it is not books nor land nor even its gold that holds value. It is its people." Ramon and Elizabeth stare at each other intensely. It takes over a minute before Ramon blinks, breaking their eye contact. Sitting back, he accepts Elizabeth's words at face value.

"Then we are done here. The cards are on the table. Now, all I can do is hope the rest of this game plays out in our favor. Until then, let's drink; when we're done drinking here, we head to shore and drink some more and some more after that. And if we're lucky, we'll fall asleep shitfaced and wake up at the start of a new age."

Ramon stands, drink in hand, and calls for a toast. The others follow, each standing and raising their glass, eyes passing over each of the others. The night has strengthened their bond once more, now a fellowship with a common goal. Before they down their drinks and head to the festivities waiting for them by the sea, they sum up their ambitions in a simple phrase:

"To a new world…"

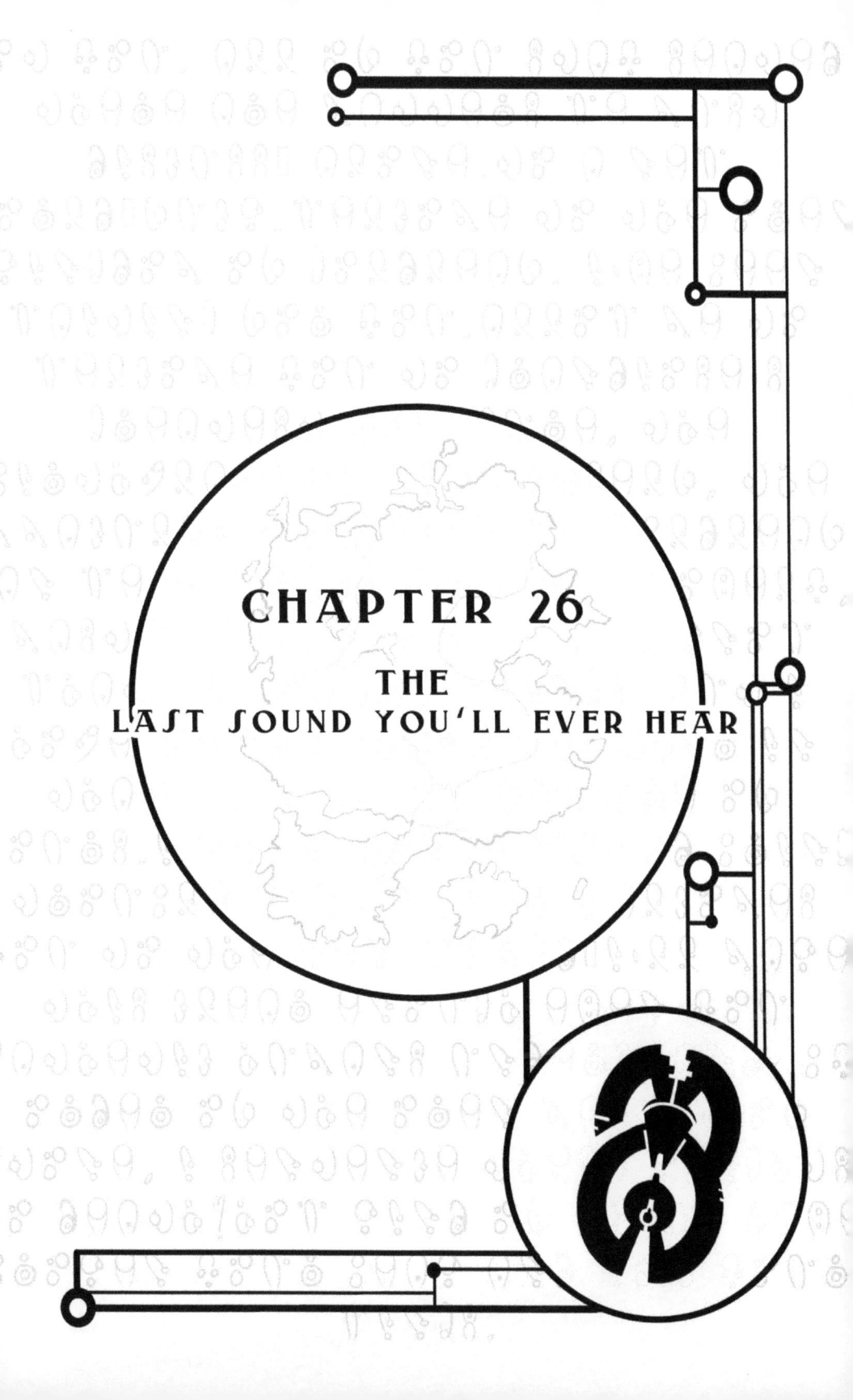

CHAPTER 26

THE LAST SOUND YOU'LL EVER HEAR

Chapter 26

The Last Sound You'll Ever Hear

As he watches the orange lights bounce off the ocean water, Creed realizes how unforgettable the sunrise over Riverhaven truly is. Creed sits in solitude, his feet soaking in the saltwater as he enjoys the warmth of the sand. As he ponders the revelations that came to light the previous night, he notices a handful of families happily cleaning up the debris left behind from the festivities. Riverahven's camaraderie amazes Creed: it is even more beautiful for him than the sunrise. He turns his head back to the ocean, where he now finds himself mesmerized at the sight of the *'Void.'*

Now, in its presence, Creed understands why the *'Void'* has become one of Grandiose's great wonders. This ancient island can only be seen from the coast of Riverhaven, yet its legend is well known all across Grandiose. Gaining infamy as a one-way trip, the *'Void'* is surrounded by six stone towers connecting a mystical barrier that allows entrance onto the island but also locks them there. Creed sees the perfect example of this curse when a flock of four-winged sparrows flies through the back end of the *'Void,'* only to be incinerated when they try to exit through the opposite side. Surrounding this deadly mystery is a flotilla of ships, led by Ethan, all studying the phenomena in hopes of breaking down the barrier one day, an effort that has yet to bear any fruit.

Liam's voice breaks through his thoughts. "Hell of a view, isn't it?" he chuckles, extending his hand to help Creed stand.

"One I definitely won't be forgetting anytime soon," Creed says solemnly, grunting as Liam pulls him to his feet. He dusts the sand off his legs and continues, "This must have been a memorable place to grow up in."

"It was, but not for the same reason. Chief Ramon's father, Chief Umaga, was a ruthless and hateful man, determined to shape Riverhaven in his image by any means necessary. Under his rule, struggling youths like myself were sent to the gallows. Undoubtedly, Ramon would never allow that to happen nowadays."

"That history is surprising to hear. I guess Riverhaven isn't the paradise it seems to be."

"On the contrary, once Ramon seized the throne, he rehabilitated Riverhaven rapidly. Ramon has done so much to better this place; the loyalty he has garnered from his people strikes fear in the other crowns. Obedience can often fall short of devotion on the battlefield after all."

Creed halts in place, and Liam's brow furrows as he looks at the man. Creed looks back at the *'Void,'* pausing briefly before asking a simple question: "If you could, would you stay?"

Without hesitation, Liam answers, "Absolutely. Wouldn't you?" Rather than responding, Creed just stares off into the horizon. "Maybe I should rephrase that question. Creed, why don't you stay?" Liam asks, his voice softening as he lays his hand on his companion's shoulder. Creed's eyes widen, relieved that Liam could tell what had been racing through his mind without needing to voice it aloud.

"You know," he says, bending over to scoop up a handful of sand. He lets it run through his fingers into his other hand, then repeats the soothing distraction. "There's a misconception about us Shadowbloods. Everyone thinks that we can become whoever we want when we shift, as if we use human flesh as a closet full of disguises, but they're wrong in every way possible. For starters, we only have two faces: the scaly one and the not-so-scaly one. This is my face, no matter how many times I shift. This is me. But what's most upsetting is that everyone thinks this is a disguise." Creed lets the remainder of the sand filter through his fingers and back to the beach at his feet. Liam notices a single drop of water plop into the sand, and when he looks back at Creed, he sees tears filling his eyes. "I may have been born a Dargone, but it wasn't until I shifted for the first time that I felt alive. The outside finally matched the inside, yet the whole world hates me for it. They'd rather me live a lie that fits their mold than disturb it, even if only long enough to defend myself."

"So you've spent a lifetime running."

"What choice did I have? My very existence is a crime in my own birthplace. Hell, I'm no saint. In fact, the thing I'm best at is pissing people off. But then... then, I run into you lot, and everything changes." Wiping his eyes, he kicks the sand up in frustration. "First, you all welcome me with open arms. On top of that, I show my true colors and you go and act like it's no big deal. Bloody hell, do you know how many others have treated me that way? One! One person in all my life treated me like a normal living being before you guys. And now you have brought me to a whole kingdom full of people like you, and you expect me to leave. Some friend you are."

Even though he can hear the frustration in Creed's voice, Liam lets out a laugh, and his companion softens the tiniest bit. "Creed, we expect nothing from you. If time has taught me anything, sometimes standing still can get you much further than running."

Liam's words are the exact blessing Creed was hoping for. He pulls the old knight close with relief, embracing Liam as a son would a father. To his surprise, with the morning sun rising above them, Liam echoes his embrace and utters words Creed thought he'd never heard...

"Welcome home Creed...welcome home."

*****

With morning behind them, the party says goodbye to Creed outside the swamp connecting Riverhaven and Goldleaf. One by one, Elizabeth, Marcus, and Helena try to convince Creed to finish the journey with them, but each time, he reassures them that he has made up his mind. In response to Creed's rejection, Marcus jokes about how much better off they are now than he is, to which Creed reminds him who saved his ass not too long ago. Their banter lifts the sadness that has blanketed the group at leaving their newfound friend behind.

"Happy to see last night's festivities have left everyone joyful." Ramon's resounding voice demands everyone's attention as he approaches with Hornet. A grin lights across Liam's face as he sees Hornet again running at total capacity, equipped with new parts and a new paint job. The locals went as far as to give her tattoos mirroring Riverhaven's traditional designs. Once she notices Liam, Hornet bounds over and nuzzles her nose against him.

"She is a fighter, Liam. Between your run-in in the desert and the piss-poor Dargone engineering, I wasn't sure she'd ever look this good again," Ramon says, leaning against Hornet's side, and she nuzzles up to him. The chief points out yet another addition his team has made to her for the journey ahead: "There's no way your carriage could make it through the swamp, so I had my finest craftsman design this saddle and storage apparatus. You have to travel lighter than before, but as I assured Miss Elizabeth this morning, all your essentials, including the offering for the Elder, are here. " Elizabeth double-checks the cargo, and then Helena helps her mount Hornet.

As the others embrace in their final goodbyes, Creed offers one final warning: "Luna says the swamp is the most dangerous place in all of Grandiose, but she's confident that if anyone can survive, it's you all. Then again, she said that thinking I'd be by your side, so I can only imagine your chances have greatly decreased without me," Creed laughs, and Marcus rolls his eyes. "Joking aside, Luna did mention the path from here to Goldleaf is pretty much a straight shot, but it's dense and dark, smells like shit, and, most importantly, it's infested with hordes of flesh eating creatures."

"Well, that's encouraging," Marcus mocks facetiously as he adjusts his armor, readying himself to head into the swamp.

"Look at the bright side: at least we know it'll be fun," Helena knocks her shoulder into Marcus, forcing a smile onto his face at her antics.

"As much as I hate to bring the mood down," Liam interjects, "I need you both to take Luna's warning to heart. Even as a boy, we were told never to step foot near this swamp. There's a haunting hiss that comes from this place. If we are not cautious, it may be the last sound we will ever hear."

Marcus and Helena acknowledge Liam's wisdom as a sign to prepare for the worst. Each prepares their weapons, then moves to opposite sides of Hornet. Liam says goodbye to Ramon one last time but assures him he'll see him again when their mission is complete. As he makes his way to the front of the group, he gives Elizabeth a wink, assuring her they will keep her safe.

"Into the unknown, my friends."

Once they enter the swamp, they realize how accurate Luna's warning had been. The swamp's ankle-high water is so thick it is like treading through snow banks, and the black-leafed trees reach so high that they block out most of the sun. Even Hornet struggles to move, and if it weren't for the lights illuminating the knights' armor, it would be near impossible for any of them to see where they're going.

"This place seems endless. No wonder so many get lost," Elizabeth coughs. "It's a miracle anyone has survived."

"If Luna is an indication, the Orens are a resilient lot. Actually, now that I'm thinking about it, that's likely where your resiliency comes from, Elizabeth. You're born a survivor."

Helena compliments Elizabeth without turning, continuously scanning their environment for threats.

"I suppose that's one way to look at it. Although you give me too much credit, I'm only half Or–"

Before Elizabeth can say anymore, Liam abruptly halts the convoy. He grips his spear tightly as Hornet's ears perk up. Marcus follows suit, slowly drawing his blade, as a sound slides through the air.

Hiss.

Hiss.

Hiss.

The branches begin to rustly, leaves falling like rain over their heads. The hissing grows louder each moment until it finally hits its peak, surrounding them. The hiss morphs into disturbing laughter, madness incarnate. As the haunting sound echoes throughout the swamp, dozens of vicious smiles break through the shadows, crazed reptilian eyes above each grin.

A sense of doom fills the air, and the knights take formation, ready to once again put their lives on the line to protect Elizabeth and the mission. The laughter then stops, and a somehow more haunting silence takes its place. Time stands still before a monstrous beast leaps from the waters towards them. If only by instinct, Liam catches the attacker mid-air, tossing it into a nearby tree. The force is enough to split the tree at its base; it would have instantly killed an ordinary commoner. Yet, to everyone's shock, the beast simply begins to laugh, raising itself once more.

Knowing the battle they now face, Liam charges his spear. The light produces enough brightness to give them a clear view of their surroundings. Trees and the water are full of identical beasts, each roughly half the size of an average man, covered in black fur with reptilian limbs and a tail to match. There is a murderous hunger in each of their eyes. Each creature draws its claws, laughing as they do. In response, Liam and the others brace themselves for the battle ahead, and he utters the only word fitting to the situation:

"Fuck."

CHAPTER 27
THE DISCIPLES

Chapter 27

The Disciples

Slash after slash, Liam deflects the onslaught of attacks from the swamp beasts. At his back, Marcus fights off an equally aggressive barrage. To thin the hoard, Helena uses her agility to discharge countless ice arrows into as many of the beasts' throats as possible. Even Hornet, although greatly limited by the cargo on her back, tries to maul as many creatures as possible. For all their effort, though, the devilish creatures' numbers continue to grow, seemingly coming from the shadows by the dozens.

Before long, the hoard manages to pull Liam and Marcus away from each other. Suddenly, Liam is blindsided by a vicious bite to his shoulder, and several of the swamp beasts maximize this moment of weakness to leap on top of him. Liam's anger builds as the monsters crawl and bite away at his skin, and he manages to tighten his grip around his spear then begins to rev it. The sparks build, and he grinds his teeth, enduring the endless pain as he readies his attack.

Once Liam's spear is fully charged, he bursts through the monsters, adrenaline silencing the pain he is in. Lightning bolts fly from the tip of the spear as he spins it above his head. He rapidly clears the area, creating a vortex of electricity that shocks and slashes open any of his attackers. Techniques like this have made Liam a legend among his peers, an unbridled master of a regular spear, and this one only made more deadly by Q.A.S Tech. In the blink of an eye, Liam dashes forward, simultaneously impaling three swamp beasts. As he revs his weapon once more, he lets out a heroic cry so tremendous it sends ripples through the swamp waters. With his next move, Liam circles the spear around him, the beast he just stabbed still impaled on its end, before swinging it high above his head and hammering it down in front of him. The impact causes a wave of discharged energy that electrocutes dozens of beasts in his vicinity.

For a moment, the swamp is silent, and the swamp beasts slowly inch back into the shadows. The victory, however, is short-lived. Just as it seems the battle is over, Liam falls to his knees, bloodsoaked and exhausted. After expending all of his energy on his display of grandeur, he cannot continue. The swamp beasts cheer in unison, celebrating victoriously, and return to their assault. Despite their efforts, Marcus and Helena are again surrounded. Licking their lips rabidly, more monsters move toward Liam, confident in their kill. With blood dripping from every cut and bite, Liam grinds his spear into the ground and lifts himself defiantly. He bares his teeth, preparing for one final battle.

One of the swamp beasts takes the lead and charges forward, but a voluptuous Oren woman bolts past him before Liam can lift himself from the ground. With lightning radiating off her body, the Oren clotheslines the charging beast, decapitating it. Easily matching, if not exceeding, Liam in height, she he towers over the remaining beasts. He stares in awe at the traditional Oren tattoos decorating the skin not covered by the naturally-dyed Oren attire with authentic gold lacing. Her fair skin is offset by her jet-black hair, tied in a thick ponytail cascading down the length of her back. The beast pack trembles in fear, and the leader lets out a shriek, and some of the monsters begin to disappear into the darkness surrounding them.

The woman looks over her shoulder at Liam with a playful smile. "I like your style, old man, but we'll take it from here."

Liam watches as their savior bolts around him, eradicating the remaining creatures with electrified tackles and grapples. From bearhugs that snap the spines of the beasts to suplexes that shatter their heads on impact, she displays a level of athleticism that would make even the gladiatorial wrestlers of old shake in fear. The swamp beasts share this sentiment, for with every electrifying move, they withdraw from their attack.

Seeing an opening, Marcus shifts stances, allowing him to use the flames from his hilt to thrust himself away from his attackers. Certain of his relative safety, he then rushes over to aid Helena, who has broken free from her attack. Together, they manage to horde a group of the beasts into one area. Before Marcus can attempt a fatal blow, the ground beneath them rumbles. Mere moments later, an enormous stone hand erupts underneath the swamp beast, lifting them into the air before crashing them into its palm. In shock, Helena and Marcus watch as the stone structure retreats into the ground, leaving nothing but blood and innards flooding the swamp water.

With the swamp beasts now all trembling in fear, three more Orens, wearing simpler garments than the first, emerge from the tree line. The first is slender yet athletic, his head shaved clean to match his hairless body. At first, he seems relatively unremarkable save for his trick bifocal: under the right light, it completely hides his emerald eyes. To his left, a sprightly Oren sports an ember mohawk and an infectious, youthful smile. Orbiting around this Oren are five palm-sized flaming spheres, and he continuously plays with them as he observes their group. The last of these is a sultry female with almond skin and the most beautiful golden brown curls draped down her shoulders. Every step she takes leaves an arctic mist in her wake.

"Damn, Nigel. Looks like we're late. Rhea seems to have this situation under control," the mohawked Oren complains, nodding toward the lightning-baring Oren. She launches the carcass of a swamp creature toward him in disdain, continuing to make waste of more creatures in her way.

"Don't be so eager to fight, Chili, it's our way," the bald Oren replies.

"Don't be so prude, Nigel," the ravishing Oren defends the anxious Chili. "It's been ages since we have gotten to stretch our arts. Let the boy have fun."

"Fine, let's do this quickly," Nigel begrudgingly agrees. "Chili will handle the rattlers attacking the woman and the mechanic beast while Isla and I finish off what Reha hasn't."

With permission and utter excitement, Chili backflips onto two of his flaming orbs, grabbing two others before using them to propel himself into battle. Isla follows him into the fray, taking a deep breath, and a cold air fills the area. As she exhales, icy armor coats her chest and works its way down her arms to her nails, extending past her knees. Ready for battle, Isla casually struts towards the beasts; she is simultaneously intimidating and intoxicating. After watching his peers join the fight, Nigel prepares himself by summoning ten stone hands, floating five on each side from the ground. Once equipped, Nigel simply points toward a beast to fire one of the stone hands towards them, where it either punches through its chest or crushes their head before returning to Nigel's side so he can repeat the act.

In a matter of moments, the Orens shift the scuffle to a one-sided affair, slaughtering the beasts at an unprecedented rate. Marcus and Helena use the opening to rush to Liam.

"Hang in there, old friend, we aren't going to let you die in this shithole swamp," Marcus assures Liam, who, with his allies by his side, finally succumbs to his wounds and passes out into their arms. Helena strokes his hair, and Marcus gulps before shifting his attention, quickly glancing between his friend's figure and the Oren's battle to ensure no more monsters have snuck up on them during the massacre. While he's not entirely sure that they can be trusted, he's more worried about his friend making it out of this battle alive.

The Orens make quick work of the swamp creatures. They move gracefully and precisely, something the party could not have appreciated during their previous encounter with an Oren. From the speed at which Rhea bolts through her targets to how Isla extends and retracts her icey nails through their skulls, they move as if weightless. Yet, as unique as they are, Nigel stands out: the accuracy with which he manipulates the earth around him is jaw-dropping. He shifts the stone fists around from shape to shape as if they were made of clay; one moment, fists, the next, an assortment of stone blades, only to quickly combine them into a giant hammer, which he uses to crush the beast beneath it. Nigel is so impressive that Marcus and Helena can't help but wonder if they have encountered him before.

"Marcus... could that be him, the Terra King?" Helena whispers.

"I'm not sure, but let's appreciate him being on our side for the moment. Our priority needs to be getting Liam help," Marcus says, grinding his teeth and gripping the scar from their previous encounter with the Terra King. "After that, I'll make sure to ask him myself."

Meanwhile, as Marcus and Helena watch the Orens, Elizabeth still fends for herself from atop Hornet, who is still surrounded by the beasts. Luckily for them, Chili quickly makes his grand entrance and tosses his fire orbs at the beasts, causing them to combust instantly.

"Hello, love, the time to worry has now passed! Your savior Chili is here."

His boastful arrival is punctuated by the combining of two of his orbs, making it larger than his head. He tosses the orb into the air and, before it hits the ground, kicks it with such force that it flies through the stomachs of a few dozen beasts before hitting a tree and causing a small explosion. Amused by his antics, Chili laughs aloud as he bounces around, tossing flaming orbs at the creatures as they run away in fear. Unlike his peers, Chili's movement is somewhat chaotic, yet still elegant. With most of the beasts on the run, Chili ends the scuffle with a flashy display of power.

"You poor rattlers spend your whole lifes in the dark, so let me leave you with a parting gift..." Chili leaps into the air once more and combines all five orbs to create a massive fiery sphere at least three times his size above his head. "Say hello to the sun!"

The heat from Chili's attack radiates throughout the swamp, melting Isla's icy armor. Knowing they are defeated, every remaining beast turns its tail and flees into the darkness.

Although there is no one left to attack, Chili still attempts to release the orb upon the swamp.

"Enough!" Nigel quickly summons a gigantic fist, grabbing the flaming orb and extinguishing it immediately. "Chili, your arrogance will be the death of us."

Like a child, Chili falls back to the ground in front of Nigel and immediately pleads his case. "Oh, c'mon, Nigel. I've never gotten to use that move before. I just really wanted to see what it does." Chili crosses his arm in a frump as the others return to their group.

"Don't be upset, little man. One day you'll get to see it in all its glory," Rhea attempts to cheer up the youth.

"Yeah," he pouts, "maybe in a few hundred ages when we're let out of the stronghold again."

"Maybe by then, you'll have a handle on it," Isla shoves him sisterly, and Chili quickly jumps up to wrestle her back.

"If you're done making light of the situation, we do have a mission to finish," Nigel reminds them. He pushes his glasses and turns his attention to the knights, who have regrouped around Hornet. The Orens watch as Marcus and Helena lift Liam onto Hornet's back, then do their best to patch Liam's injuries. As the knights tend to their friend, Elizabeth stiffens, noticing the Orens approaching them. Marcus immediately notices that her demeanor has shifted and immediately draws his sword. His eyes scan the Oren warriors, unaware of their intention. Before they can get too close, Marcus points his blade directly at Nigel's neck, his intention clear.

"Put your toy away. Why would we go through the trouble of saving you fools if we had any intention of hurting you in the first place?" Nigel demands arrogantly.

"Only the ignorant assume the intentions of a man he has never met," Marcus insists, standing his ground.

Adjusting his glasses again, Nigel sighs, "You humans are an aggravating species. If it's a proper introduction you must have, so be it. You are in the presence of Nigel Nocturn, Master of Stone. My colleagues," he continues, gesturing to the Orens around him, who each incline their head at their recognition "Lady Isla Rose Master of Ice, Lady Rhea Coloso Master of the Storm and youthful Chili Surlefeu Master of the Flame. We are four of the great Oren Disciples. And, if I am not mistaken, you are late for a very important audience with our Elder. The older one among you," he pauses briefly, his initially haughty tone shifting to concern, "could benefit from meeting with our healer."

Marcus lowers his blade at Nigel's final remark, choosing to believe his intentions are pure enough to trust that Liam would be saved. Acknowledging the truce, Nigel approaches Hornet to examine the severity of Liam's wounds. He is unfazed as Hornet growls defensively.

"Tell your machine to stand down before I put it in its place," Nigel demands, and the knights begrudgingly obey. "Your companion is in rough shape, but if we're quick, he should survive. He'll need our best healer to do so. Rhea, run ahead of us and have Master Zayn ready at the gate." Rhea nods before sparks engulf her body, and she speeds off with a flash into the forest. "As for the rest of you, get in line. This swamp is a labyrinth of death, but luckily, now you have a guide to show you the way."

The three remaining Orens take point and head into the forest. Elizabeth and the knights look between each other before hesitantly following the warriors. Their slow steps are suddenly interrupted when an impatient Nigel turns around and summons stone chairs beneath Marcus and Helena. As soon as they fall into the seats, he motions to the chairs and to the ground underneath Hornet, lifting all of the company into the air before swiftly forcing the floating arrangements into a straight line.

"Did you miss the part when I said to be hasty about the situation, or are you humans too lazy to even put the slightest effort into an attempt to save one of your own?" he asks, but continues before anyone can answer. "Either way, I'll take control of the matter and move you myself. I will not be scolded by our Elder over human shortcomings." Nigel again heads into the forest, this time with the knights and Elizabeth forcedly hovering behind him. Isla and Chili giggle, whispering amongst themselves as they watch Nigel groan under his breath.

They travel deeper and deeper for hours before Nigel and the other Oren suddenly stop. To Marcus and the others, this part of the forest looks no different than any previous one. Fearing that they have been led into a trap, Marcus lashes out.

"What the hell is going on?! Are you lost or something? Because this sure as hell isn't any kingdom I've ever seen!"

Their stone vehicles immediately disappear, and the knights fall to the ground without warning, only increasing his anger. "Son of a bitc–"

Before Marcus can reach his feet, the trees around them begin to move. Suddenly, the dark, empty forest twists and turns into itself, and a clear path stands before them. The Orens go down the path, and Marcus and the others follow, fascinated. As they make their way to the end of the path, the trees behind them once again shift back into place. Before long, they reach the end, where they now stand in amazement, for the dreary swamp no longer surrounds them. In its place is a beautiful forest kingdom with lush trees coated in gold.

At the kingdom gates, Rhea waits, accompanied by a handsome male, Oren, in similar clothing. This mysterious Oren seems to glow in the now abundant sunlight. This Oren is well-built and has a natural handsomeness to him. While his skin tone and build is identical to Nigel's, he is notably younger – yet not as youthful as Chili. His eyes are piercing emerald, and his hair is cut thin, though he is not completely bald. He steps forward, walking right past Marcus and Helena and directly to Elizabeth, who he helps down from Hornet's back. He looks deeply into her eyes, and she can't help but do the same. With Elizabeth entangled in Oren's gaze, he blesses her with the warmest smiles and finally speaks:

"Welcome to the Oren kingdom of Goldleaf. I've been waiting for you."

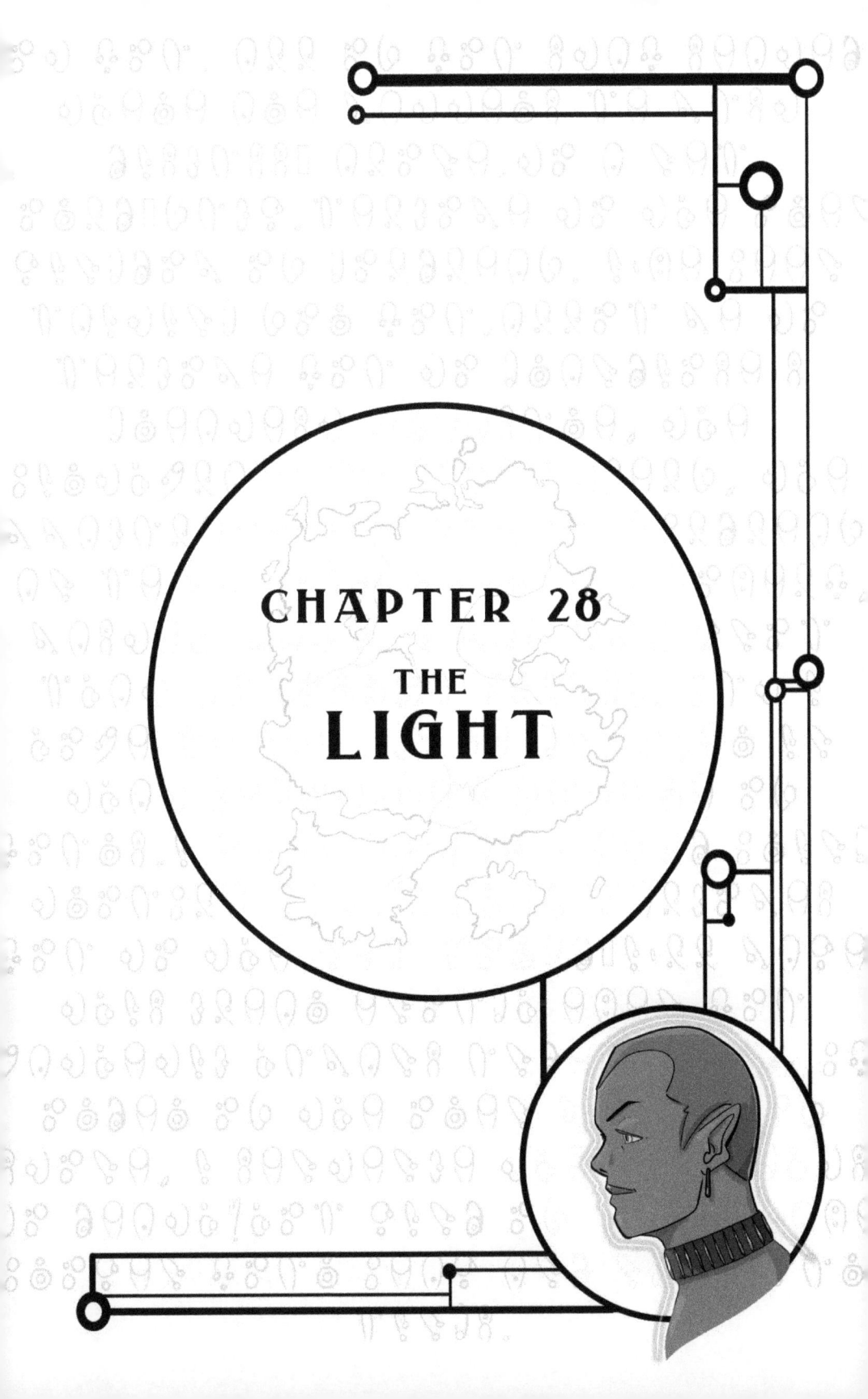

CHAPTER 28
THE
LIGHT

Chapter 28

The Light

A single bronze leaf falls to Helena's feet, her body tensing as she watches this unidentified Oren, who continues to eye up Elizabeth. Though he appears friendly, Helena can't help but feel unease around him, but she cannot act on her intuition before he speaks again.

"Oh, my dear, you have no idea how much I have looked forward to speaking with you," he swoons, walking her to the city entrance. "When I heard someone like you existed, my mind raced excitedly. My dear, do you understand how much you could change this world?" He speaks so quickly that she never has a chance to respond. "And that first time I glanced upon you...your beauty...it stopped me in my tracks."

Elizabeth finds his admiration troublingly familiar, but she's most taken aback by his last words. "The 'first time'?" she asks, confused. She is confident this is the first time the two have met.

"Oh," he chuckles, waving his hand, "forgive me. I meant just now, when the forest opened and saw your party here. Your presence is so... you, my dear, radiate in the sunlight. I couldn't help but see you first."

Helena has heard enough. Watching Elizabeth's discomfort, she is validated in her intuition and refuses to allow this Oren to continue. She pulls Elizabeth away before addressing the Oren in quite an uncharacteristically unfriendly manner.

"Are you the Oren who can aid our companion? If not, could you move out of the way so your peers can take us to someone who can?"

The unfamiliar Oren looks over Helena's shoulder, noticing Liam's blood-soaked and unconscious body, and is reminded of why Rhea summoned him to the gate.

"Oh yes, my apologies. I've clearly put my foot in my mouth and forgotten all my manners as well as my purpose. I am indeed the Oren you seek. Allow me to introduce myself: I am the First Disciple, Master of the Light, Sir Zayn Yeshin. Among many other things, I will be your host during your stay. More relevantly, I am this kingdom's leading physician. Allow me to see to your friend's needs." With that, he is silent for the first time, moving quickly to Hornet's side to look into Liam's wounds.

Nigel excuses Chili and Isla and allows them and Rhea to return to the kingdom. As Zayn examines Liam, Nigel gathers Marcus, Helena, and Elizabeth at his side.

"Forgive Master Zayn," he says. "He is the most intelligent of us but, in exchange, his social skills are lacking, to say the least. Once he's done with your ally, he and I will escort you to the castle, where we can discuss further matters. If we are lucky, your stay here will be a short one." Nigel nods once, then recedes to the kingdom gates, leaving the others to watch as Zayn begins to treat Liam.

Zayn looks over Liam's wounds before sitting beside him, legs crossed. The healer places one hand on Liam's chest and the other on his own. Zayn's eyes begin to glow with a cool white light while a calming quiet fills the forest. As he steadies his breathing, the air around him matches his breath. With the world around him at peace, Zayn gently pushes down on Liam's chest, and all of the knight's wounds glow with the same cool white light.

"My understanding is that humans believe this art, or magic as you call it, is simply the manipulation of *'light.'* Although my gift does allow me to illuminate the dark or create simple illusions, what you understand as *'light'* is a mistranslation. In the context of the Oren language, a more fitting description would be *'soul'* or *'spirit.'*" As Zayn speaks, Liam's wounds slowly close, sealing the light behind them. "The *'light'* within us all, our will to live, that is what my gift can truly manipulate. Luckily, your friend is quite the fighter. He's not ready to leave this world. Makes healing him much simpler."

After all of Liam's cuts are closed, Zayn removes his hand and stands. As he does, Liam shoots up, blinking quickly as his eyes adjust to the light and sights surrounding him. In such a short time, he now seems completely fine. Noticing one new face, Liam immediately identifies that this must be his healer and thanks Zayn for saving his life.

"No reason to thank me. Frankly, I rarely get a chance to use my gift to its full extent; I was starting to get quite restless. But, if you don't mind, try not to get so badly injured any time soon. Patching you up took a fair amount out of me. I'm not sure I could fix you up so fast next time," Zayn laughs off Liam's near-death experience as if it was nothing more than a simple scrape.

With Liam back in good health, Nigel waves them to the gates to reach the intended destination.

"Nigel, come on, these people clearly need time to rest," Zayn huffs, annoyed at the other's commitment to procedure. "Maybe let them clean up a little before meeting with my father."

"Do you think me a fool, Zayn? You don't give a damn about them bathing or getting sleep, you just want more time to drool over that obscenity." His eyes dart over to Elizabeth, and Liam stiffens as he becomes aware of what transpired while he was unconscious.

Marcus and Helena stand protectively in front of Elizabeth, glaring at Nigel once more. Before they can say anything, though, Zayn pushes his way through them to confront Nigel himself. The two Orens argue at the front gate in their native tongue, a rhythmic language that shares few words with the human language. While their facial expressions indicate their argument, it sounds more like individuals reciting poetry to each other.

"If not for them, I would have died, wouldn't I?" Liam ponders, and the others turn to look at him.

"If not for them, we'd all be dead," Helena answers somberly.

"Uther used to tell me stories of the Great War and man's great victory over the Orens. He showed me a library full of history books that speak of it as a triumphant, one-sided battle that gave humanity control of Grandiose. But after every tale he would remind me they were nothing more than lies. He made it clear that man only won because the Orens refused to fight." Elizabeth speaks a truth that many believe but would never admit. Man's history is full of self-serving propaganda, and the Great War might be the worst of it.

"For our sake, I hope you're one hell of a negotiator," Marcus whispers, concerned. "We have only seen a handful of Orens in action, but between these Disciples and what we faced in the desert, I'd imagine it would take the entirety of Grandhaven's army plus a few of the Academy's reserves just to even the battlefield."

"Uther agrees. He fears them just as much as he admires them. Thankfully for all of us, I have no intention of failing here." Elizabeth speaks with the utmost confidence, gripping her necklace as she does. Helena eyes her friend curiously but says nothing.

Nigel and Zayn continue to argue briefly before agreeing on what to do next. They approach the group, where Nigel is the first to speak.

"Let me start with an apology," Nigel says, adjusting his glasses again. "It seems my use of the word *'obscenity'* came off as insulting. Forgive me; the language of man is something I rarely use. I only meant to refer, that the young lady is somewhat of a... curiosity." Nigel's apology lacks an ounce of sincerity.

Under his breath, Marcus whispers, "Sounds like you speak it just fine to me." Unbeknownst to him, Orens have remarkable hearing, and Nigel is aware of the knight's disbelief in him.

Zayn quickly interrupts, noting the tension between Nigel and the knights. "As a sign of good faith, we have agreed that it would be best to allow you to spend the night in the castle, getting some well desired rest, some Oren delights, and a decent bath before meeting with my father."

"Your father? You have said that twice now. Are we safe to assume the Oren Elder is your old man?" Liam asks.

"Indeed, Elder Yeshin is my *'old man,'* as you say. I hope that doesn't have you questioning my authority? I was a success in my crucible just like every decipher before me. In fact, I was more determined to be a success because of it." Before Zayn can continue or make any more inquiries, Nigel insists they enter the kingdom. Apt at idle conversation, Zayn is annoyed at being cut off, but he looks to the sky, commenting on how the day has gotten away from them.

The knights gather their things, sitting Elizabeth atop Hornet once more. With Zayn and Nigel as their guides, the party becomes the first humans to step foot in Oren territory in countless cycles. Once they are all within the kingdom's wall, the forest outside the gate shifts back to its original state, a massive blockade of trees that makes it impossible for anyone to enter or exit. Before they can go any further, Nigel stops and turns to the group, formally introducing his home:

"Allow me to welcome you to Grandiose's greatest treasure, the birthplace of life itself, the immaculate Kingdom of Goldleaf."

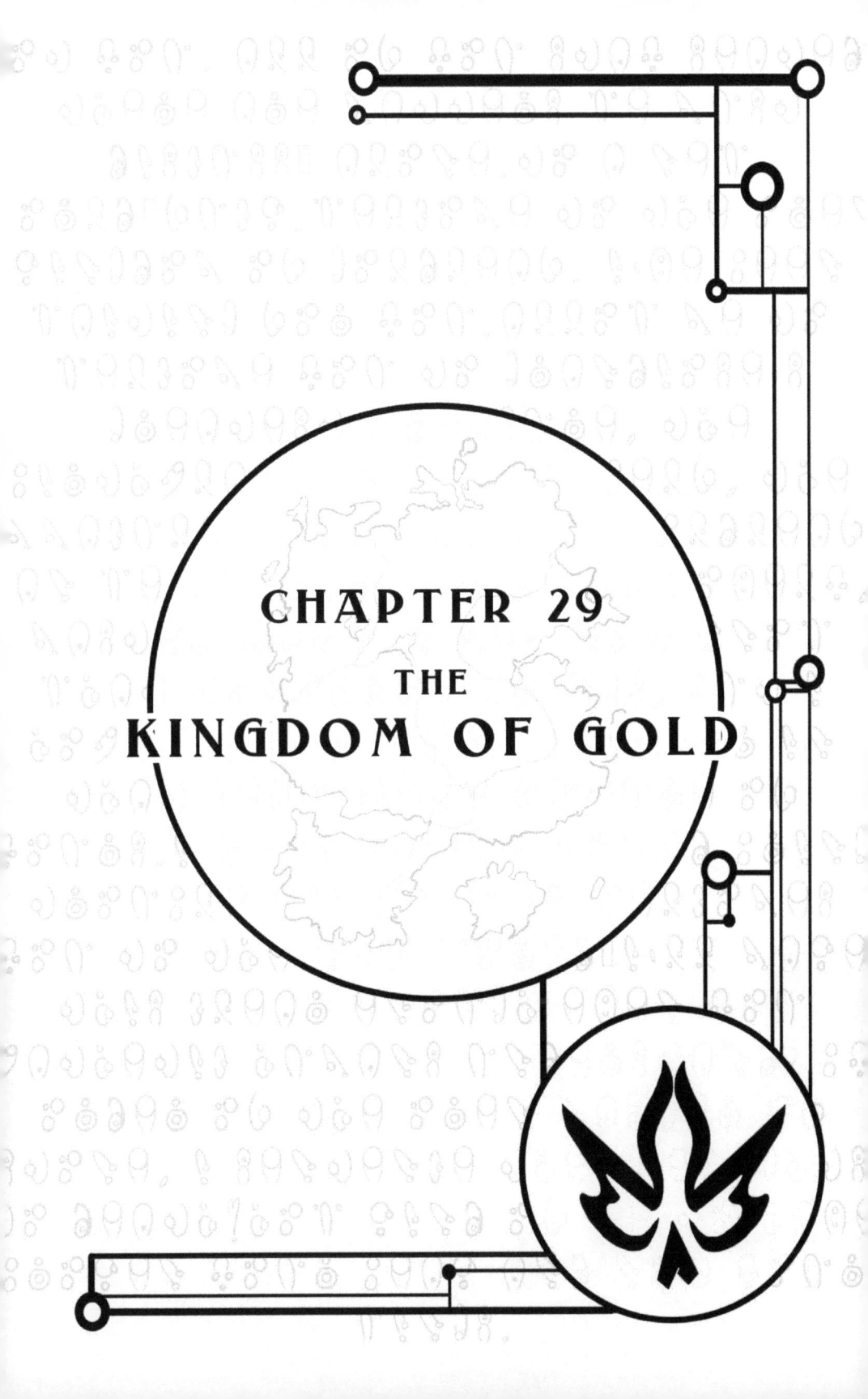

CHAPTER 29
THE
KINGDOM OF GOLD

Chapter 29

The Kingdom of Gold

Commonly referred to as *"A city paved in gold"* by the outside world, Goldleaf is a kingdom so ravishing that even the most flattering rumors pale in comparison. Ironically, no structure is *"paved"* with anything in Goldleaf; instead, the kingdom is entirely natural. Orens use magic to manipulate and accelerate the growth of the forest's rare golden trees, shaping them into the many homes, shops, and other establishments now entangled with the beautiful forest skyline. Unlike the architecture found in nearly every other kingdom within Grandiose, Goldleaf's buildings are spherical. Some hang down from enormous branches, while others are nested deep within the massive trunks of the golden trees.

While the kingdom's skyline is the first thing many would notice, Goldleaf's ground level is just as fascinating. Its many weaving dirt paths are covered with golden leaves that have fallen from above; rustling among those leaves is the most peaceful wildlife man could ever find. Tigermunks scuttle about looking for berries or nuts to take back to their young, while moss elks mingle with Orens as they go about their days. Hidden within the treeline are various ponds and waterways, some only big enough to get a refreshing spit from. Others are large enough to swim or bathe in, a common pastime of the more spry Orens.

Goldleaf's first impression is otherworldly. Nothing outside its walls is as stunning, and its air alone has an exotic taste. Its atmosphere is welcoming yet so perfect that you wish to never enter in fear of disturbing it. Its juxtaposition to the surrounding swamp is unbelievable, to say the least, but these first steps are only the beginning of its splendor.

To the newcomers' surprise, it takes nearly four hours to make it to the Oren castle. Luckily for them, during those four hours, Zayn would act as an enthusiastic tour guide, introducing the party to local foods like sugarcorn and lush pumapple. He eagerly educates them on Orens' day-to-day life, everything from their mostly vegetarian diets to their love of farming and agriculture. Each small nugget of information leaves the group wondering more, which only excites Zayn further. Every time he promises a more in-depth history lesson at the castle, Nigel scoffs.

Nigel is not alone in his disdain of their presence. Nearly every other Oren who passes greets them with a sneer or gasp. Others hide away in the tree line as if they have brought some plague upon them. The knights acknowledge their behavior with a low nod, understanding how their presence would bring up more unsavory feelings; the last time many had seen a human was during the war. The younger Orens who escaped the trials and tribulations of battle have grown up with the stories of how man stole their land and murdered their forefathers, and they harbor more hatred for the humans. However, as each unpleasant interaction passes, Zayn ensures them that, given the time, he believes his peers will welcome them as he has. Zayn's optimism makes time pass quickly, and before long, a gorgeous meadow sprawls before them filled with thousands of flowers and burgundy buffalo roaming freely. In the meadow's center stands the most extraordinary tree anyone could imagine, and atop it rests the great Oren castle.

This enormous wonder, known as the heart and soul of Goldleaf, is home to numerous Orens but, most importantly, the Oren Elder and all his Disciples. Each of their living quarters is housed inside. While each Disciple is awarded their own wing of the castle and housing for any apprentice they choose to take on, the Elder's chambers rest at the center of the castle. A home that is four or five times larger than any other home in Goldleaf, it is blessed with the only synthetic architecture in the kingdom. Beautiful stained glass windows rest inside any opening in the spherical chamber. Each of these works of art glistens in the light, and, thanks to Zayn's constant stream of information, the group recognizes how each panel depicts a different Elder's reign and his accomplishments through the ages.

"Our humble abode awaits," Zayn eagerly continues, waving them onward. A less enthusiastic Nigel holds his hand up, stopping them, and informs the groups of the ground rules for their stay.

"While under our roof, there will be some basic mandates expected of you. First, all of the castle and its accommodations will be made available to you, barring the Elder's personal chambers. You will only be allowed access there with our company tomorrow morning. Second, you will not leave this meadow until after said meeting. To ensure this, there will be guards on patrol until further notice. Finally, before entering, you will relinquish all your weapons to my fellow disciple, Titus, and leave your steed behind to spend the night here in the meadow."

"Ha," Marcus snorts, his distrust shining through. "Let me get this straight: you want us to stay in your home with no way to defend ourselves and guards blocking any exit. I may not be the brightest one here, but this sounds like a trap." He steps towards Nigel but fails at intimidating the Oren, who stares down his nose at the knight.

Helena steps in quickly to defuse the situation. "No, Marcus. We are guests here; it's best that we obey their wishes. We've come this far, and there is no reason to ruffle any feathers this late in our journey." As usual, she can prevent Marcus from succumbing to his short temper. He begrudgingly steps back into their group.

Nigel takes a deep breath in, adjusting his glasses and glaring down at each knight in turn before smiling dangerously. "That fact that you believe your weapons could do anything to stop us from having our way with you is ignorant at best. Weapons of any kind are banned in all of Goldleaf. It's only because you are outsiders I've allowed them to get this far."

"Nigel is correct; it is Oren law that weapons of any kind are forbidden." Like Helena with Marcus, Zayn steps in front of Nigel in hopes of clearing up any animosity. "But my father and I had discussed the matter before your arrival and felt that, to respect your customs, we should allow them everywhere but inside our castle walls. Do forgive me for not mentioning it earlier."

One could easily think Marcus and Nigel host years of hostile history amongst them from the tension that lingers in the room. As the group makes their final steps toward the castle, Marcus continuously mocks Nigel under his breath, Nigel insulting Marcus in his native tongue in return. The others find sweet relief in their quick arrival at the castle doors, where a large dark-skinned Oren waits.

As Nigel had warned them, this is the last of the Oren masters, Titus. He stands a full head taller than any other Oren the knights have seen. His stoic presence does nothing to mask his intimidating aura: Titus is undoubtedly a person you wouldn't want to get on the wrong side of. The parts of his face that are not covered by his large gray beard are decorated with beautiful tattoos, many of which share similarities with the roots of the forest trees. He stands shirtless, his massive muscles only disturbed by a few handmade sets of jewelry. His necklace, made from intertwining branches and golden leaves, stands out amongst the rest, glistening against his skin. With the party drawing near, Titus steps forward, his bare feet pulling away the earth from below him as if he has been standing in place for weeks.

"Weapons, please," Titus says, introducing everyone to his sultry baritone voice. Already warned of his request, Marcus, Helena, and Liam oblige, removing their weapons and offering them to the master. To their surprise, Titus does not reach for them; instead, he raises his hand, after which an array of roots and vines grow from the ground below the knights and take the items in his place.

"Do not worry; I am merely transporting them to a safe hold within the castle. You have my word no harm will come to your belongings." As Titus speaks, he makes sure only to make eye contact with Helena, and his enticing tone pulls a smile out from her hesitancy of handing over her weapon. Marcus, already displeased with Oren interactions from his time around Nigel, prickles at the observation, jealousy apparent as he takes two steps to noticeably position himself between the Orens and Helena, glaring. When the vines are fully grown around the weapons, Titus lowers his hand, and the weapons are pulled into the ground, now impossible for the knights to obtain.

"With the formalities out of the way, I will be taking over as your guide for the night. In addition to my duties as the Disciple of Growth, I have also been appointed as lead guard to Elder Yeshin, so I must know where you are at all times during your stay. If you feel roots around you moving or a vine tapping you on the shoulder, do not worry; it is only me making sure of your safety." As he finishes, a small vine grows by Helena's side before blooming into a beautiful flower, again bringing a smile to her face.

"I think we're perfectly capable of keeping ourselves safe," Marcus snarls, "and if you don't mind, I'm starting to feel the length of this journey. Would you give us the pleasure of showing us to our rooms?" Liam and Elizabeth can't help but snicker at his jealousy..

"Who am I to doubt the skills of such fine knights as yourselves? My apologies. You will be staying in Disciple Zayn's wing of the castle. He has yet to take on any apprentices, so there is space for each of you to have your own room."

"Yes, this benefits us all. This way, if you have any questions – and I do mean any – feel free to stop by my quarters. I will be happy to answer anything. And don't worry about getting lost; my room is attached to the massive library we have in the castle." Though spoken as if it is meant for the group, the offer hangs in the air between Zayn and Elizabeth, his eyes focused on her.

"The two of you seem to have things in order, so allow me to excuse myself. My wife is waiting for me in my quarters, and I'd like to wash away the filth we've acquired throughout the day." Before walking away, Nigel makes direct eye contact with Marcus and whispers a handful of words in the Oren language (which roughly translate to 'except for that which we are giving a bed to'); even without speaking the language, Marcus can tell this is an insult, returning the gesture by giving Nigel the finger as he walks away. Before any other Oren can notice, Liam smacks Marcus behind the head, helping to save face and avoid any more confrontation.

Flirtatiously, Titus uses his magic to unload Hornet before he and Zayn walk the party to their rooms. The interior of the castle is similar to the forest itself: its floor and walls are made from the interweaving roots of the massive tree that houses it, with beautiful floral arrangements dropping over any window opening. Each knight is given an identical room, with a fair-sized bed in the center where all the sunlight meets. The bed is one of the most comfortable pieces of furniture any of them have ever been on, with hand-quilted sheets and animal fur-filled pillows. The rooms also accommodate a small living area with a table, stools, and a reasonably sized wash area. Overall, the Orens have provided a more than adequate place for the knights to stay.

Elizabeth's quarters are quite the contrary. Her room is so elaborate that most royalty would find it over the top. The bed is twice the size of the others, and her living area has a small bookshelf and a handful of instruments. Adjacent to it is a dining room with a full dinner table and a matching kitchen stocked with food. Where the others have a wash area, she has a full bath with a waterfall flowing fresh water into it at all times, a feat none of the humans can fully comprehend. An endless assortment of flowers and several Oren dresses also fill the room. Titus informs Elizabeth that her room was indeed Zayn's private quarters, but he had opted into staying in another room so that she could have accommodations "fit for her elegance."

With everyone shown to their room, the sun sets, and the party begins their first night in the Oren castle. With the world quiet around him, Marcus decides to take a moment for himself. He is finally using the time to wash himself, removing weeks of dirt and grime. As the water flows over his stab wound, he grits his teeth. No longer deadly, the scar still aches. Fresh from his bath, Marcus grabs his undergarments and sits on the bed. He can't help but feel like the Terra King is hiding in Goldleaf. Without clothing himself, he starts to clean his blade when there's a knock on his door. Marcus grabs a towel and makes his way to the door. He opens it, and to his surprise, Helena stands before him. As always, Helena is ravishing, her red hair sparkling in the moonlight. She smiles at Marcus before asking him a concerningly simple question:

"Can we talk?"

CHAPTER 30
THE
NIGHT BEFORE

Chapter 30

The Night Before

While Marcus stands frozen in awe of Helena, she pushes past him before he can invite her in. With her now in his room, Marcus slowly makes his way to his clothes, hoping to make himself decent while also taking advantage of the moment.

"Here to keep me company in this oh so lonely castle?" Marcus flirts, pulling his clothes on, staring directly into Helena's eyes with each move.

"Only in your dreams, Marcus," Helena shoots him down with a smile.

"That is indeed a dream of mine; I'd be lying if I said otherwise. But if you're not here to keep me warm tonight, what do I owe the pleasure?" Marcus questions, pouring them both a drink. After passing hers over, Marcus lingers next to Helena. She steps close to him and roves her hand up under his shirt. A deep blush spreads across his face, and he grins sheepishly.

"I came to talk about this…" she says quietly. Marcus locks eyes with her, hoping this will become a night he'll never forget. Suddenly, she slaps him right where his stab wound is, shocking him out of his reverie.

"Damn it! Why the hell would you do that?" Marcus cries out as Helena sits on his bed.

"To remind you that you're better than this. The Marcus I know would have never let that blade hit him." Helena pauses for a moment before tapping the bed next to her, as though it's hers to invite him into. Marcus wonders if she knows that he would give her the bed, or anything else she wanted, just to see her smile. Marcus sits next to her, and she grabs his hand. "I need to know where your head's at. I can't shake the feeling that things are about to shift. We need to be on the same page."

"Love, we are always on the same page. Don't waste energy worrying about that," Marcus says with an unconvincing smile.

"Are we, Marcus?" Helena exclaims angrily, seeing through his facade. She stands abruptly, continuing, "We nearly lost you, and you haven't said a single thing about it since we got you back! You seem determined to pick a fight with one of these Orens, which, if you ask me, doesn't seem like your brightest idea, either."

Marcus downs his drink before standing up to defend himself. "First off, that Nigel guy is a prick and deserves a good ass-whooping. Secondly, what the hell do you want me to do, prance around here with pride that I got laid out in the desert by a bloke in a mask? I'm supposed to be this squad's leader. I'm supposed to be the one doing the saving not being saved! If I fail here and now, what chance do I have of keeping us together later?"

"There is no 'later' if you're dead, you fool!" Helena barks, her hands quickly finding his chest again and shoving him back onto the mattress. "I understand the stakes here as much as you do, but we need to be realistic here. Whether we want it or not, this is likely our last mission together. They are going to separate us whether you get promoted or not, and I would rather we live in a world where I get to see you in passing than not at all." Her anger waning, Helena again sits on the bed next to Marcus. Her voice barely registers as a whisper when she chokes out, "Marcus, I can't lose you too."

He watches as a single tear rolls down her face, splashing into her drink.

"Helena," he says softly, taking her face in his hands. "I don't want to lose any of you. We are family and, with Nolan gone, I'm supposed to be the head of the table. I'm supposed to be the one who keeps us together, and I'm going to fail at that, aren't I?" This time, it's his breath that comes out ragged. "Nolan taught us to be strong, to see right from wrong even if the rest of the world is telling us otherwise, to keep moving forward when times are hard. Yet here I am, and honestly, I can't see the forest through the trees. I can't tell what's next. All I see is us parting ways, and the best part of my life being over. So you're right, I got over excited out there in the desert. I saw the opportunity to bring in the most wanted man in all of Grandhaven just hoping it would bring enough clout to keep this," he gestures between them, "going. To continue the life where I get to wake up and see you everyday, one where I can still sit under Liam's learning tree... One where I live up to Nolan's legacy."

"Nolan never wanted you or anyone else to 'live up to his legacy,' Marcus; he wanted us to make our own." Helena lifts her hand to her face, wrapping it tightly around his before pulling them in front of their faces. "I know we want to do good by him; hell, we wouldn't be on this little adventure of ours if we didn't, but Nolan would not want us dying for his burial." Helena stands, pulling Marcus to his feet, her loving eyes on him. "I care about you, Marcus, and I see the same greatness in you that Nolan did – but you can't get yourself killed rushing to it. None of us knows what the future holds, but the winds of change are among us, and we need to protect each other now more than ever. If we are lucky, destiny will keep us intertwined."

"I haven't been the best at trusting destiny, you know." Marcus slowly pulls Helena closer. "Outside of you, all it tends to give me is the short end of the stick. So forgive me if I'm a little impatient."

Helena and Marcus lean in closer to each other. Though she knows he wants more, Helena simply kisses Marcus on the cheek and tells him, "The best things in life are worth waiting for," before gathering herself and walking to the door. "Your legacy will be one of legend, I have no doubts about it. Stop trying to live in Nolan's shadow and create your own."

Before she can leave, Marcus calls out to her.

"Yes, Marcus?" she answers, also somewhat hesitant to leave.

"Thank you. Truly, I don't know how I would have made it this far without you. And I promise not to prove you wrong. It may not be traditional, but I'll find a way to make destiny my own – even if only for a few more moments by your side."

"I'd like that, Marcus, I truly would," Helena confesses, her hand on the door as her heart skips a beat.

"You know, you could stay…" Marcus says playfully but with pleading in his eyes. When Helena meets his gaze, her heart leaps into her throat at the love in his eyes. She smiles softly, the blush spreading across her face, revealing her genuine emotions. Helena turns to leave, but before she walks away, she tosses her hair back over her shoulder and teases,

"If I did that, your dreams wouldn't be nearly as intriguing."

*****

With Marcus still on her mind, Helena returns to her room. As she does, she crosses paths with an Oren handmaid she hasn't seen before. Out of curiosity, Helena waits in her doorway, watching as she approaches Elizabeth's room. The handmaid knocks several times; receiving no answer, she leaves a letter on the small table outside the door, placing a golden rose atop it before scurrying away. Once the handmaid is gone, Elizabeth finally emerges from her room, picks up the letter, and reads it before returning inside. Thoroughly intrigued by these events, Helena waits outside her doorway for a few minutes, and, to her surprise, Elizabeth once again comes out of her quarters. This time, though, she is dawning one of the beautiful Oren gowns left behind for her. Needing to know what's going on, not as a knight assigned to protect her but as a curious friend, Helena sneaks up behind Elizabeth,

"Where are you going?"

"Oh my! Don't scare me like that," Elizabeth exclaims, frightened by Helena's sudden appearance. "But – if you must know – Master Zayn has requested my presence for a late-night dinner in the library."

"Did he also request that you get so dolled up for said dinner?" Helena mocks as she tugs on the elaborate dress Elizabeth is wearing.

"No, not exactly, but they were left here for a reason. Figured I might as well," Elizabeth jokes as she pulls the dress away from Helena.

"Well, it does look good on you. I just didn't take you as the type to sneak away in the middle of the night to be alone in a library," Helena says with a wink.

"It's not like that! I see this as an opportunity to get more intimate with our hosts. Maybe get insight into what they get out of this whole ordeal."

"I have a feeling Master Zayn would love the idea of getting more intimate with you," Helena laughs.

"Will you stop it? Uther would have your head for talking like this. And, if my eyes aren't mistaken, you're flaunting about in the middle of the night as well," Elizabeth snaps back, catching Helena off guard.

"Well – well–" Helena sputters, "I was on official knight duty..." She blushes fiercely.

"Yeah, yeah, I bet," Elizabeth jests.

"Maybe you should go before you're late for your dinner. Or worse, I incriminate myself any more than I already have. Just know I am here if needed," Helena reassures Elizabeth.

"I'm a big girl, love. I'll be fine. But maybe stop by afterward so I can fill you in on all the details," Elizabeth winks before making her way to Zayn's quarters.

Once there, Elizabeth lifts her fist to knock on the door, but Zayn swings it open before she can, clearly excited at her arrival.

"You came!" Zayn says, baffled.

"Well, you did invite me to," Elizabeth answers as she enters the room.

"No, no, no. I just wasn't sure with the time and the importance you'd even... never mind all that, allow me to get ready."

Zayn glides toward a chest in the corner of the room next to a makeshift bed. Since he had given up his room for Elizabeth to stay in, this is actually his tiny office. Scattered about the room are scrolls and notebooks, among other workplace clutter. The walls are covered with maps of Grandiose and paintings of timelines and star charts, each with different drawings or notes scribbled among them. Some are written in the Oren languages, while others are entirely illegible. The place is quite a mess; Elizabeth would have thought a madman lived there if she didn't know better. She was starting to question whether one did. It is a stark reminder of how different it was back home, Uther's office the antithesis of this disorder.

"How do you find anything in this mess?" Elizabeth questions, picking up an assortment of mismatched papers.

"I have my own system, you know. Plus, no one ever comes down here anyway," Zayn jokes, struggling to get his shirt off quickly before Elizabeth can see, but he fails miserably.

Zayn stands in front of Elizabeth bare-chested, giving her a full look at his physique. His body is a work of art for someone who spends all day with his head in a book; his chest and abs seem chiseled from stone. On his shoulder, he has the Oren symbol for *'light'* surrounded by more traditional Oren tattoos. As Elizabeth examines his body further, she notices a peculiar leather bag hanging from his waistside.

"What's that hanging from your belt? Hopefully, that's not hiding the dinner you promised in your invitation," she asks, almost expecting the latter to be true.

"No, dinner is next door in the library. I didn't think you'd like eating among my work." Zayn finally pulls a well-fitting shirt on before showing Elizabeth the bag's contents. "This is more of a hobby of mine."

Zayn opens the bag. Inside are a handful of tiny stone busts and an assortment of six—and twenty-sided stone dice. The busts are in the shape of animals, with a few modeled after the other Disciples.

"It's a game we Oren play called *'Nunasetsu,'* which roughly translates to *'Legends of the Land'*. In our youth, it teaches us about our forefathers and the world around us. Many grow out of playing it regularly as they age, but I have not. I find comfort in it, a reminder of easier times. Unfortunately, I've run out of youths to play it with. Chili is one of the city's youngest Orens, and he is nearly two hundred. To be honest, that's actually why I asked you to dinner," Zayn explains, his voice sincere.

"To play your game?" Elizabeth replies facetiously, knowing that's not what he meant. She turns, hiding her smile: she finds the hobby extremely cute.

"Not exactly. But if we have the time, I'll gladly teach you." Zayn's innocence elicits a smile from Elizabeth. Then, he rushes over to move his bed out of the way, revealing a door. "Let's sit, and we can talk while we eat."

Zayn opens the door, and behind it lays the great Oren library. Even though she knows the size of the castle, Elizabeth is amazed at the enormity of the library. Thousands of books sit on endless golden shelves, and wooden statues as tall as an ordinary man's home are scattered around its numerous halls of knowledge. Unlike Zayn's office, the library is pristine, without an ounce of dust on any surface. Every book is filled perfectly by age or author, and even the scent of fresh flowers fills the air.

"This place is amazing," Elizabeth says in awe.

"Thank you. I try my best to keep it orderly, but as you can tell by my office, sometimes I can let things go a little," Zayn confesses.

"Wait, you take care of this library all on your own?" Elizabeth asks shockingly.

"Well, yes. It's one of my duties as the Master of Light. Normally, my apprentices would help. But seeing as how I don't have any, I've been keeping it up myself these last few hundred cycles," Zayn explains, nervously wiping down an already clean table.

"Why don't you have any apprentices?" Elizabeth inquires, perusing through the books.

"Ah, well. A few reasons. First, there haven't been many Orens born to the mark of light in some time. It's the rarest of the birthrights, but mostly, I guess I'm just not very liked. See, I am not what you'd call a traditionalist. As much as I like learning from the past, I'd much rather use that information to improve the future. That's kinda taboo around here," Zayn goes as he ushers Elizabeth toward where he has a dinner set up.

"Birthright? Mark of light? You must forgive me, but those terms have no meaning to me. I don't understand." Elizabeth sits at the quaint little table Zayn has set up. There isn't much food, but what does sit before them looks delicious as it sparkles in the candlelight.

"I figured as much, so I wanted to have dinner with you. Tomorrow's audience seemed pointless if you didn't understand why it meant so much to me. As beautiful as Goldleaf is, it's nothing more than a prison. One that Orens have been trapped in for more than three hundred cycles. I want to change that, not by war or aggression but with the promise of knowledge and camaraderie." Once again, Elizabeth finds Zayn's plea eerily familiar.

"Knowledge can be just as dangerous as war," she warns.

"You are absolutely right, we learned that lesson ages ago. I have a feeling that, outside Goldleaf, you can't say the same. But we can teach them that. It would not be an easy task, yet putting the work in as a teacher is better than the alternative."

"The alternative?" Elizabeth indulges, unsure if Zayn's words were meant as a threat.

"A second *'Dark Massacre'*. Without our warnings, without our library's cautionary tales, I fear history will repeat itself." Zayn's words are spoken with such passion that Elizabeth knows his wishes are sincere.

"Again, my ignorance has led us to a crossroads. What is this *'Dark Massacre'* you warn of?" Elizabeth asks, remembering that Luna also said such a thing in Riverhaven.

"Come with me." Zayn gets up from his chair and grabs Elizabeth by the hand. He leads her down a hall of books, each getting older and older the deeper they go. Although the books are all written in Oren, Elizabeth notices they look similar to the journal Uther has grown fond of. At the hall's end, a large painting depicting six hands pulling a beautiful Oren child from a sea of darkness is hung. Each of the hands has a mark upon them, and she recognizes one as the same marking Zayn has tattooed on his shoulder. The sea of darkness comprises five symbols, none matching those on the hands in the painting, or any others Elizabeth has observed while in Goldleaf.

"This is called the *'Divine Future,'* and although time has made some of its meaning obsolete, the tale that led to its creation still has great value. You see, hands represent the arts which we Orens master," Zayn points to each symbol as he speaks. "*Fire*," a rudimentary flame with a devilish grin splitting in half. "*Stone*," a mountain with boulders flowing around it. "*Light*," a hollow circle with rays pointing to its center. "*Growth*," a simple leaf with a diamond-shaped vine around it. "*Storm*," an animal head made of lightning, the fiercest of all the markings. "And lastly, *'Ice*,'" a snowflake made of daggers.

"These arts are our way of life, our purpose. Upon birth, we meet with the Elder and are presented with a stone housing the essence of each of these arts. Whichever one reacts strongest to the child is their marking. From that day forth, that is the sole art that Oren may practice. They become apprentices to the matching Disciples if they show great promise. Once that Disciple decides to become Grandiose or is chosen to become Elder, their greatest pupil takes their place. This is the life cycle of an Oren. But it wasn't always that way," Zayn explains, pulling a book from the shelf that looks older than time itself before placing it on a podium in front of the painting. He opens it to a page full of old Oren text with a picture of Orens slaughtering each other as a shadowy figure watching over them.

"Before the *'Dark Massacre,'* there were more arts. Time has left them with the title of dark or forbidden arts, but once, they were as common as the ones we see today. They were known as *'Shadow.'*" Zayn again points to the painting, but this time to the markings that make up the black seas, gesturing first to a black wave crashing into a claw. *"Water,"* a droplet with a skull inside it. *"Air,"* a circle with a spiral within it. "And lastly, the most dangerous of them all, *'Whisper,'*" a mouth with its tongue sitting out with an eye at its end – easily the most ominous of any of the painting's symbols.

"Unlike today, during the old ages Orens lived divided. Those who practiced fire lived amongst each other, while those who practiced water stayed together, and so on and so on; all except those who practiced the whisper. The 'voices,' as they were known, were nomads traveling from settlements using their gifts to persuade evils from others' minds or helping those who had fallen to the depression of time find their way back."

"So they were like traveling witch doctors?" Elizabeth interrupts. She has learned that Zayn will talk himself breathless, excited to share his knowledge with anyone who will listen. Her question gives him a quick moment to breathe.

"Precisely. But, like any good doctor, they never use it for their own gain – at least, not until the Shaman Sorro. Sorro discovered a new art, that of 'Death.' After being corrupted by said art, he used his mastery of 'whisper' to spread that corruption. Before long, the settlements of shadow, water, and air fell to Sorro's persuasion, and together, they waged war against the others. This war is the 'Dark Massacre,' a near endless age of suffering that only ended when all Orens united to defeat Sorro's army and bury them deep within the island now sealed behind the void."

"Were there any survivors from Sorro's side of the war?" Elizabeth asks, but she is relatively confident of the answer.

"A handful, but those who remained were swiftly exterminated. In an act of prevention, those arts barred and any other 'voices' unfortunate enough to survive the massacre, were hunted down and publicly beheaded as a warning that anyone else who ever tries to practice these dark arts would meet the same fate."

"Depending where you stand, one may say the wrong people won the war." Elizabeth chastises as she flips through the rest of the book pages. Each turn reveals a more gruesome depiction of the events after the war.

"You may be right, but that is not the point of this story..." Zayn closes the book, places it on the shelf, and brings down another. He opens this one to a mural showing all Orens together peacefully, helping one another. "From great tragedy came harmony; all came together as one. Orens of every background live together using every art available to build a utopia. Even after the other races of Grandiose made their presence known, we still lived in peace. At least, until man arrived." Zayn also closes this book, putting it away, and escorts her to the dinner table.

"So what's your endgame? Free yourself of the prison that is Goldleaf? Take revenge on the humans and get your paradise?" Elizabeth questions, no longer sure of Zayn's intent.

"Not at all. I do not want to drive people apart; I want to bring them together. I don't want a war to be the cause of it. I want us to learn from the past to avoid repeating those same mistakes. I've had dreams...nightmares...no, visions of the future; of another 'Dark Massacre.' Sorro's return in a new form. And whether we like it or not, Goldleaf's wall will not protect us. Instead of waiting for the slaughter, let's get in front of it: if man and Oren can put aside their past for a better tomorrow, then all Grandiose can. You're living proof of the beauty that can come from a united world." His compliment strikes Elizabeth at her core. Compared with the few from Uther, Zayn's feels genuine.

"So you plan to go on some grand crusade for peace, and hope everyone listens? It's a novel idea, if not foolish. You've been locked in here too long; the world loves the idea of peace but doesn't want it. It would much rather hide behind the facade while turning a blind eye to all the murder, rape, and children dying in the streets." Elizabeth downplays Zayn's ambition, even though she actually finds it quite attractive.

"I'd rather live the rest of my days out there crusading than waiting here. Orens should be a part of Grandiose, and we should be out there sharing our wisdom with every other living creature. It shows them that a better way awaits them and that it doesn't need too much bloodshed. Is it a dream? Yes, but it's a dream that can be a reality. It will take work, I know that much. I'd be lying if I said I didn't almost give up on it myself, but then, I heard about you." Zayn rises from his seat, kneeling next to Elizabeth and taking her hands in his before continuing. "I had all but given up, becoming content with my life as a librarian when chatter of an unique young girl living among the filth of Grandhaven made it to my ears. I knew if the stories had made it this far, there had to be some legitimacy to them, so I did everything in my power to seek you out, but I was too late. By the time I knew your location, you were already in the arms of the king. But knowing you were real was enough to spark my flame once more, and I've spent every waking moment working to make this dream come to fruition." The words tumble from his mouth like a waterfall, passion overflowing with every word. "When King Uther's request for an audience came to us, my heart nearly stopped. I had hoped that a successful first meeting would have led to a future meeting, but then I heard that it was you making your way here, and it was like fate itself had intervened. Then I had the pleasure to see you with my eyes,, and your presence had me frozen. You embody everything I've dreamt of."

"Your admiration is overbearing," Elizabeth stands, removing her hand as she does. "Contrary to popular belief, I am not some holy grail to be fought over."

"That's where you're wrong, Elizabeth. This library is full of stories about how all life comes from one another, particularly how we were all once Oren but through magic or evolution or chance circumstance we became Dargone or Crow or whatever we may be? Hoopla and propaganda. None truly knows how we started, hell the Dargone believed in some sun deity, the Orc thought their blood was infused with the earth itself, and only the heavens know what tragedy led to the Crow. But here in front me stands what our future could be – no, what it should be. And if the world out there is as horrific as you say and it still leads to something as wonderful as you, just imagine what a new world of peace could bring us." Elizabeth, taken back by Zayn's onslaught of ideals, makes her way to the door.

Realizing her discomfort, he quickly interjects, "Forgive me, I came on too strong, and I inadvertently disrespected you. But I promise I am no madman, nor do I have any other intent with more than what I have presented to you this evening. I truly want nothing more than a future deserving of your grace."

Without saying a word, Elizabeth glides out of the library, never looking back. Zayn sits back at the table in defeat, scared that he has squandered his chance at fulfilling his life's purpose. In the deepest hours of night, he cleans his plate and ponders how he could have better approached things, lost in his own self-pity for over an hour before he finally forces himself to bed.

As he lays down, intrusive questions about the evening ringing through his head, he hears knocking at his door. Zayn rises to answer, but a folded letter is slid underneath the door frame before he can reach for the handle. He opens the door but finds no one there.

Now baffled, he picks up the letter and reads it. This harmless piece of paper brings him an unfound amount of joy; it is from Elizabeth and simply reads:

"Dinner was lovely, Master Zayn. I may not know what tomorrow brings, but I hope we can share another in that beautiful future of yours."

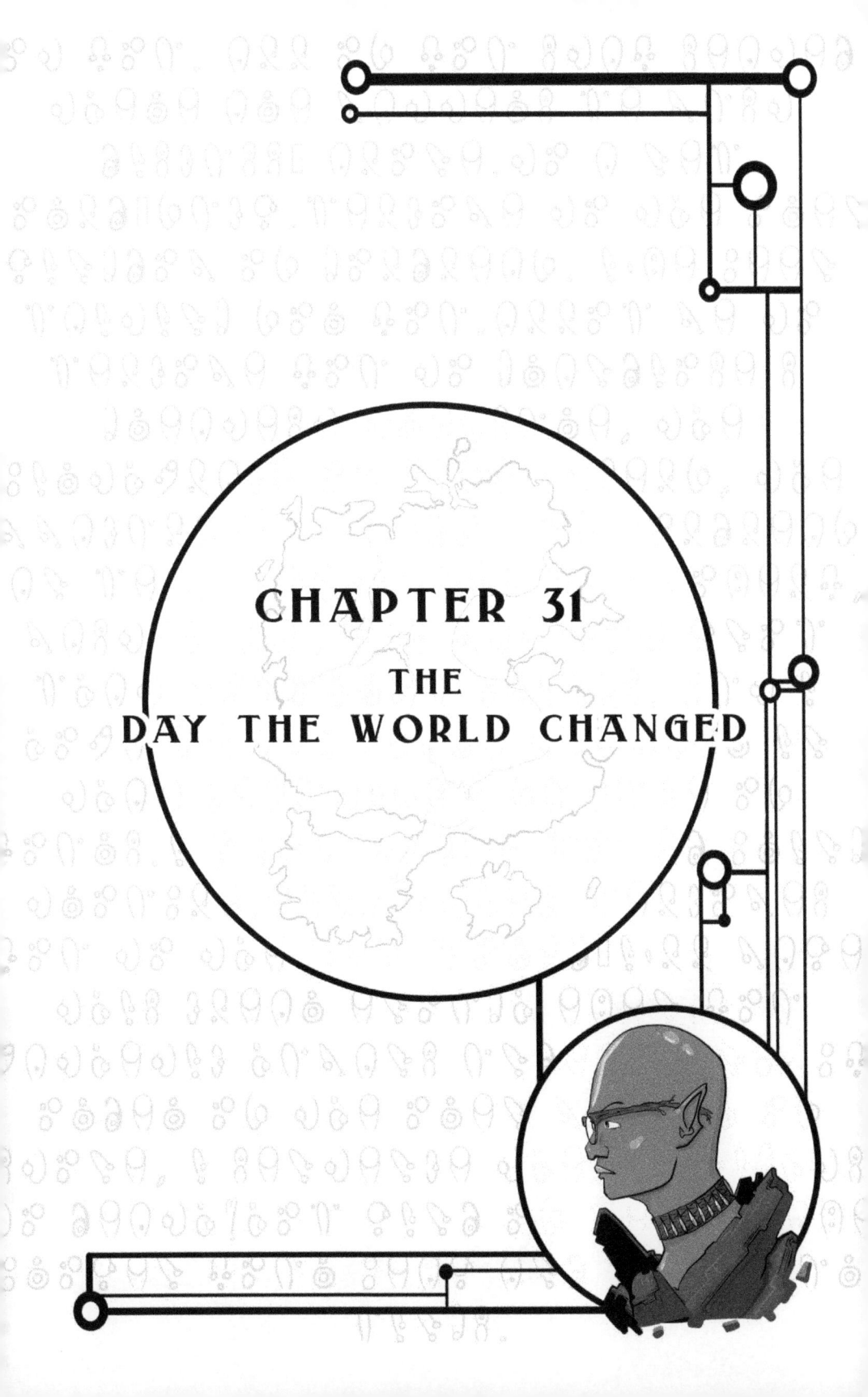

CHAPTER 31
THE DAY THE WORLD CHANGED

Chapter 31

The Day The World Changed

With the dew fresh on the grassy meadow outside of the Oren castle, Liam makes his way to Hornet, who is spending this very early morning playfully chasing the burgundy buffalo.

"Come here, girl," Liam calls Hornet, and she immediately leaves her hunt, bounding over to his side. The knight starts his daily routine of tinkering on Hornet as the sun rises. While he works, Liam notices a few flowers blooming up around him before retreating into the ground: a flashy reminder that he is being watched, and something he doesn't take kindly to. Unfortunately for him, his presence in the meadow is more unwanted than he thought. Before long, Nigel strides up to him, his arms crossed as he glares down at the knight.

"Is there a reason you are outside your chamber at such an early hour?" Nigel scoffs, raking his fingers through his hair and tugging at his clothes to appear presentable.

"Hornet needs my attention in the morning. If I hadn't shown up, she would've ransacked this entire forest looking for me," Liam answers, his eyes firmly fixed on the mechanical hound.

"Then you should have programmed it better. I have a long day ahead of me, andI did not plan to spend the early hours babysitting you," Nigel bitches, still fumbling with his clothing.

"You can't program an animal; you train them, and even then, their emotions can get the better of them," Liam disregards Nigel's complaints, continuing to work on Hornet as though the Disciple's presence is nothing more than a gnat flying past his head..

"Emotions?" Nigels mocks. "Human hubris has no limits. To think a machine could have anything resembling the beauty nature provides is laughable."

"You Orens speak down to us like you know everything, but it's clear your isolation has left gaps in your all-knowing facade." Liam finishes his work and taps Hornet, permitting her to return to her play. As she runs off to chase the buffalo again, he finally stands and faces Nigel. "Hornet is far from a machine. There's more beast under that armor than you think."

Liam towers over Nigel, his silhouette casting an impressive shadow across the meadow. Liam was unconscious when the Orens initially interacted with his friend group, and Nigel's haughtiness settles a bit as he sees Liam in his full, restored glory for the first time. Liam's authority radiates off of him, and he is not intimidated by Nigel, or any other Oren for that matter.

Somewhat impressed by Liam's resolve, Nigel says, "Alright, then. Enlighten me."

"Under all that metal, there is the brain and the heart of an actual animal. When our earthly companion's body fails them, our scientists harvest their mind and working organs, giving them a second life in an everlasting body."

"So you played god just to spend a few more cycles with your little doggy. It seems very short-sighted and self-indulging if you ask me," Nigel downplays the achievement. Whether he likes it or not, Liam must admit that he's argued a valid point. "Your human lives are finite, yet you build these creatures that will outlast you. You say its emotion will get the best of it if you are not here to greet her in the morning, but what happens when you're dead?"

Liam contemplates his answer before being relatively straightforward with the Oren. "Honestly, you're right: we don't think that far ahead. We make them so we can live happier, rarely questioning the consequences. That is, indeed, a great human flaw. Most humans will just power them down before their own time is up and sell them off for parts so they can live comfortably in their twilight."

"Is that what you will do?" Nigel asks, his nose crinkling in disgust.

"I would not dare do that to Hornet. I'd once hoped to pass her down to a child, but that opportunity has long expired. Luckily for me, when my time comes, I'll have Marcus or Helena to take care of her. After that, hopefully their kin will do good by her."

"A noble thought for a human. Didn't know your kind was capable of such things," Nigel mocks.

Liam turns to him in response, calling Hornet over while never breaking eye contact with the Oren. With Hornet once again by his side, Liam opens a small hidden compartment, removes an item wrapped in cloth, and hands it to Nigel. His eyes never stray from the Oren's gaze.

"Not all of man is evil, nor are all Oren peaceful, it seems," Liam's words drip with threatening weight, and the air around them shifts with the tone of their conversation. The time for pleasantries has ended.

Nigel unwraps the cloth to find the dagger the Terra King used to poison Marcus in the desert. He freezes momentarily, baffled that the knight would own such an item. Liam, though, doesn't notice the pause; he sees how the Oren's nostrils flare out slightly. It is clear he recognizes it.

"Why are you attacking my people? And why attack us directly after inviting us here?"

"Attack your people? How dare you accuse me of such an act!" Nigel scoffs, tucking the dagger inside his sleeve. "Not only would I have to step past our agreed boundaries to do so, but I would also be using my gifted arts for unprovoked violence. Just one of those acts would have banished me, the two together... I would be one with Grandiose by day's end. And the fact that you think I'd give up everything coming to me to exterminate a few insects? It's belittling!"

"Maybe it's not you, but you carry yourself as the kind of gentleman who would know who it is. At least, you should know." By stroking Nigel's ego, Liam hopes to get more answers.

"Our home is impenetrable; no one comes or goes without me – or, more importantly, Titus – knowing. Now, if you don't mind, I have wasted enough time with the likes of you," he changes topics quickly. "Get back to your chambers and wait for our summoning. Today needs to be flawless so we can all be done with this pointless charade tomorrow. I can return to more important matters, and your kind will no longer be dirtying my meadow!" Nigel storms off in anger, but Liam can see through the act; he can tell Nigel knows more than he says. With that in mind, Liam again takes a jab at his ego.

"There's a crack in your wall of trees, Master Nigel. If I were you, I'd start investing in my students first. I've seen this Terra King firsthand, and one thing is clear: if it isn't you behind that mask, there's an Oren in your midst more fitting of the title of Master." He enjoys the look of pure irritation on Nigel's face before the Oren storms off. Liam pets Hornet one last time, telling her to return to her fun, before making his way inside. Before he goes, he leaves her with somber words of wisdom:

"Enjoy this peace and quiet, old friend. It will not last much longer."

*****

Blood boiling, Nigel slams his chamber door behind him. Contrasting his stony demeanor, his chamber is filled with colorful tapestries and beautiful paintings. A small garden full of the ripest fruits and vegetables grows in the corner. Sitting in the kitchen, his wife sips her morning tea while their breakfast cooks. She's a quiet Oren, calm and caring, the perfect contrast to Nigel in every way.

"Your frustration is showing earlier than normal," she laughs.

"Don't patronize me, love. You have no idea how frustrating these intruders are. So primitive, yet so arrogant. They act as if the only reason they own Grandiose isn't because we chose not to fight. A handful of us could crash it in an instant." Nigel sits at the table, pulling down on his face in anger.

"Who's primitive now?" his wife questions, taking another sip.

"No, you're right, my love. These thoughts are beneath me." As he calms himself, Nigel pulls out the dagger he had snuck away from Liam and looks it over. "If anything, our current plague has unearthed a new mystery." Nigel continues to examine the dagger when someone knocks on his door. To his surprise, Titus awaits him, holding several soft, hand-woven blankets.

"Good morning, Nigel. I came bearing gifts for the lady," he grins, and Nigel's wife playfully shoves her husband out of the way as she thanks the Disciple for the gifts.

"I had my students prepare them from our finest harvest," Titus explains, watching her open a small pantry full of clothes and toys. "But aren't you a few cycles early to be preparing for the new addition?"

"You can never be too early when it comes to these things. Speaking with this harvest, I found it to be warm and pleasant, perfect for blankets," she responds, placing them on a shelf and closing the pantry.

"Your timing is impeccable, Titus. My unfortunate meeting this morning led to an interesting discovery." Nigel hands the dagger to Titus. "Is this not from your armory? The human said they were attacked by an Oren wielding this. And he accused me of being that Oren. I'm not one for a knife or sword, but that's the point, isn't it? How did an Oren weapon of any kind get to the outside world?"

The flirtation Titus is known for fades from his smile. His brows knit together as he studies the knife, first in confusion and then in anger.

"This is one of mine. How anyone could take it without my knowing warrants investigation." Titus calls forth vines in the ground to take the dagger away. "There are few with access to the armory. Once today is behind us, I will interrogate all of them. I take great pride in being the eyes and ears of our land. If there is an Oren breaking laws, I will ensure that justice comes to pass."

"The human mentioned their assailant was more than proficient in the art of stone, so I, too, will question my students. We must get to the bottom of this quickly," Nigel announces before pausing to think for a moment. "It may be best to inform the Elder of this before today's meeting, just in case this is some kind of human trickery. Wait a moment, and I'll get my things."

"No, stay and enjoy breakfast with your wife. You have more than enough on your plate for today. Allow me to inform our Elder; I was making my way there next, anyway," Titus says. Looking over to his wife, Nigel knows immediately that leaving early is not an option, so he accepts the offer.

After saying goodbye, Titus leaves and travels to the Elders' chambers. As he walks, he again summons vines from the ground to return the dagger to him. He looks over it once more, his face filled with concern, and mutters to himself,

"I knew today would bring trouble."

CHAPTER 32

THE DAY THE WORLD CHANGED
PART II

Chapter 32

The Day The World Changed Part II

With the morning events behind him, Nigel makes his way to the Elder's chamber. Although he is against the meeting, he does his best to present himself well, now dressed in more formal attire. These prestige garments are more restricting than the typical day-to-day Oren clothing, but are even more eye-catching. His high-collared shirt, woven by the finest Oren seamstress, displays the Oren symbol for *'stone'* embossed on the chest. The pants are made from burgundy buffalo leather, glistening crystals sewn down the side. An assortment of jewelry, ranging from golden bracelets to white-gold earrings made from tree leaves, completes the ensemble.

As he approaches the chamber, Zayn greets him with a cheerful smile. The only major difference in their clothing is that the Oren symbol for *'light'* is embossed on Zayn's chest, his signature pouch of *'Nunasetsu'* pieces attached at his side.

"Where are your guests, Zayn? I'd prefer not to spend all day on this charade of yours," Nigel bickers as he reaches the chamber door.

"They will be here shortly. I sent a handful of guards to collect them from their quarters," Zayn answers, pulling at his collar in discomfort.

The two of them wait silently before a group of guards finally arrive. The guards travel in formation, with a pair walking ahead of the knights while a second pair follows behind, carrying the chest filled with Uther's offering.

In honor of the day's events, all three knights spent the morning cleaning and waxing their armor, each taking great pride in representing the human race in such a historic moment. Presenting herself with just as much class, Elizabeth dawns an elegant white dress that glistens in the light, a golden scarf with the sigil of every human kingdom embossed on it draped around his shoulders. Her neck and arms are covered in the finest jewelry, but the necklace that Uther gifted her is the most prominent.

"Now this is a sight to behold! My father will surely be impressed," Zayn exclaims, greeting the group in turn.

"We are honored to be part of such a tremendous moment. I speak for my peers when saying, we hope history speaks fondly of today." Helena proclaims as she, Marcus, and Liam bow.

"That chest," Nigel demands, pointing to it. "Open it."

"As much as I'd like to, we don't have that authority. By law, only a king can open a gift from another king – or an Elder, in your case." Marcus informs Nigel, remembering how he was once rejected when attempting to get a peek.

"I don't give a shit about your laws," Nigel responds bluntly. "Nothing enters the chamber without my approval, so open it or we can call today's meeting to a close early." He chuckles briefly before saying, "I'd much prefer that."

The knights turn to Elizabeth, uncertain of what to do. Elizabeth pauses, glancing between the Orens and the knights, thinking over the best move. Concluding Uther would be much more upset if the meeting never happened over such a trivial thing, she decides it is best to open it. Nigel instructs Elizabeth and the two guards carrying the chest to come forward. The guards place the chest down in front of the disciple, a thud reverberating down the hallway from its weight. Everyone waits with bated breath as Elizabeth turns the lock on the front of the chest. Once unlocked, she slowly lifts the lid, building anticipation.

Once open, Nigel takes one look at its contents and scoffs, "Pathetic."

The others do their best to sneak a peek. Within the chest rests a small fortune of jewels, gold, crystal goblets, and other treasures. The knights are baffled by Nigel's remarks, since the content of that chest could fund a small village for years or instantly elevate a man to the highest rank among the elite.

"Human arrogance is fascinating," Nigel announces as he slams the chest shut. "Your obsession with the material is a prime example of how primitive you are. In a world of endless resources, only fools would base their society on such meaningless trinkets. As long as your kind continues to value individual worth over the benefits of all, your lives will stay meaningless."

"Master Nigel, your words are too harsh," Zayn interjects. "Humans are far from perfect, but so are we. Today's gathering comes in hopes of lifting each other up, not belittling one another. So I ask you to refrain from such negativity for the remainder of the day."

Nigel turns his back on the group before begrudgingly reviewing how the meeting will be handled. "Once you enter this chamber, you will be Elder Yeshin's official guests. When he speaks, you will listen; he will tell you his intention, and once done, your ambassador – and only your ambassador – will speak hers. After this, the Elder will make his declaration on behalf of all Oren. If, by some unfortunate notion, he decides a new partnership is indeed best, we will make our way to the dining hall, where we will break bread tonight before spending the rest of the evening discussing the final details of the matter.

"However, if the meeting goes as I expect, he will find all this futile, and once he has made his decision, Zayn and I will escort you back to your quarters so you can rest for the night and prepare for your leave in the morning. Is that all understood?" They all nod in agreement.

Once the guards open the doors, Elizabeth enters the chamber with Liam, Marcus, and Helena close behind. The chamber is nothing more than an open room with seven wooden thrones at seating curved at its center. Every throne grew directly from the tree itself, and each was identical. The chamber is relatively modest for a room of such importance, but the massive stained glass window above them is more than impressive. It is as if, by magic, the window correctly streams light the color of the corresponding Oren over each throne, no matter where they sit.

Each master sits on their throne, and Chili, Rhea, Isla, and Titus all wait for the others to enter. Each of them is dressed in clothing similar to Zayn's and Nigel's. The most renowned Oren, Master Elder Yeshin, the *"Fire Breather,"* sits at the center throne. Unlike most other Orens the group has met so far, who look youthful despite their age, Elder Yeshin wears his age as a badge of honor, looking several centuries old and entirely unbothered about it. His exposed chest is covered in a mane of white hair, but what skin can be seen is wrinkled and covered in age spots. Above his large mouth, he sports a white mustache that has grown down far past his face. As the party makes their way to the center of the chamber, his gaze could burn a hole through them, but he occasionally coughs to clear his throat. When he does, a small flame comes out, each one morphing into a shape, such as a bird or insect, before dissipating.

Once Nigel and Zayn take their seats, the guards drop the chest in the center of the room before two of them stand at the door they enter from, while the other two do the same at the second door at the opposite end. The guards lock the chamber as Elizabeth, Marcus, Liam, and Helena take their place before the masters. As custom dictates, the knights bow and then take to their knees in respect. Now behind the chest, Elizabeth opens it again, presenting the gift to Elder Yeshine, a gesture that signals she is ready for the summit to begin. In response, Yeshine clears his throat again, the flame shifting into a skull.

"Let me make this clear," Yeshine speaks, his voice deep and trembling. "Despite my age, my memory is as sharp as it has always been. I remember with ease watching men murder my brothers and sisters, cutting through them as they stood still in peace and filling our homes with blood to then claim them as their own. Though ages have passed, I doubt man has gotten any wiser. I honor your meeting request because my son asked me to do so."

Yeshine cracks his neck and back before continuing. "Master Zayn thinks highly of your kind, insisting that our futures are better intertwined as allies than enemies. Admittedly, I think he's a fool, blinded by the ignorance of youth, but before he can take his place as the next Elder, he must experience success and failure. Which one will it be today? Now, that is up to you, young lady."

Elizabeth attempts to hide her nerves, desperately trying to swallow her fears without everyone in the room hearing her gulp. She tucks her trembling hands behind the skirts of her dress. As she scans the room, she notices that most of the masters pay little mind to the conversation. It is clear they all have already decided how things will go – save for Zayn. When her eyes lock with his, he gives her a warm smile, easing her mind with reassuring nuance.

Immediately, Elder Yeshine notices the chemistry between them. He's exceptionally perceptive to the longing look in his son's eyes.

"When your King's request came, I was so surprised that I ignored it. That is, until my son told me about you, Lady Elizabeth. The half-Oren." Yeshine continues, "Master Zayn is fascinated with your existence; I'd imagine he and King Uther have that in common. And while I may not be as eager to eat from another's pantry, you do intrigue me. I'm old enough to know that you're not the first of your kind, but you are the first halfling I've met in all my time. So, without further ado, tell me your story, your purpose. Tell me why King Uther is willing to risk losing someone so rare for this proposition." As Yeshine stands up tall from his throne, he commands the attention of the masters seated around him, who are finally forced to take notice of all that is transpiring in front of them. "Lady Elizabeth of Grandhaven, convince me this gathering is not a waste of my time!"

Elder Yeshine drops back onto his throne and opens the floor to Elizabeth. Silence fills the room; the knights know this is the moment their journey has led to. Here, Eizabeth's words can change the course of history. With this in mind, Elizabeth takes a deep breath, closes her eyes, and grips the necklace Uther gave her.

"Elder Yeshine, you asked for my story, but I fear it is a tale that is not worth your time. I am a product of a forbidden courtship. Orphaned by both my bloodlines, thrown to the street where I was meant to die." Elizabeth opens her eyes and begins to pace the room. "Yet when you talk of men as butchers, I have embraced them as saviors. For it is a human King who took me in, and now, it is a human King with whom I share my bed. As your son said before we entered this chamber, we are all far from perfect; many of human's flaws can outweigh their pleasantries, yet they are the cunning pursuit of innovation." Elizabeth returns to the chest and slowly removes the necklace from her neck, trained enough that no one takes notice of her action.

"They conquered these lands – albeit, yes, forcefully – and, in a short time, built kingdoms that towered into the heavens. When they saw weakness in themselves, they forged armor that could rival even your magic. Now, while many find comfort in their current place in the world, there are still those like King Uther and myself who long for more." Elizabeth stands next to the chest with her necklace precariously at her side. "While you may see that as greed, I find ambition attractive. That hunger for more has led to a world where beast and machine are now one; a world where leaders speak to one another while lands apart; a world where something as simple as blood can be more deadly than a blade…"

In an instant, Elizabeth drops to her knees, slipping her necklace into a hidden groove on the side of the chest. Moments later, several secret compartments on the chest burst open, releasing clouds of poison into the room. Before anyone can react to the sudden attack, the chamber is filled with toxic gas. Marcus, Liam, and Helena are the first to collapse, the guards shortly following. The Oren masters try their best to react, but they find it difficult to resist. Oddly enough, while the others try to attack Elizabeth before falling, Zayn uses his last moments of clarity to reach for the sack of game pieces on his side. Being the strongest of them, Elder Yeshine withstands the toxins the longest, burning as much away with his flaming breath as he can.

With the Elder distracted, Elizabeth spreads her wings for the first time. As she lifts herself into the air, the gust of wind from her wings pushes away the gas like small tornadoes erupting from her body. Now, in the air, her silhouette blocks the light for the window, causing shadows that Elder Yeshine has no choice but to take notice of. He looks up at her in awe. Though he should be frozen in fear, he is mesmerized by her angelic beauty instead. Elizabeth's white dress sparkles in the light and her wings release snow-white feathers, as if the room is trapped in the middle of winter. She extends her nails before piercing her palm to cover them in blood. Now equipped with her deadliest surprise, she drives toward Elder Yeshine with the speed of an arrow shot from a bow.

Before he can protect himself, Elizabeth is face-to-face with Elder Yeshine, her claw deep in his chest. She retracts her nails, releasing him from her attack. Yeshine again drops onto his throne, looking down at his wounds to find infection already spreading. Before he can succumb to the poison, Elizabeth leans in to whisper a message destined to haunt him even in the afterlife:

"King Uther welcomes you to the new world…"

CHAPTER 33
THE
COST OF FREEDOM

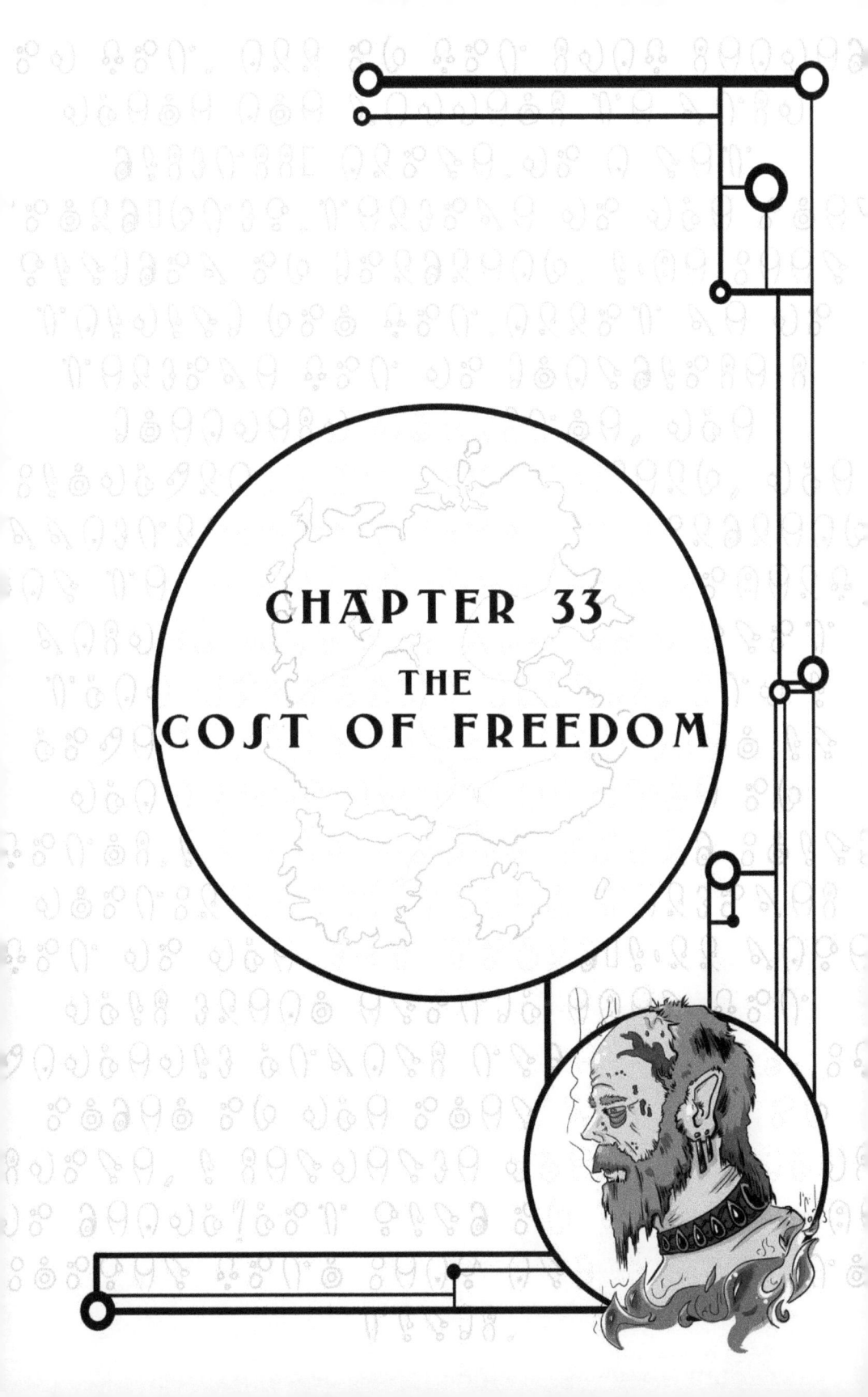

Chapter 33

The Cost of Freedom

Elizabeth watches Elder Yeshine's life fade from his eyes while the knockout gas swirls around the chamber. She stands there, cold and numb to what she has done, while the Elder's blood drips from her hands. After retracting her wings back into her arms, she looks around at all the others lying unconscious.

"Well look at that Red, your plan worked. Everyone but me is out cold. You really did make my blood one hell of a weapon – not that it wasn't already deadly before you toyed with it," Elizabeth says to herself as she makes her way to the door, passing by the bodies of Liam and Marcus.

"I know you can't hear me, but I want you to know this wasn't personal. I am going to miss all of you, especially you, Hele–" Suddenly, Elizabeth realizes Helena's body is not with the others. Before she can act on her discovery, a fist comes flying through the gas, cracking her across the jaw with such force that she flies to the other side of the room.

Elizabeth manages to brace herself before slamming into the wall, lessening the impact just enough to stay conscious. While she remains on her feet, the punch left her rattled. She spits blood from her mouth before once again spreading her wings. Using her wingspan once more, she sends a large gust of wind toward her attacker. The gas clears just long enough to confirm her suspicion: Helena, furious, is ready for another attack. Even with their eyes deadlocked, Helena can still rush Elizabeth, landing a fury of attacks, each one more painful than the last. She knew Helena was strong, but Elizabeth had unleashed an overwhelming rage. She takes flight in a last-ditch effort to survive, her blood covering her wings. She hovers above the smoke, looking for an exit while attempting to watch Helena down below.

"The window, it's my best bet, but how do I break through?"

"TRAITOR!" Helena cries out as she leaps into the air, landing a swinging kick at the center of Elizabeth's back, powerful enough to send her crashing into the ground. Elizabeth tries to recover from the attack, but before she knows it, Helena drives her knees into her back, pinning her to the ground. Helena rolls away as Elizabeth flips to her feet. Then, she punts Elizabeth in the ribs again, sending her flying into the wall. Elizabeth lays on the ground in defeat, her ribs likely broken, blood dripping from nearly every orifice. She is shocked when Helena approaches gingerly with tears in her eyes, expecting a killing blow.

"Give up! I don't want to kill you," Helena begs, struggling to breathe.

"So the gas is getting to you after all. Here I was starting to think you were special," Elizabeth taunts, trying to rise to her feet.

"Cut the bullshit, Elizabeth. You and I both know that even in this condition, I can end your life." Helena inches closer, but Elizabeth notes her ragged breathing and the droop in her eyes.

"Then do me a favor and end it already. Chances are, if you don't, he will." Elizabeth falls to her knees, too weak to stand.

"If you believe that, then why the hell do his dirty work? Why throw your life away for this?" Helena questions as she drops to her knees less than an arm's length away from Elizabeth.

"You have no idea what Uther is capable of. He's bringing the fury of Hell to every doorstep in Grandiose, and nothing will be able to stand in his way. So forgive me if, for the first time in my life I'm deciding my own fate. Damn it, if I've learned anything in this life, it's that I'd rather be by the devil's side than on my back while another one takes advantage of me." Elizabeth tears up as she tries to justify her actions.

"I didn't think you were so foolish, Elizabeth. This is not controlling your fate; you're still nothing more than a puppet. All Uther did was trade your string for fancy bed sheets. You aren't standing by his side. You are nothing more than a toy. In time, he'll throw you to the curb, just like everyone else has before." Helena reaches out her hand, hoping to break through to her, but Elizabeth smacks it away.

"Oh, but not you, Helena? Am I to believe that we are friends? That our companionship was not merely a matter of circumstance? Do you want me to subscribe to the notion that our smiles meant we cared for one another? Well, I am sorry, dear, but that's not the world we live in. And if you think it is, then you're the biggest fool here." Her tone is harsh, but Elizabeth immediately breaks out in tears, with no belief backing her words. She'd gladly spend her remaining life by Helena's side, but she's in too deep at this point. Entangled in a conspiracy of evil, she knows there is no escape from it.

"Then it seems we are both fools, and I would have it no other way." With those last words, Helena gives in to the gas and collapses onto Elizabeth's lap.

"Damn it! Why the hell did he have to choose you assholes for this?" Elizabeth cries into her hands, breaking down as the weight of the reality of what she has done crashes over her. "This was supposed to be simple: I do my part, and Uther embraces me with open arms. I live the life of a queen while he gets off on his power fantasy. I knew people would get hurt, but I wasn't supposed to care." Elizabeth punches the ground in anger. "I wasn't supposed to care…"

Just then, a massive fireball hurtles towards Elizabeth. She throws Helena to safety with all her might, barely making it out of the way herself. As the wooden walls start to burn, Elizabeth is shocked to see Elder Yeshine on his feet. His eyes are soulless as the infection still spreads through his body. While the Elder is not dead, he is far from living. This attack is an act of pure instinct. His body trembles as he takes a deep breath and takes in the toxic gas as if it were nothing. He then spits out several fireballs, all radiating so much heat that, as they fly toward Elizabeth, the gas around them burns away. Her adrenaline gives her enough strength to take flight one final time to avoid the attack.

With the chamber now going up in flames, Elder Yeshine prepares one final attack. He takes a massive breath so deep that his chest seems to inflate with air. As he inhales, he cries, *'I will protect my people'* before unleashing a whirlwind of flames. This tornado of fire comes spiraling towards Elizabeth with such force that whatever gas doesn't burn away is vacuumed up while clearing the room. She floats, frozen in the air, ready for the flame to take her life, when suddenly, a hand grabs her leg and pulls her to the ground. Elizabeth hits the ground to find an unconscious Helena holding her by the ankle. Above her, Elder Yeshine's attack continues to burn, finally making contact with the large glass window until it finally breaks through. The shattered glass falls around Elizabeth, a handful of the shards cutting her as they drop. She frees herself from Helena and goes to the opening Elder Yeshine has unknowingly made for her. Reserving her energy, she dodges falling flames and mottled glass, leaving a trail of blood behind her.

Finally, Elizabeth makes it to the window, where she waits for the flames to stop. Luckily, she doesn't have to wait too long for an opening, as the Elder Yeshine's body finally runs out of energy, falling face-first to the ground. Yet his attack was not in vain, as it managed to clear all the toxins from the room, allowing the others to wake. Elizabeth gathers all her strength and takes to the air, flying away with all the speed she can.

None of the Masters can come to their senses in time to stop her, but they answer the call to arms even with partial power recovered.

"Rhea...after her..." Nigel orders. Rhea bolts after Elizabeth as the others rush to the Elder's aid, his son attempting to heal him as best he can. Shortly after, Marcus and Liam also awaken, but before they have time to realize what has happened, Nigel encases them in a stone cage.

"What the hell are you doing?" Marcus demands between futile attempts to break free.

"What am I doing? How dare you ask me such a question after you bring death to our home!." Nigel shouts angrily, slowly pushing in the cage bars to make it harder and harder for Marcus to move. He grabs Marcus by the collar, pulling him into the bars so hard that it cuts a gaping wound across his forehead. With the guards now also surrounding the cage, Nigel makes his order:

"I'll make this clear enough even you pathetic humans understand: by order of the Oren Master of Stone, I sentence these knights to death!"

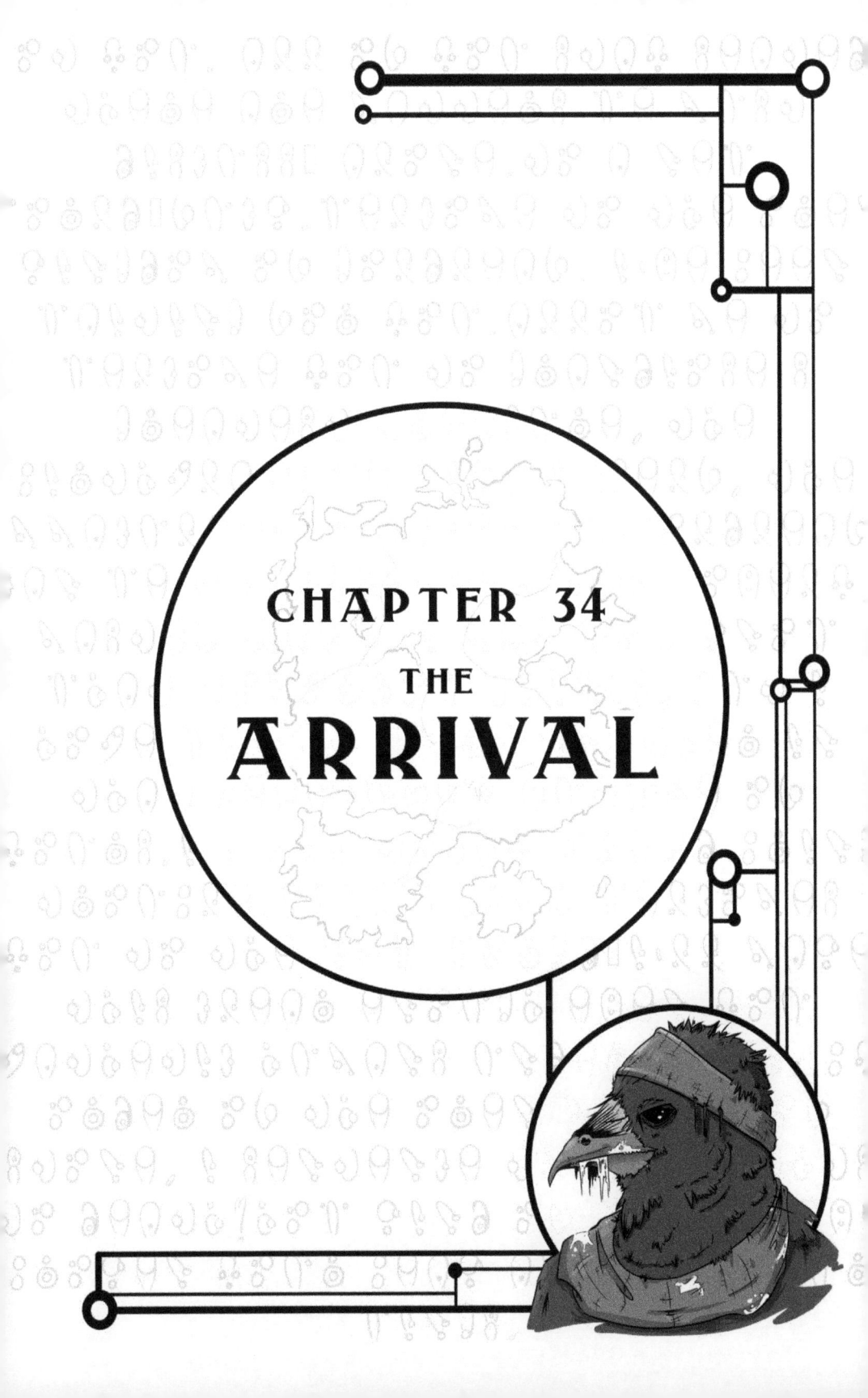

CHAPTER 34
THE ARRIVAL

Chapter 34

The Arrival

"Fear not, great people of Grandhaven, what you are witnessing is no act of god but the first step towards a glorious future." From a perch atop the castle gates, Uther addresses an increasingly growing crowd outside his castle walls, with Red and Callahan at either side. The citizens of Grandhaven are enamored with his every word while simultaneously concerned at the colossal flying warship blocking out the sun above them.

"Understandably, its arrival may cause concern, but there is no need to fear! This is no vessel of war. Instead, you lay witness to the greatest invention of transportation." Uther's lies do little to reassure the crowd as the intimidating warship docks atop the high tower of Castle Whitelion. The massive vessel is jet black, similar to a knight's armor, which should be no surprise as they are made from the same metals. Keeping the ship afloat are six giant Q.A.S engines, three on each hull. The glow from these engines illuminates the sky with a haunting mix of yellow and red lights while with a roar that echoes down the kingdom's streets.

"It may cast an impressive shadow over us today, but trust me when I tell you, this is the light that will lead us to a new age. This beautiful spectacle of engineering has the capacity to house not hundreds, but thousands of men as we cross Grandiose. It can also carry weeks' worth of supplies for each of them. You will be able to make the trip from here to Riverhaven in days compared to the near quarter of a cycle it currently takes." Uther's words finally earn him some applause, as the prospect of making such a trip so easily fuels the people's imagination.

"This sh– this skycraft," he quickly corrects himself, holding their imagination, "has been a dream of mine for ages, but your loyalty, willingness to pay our fair tax wages, and trust in my decisions behind closed doors made this a reality. I take this moment to thank you, and I promise you will reap its benefits. From the luxury of travel to your increased access to exotic merchandise, this is the tomorrow I have given you!"

With that, Uther's charisma wins over the crowd, the majority ecstatically cheering as they feast upon his false promises. Both Callahan and Red find the people's naiveté amusing. It doesn't go unnoticed by Red that neither Uther mentions him nor his brother Black. Instead, he acts as if he alone created this impressive warship.

At this point, the vessel completes its docking sequence, locking itself atop the tower with a thunderous thud. Its engines power down, not entirely shutting off, but their roar is now nothing more than a muffled whisper. Uther takes this as a sign to wrap up his speech and return to important matters.

"Now, now, calm yourselves! I find your excitement intoxicating, but please allow me to take my leave so that I can inspect this beauty and ready it for its inaugural voyage. To our glorious future!"

Uther steps down from the perch as the citizens of Grandhaven cheer his name. Callahan and Red follow, and once they are out of others' sight, Uther's demeanor drastically changes. His excitement is quickly washed away by his anger as he calls Callahan to issue his demands.

"You get your ass up there and find whatever fucking birdbrain decided bring this warship early and keep them there until I decide whether to fry or roast them for dinner. Am I understood?" Callahan nods and rushes off to oblige. Then, Red steps in to ease Uther's temper.

"My lord, I commend your handling of the situation. If not for your foresight, we would never have had the dock ready. We would have found ourselves in quite the predicament due to President Newson's rebellious act."

"Have I gone mad, Red? Have you not witnessed me tell that bastard Crow not to make any movements until I ordered so!" Uther's fury is palpable; with every word, his eyes flicker violet, and the glow from the carvings in his skin shines through his clothes.

"You're absolutely justified in anger, my lord. But I do warn you against any rash actions at this time." Red's admonition infuriates Uther to the point where he promptly grips Red into the air by his neck before belittling him.

"Who are you to tell me what actions to take? I am the president of change in a world where you are nothing but an insect that I have given the luxury of standing by my side!"

Uther's anger vibrates through his hand as he slowly chokes the life from Red, his eyes solidly aglow in violet light.

"My lord, you misunderstand my intentions," Red chokes out. "I am merely doing my duty as your advisor. You are so close to your goal. I would not want to see a pawn like Newson spoil your effort." His groveling satisfies the King, and he throws Red to the ground, releasing his neck.

"As if a damn Crow could do anything to thwart my mission. Yet maybe you have a point. I'll punish him after I finish what I've started." Uther cracks his knuckles on the hand he used to choke Red as the color in his eyes dissipates. "But if Newson was foolish enough to come here today, I must ensure he leaves knowing his place. Clean yourself up and meet me atop the tower. There's something I need to retrieve before I make my presence known."

Red lies on the ground, catching his breath, as Uther enters the castle. Once he has faculties in order, he does as Uther instructed, lifting himself from the floor and dusting his clothes off before making his way to where the warship is docked. Once on top of the tower, he notices Callahan watching over a traditional Crow carriage, its two carriers held hostage by the King's guard. These carriers are a unique form of transportation used solely to get a person to and from the heights of the Nest: a simple, small carriage where one or two people can sit while two to four Crows are chained to the outside of it to lift it into the sky.

"You look like shit. What the hell happened?" Callahan asks as Red approaches him.

"He's getting worse," Red answers as he rubs his neck.

"That's why I keep my mouth shut."

"Who's in the carriage?"

"Believe it or not, Newson is as dumb as we thought he was," Callahan laughs, knowing what chaos is about to ensue.

"Oh, what an idiot. How does an entire city elect such a moron?" Red rolls his eyes, knowing what awaits the Crow leader.

"I have an inkling they will get the chance to elect a new one soon enough," Callahan says ominously..

As they wait for Uther's arrival, the heat from the warship's engines becomes unbearable. Every knight has sweat rolling down their armor, and the Crow carriers fluff their feathers to cool themselves down. The carriage itself is becoming an oven.

"Enough!" The doors of the carriage burst open with a frustrated President Newson following. "Enough already! Where the hell is he? Uther has no right keeping me here to burn my ass off." Newson is always appalling and chaotic. With each word, spit flies off his beak, hitting the faces of the knights he continues to criticize. It is not until Uther finally makes his way to the tower's peak that Newson shuts up.

Uther walks past Callahan and Red without even a passing glance, and Callahan notices Uther has his gauntlet equipped with its gemstones glowing. Uther strides towards Newson, whose complaints have quieted at the King's arrival. Despite the heat, he trembles as though outside in the deepest winter. The Kingsguard clears the path for Uther, and he makes his way to Newson. The president stumbles to Uther, dropping to his knees immediately, begging for forgiveness.

"Uther, you have to understand, I could no longer hide this. My people are too often questioning where the food has gone and why so much of our workforce has been sent underground but not returned. I had to show them something, I mean, anything. Now, they can see what we have done. They will understand. They will cheer like your people do. If not, I would have never been reelected... I would be useless to you," he rambles, trying to defend his actions.

"What I have done." This simple statement is uttered so terrifyingly that even Callahan looks away..

"Excuse me? I – I don't understand," Newson stutters, standing up.

"You said they will see what 'we' have done," Uther snaps. He quickly grabs Newson by the beak with his gauntlet-covered hand and slams him into the carriage. "You have done nothing. This is my legacy! You are nothing but a pawn I have decided to place on the board, one I will easily take off if needed!" Uther grips down on Newson's beak to the point where it starts to crack. " I will leave with your life today, and you will never disobey me again! Do you understand?" He cracks the president's beak further as he struggles to respond.. "Answer me!" As Uther cries out, his body once again radiates that horrifying violet glow. The air changes, and everyone atop that tower is struck by fear of what this King is capable of.

Newson uses the little strength he has mustered to cry out, "YES!" At this acknowledgment, Uther loosens his hold on the Crow. Before releasing Newson completely, the King breaks his beak completely, and blood begins to pour down the president's face.

Ignoring Newson's cries of pain, Uther turns to the Crow carriers. When he clenches his fist, a collapsible katana appears from the crown of his gauntlet. The katana has the same carvings as the gauntlet and shines the same menacing violet. Just as everyone starts to admire the blade, Uther makes one quick movement and relieves both carriers of their head. Each body drops to the ground, and their blood flows over to Newson, coating his feathers in red.

As he trembles in fear and pain, he looks up at Uther, making his way back inside the castle, and asks, "How do you expect me to get home now?"

Uther picks up one of the Crow carrier's heads, pulls a handful of feathers, and uses them to clean his katana. While he pushes the blade back into its hidden chamber, Uther answers Newton,

"How kind of me to have broken your beak and not your wings."

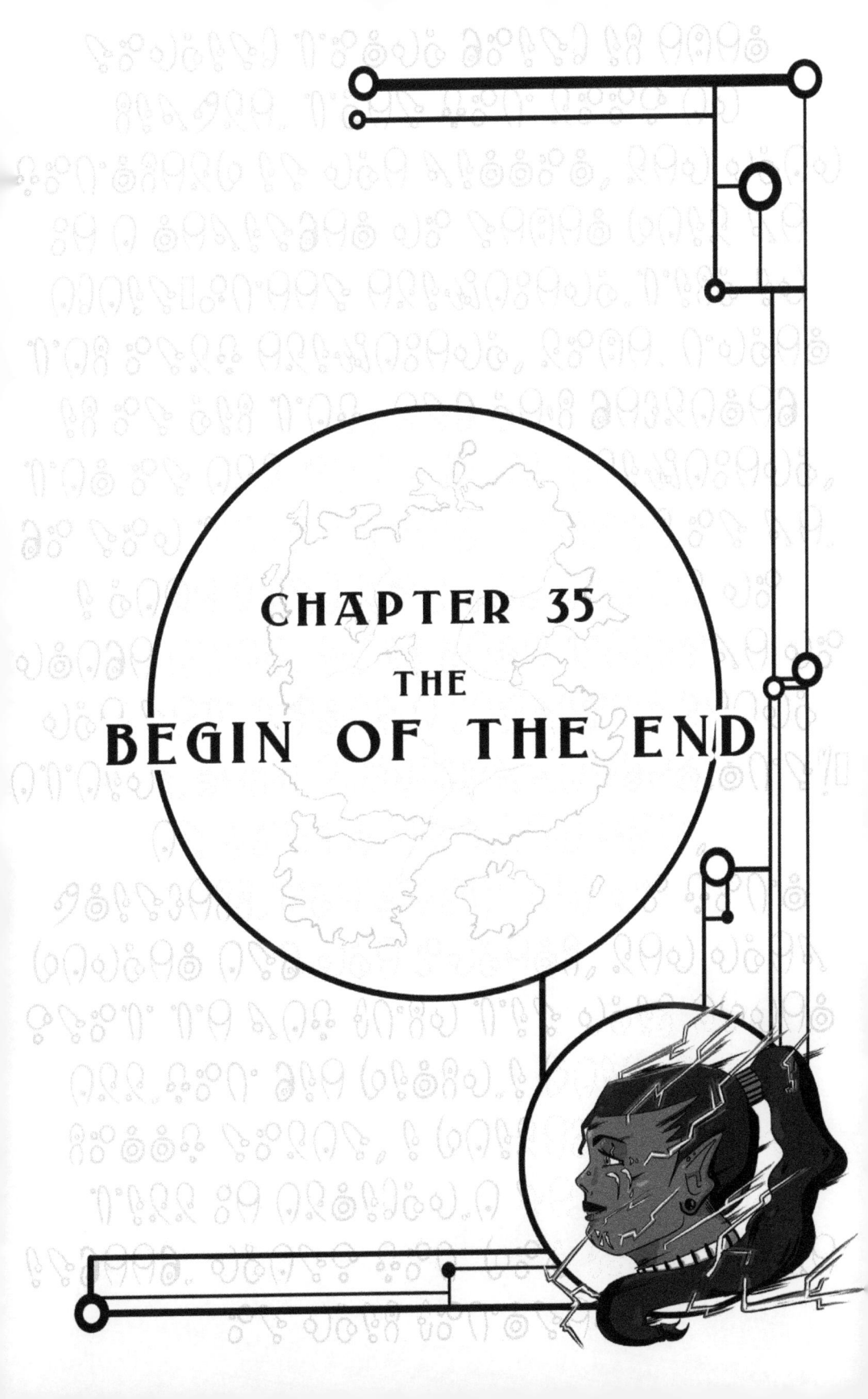

CHAPTER 35
THE
BEGIN OF THE END

Chapter 35

The Begin of the End

"Two seasons, a full cycle if you're lucky."

Callahan expected these words, yet hearing the doctor say them out loud cuts deep. The doctor in the royal treatment center continues to review Callahan's charts; with each turned page, his face winces a little more. He places the papers down, shakes his head, and addresses Callahan once more.

"I'm sorry, but there isn't much more we can do. Modern medicine is good, but this is beyond its reach. The disease is spreading faster than we can heal it."

"So what now, doctor?" Callahan asks. He knows the answer, but some part of him needs to hear it spoken aloud. As formidable a knight as he is, he isn't brave enough to say it himself.

"What now? You go live what life you have left. Hang up the shield, maybe get King Uther to send you on a trip on that new airship of his. Callahan, you have spent your life seeing Grandiose as a soldier, now enjoy the luxury of ending it as a citizen. Visit your favorite places, but this time, stop and smell the roses. Take a knee and breathe in the peace and quiet."

The doctor's words are meant to comfort Callahan, but all he can hear is the word 'coward' spiraling around his head. His mind races as he leaves the doctor's office, heading to a local bar. Bottle after bottle, he washes away the hours, drowning himself in depression and alcohol, lamenting not that his life is ending but how mindless his death will be. With each drink, he becomes more belligerent, continuously cursing at the bartender while mumbling to himself how disappointed his father is with him.

Callahan's demeanor is enough to sour the bar's atmosphere, and most patrons leave. Not even a spectacular performance from a local singer can persuade people to stay, leaving the bartender no choice but to ask him to leave. Callahan responds to his request by swiftly punching him in the gut, then demands another beer. Not long after, a drink arrives. When he looks up, he finds Red's face in place of the bartender's, a pitcher of refreshments bridging the space between them.

"Productive day off, I see."

"Fuck off, Red. I'm not in the mood," Callahan nastily greets his colleague, downing another drink.

"Word is you're having a rough day," Red mocks as he hands Callahan another glass.

"What part of fuck off didn't you understand?" The anger in his voice does not stop him from taking the drink from Red. He upends it, guzzling down the booze, before sliding it back to Red and signaling for him to fill it again.

"I can understand how today's news can be devastating, but this is no way for the highest ranking knight in all of Grandiose to present himself." Despite the rebuke, Red refills the glass and slides it to Callahan once more.

"You don't understand, shit geezer! Don't come in here acting like we're old buddies, like you'll give me some rousing pep talk to lift my spirits. We aren't friends, Red. We're just two guys who got dealt different variations of the same bullshit hand." Callahan downs another, and just as quickly, Red refills it. Before drinking this one, the knight pauses, staring into his blurred reflection in the golden-colored liquid. Once again, the word *'coward'* races inside his head.

For the first time in hours, he sits upright in his chair. His reflection heard what his body had missed. Despondent, he asks, "How the hell do you know about today, anyway?"

"Before ever teaching us the art of science, our father instilled in us a defining principle that me and my brother follow to this day: *'Know all about everyone but do not give anyone that luxury about yourself.'*"

"Some good that's done you. From my view, your old man did you dirty." Callahan finishes his drink. This time, instead of filling the glass again, he reaches across the bar to pull the entire pitcher over. "He gave bullshit advice that led you to a life where you might always be the smartest man in the room, but you're also the one with the least amount of power. Like I said, variants of the same bullshit hand, you and I."

"Like so many others, you fail to see what power the Regalia's truly possess. But, as you said, we are not friends. Enough with the pleasantries, then. I am here on business."

"What the hell does Uther want now?" Callahan mumbles as he finishes what's left of the beer directly from the pitcher.

"You misunderstand. Today, I am here on behalf of my own family." Red reaches into his coat pocket and starts to pull out a scroll sealed with an unfamiliar symbol: a spear facing down whose point extends in the letter V with wings to each side. "What if your life didn't have to..."

Although Callahan is eager to hear what Red says, they are interrupted by a young knight barging into the bar, looking for Callahan before he can finish.

"Forgive me for disturbing you on your day off, Sir Callahan, but I come to you with an urgent matter," he declares in a panic as he salutes Callahan and Red.

"What is it, boy?" Callahan quickly wipes his face and stands swiftly, somehow compartmentalizing his drunkenness to transform into the fierce knight he is known to be.

"Just before sundown, my squad was asked to investigate an unusual disturbance at a farm just outside the castle walls. The couple who owns it reported that a large object had fallen from the sky and crashed into their barn, but when they went to see what it was, they heard cries of pain coming from within. They are an older couple so they requested the knights' aid before going in." Red shuffles from the bar to Callahan's side, returning the scroll to his pocket as he does. Together, they listen to the young knight's tale.

"Once we arrived we made our way into the barn to find what was believed to be a badly injured Oren but upon further investigation, the woman not only Oren but some kind of Crow hybrid. We have never seen such a thing. Just an Oren this close to Grandhaven would have been worth bringing to your attention, but this seems like a matter that needs to be handled only by someone of your rank, sir."

Callahan and Red look at each other silently, understanding the truth of the situation.

"Where is the woman now?" Callahan questions.

"She remains unconscious in the barn, sir. We did not feel equipped to assist the matter any further without you, sir."

"Who else knows about her?" Callahan follows up.

"Only the owners of the farm, myself, and my squad, sir."

"Keep it that way. Head back at once and inform everyone to stay where they are. I'll be there shortly with my steed to handle things. I'll debrief you and the squad then. That's an order, is it understood?"

"Yes, sir!" The young knight leaves in haste, following Callahan's order without question.

Red watches as the young man fades from view before addressing the situation. Shaking his head, he says, "I'll have to come up with a hell of a story to explain the death of a whole squad of knights and a little old farm couple. It's a little too close to home to blame our normal scapegoat."

"I'll have Moses tear the bodies apart, devour some of the livestock, and we'll blame it on wild bearturtles," Callahan suggests while gathering his belongings, leaving many credits on the table for all the trouble he has caused.

"Bearturtles? This late in the cycle no one is going to believe that, not to mention how pathetic your knights would look. If they can't handle a bearturtle, what good are they at protecting the people?" Red paces a bit as he ponders another plan. "Look, tear apart the bodies like you said and throw them in the barn. Just make sure to bring the armor back with you. I'll pay off some Crow hoodlums to make themselves at home for an early morning feast. Before they can make it back to the city, I'll report a robbery at the farm house and a new squad of knights can make quick work of the Crow."

"I liked my plan more; it was simple."

Rolling his eyes, Callahan strides out of the bar, his day off officially ended. Red stays behind, pocketing the credits Callahan left on the table. Before putting away the last of the credits, he stares at the coin; on one side, the symbol for Grandhaven; on the other, the head of a tri-horned lion, a mythical beast representing the Whitelion family. He laughs,

"Nothing worth doing is ever simple."

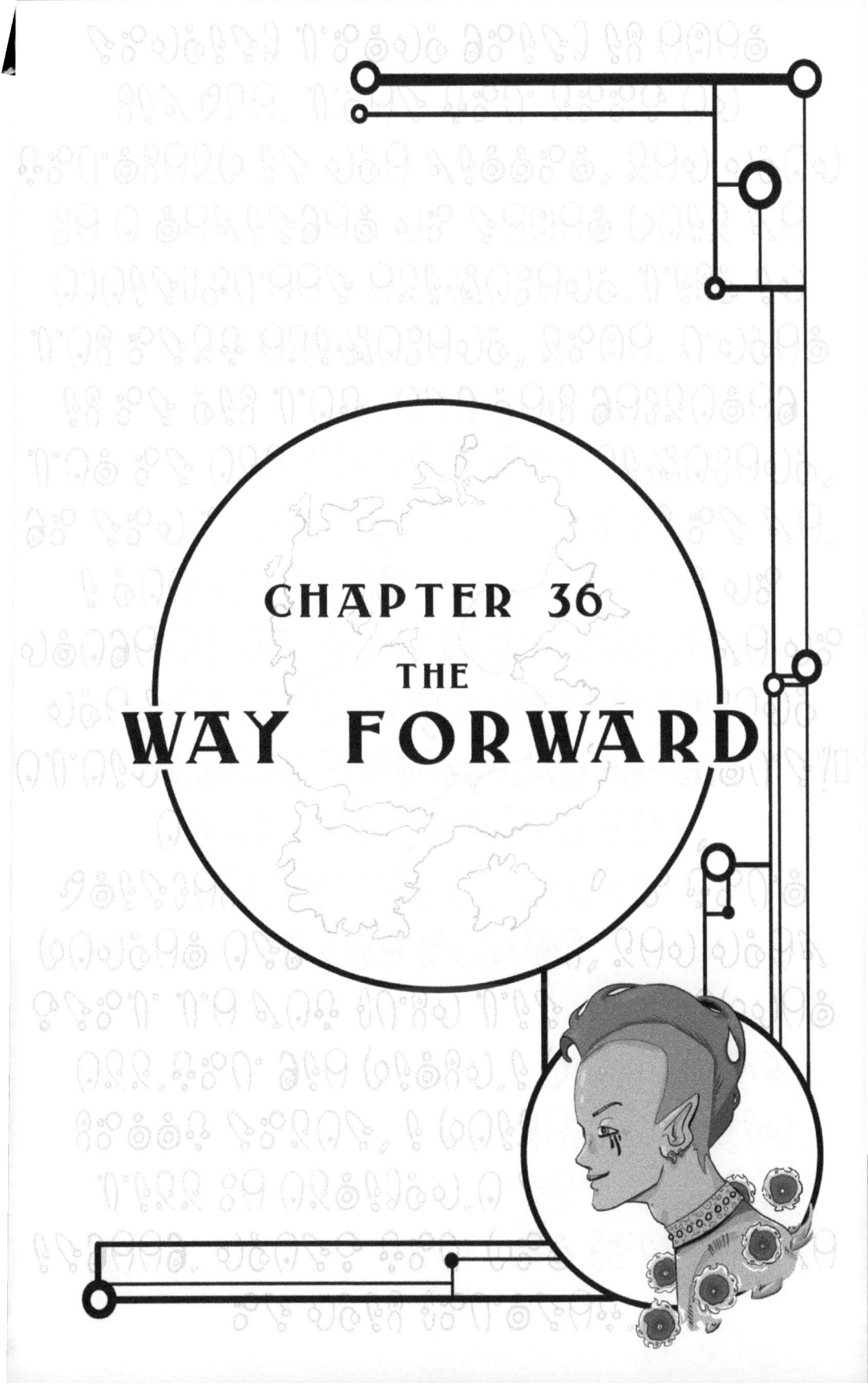

CHAPTER 36
THE
WAY FORWARD

Chapter 36

The Way Forward

Dreadful silence fills the room. In the week since Elizabeth returned, Uther has not spoken to a soul. Silently summoning Callahan, Red, and Elizabeth to his office, he sits at his desk, irate. For hours, they watch as he flips through the pages of Sorro's journal without a word. Then, suddenly, he slams the book shut, the thud echoing off the walls of the study. Uther taps his fingers on its leather cover menacingly, the clang of his war gauntlet conducting a symphony of concern. With each tap, the candles around them dance to the beat, their flames shifting from red to purple.

Finally, Uther speaks. "I have sat here hushed for some time now, processing the report, I was handed upon your return, Elizabeth. And I can't help but be sickened by your capacity for failure." Uther stops tapping, and the gauntlet begins to pulse dark violet. "I have spent my adult life planning for this moment, took two cycles training a mutt my father *'blessed'* me with, spent endless riches to equip her with every tool needed for the job, and still, you wallow in defeat!"

In an intimidating act of rage, Uther slams his fist on his desk, splitting it in two. As he stands, his eyes glow purple, and a ghostly aura sinisterly seeps from his body. The room gets cold, and the air is so thick that it's hard to breathe. Uther moves closer to Elizabeth; with each step, a burning fills her bruises and her cuts slowly rip back open. Although she is his focus, Uther's malice affects everyone in the room. Red's bones stiffen as his muscles constrict, locking him in place. Next to Red, Callahan stands quietly in agony. His organs slow down while the taste of blood creeps its way into his mouth.

Now, with Elizabeth within arms' reach, Uther opens his hand. His gauntlet bursts into a violet flame, and every wound, cut, scrape, or imperfection on Elizabeth's body glows a matching shade. She falls over in pain, her cries of torment shaking the halls of the castle.

"It was a simple plan. Get them to open their doors, kill their leader, and while they mourn, I fly in with the most dangerous weapon ever made and claim the future I deserve!" Uther's rage sends Elizabeth falling into the office door, the focus of which drops both Red and Callahan to their knees. "But now, here we are in a world where their Elder still reigns, where there are at least three witnesses to your crime still living, and, instead of mourning, they are undoubtedly preparing for war!" With his new mastery of this dark magic, Uther tugs on Elizabeth's injuries, pulling her back to him. Now, with his hand around her neck, Uther starts to choke the life out of her. Lucky for Elizabeth, Red speaks before life fades from her eyes.

"Not all is lost, my king. Your future is still within reach," he huffs out.

Uther drops Elizabeth and turns his attention to Red. Stomping over, the King pulls his adviser to his feet by his hair.

"Enlighten me, old man."

"Even if they prepare for war, they know not of your true strength. If we act fast enough, with your overwhelming might...the probability of your success is still quite high."

The flame on the gauntlet fades, and the weight of the air lessens as Uther ponders over what Red is suggesting.

"Time is not on our side, nor would the Council approve of me taking an army of knights to fight a war I started."

"Who's to say they didn't start it?" Callahan speaks, wiping the blood from his lips. "At this moment, the Council knows nothing. Not even Chief Ramon is aware of Elizabeth's return."

"Callahan is right. There are whispers, but as of now, that is all there are: whispers." Seeing an opportunity, Red supports Callahan's idea. "If we act hastily and tell our story before anyone else can, what proof would anyone have to deny it?"

Uther begins to pace the room, circling a barely conscious Elizabeth, and then asks, "And what is our story?" Callahan and Red look at each other, thinking quickly about the best tale to please Uther.

"We sent an ambassador to Goldleaf in an attempt to broker peace, and this is how they returned her." Red points to Elizabeth, making eye contact with her. It's only a passing glance, but she recognizes that he is trying to save her life as well as his own.

"We tell the people that they slaughtered our knights – and even if they haven't, we'll make sure only their bodies return," Callahan adds. "Our time bolstering the infamy of the Terra King may not have swayed the Council as planned, yet it has the people on edge. We can morph the public's fear into bloodlust, convincing them that striking now is the only way to keep them safe."

Uther continues to pace, but the violet has dimmed almost completely, and the anger in his face is replaced with intrigue.

"I'll have the people's support, but the Council won't fall in line as easily. They'll want to investigate before giving me access to all of Grandiose's armies," Uther thinks aloud.

"You don't need them to fall in line just yet. We only need them to stay out of the way," Red pushes. "We won't be given access to the knights outside of Grandhaven, but we have an ample amount with our own walls at your disposal."

"And in times of war, I can promote anyone to kingsguard," Callahan supplies. "By law, no kingsguard can leave their king's side, not even by order of another royal. The Council would be powerless to stop you from bringing them with you to Goldleaf."

"Interesting," Uther mumbles. "With that many knights and the corpses we have stored, it would be quite the force." His mood shifts as he starts to see the plan taking shape. "But wait, the *'Royal Shield Law'* can only be invoked if there's been a direct attack on a royal family member. And I have not been attacked."

Both Red and Callahan struggle to find a solution to this dilemma, convinced that with no other solution, it is only a matter of time before Uther's rage returns.

Just as Uther's disposition begins to sour, Elizabeth mutters, *"Or their betrothed..."*

Everyone stops and looks at her. Both Uther and Red echo how dangerous and cunning her idea is.

"She is right, my King. Even before an official courtship, as long as you are engaged to another, they are considered a royal family member." Red seconds the idea, knowing the suggestion alone could anger Uther all over again, but hoping against hope that he will take to this idea.

"Together, the two of you would have to make a public statement, but after that, she'd fall under our protection," Callahan encourages. With his adviser and most trusted knight agreeing to this plan, Uther begins to truly consider it.

"Betrothed... It's so simple. Just tell the world you are to be my queen," he rambles, his tone unidentifiable. Staring down at Elizabeth in a heap at his feet, he takes a moment to contemplate."You've always been smart – found your way from the street to the castle, after all. And you either face death or a crown."

Uther bends over, grabs Elizabeth's chin, and looks into her eyes. The room once again goes silent, everyone awaiting Uther's next move. They wait for what feels like an eternity before the whistle of a blade cuts through the air, breaking them of their trance. With a hidden blade from inside his gauntlet, he quickly slices Elizabeth across the face. She screams as her eye falls from its socket and blood spills to the floor. Unaffected, Uther turns his back to her and cleans off his blade. Red and Callahan stand frozen in fear and shock as Uther announces,

"When you look at yourself in the mirror, let that be a reminder to never fail me again...Queen Elizabeth."

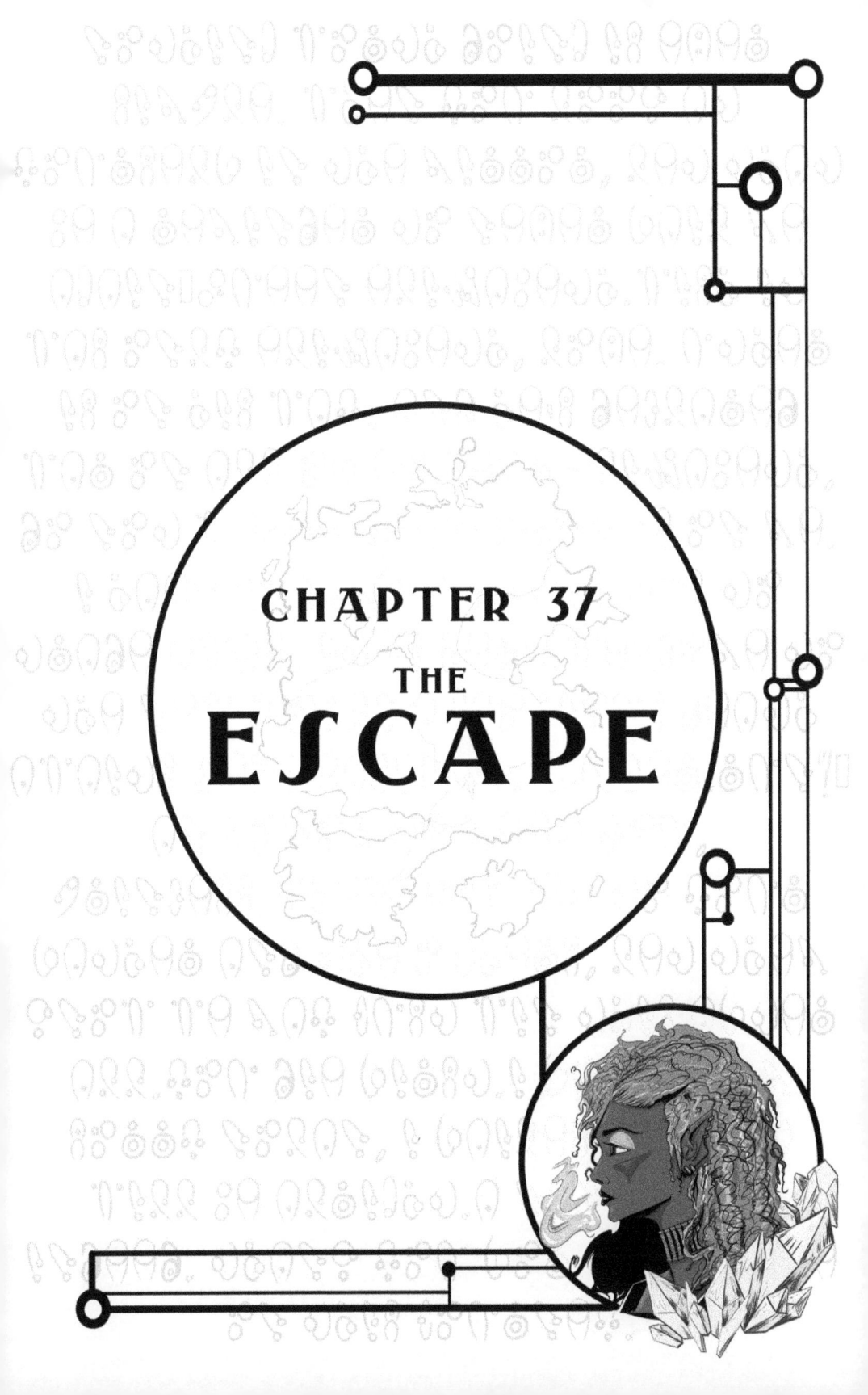

CHAPTER 37
THE ESCAPE

Chapter 37

The Escape

Days have passed, and smoke still seeps from the Oren Elder's chamber. As small flames smolder inside this sacred place, the Orens fear for their lives again. After ages of peace, the kingdom of Goldleaf is in panic. The youth question what happens next, while those unfortunate to have lived through the Great War warn of history repeating itself. Yet, with the world around him in chaos, Nigel only fixates on Zayn.

Since Elizabeth attempted to assassinate the Elder, he has sat within his chamber every waking hour, watching as countless Orens come to give Zayn their condolences. The current one is Master Titus, who has spent the last few minutes speaking with Zayn as they look out across Goldleaf from the open ruin created during the assault. With every passing word, Nigel's frustration grows, and his mind cannot understand how everyone can forgive Zayn for welcoming the outsider into their home. For him, if not for Zayn's ignorant ambition, their house would not be in flames, the Elder would not be on his deathbed, and the future would not be so bleak.

Just as Titus and Zayn's conversation ends, Nigel's intolerance for the situation reaches its apex. He waits for Titus to leave before approaching Zayn in anger, determined to reprimand him until he finds a way to fix the damage he has done.

"Admiring the paradise you have created?" Nigel questions obnoxiously.

"Not now, Nigel," Zayn requests. HIs melancholia drenches his room and words, but his plea lands on deaf ears.

"If not now, then when, Zayn? How long do our people have to wait in fear thanks to your actions? How many more homes have to burn before you put aside these ignorant notions of peace and equality?"

Are we not meant for more than this life hidden away from the world we created?" Zayn snaps back, unwilling to let Nigel continue to belittle him. "The Great War has been over for ages, and while they prosper and evolve, we stay stagnant, unwilling to look inward on ourselves. You of all people should understand how barbaric so-called traditions can be."

"Therein lies your problem, Zayn. You believe the Great War ended, but you are wrong. It's ongoing. We were just wise enough to remove ourselves from the conflict. But now here we are right back in the crossfire, thanks to the man who is meant to be our leader." Nigel's anger grows, and so does his voice. "And what pisses me off more than anything is that everyone still wants to coddle you like a child who has dirtied his clothes. But not me! I am here to make sure you see the damage you have done. Our traditions may not be ideal, but they have kept us safe for ages. Yet you want to throw them away just so you fraternize with the enemy."

Enraged, Nigel pulls Zayn close to him by his clothes, determined to make his point as straightforward as possible. "It is time you fall in line, put aside your childish beliefs, and lead our people or, mark my words, your father will not be the only Yeshin buried in the near future."

Nigel drops Zayn to the ground with enough force to break open his sack of stone playing pieces, scattering them around. Nigel looks down at Zayn before kicking one of the pieces back at him.

"You have played games so long that now there's blood on your hands. So ask yourself, what do you do now as the world around you turns to ash?"

Nigel walks off, slamming the chamber doors behind him. Zayn stays on the ground for some time before collecting himself. Again, he looks out at Goldleaf; as he does, the stone playing pieces scattered around start to tremble. Soon, they rise from the ground, slowly orbiting around Zayn. He reaches out his hand, and the small stone totems gather in it. The game pieces reshape like clay, slightly hovering above the palm of Zayn's hand. Moments later, they are one solid infamous object, the mask of the Terra King. The mask rotates as it moves up to Zayn's face. It then slowly wraps around his face, tightening itself to his skull.

Now embracing his alter ego, Zayn speaks to himself,

"Do not worry Nigel, I know exactly what I *have* to do."

*****

Night falls over Goldleaf, and while the Orens try to contemplate their future, Marcus, Liam, and Helena await death inside an Oren detention center. The cell is dirty and unkept due to its rare use, without even a pot to piss in, let alone a place to sit or sleep.

"It's safe to say we are not getting a last meal, are we?" Marcus mocks, his stomach rumbling.

"Do we even deserve one?" a defeated Helena replies. "We walked right into their most sacred place and used our armor to protect a murder."

Among the three, Helena has taken Elizabeth's betrayal hardest, her feelings increasingly complex as she reflects on what she considered a friendship. She can't stop replaying the events, looking for each hint she missed that something was off, chastising herself for not noticing sooner. She should have seen through the deception.

"We were following orders; nothing more. But maybe the reward at the end of this journey blinded us to the reality around us," Liam says remorsefully.

"You're both being too hard on yourselves. We were told we were on a peace mission, so how were we supposed to know there was a wolf among us?" Marcus attempts to console the others to no avail. Quickly recognizing that the mood will not shift, he sits on the ground beside Helena. The sound of his metal armor hitting the rock floor when he sits echoes down the empty hall. "Look at the bright side: at least they honor us enough to let us die in our armor."

The knights gather close, falling asleep from hunger and exhaustion. Deep into the night, they are awoken by the sound of footsteps. Instinctively, they reach for their weapons only to quickly be reminded they were stripped of their arms. The footsteps grow louder and faster before suddenly fading away. The knights work their way to the cell gates only to find the empty hall. Their confusion doesn't last long, though, as the floor below them quakes. Then, in the blink of an eye, a large stone pillar grows from the ground, creating a large opening in the cell ceiling before retracting back down to create a stairway out.

Marus, Helena, and Liam take a moment to ponder what to do before a familiar voice calls out, *'I'd hurry if I were you.'* They take the voice's advice and make their escape. Once outside the cell, they find themselves deep within the forest surrounding Goldleaf. The knights have no idea where to go next between the labyrinth of trees and the pitch blackness of night. Lucky for them, the voice once again calls out, *'This way...'* and then, as before, the trees move swiftly, making a clear pathway out.

With haste, they make their way through the pathway, each time hitting a dead end, only for the voice to guide them once more before a new path opens up. After what seems like hours, they find themselves in a small forest grove where two figures await them. The largest of the two is none other than Master Titus. Standing next to him, though, is none other than the Terra King himself.

Without hesitation, Marcus charges forward to attack, quickly reminded of their last encounter. But before he can get within swinging distance, a mix of stone and vines entangles Marcus's legs, stopping him where he stands.

"Do you truly believe we'd go through all this trouble just to fight you?" Master Titus asks as he and the Terra King come closer. Helena and Liam move quickly to defend Marcus, unsure of either's intent.

"Contrary to our prior engagement, we may be on the same side," the Terra King says, putting his hands up as a symbol of peace.

"Same side! You nearly killed me, you bastard!" Marcus cries out as he tries to free himself from the vines. The more he struggles, though, the tighter he feels the vines wrapping around him.

"An honest mistake. I attacked thinking you carried dangerous cargo. And in fairness, I was correct about that... even if neither of us knew it at the time," the Terra King mocks, moving to face the knights. "I'm not the villain you believe me to be; only days ago, I saved Liam's life."

The Terra King points to Liam before morphing his mask into a chest plate, revealing Zayn's face to the knights. Liam and Helena glance at each other, neither surprised by the revelation.

"What the fuck!" Marcus exclaims.

"So why attack us in the desert? Was your call for peace as much of a charade as Uther's?" Helena asks, unsurprised but still curious. She leaves Marcus alone in continuing his attempts to free himself.

"Not at all, my dear. My call for peace is as genuine as my presence in front of you. It's a goal I and a mutual friend of ours have been working towards for cycles. But right now, I need you to trust me long enough to get all of you out of this forest, through the swamp, and back to Riverhaven."

Understanding the severity of the situation, Liam and Helena agree. Titus and Zayn free Marcus, who again attempts to charge Zayn but is held back by his allies. After cooler heads prevail, the five of them leave the forest. Master Titus makes a point by using his gifts to clear the trees from their path. They stay silent for some time, but once they are far enough away from Goldleaf that Zayn feels safe, he enlightens the others about his intentions.

"There's a movement among Oresn, especially among the youth, that would like to see a change in our sacred tradition. There's no secret to what we do to the Oren born outside of our *'Life Ritual.'* For most of my life, I turned a blind eye – but that's a lie." Zayn's tale is similar to Luna's and just as heartbreaking. "During one of my father's attempts to have me recruit others to my school, I stumbled among this group of revolutionaries but it wasn't until the issue hit close to home that I took action."

"You lost a child?" Helena asks sympathetically.

"No, I did," Titus confesses. "I have always had a weakness for the other sex, and a little over a decade ago my promiscuous ways caught up to me. At first, I thought I could follow tradition and do what we are ordered to do but the mother couldn't live with the idea of losing the child." Titus' story continues with tears running down his face. "We hid the pregnancy intending to raise the child in the shadows but the moment I saw that little girl I knew that wasn't the life I wanted for her. So I asked an unreasonable favor from my friend."

"And without hesitation, I agreed." Zayn takes over. "The plan was simple. Under the cover of night, I would escort Titus, the child and her mother much as we are doing now but our isolation from the world left us unequipped for the journey. We made it out of the forest only to be attacked by creatures that fill the swamp around it. My light can heal but is quite useless in a fight, but even Titus' strength was not enough to protect us all. We stood our ground long enough for the child and mother to make an escape but could not make it out ourselves."

"Being Disciples, our absence led to a search party that found us before our wounds could end us," Titus speaks again. "After awakening from a short coma. Zayn had taken blame for the excursion, convincing the others that his academic curiosity had led him into danger and that it was I who came to his rescue. I've been in his debt ever since."

"Since that day, I've made it my mission to never let such an innocent thing happen again. It started by building a network to help others escape with their children but, as my more aggressive talents evolved, I would guide them myself," Zayn continues. "Those ventures lead to a partnership with the monarch of Riverhaven. The mask became a tool to keep my identity secret for the few times we had to meet in person, and that's where the 'Terra King' was born."

The Oren's story wins the knights over, but they still have questions. Unfortunately, they will not be able to ask them, for they have now reached the forest end and the edge of the swamp.

"This is where we part ways," Titus tells the group. "Zayn will continue with you, but I need to return before sunrise to protect our alibi. I've had my vines reach out to Riverhaven and they have sent an escort of their own to meet with you. Speaking of my vines, I believe you need these."

The trees around them shift shortly, and a group of roots rise for the ground holding the knights' weapons. Helena, Liam, and Marcus rearm themselves and thank Titus for his help. Titus then shifts the forest around them, creating a pathway. To everyone's delight, Hornet emerges, reuniting her with her family. No longer defenseless and with Zayn as their guide, they once again trudge through the swamp, carefully listening for the haunting laughter that leads to their agony on their maiden journey.

All is going well until the devilish rattling once around surrounds them. The shadows around them once again reveal eery smiles. The monsters' yellow eyes again pierce from out the tree tops. The knights draw their weapons, assuming a defensive position, and Zayn dawns his mask once more. As they ready themselves for the attack, the devilish smiles turn fearful, and suddenly, a massive figure leaps from the darkness, grabbing one of the creatures from the trees and slamming it to the ground before tearing it in two.

Their savior is none other than Creed in full Dargone form. He lets out a furious roar, causing ripples throughout the swamp. Fearing for their lives, the creatures flee.

"That's what I thought, nothing more than a bunch of cowards." Creed laughs as he tosses half of the creature in his hands into the treetops. He turns to his friends, continuing his smart-ass ways. "I can't leave you all anywhere. I take a few days to myself and you go and start a war."

Helena and Creed hug, excited to be reunited, and then Liam embracing the lovable giant. Marcus even offers Creed a smile.

"Well, if your lazy ass didn't want to retire to a life of tanning on the beach all day, we may not be in this mess," Marcus quickly mocks.

Zayn removes his mask, attempting to approach Creed as well, but the Dargone growls menacingly.

"Hold on! I am on your side, big guy. Did you not get our message?" Zayn pleads with his hands up, backing away.

"Oh, we got your message, but it doesn't change the fact I still want to finish the ass whooping I was handing you in the desert," Creed threatens. "Unfortunately, there's more important things to deal with, so it will have to wait."

"It's Elizabeth, isn't it?" Helena's questions with concern. "Has she gone after King Ramon as well?" Creed turns to her and shakes his head, letting everyone know what true terror comes their way:

"Wish it was only Elizabeth, love. Uther is on his way, and he's declared war on all of us."

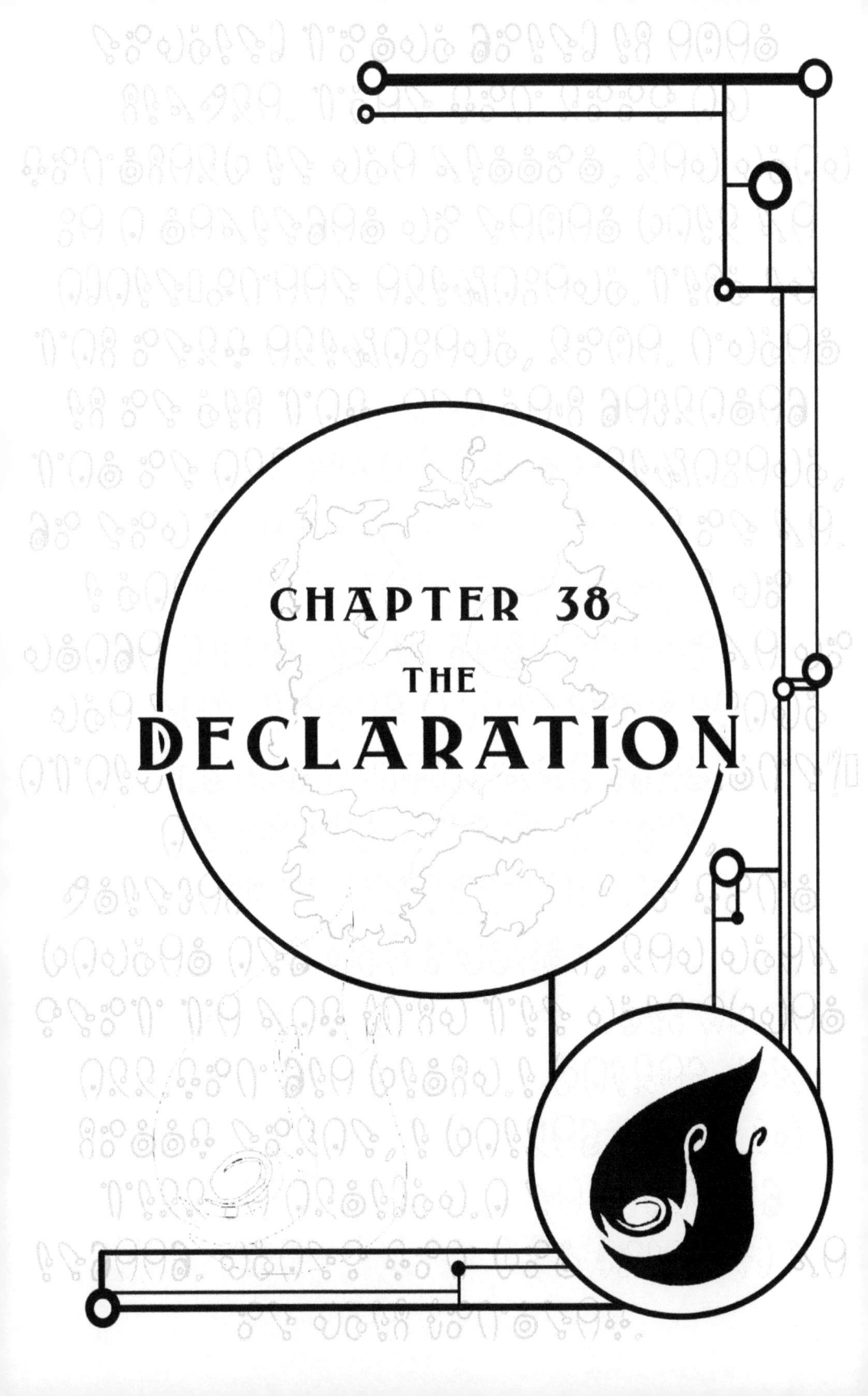

CHAPTER 38
THE
DECLARATION

Chapter 38

The Declaration

The knights of Grandhaven herd the populous towards the castle gates like cattle. Even those unable to travel alone are being forced onto wagons, so they, too, can hear King Uther's declaration. None of them knows what awaits at this royal summit. District after district surrounds the castle wall until every citizen stands before it. Then, once the sun reaches its highest point, Commander Callahan makes his way to the podium.

"Our King has gathered us here so that we can all usher in a new age together. From this moment forward, all that we know will change. The words you are about to hear will lay heavy upon the threshold of time. So stand, give praise, and allow me to delay our destiny no longer as I introduce his majesty, fourth of his name, King Uther Whitelion!"

Uther, sporting all-black attire, approaches the podium to unanimous applause. Red is at his side customarily, but the crowd immediately notices a figure locked arm and arm with Uther. Elizabeth stands before the public for the first time, wearing a flawless white gown with a golden tri-horned lion embroidered down its side. Her face is covered by a white veil topped by a crystal tiara. Together, they fulfill every citizen's picture of a fairytale romance.

"My loyal subjects, I had planned for this to be a day of celebration. One filled with bright futures and surprise matrimony, followed by a festival that would leave no belly empty nor any lips untouched by the finest wines." Uther's lavish approximation causes the sea of people to break into fervorous glee, blissfully ignorant of his true intentions. "Alas, instead, I stand before you in mourning." The crowd's mood swiftly changes, and the cheers become eerily quiet. "Yet before I can go any further, there is someone I must introduce."

Uther removes the veil from Elizabeth's face, revealing her double-pointed ears and harder nose bridge. A new gold-trimmed eye patch covers the scar Uther gave her. With her face exposed, the nearby crowd erupts into gasps, quickly passing their gossip to those behind them. Some express confusion while others discuss with intrigue, but the majority talk amongst themselves in disgust. Before the chatter can become uncontrollable, Uther reins them in. *"Silence!"* With one word, the entirety of Grandhaven goes quiet.

"I understand, my dear Elizabeth's mere existence welcomes question. I, too, stood awestruck when my father brought her to me so many years ago. Yet in time, I grew to love her." Uther's affection was once something Elizabeth longed for, but today, the false words bring pain, harsh reminders that she is nothing more than a pawn in his game. "With every passing day, I find her uniqueness more and more intoxicating. I have learned that even without a royal upbringing, she possessed the poise and elegance of a queen, and as I mourned the passing of my parents, it was her shoulder that I cried upon. This sophistication and gentleness, the safety she's provided, has given me no choice but to ask her hand in marriage."

Once again, Uther's silver tongue wins over the people, many now feeling like they had just been shown a newborn child. He pulls Elizabeth closer to feed into the charade, kissing her on the head, and the disgust that remains is silenced under tremendous applause. Knowing her steps in the dance, she smiles and waves to the crowd, a simple gesture that buys her favor with the people.

"When she agreed, I was elated. I was so eager for my people to know her splendor, but then I realized that would not be that case. As humans, we are born with privilege, welcomed into this world with acceptance and understanding – but not my dear Elizabeth. She was born as what many would call an abomination, a series of mistakes with a misfortunate outcome. I knew that, if we wanted to live in harmony, I must first change this world."

With each word, the people of Grandhaven fall further into Uther's trap. Red and Callahan cannot pity the people's ignorance, both knowing the truth behind the farce. Even Elizabeth's stomach sours at the thought of this loving affair Uther has concocted.

"So I used my position to put a plan for peace in place. In our dream of this new world, we knew we needed to welcome those who have been shunned the most: the Orens." Again, whispers erupt throughout the crowd. The idea of Orens walking side-by-side with man allows fear to creep into the humans' minds.

"Your concern is understandable, but how could I build a home with this woman if her people are locked behind a forest wall? With the help of my associates, President Newson and King Regalia, I was able to set up a meeting with the Oren leadership, an opportunity I jumped at. The airship housed upon my tower was built with the hope of carrying our two races back and forth from each other's homes. After cycles of preparation, the day had come that my beloved Elizabeth would cross Grandiose with my blessing, the promise of tranquility at the end of this journey. Yet, all she found in her homeland was pain." Uther now has his hooks in his subjects. As much as a sob story can get their attention, a tale of suffering is even more tempting.

"After what felt like ages, my dear Elizabeth did not return to me with good tidings and a bright future, instead covered in blood, bruises, and only one of her beautiful eyes," Uther says, his tone becoming sinister, and anger murmurs through the citizens. "With what I thought would be her final words, she told me about the trap the Oren had set for us, how our request for peace was met with slaughter. How the Oren led waste to the knights who gave everything to protect her, and how all that kept her out of death's embrace was never being able to see my face again. With all that she had left, she fought off her captors and flew back to my arms, where, thankfully, Lord Red was able to nurse her back to health." The crowd cheers as Red offers them a slight bow only he knows is mocking.

"With my dear back in good health, I knew I couldn't let this act go unpunished. Thus, I reached out to my fellow Council members and requested their aid. Although some were quick to take my side, others refused. I now fear that some of them may even be aligned with our enemy." Uther's accusation leads to notable gasps. "Because of these traitors, I am unable to call upon the great armies of Grandiose to defend my betrothed's honor. But I am not a leader who lays idle, especially when someone tries to burn down my home. So I enact the law of *'Royal Shield.'* I will don the armor passed down by my forefathers, gather my royal guard, and stomp out this threat before it harms my people!"

With that declaration, Uther has won over the people. In a short time, he convinced them that Elizabeth was their queen-to-be, and they were willing to go to war for her. The King's master manipulation is greeted with unanimous cheers, a sickening song that brings him the utmost delight. He leaves the podium again with Elizabeth in his arms, followed by Red and Callahan. The castle door closes behind them while the crowd still chants Uther's praise. Once out of the people's sight, he throws Elizabeth to the side, angrily brushing himself off.

"All seems to have gone as planned, my Lord," Red says in hushed tones. "By the time the others become wise to your plan, it will be too late. Soon, you will seize Goldleaf as your own." Uther looks at Red and Callahan with a devilish grin, an overwhelming sense of pride washing over him, and announces,

"It is time for the true fun now: war."

*****

For the remainder of the day, the citizens of Grandhaven watch as a few hundred knights file into the massive airship docked atop the castle tower. Inside, the hum of its engine echoes down its many halls, filling the enormous space. Callahan marches the knights down these corridors, their armor reflecting the many Q.A.S powered lights on the walls. Their journey ends when they reach a large, open room where the knights can all stand in formation. Once all the royal guards, roughly one thousand men and women, are in place, Callahan takes his place before them to give them their final orders.

"Knights of the royal guard, stand and salute, for your actions from this moment forth will earn you your valor. Our mission is honorable: to protect our King and his throne at all costs. We must stand face-to-face with fear, prepared for the weight of battle as we quench the hunger of death. To those who return, the title of legend awaits, and for those you who perish in this fight, your name will live in immortality. To King Whitelion and kingdom of Grandhaven!"

Callahan's speech is met with applause, then followed by beating one fist on their chest to acknowledge their leader. He quiets them before walking over to a panel of buttons and levers. Callahan pulls one down, and a pulse of electricity surges across the floor beneath the knights, magnetically locking them in place.

Inside the castle, Uther's handmaidens prepare him for war. First, they tighten his aketon, a beautiful white undergarment with a golden royal crest sewn throughout it. Next, they braid his hair, weaving diamond lace into each one. They then bring him his armor. Each suit piece is plated in gold with flawless black leather holding it together. Last, they bring him his cape. On the outer side, diamond white fabric shines with royal purple peeks out from the interior. The handmaidens attach it to his armor with two lion-head shoulder plates, a gold and white mane chain between them. Fully equipped, Uther calls for Red.

His adviser enters the room carrying two ornate casse, two other handmaidens following in his wake. Sitting it on the table between himself and the King, he opens the first case and removes Uther's infamous gauntlet before placing it on Uther's arm. The sleek black of the gauntlet clashes against the rest of the golden armor harshly. Then, he opens the second case to reveal a custom belt housing several purple quartz stones, Sarrow's journal secured to its side with golden chains. The handmaidens place it around Uther's waist, causing the armor's edges to illuminate that sinister violet glow.

Uther allows the power to take over as the smell of death fills the air. Many of the handmaidens fall to their knees, unable to handle the ever-growing heat of the atmosphere. Red, too, finds it hard to breathe, but holds his ground, while Uther finds the change intoxicating. Uther lets out a deep breath, and the room returns to normal. As the handmaidens return to their feet, Red and Uther take their leave.

Together, they continue to the roof, where Elizabeth and yet another handmaiden await. This handmaiden holds a large pillow with Uther's morningstar on it. Uther takes the weapon before hanging it from the opposite of Sorrow's journal, then dismissing the handmaiden.

Leaning in close to Elizabeth, he whispers, "When I return this will be a new world and you will be its queen. But remember: I will be its god, so if you want to be a part of it, it's best you learn to worship me." Elizabeth feels sick at the thought of what her life will be like once he returns, yet for now, it's a fate better than death.

"While I am away, the people will look to you, Red," Uther says, his voice normal once more as he turns from Elizabeth. "But don't let that go to your head, old man. You are merely a placeholder. With that said, once all this is done, I will ensure you are compensated for your aid in my rise."

With that, the cocky King makes his way to the ship's helm, leaving Elizabeth and Red behind. Once inside the ship, Uther takes his place in the captain's chair. This throne-like seat lies in a private room away from the knights. From this seat, Uther can look out the massive airship windows as he uses a series of controls to pilot. Before he takes his throne, he removes his morningstar's top from its head and inserts it into a slot at the side of the chair.

With the weapon locked in, the airship comes to life. Its hull shifts open, allowing bright yellow lights to flood out. The enormous engines fire up at the ship's stern, lifting it into the air. Uther's throne locks him in place as he pushes his morningstar forward, and with that, he and his army are on their way to Goldleaf.

Red and Elizabeth watch from the castle tower as the airship fades into the horizon.

"And so it begins," Red says, temporarily safe from Uther's rage. "The end of the world as we know it. Shame things won't go the way he plans." Eyes wide, Elizabeth looks over at him. "I have to give you credit, my dear. You've worked your way into quite the comfortable position. I honestly didn't think you had it in you."

As he turns to leave, he notices Elizabeth staying behind. "Aren't you coming? It's cold out here at night, and I doubt you worked this hard to freeze to death."

"I have to take care of something," Elizabeth answers, looking out across the distance.

"Don't be a fool, Elizabeth. Your role in all this is over; let the swords of destiny sort things out now. Come, enjoy the prize you have earned." He is acutely aware of how she brushes his words aside, and he shakes his head, knowing precisely what Elizabeth plans to do.

"A friend warned me I was trading my soul for fancy bed sheets," Elizabeth confesses, the regret clear in her tone. "I wish I listened to her. Don't make that same mistake, Red."

Red finds her warning amusing. After all he has done, she still wishes him the best. Feeling this very well may be the last time that speak to one another, he lets his guard down, giving her a glimpse into his ominous outlook:

"Dear Elizabeth, do not waste your lessons on me. I have long not had a soul to trade away."

CHAPTER 39
THE
IGNORANCE OF HOPE

Chapter 39

The Ignorance of Hope

With great haste, the citizens of Riverhaven make their way to the kingdom's docks. Overwhelming panic sweeps over the people; Chief Ramon has never before ordered a complete evacuation. Yet, without notice, the handful of knights living in Riverhaven begin escorting everyone into ships, hoping it would be safer out at sea. Even with their fleet, many of them will be left behind to face whatever horror awaits. Knowing that, most of those who are capable of fighting have taken up arms, choosing to stay behind and defend their home.

While the ships sail off to rendezvous with Ethan's research department outside the Void, the remaining citizens stand guard around the dining hall. There, Chief Ramon and his daughter Luna meet with Marcus and his cohort.

Irate, Ramon slides a declaration across the table to Marcus. "The bastard has declared war on the whole Oren race. And I have no doubt he plans to go through Riverhaven to get to them."

Creed, Liam, and Helena join him in reading the papers over:

"The following document is the first and final warning of an approaching fleet led by King Uther Whitelion, fourth of his name. Due to the heinous attack on King Whitelion's betrothed, Lady Elizabeth, that led to the death of three of our finest knights, the King has enacted the law of 'Royal Shield.' With this ruling, King Whitelion hereby lays claim to the city of Goldleaf and all who reside there. Any and all resistance will be met with force, and anyone caught aiding and abetting the city or its Oren citizens will be deemed enemies of the monarchy. By the power of our King, we will prevail."

Marcus rips the paper in half before tossing it to the ground.

"It is almost impressive how much bullshit can fit in so few words," Liam mocks, equally frustrated. Still, he picks up the pieces and places them back on the table.

"Those same few words will cost countless lives," Helena reminds them.

Standing in the corner of the room, Zayn makes his way to the table. While his forehead is created in concern, his shoulders droop. Each person in the room can sense his regret.

"We knew Uther wasn't to be trusted, but this? I fear we may have waited too long to act."

"No shit!" Marcus punches the table before confronting both Zayn and Chief Ramon. "I don't have to be the smartest man in the room to see that you both know more about this than you're letting on. I shouldn't be surprised that the Oren who has been slaughtering our men for cycles is also a lying prick. But the Chief leading us into a death trap? That really pisses me off."

Offended at Marcus' words, Zayn confronts him, willing the ground to shake as they face each other.

"I am no murderer! In fact, I have been risking my life, the trust of my people, and now my home in hopes of peace between us. It's man's ignorance and greed that once again lead to war!"

"Don't try to play that hero shit with me! I have the scar that proves just who you are. I think it's time I repay you for our little dance in the desert," Marcus snarls, reaching for his blade. Before the fight goes any further, Liam's spear stabs the space between them, separating the two..

"Enough!" Liam pushes between the men, forcing both to take their seats. Then, he turns his attention to Chief Ramon, who has been uncharacteristically silent. "Although I disagree with my colleague's choice of words, his concerns are valid. You and I have broken bread many times, Ramon; I trusted you. We trusted you. Why wouldn't you warn us there was a snake among us?"

"You misunderstand, old friend. I knew trusting Uther was dangerous, but Elizabeth's treachery is just as much of a surprise to me as it is you. Though I must admit that I have been less than transparent with you," Ramon nods to Zayn.

"As I have mentioned before, long have I had a network of informants keeping an eye on anything suspicious across Grandiose. A handful of cycles ago, one of them noticed several unmarked and undocumented supply carriages traveling across the country. So I asked my best to look into it. Nolan." Just the mention of his name buys Ramon the attention of the others. "It took him some time, but he was able to infiltrate their route and return with a sample of its cargo." Zayn removes a small indigo quartz from his pocket and sets it on the table. Though the knights have seen many different colored stones in their work, they have never seen this particular hue.

"I've been around since the dawn of Q.A.S. Tech, and the Council has always been told the machinery could only handle red, white, blue, and yellow stones, so why would someone be secretly shipping these?"

"With nowhere else to get an answer, the sample made its way to me," Zayn interjects, continuing the story. "Immediately, I knew what it was, a natural element infused with magic. The real concern is the type of magic." Zayn picks the stone up from the table, explaining, "This little gem is filled with death magic. Something – or more importantly, someone – is hoarding a lot of it."

"I guess it's safe to assume that's a bad thing?" Marcus questions.

"Very bad," Zayn replies. "Death magic is one of the forbidden dark arts. Toying with it drove Sorrow mad and led to my people's darkest age. To this day, we still don't know all its capabilities and, personally, I didn't want to find out."

"So we took matters into our own hands," the Chief takes over. "I had my informants feed the route details to my Oren allies, and the next time they attempted a delivery, the Terra King debuted."

"I destroyed cargo but didn't do any lasting harm to those carrying it," Zayn defends himself. "I knocked some out and incapacitated others, but I never killed anyone. My sole mission was only ever to stop the shipment and intimidate them into not having another. And it worked at first; it was some time before reports of another shipment. But with each assault, they got wiser, moved the routes, used decoys; they even went as far as having outlaws as escorts. For cycles, I did everything in my power to prevent those carriages getting to their destination, but I swear, I never ended a single person's life."

"As he dealt with the cargo, my informants, including Nolan, and I tried to find out who was behind all this, to no avail. Every trail went cold, before one day, it all stopped," Ramon explains. "The shipments stopped and everything just went quiet. With nothing to chase, the Terra King wasn't needed, so Zayn and I returned to helping the Orens search for freedom.

"A few moons later, Uther came to me proposing his plans for a united future. Although he had always been my prime suspect, as I said before, I couldn't give up the chance of giving my little girl a better life." Ramon reaches out for Luna's hand, giving it a loving kiss. "So, with Zayn's aid, I started working on the additions with the Orens, and suddenly, new reports of the Terra King arose, each one progressively more violent than the next. We knew for a fact they were some sick charade, but how could we prove it without exposing ourselves? Just as I started to wrap my head around it, the incident with Nolan happened. But before I could even come to his aid, he was at the end of a chain."

At this moment, a morbid thought washes over Marcus, Helena, and Liam..

"Wait," Helena gasps, "You don't think?"

"At first, no, but it's becoming ever more apparent we are merely strokes in a much bigger painting." Ramon's revelation hits them like an arrow to the chest. Anger, despair, confusion, and fear race through their minds. "The cargo, the false Terra King, the bar... Nolan's execution has all been a part of Uther's plan."

Marcus erupts from his chair, tossing it into the wall in anger. "Son of bitch!" Though Liam tries to calm him, he is met with only more vexation. "Don't! I'm tired of being calm! Our family has become tools in some sick war game, and Nolan is dead because of it! And as we rest at the tip of that same blade, you expect me to stand proud and restrained? Fuck that! If Uther wants a war, so be it – but he's going to have to go through me to get it."

Before Liam can try to reason with Marcus, Helena stuns the room with her own words. "And me too..."

"Helena, not you too," Liam interjects, surprised at her outburst. She had always been the one he could count on for level-headedness. "I share both your anger. Nolan was my brother. But you're talking about warring against the most powerful man alive. I've seen firsthand how this ends, surrounded by nothing but dead bodies, widows, and orphans. There has to be another way. Ramon, please tell them the Council is already planning something."

Ramon shakes his head.

"He has found a loophole. As of now, he hasn't done anything wrong; at least, not on a legal level. Even the members who know it's morally bankrupt aren't willing to risk their people's lives for that of the Orens. It is easier to turn a blind eye to a war from afar than from within."

"Stop saying this is a war!" Once again, Helena demands the room's attention. "It's genocide. Uther doesn't care about the glory of battle or honor of victory; he wants the destruction of innocent people. And I, for one, would like to believe no one in this room would stand for that."

"Marcus may be irrational and naive, but at least he's ready to fight. As knights, we are meant to be Grandiose's shield, all of Grandiose. We are to fight the battles they can't, not just the ones we know we can win. Uther's actions may belittle the idea of a united country, but that is still a notion I wish to see made real. Why should Luna live her life in fear? Why should Creed be forced to wear skin he doesn't belong in? Why can't Zayn's people walk freely in the lands once called home? Why can't I–" Helena chokes on her own words, but she has already said enough to win over the room. Liam places his spear on the table in front of her.

"As always, you are the voice of reason. It is our duty to protect, and if I must fight, then I will gladly do it by your side."

Marcus' sword clatters to the table, too. "We will win this, even if it takes our last breath. There's no other choice. If we fail here, Nolan died for nothing."

Joining Helena's side, Creed says, "I may have just moved in, but I'll be damned if I let a man burn down my new home." He pats her hand reassuringly.

Lastly, Zayn places his Terra King mask on the table. "I believe it is time Uther and I meet face to face. Let him bear witness to the fact that the myth he has created is nothing compared to the truth."

The five of them embrace, and Ramon is unable to hide his smile, realizing why Nolan had brought them together. They are not only knights and they are more than just family. They are greater than heroes. They are hope embodied – and, he realizes, they are the future he envisions..

"Seeing that everyone is ready to walk into the house of death, the least I can do is give you an idea of what you are going against," Ramon says, pulling a scroll from beneath his chair and handing it to Luna.

Taking up their arms, everyone huddles around his daughter in intrigue as she rolls it across the table. Laid out before them are blueprints for a large ship. It contains notes on its size, holding capacity, max speed, and estimated build time. The plans paint the picture of an immense machine to the naked eye, but overall, they appear to be nothing more than standard blueprints.

"Throughout our entire investigation, we could never put the whole puzzle together. We knew the what and we had a fairly good idea of the who, but we couldn't figure out the why. To be completely transparent, until a few days ago, we still had no idea," Ramon reveals. "Then, one morning, I was delivered a declaration of war from one Crow, followed by an unmarked letter and a locked chest by another. The letter simply says *'The Traitor.'* After some pondering, we figured it was a clue to the chest combination. Once it was opened, all we found was this scroll."

Marcus states the obvious, pointing out that the prints are for nothing more than a large ship.

"We thought the same until Luna noticed this," Ramon says, pointing out a small, nearly invisible tear at the top corner of the scroll. Luna holds down the opposite corner and pulls at the tear. To everyone's surprise, she peels away the parchment's top layer, revealing a second blueprint. The base design of this ship is the same but with numerous diabolical 'improvements.' Unlike the first layer, many details are blacked out, the only legible word being *'Project Knightfall'* printed across the top. Yet, without being able to read any other words, it's clear to the knights that this is a warship.

"While you were in Goldleaf, word came of a one-of-a-kind airship making dock atop castle Whitelion. Uther ensured the people it was nothing more than a working prototype for a new state-of-the-art mode of transportation; a gift from him to the people, a tool to bring the world together," Ramon continues. "From the outside, it looks like nothing more than that, but from my understanding, before any declaration was even sent out, Uther loaded private guards into and is currently heading our way."

"If that's true," Liam ponders aloud, "that means a small army is making its way here at unprecedented speed. It could be here–"

"At any moment," Ramon inserts. "We came to the same realization, so I invoked the evacuation while sending Creed into the swamp with a prayer and orders to find all of you."

"Unfortunately, that's only where the problem starts." Luna directs their attention back to the blueprints, where she points out the many other additions that have been made. "Uther has armed this ship to the teeth. There are cannons across every plane, Q.A.S. Tech engines that will seemingly keep it afloat indefinitely, and a custom cockpit that somehow links the driver to the ship. That isn't even mentioning whatever this is." Luna points out a second, smaller blueprint in the left-hand corner of the scroll. It details a large cylinder-shaped object with a drive at one end and several smaller cannons housing what appears to be hundreds of sharpened quartz stones. "We believe these are some kind of ammo for the main cabinets, most likely using all the horded stone over the cycles. Other than that, we are drawing blanks."

Together, they look over the blueprints in hopes of figuring out any more of its secrets. Before they can theorize much more, the hall doors fly open, and a citizen rushes in, panting with every stride. They collapse into Helna's arms, and she quickly helps them get back to their feet. Ramon orders Luna to get them a glass of water, but as he turns for the kitchen, the citizen speaks three words that will change the course of history:

"It is here."

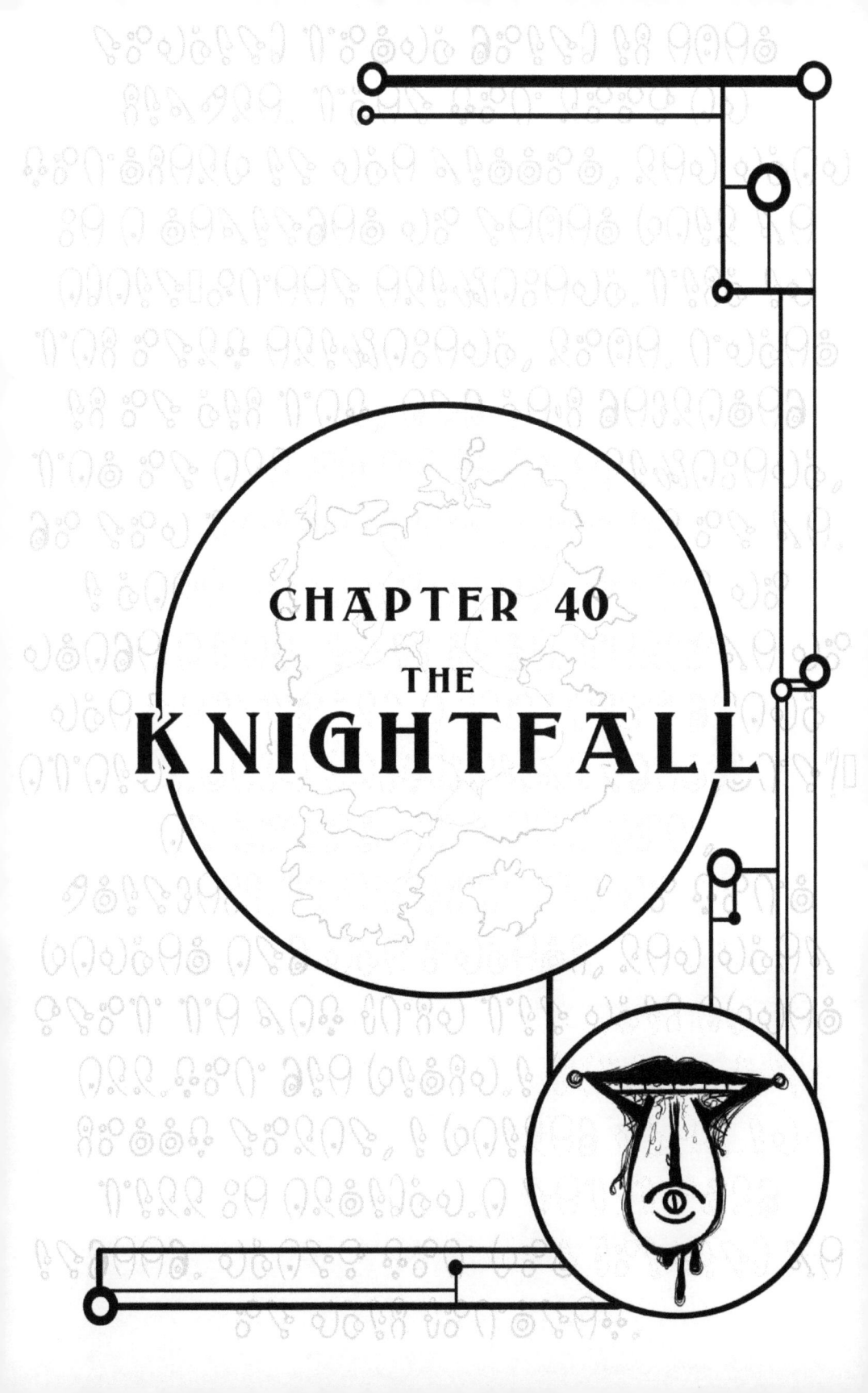

CHAPTER 40
THE
KNIGHTFALL

Chapter 40

The Knightfall

The sea trembles as the Knightfall hovers above Riverhaven. Below, the citizens arm themselves, but the wildlife around them flee in fear. From the ship's cockpit, a Uther looks down smugly at the first target in his match for greatness. He rearms himself, switching the vessel into attack formation. Callahan enters the helm as the cannons emerge and aim at the city below.

"It seems Chief Ramon has evacuated the majority of Riverhaven into the sea, yet a notable resistance has stayed behind to defend the city," Callahan reports.

"A feeble notion." Uther brushes off any threat they may oppose arrogantly. "In a matter of moments, they will be nothing more than a footnote."

"You plan to attack without warning?" Callahan questions.

"What does it matter? I could give them a full cycle to prepare, and they still would not have a chance at survival."

"My lord, a battle without honor is nothing but mindless slaughter. Victory is assured, so why stain your legacy in such brutal ways?" the knight pleads. Uther's blood-thirst initially denounces it, and he rolls his eyes before giving in.

"When did you get so soft, Callahan? Fine, go give them a chance to surrender. When they refuse – and they will refuse – I will open the heavens and rain death down upon them."

Callahan nods in agreement and makes his way to the chamber housing the rest of the royal knights. Once there, he releases Moses from her cage and makes his way to a small armory at the back of the ship. His war helmet hangs on the wall, a family heirloom passed down through the ages. Due to its age, it has a simple design and no fancy engravings, only the standard royal sigil on its forehead. Its bone-white color has faded over the cycles, and numerous dents and large repaired slices decorate its right side. Callahan runs his hand over the slice, a reminder that his father died in this same helmet.

Callahan turns to his knights and salutes them. As he mounts Moses, a large gate opens at the ship's stern. He dons his helmet, causing grooves in his armor to illuminate that haunting red. Then, as he grabs Moses' reins, her eyes match that red glow. She unleashes a fearsome roar before leaping out the back of the Knightfall. The crowd below watches as Callahan, atop Moses plummets to the ground. Before they can smash into the ground, micro-flaming engines emerge from Moses' arms and legs, allowing them to descend safely.

With an echoing thud, Callahan safely makes landfall. The citizens march to meet him; Marcus, Liam, and Elizabeth leading from the front line. Silence sweeps over the land as Callahan stands across from a small army of civilians willing to die to protect their home. The sea of people parts to allow Chief Ramon to approach the knight.

With one hand, the already intimidating Ramon carries his massive war anchor over his shoulder and, in the other, his royal helm. Unlike Callahan's helmet, Ramon's is unmistakable, a gold-plated fin on top and blood-colored tribal art on its face. Zayn, wearing his Terra King mask, stands at the chief's side. Callahan dismounts and, as tradition, bows to Ramon before addressing him.

"King Whitelion graciously offers you and your people the chance to surrender."

Ramon laughs mockingly, and his people mimic it. After a few moments, they return to stern silence as the chief continues, "Your King is a fool if he thinks my people and I would ever stand down against this obvious act of tyranny."

"Don't be a hero, Chief Ramon. Riverhaven is not His Majesty's primary target. Your people need not suffer for the Orens," Callahan pleads again.

"You understand so little, Sir Callahan," Ramon answers. "These people protect this land not only for themselves but for the ideals it represents. We cannot rest in a world where we stand idle as innocent people are laid to waste merely for the pleasure of a tyrant. So tell your King that if he wishes to address me any further, it shall be on the battlefield."

Callahan bows once more, addressing Ramon one final time. "History will remember you as an honorable man, Chief Ramon, but for the few that survive here, you will be nothing more than the fool who sentenced them to death."

Callahan mounts Moses again, directing her back a few strides and putting distance between him and the crowd, never losing his view of their opponent. Ramon reconvenes with his people before placing on his helmet, signaling them to prepare for war. Behind him, they ready their weapons. Marcus, Liam, Helena, and Zayn follow Ramon's lead while he takes points by his side.

"Ensure Luna is safe, old friend," Ramon tells Liam, a concerned plea in his voice.

"Creed has promised not to leave her side, and we have positioned a small group of our most capable men outside of the hall where they hide," Liam responds, attempting to comfort his friend.

"In that case," Ramon says before slamming his anchor into the ground several times, creating and echoing war songs that the citizens repeat. "For Riverhaven!"

Callahan admires their spirits from a distance, even though he knows it to be fruitless. He takes his shield from Moses' side equipment and points to the sky. Above, Uther acknowledges Callahan's signal and, with sinister glee, makes his way to the chamber of royal knights. Once in their presence, he addresses them as he strides to the same small armory his commanding knight visited earlier.

"My dearest protectors, I must thank you for your service. Without you, this moment could never happen. It is because of you that today, I fulfill my destiny. So take solace knowing your sacrifice has changed the world."

With those final words, Uther places his morningstar into yet another hidden slot in the ship's floor. He pushes down on it, lighting up the floor below the royal knights. Slowly, the floor begins to lower into the sky below. The knights panic as where they stand begins to rotate. Forgetting that they have been magnetically attached to the ship, they fight to free themselves in vain. Before long, the people of Riverhaven are looking up at the Knightfall with an army of panicked knights dangling upside down from its hull.

Callahan lowers his arm, and mere moments later, the magnets holding the royal knights are deactivated. Like rain, they fall to the ground with nothing to slow their descent. The bodies crash around the citizens of Riverhaven.

The more able-bodied citizens do what they can to avoid the assault of corpses, but unfortunately, those who cannot find themselves crushed. Ramon and the others try their hardest to keep everyone calm, but the unorthodox attack has led to chaos. Dead bodies hang from the roofs and blood flows from the streets into the sea. Civilians rush for cover as weapons fall from the sky, impaling them as they run. Before long, the already timid-sized army is cut in half.

Uther returns to the Knightfall helm, maniacal. Again, he takes his position at the throne. He places the attached crown atop his head, activating a podium that rises from the floor.

He turns toward it, a series of wires following him from the crown, and detaches Sorro's journal from his side to place it on the podium. The ship rumbles, and the cannons load as the engines shift from red light to the hellish indigo. The sky blackens as the scent of death fills the air. Every ache and every wound, past and present, begin to burn those below. Callahan bares down on his teeth as his body eats away at itself.

Then, without warning, Knightfall's cannons unload upon the city below. Marcus calls for everyone to take cover as the large cylinders described in the blueprints make an impact around them. Zayn erects as many stone pillars as he can to shield the people, but he can only do so much. Though only a few moments pass before the onslaught stops, it feels as though an eternity has passed. To everyone's surprise, the ammunition never causes any explosion. Debris has flown in all directions, but the cylinders have done nothing more than slightly drill into the ground, exposing most of the device.

As the dust settles, Ramon regroups the survivors. They find things to be eerily quiet as they come out from their cover. The feeling of death still lingers, but now it is more focused, seemingly radiating from the fallen cylinders. Just as they seemingly get their bearings, the devices open, and the presence of death grows immensely. It is at that moment when Zayn can sense what is coming. He tries to warn them as quickly as he can, calling for everyone to take cover once again, but he is too late. In an instant, hundreds of sharpened purple quartz stones fire from each cylinder, impaling every dead and living thing in their path.

Marcus, Helena, Ramon, and Liam can defend themselves, either dodging the assault or cutting down the stones in midair. Zayn does his best to shield as many of the citizens as he can, but their forces are drastically reduced once again.

The horror has only begun.

Above them, Knightfall's illumination intensifies. Every quartz stone begins to pulse like a beating heart. And before the eyes of those left standing, the endless number of corpses surrounding them rise once more. Zayn watches in horror as fallen once again reach for their weapons. They deadlock eyes with the living and let out a gruesome cry as all their heads burst into purple flames, burning away their flesh.

From high above, Uther marvels at this hell of his own making. His eyes blacken and his scars illuminate through his armor, purple flames replacing his braids. The poison of power no longer consumes the man once known as Uther; a demon of death stands in his place. After letting out a horrific laugh that causes the world below to quiver, this self-indulged lunatic utters his first words:

"Welcome to the new world…"

CHAPTER 41
THE BATTLE OF RIVERHAVEN

Chapter 41

The Battle of Riverhaven

Hordes of undead knights flood the streets of Riverhaven, but there are no signs of rigor mortis in their corpses; these warriors display more agility and strength than ever. A courageous Marcus charges forward in the storm, severing every limb with his sword as he makes contact. At his back, Zayn uses the earth to throw stone javelin after javelin, fighting them towards the demonic armor, pinning down as many as he can. Despite their heroics, this defense is meaningless.

Every severed limb somehow finds its way back to its host, and every javelin is effortlessly pulled from its wound. Marcus and Zayn continue to stand their ground as the horde surrounds them, purple flames rejuvenating their enemies.

"Starting to regret splitting up from the others," Marcus huffs, catching his breath while shifting his stance.

"I told you that when you suggested it in the first place!" Zayn responds, irritated, as he summons a circle of stone walls to protect them.

"I remember no such suggestion! Even so, this is no time to point fingers. Instead, why don't you stop holding back and show these assholes some of that aggression I witnessed firsthand in the desert?"

"If you insist. I just didn't want to make you look bad again," Zayn mocks before causing rows of spikes to grow from the face of the stone walls. He does not pause as he pushes the walls away from them, tearing apart dozens of the undead until they crash into the architecture around them.

Marcus mouths, "Bastard," toward the Oren. Not to be outdone, he releases his katana into the air. He then charges into the fray, kicking and punching as many skeletal jaws from their heads and guiding his blade around him. The fiery trail left behind by the blade etches an elegant painting throughout the streets, a flaming buzzsaw removing every head and torso in its wake.

Together, Zayn and Marcus thin the horde, buying themselves time to regroup. Marcus returns his blade to its sheath to recharge, and Zayn throws his mask to the ground, sweat dripping down his face. Again, their relief is short-lived; underneath the rubble, the dead rise once more. It is more than apparent they stand no chance of winning this battle. They nod to one another, choosing to live to fight another day and fleeing deeper into Riverhaven. As they race to safety, the horde follows behind. Even with his life at risk, Marcus cannot help but think to himself:

"Helena, please be safe."

*****

Far from safe, Helena fares better than Marcus. She leaps from rooftop to rooftop, Chief Ramon by her side. Even with the buildings' modest heights, the slight advantage gives Helena all she needs to pick off their pursuers. With precise aim, her arctic arrows pierce the undeads' skulls, instantly freezing the flames that engulf them.

"Your majesty, I can hold them as long as you need, but I suggest we pick up the pace to make it to the hall before any more get ahead of us."

Ramon swings his anchor, deflecting any projectiles being hurled toward them. Once the sky is clear, he aims his anchor at a rooftop ahead of them. Pushing a button on its grip, it shoots the anchor head forward, a massive chain keeping it tethered to the handle. Once cemented in the roof, Ramon pushes the button again and retracts the chain to pull himself through the air. With the Chief safely landed, Helena aims for the air. She pulls back on her bow and holds it back, charging the ice arrow until it's relatively larger than its typical size. She releases the arrow, and in mid-air, it shatters, raining down hundreds of half-size bolts on the undead. The frozen assault temporarily immobilizes their enemies and creates a giant wall of ice.

With a barricade in place, Helena and Ramon make haste towards the dinner hall. Once the building is in sight, the horrific reality before them hits. They look down at hundreds of undead surrounding the hall in an organized formation. Royal knights stand side-by-side with fallen civilians as though they'd gone to war together a thousand times. The bodies of those who did not turn into warriors are propped up like trophies to warn any other survivors of their fate.

"They're intelligent." For the first time, Helena hears the fear in Ramon's voice.

"Intelligence may not be accurate. Oren magic is complicated. The same people who were willing to die for Riverhaven now fight against it with skills that rival any of my peers," Helena asserts, hoping to comfort him.

"They are now immortal puppets, controlled by a madman, set on using us as an example of what's to come." Ramon removes his helmet and tightens his grip around his anchor. "I will die to save my daughter, Helena. I understand if you wish to leave and spend what time we have left with your loved ones."

Helena walks over and picks up Ramon's helmet, reassuring him. "I will not be leaving your side any time soon, my lord. If death is what you desire, I am afraid I will be disrupting that plan." Helena hands the helmet back to the chief, which he accepts, thanking her for her commitment. Helena readies her bow and surveys the situation once more. In moments, she notices Creed peering out one of the hall's windows. Now, with a glimmer of hope, she points him out to Ramon and reminds him:

"We still have a secret weapon."

*****

Just as Helena notices Creed, he, too, catches a glimpse of her through the dining hall window.

"About damn time, Helena." Creed turns to Luna, who trembles behind a wall of tables. "Ready yourself, dear. Our escape window is slim."

"Ready myself? Are you bloody crazy?" Luna exclaims, coming out of hiding for the first time. "Have you not seen what awaits us outside those doors?"

"You do know what I am, correct?" Creed questions.

"It doesn't matter what the hell you are, there's one of you and a small continent worth of them," Luna barks back.

"Oh, so the odds are in our favor?" Creed jokes.

Unamused by his joke, Luna rolls her eyes. "You are arrogant. It's no wonder my father has grown to like you." She crawls back behind the tables. Unlike his, her voice lacks any humor. Acknowledging that his coping mechanism only caused more harm, he sits down on the opposite side of Luna's makeshift barrier.

"I'm not arrogant, little one. Truth is, I make a fool of myself to cover up the pain, or, in this case, the fear. But we can't stay here forever. I mean, it is a dining hall, so we could stay for quite some time... but that's not the point." As Creed opens up, Luna peers over the tables. "We have to make it out of here; there's no other choice in the matter. If Riverhaven falls, something greater than us dies with it."

Once again, Luna emerges, joining Creed on the floor. "You have barely been here a fortnight, yet you're already willing to risk your life for us," she observes. It's not a question.

"I hope that's not how this ends. You may not understand but, then again, after hearing your tale, maybe you would. Either way, this world is cruel. It begs for perfection in things that are meant to be flawed. In the rare case it does get what it wishes, it finds a way to hate that, too. It wants to preach its successes while ignoring its failures. It punishes its most unique children moments after taking their first breath just because it fears that acceptance will crumble the hierarchy it spent so much time creating." Creed sighs as he reminds himself of the unjust burden his mere existence brings. "But not here, not in Riverhaven. And that's why we must win. Please forgive my arrogance; it's just that this place is needed now more than ever."

Luna takes Creed's hand, telling him, "You are forgiven; just please tell me you have a plan?'

Creed smiles, stands, and helps Luna to her feet. His bones start to crack as his skin tightens. His fangs grow, and before he completes his transformation, he reassures Luna,

"Of course...Fuck 'em up!"

*****

Stoically, the undead wait with their backs to the dining hall entrance with a single thought passing through their minds: kill all that approach. They stand still, concentration unbroken, until the ground begins to rumble. In sequence, they look to investigate, but the tremors only intensify. Then, they realize the source of which is behind them: a fully Dargone Creed, with Luna on his back, bursts through the hall doors. Before they can react, Creed picks up an undead knight and rips them in half. He unleashes a violent roar that shakes the sea, drawing everyone's attention, including Uther's from high above.

Creed goes on the offensive, using his tail to break the spines of several undead and tossing them across the skyline, grabbing others by the skull and crushing them together. The warriors try to slash at him to no avail; his Dargone scales are more substantial than any armor. As the blade shatters against his skin, those with varied weapons try their luck, but they, too, bounce off. Creed fights them off while protecting Luna at all costs. Clawing through the dead like a wrecking ball, he distances them from the dining hall. Yet with all his power, Luna's fear is justified, knowing more of the undead wait wherever they run. Whenever they are met with another threat, the ones behind them reassemble themselves. It is only a matter of time before they find themselves surrounded.

An exhausted Creed falls to one knee. Though he is ready to give up, he feels Luna trembling in fear, her tears running down his back. Unwilling to fail her, he gathers all his energy and stands tall again. Bracing himself for one final fight, he starts to charge into the horde once more when suddenly, a prominent figure crashes into the group before him. Through the debris, the head of Chief Ramon's war anchor races toward Creed's head, stopping just before it makes contact. It reverses before it can drop to the ground, blowing the dust away and numerous corpses back with it. In a grand feat of strength, Ramon spins the anchor above his head until at least forty undead warriors hover above him. He then launches them across his kingdom's streets, toppling a block of houses.

As an astonished Creed attempts to process what he just witnessed, a storm of ice rains down on the swarm behind him. Creed moves across the freezing battlefield with grace, breaking the crystallizing corpses to pieces. Moments ago, Creed thought this to be the end, but now he sees not one but two ways forward.

With tears of excitement, Luna leaps from Creed's back and rushes over to her father. With yet another mighty swing, Chef Ramon clears her path, and she jumps into his arms. The joy of their reunion is palpable, momentarily brightening the dread from the battle.

Creed turns to Helena, jokingly opening his arms for a hug, only for her to roll her eyes and smile.

With little time to celebrate, Ramon quickly informs Creed of the mission ahead. "We need to get Luna out to sea so Ethan can keep her safe."

"What about the others? Are they with you?" Both Creed and Luna inquire.

"Not yet, but everyone heard that cry of yours. They are likely heading this way as well. Unfortunately, we don't have the time to stand in one place." Helena points out, and they notice the shattered bodies thawing and reassembling.

The four of them rush to the shore, Callahan, mounted atop Moses, watches from a distance. Tightening the leather strap of his shield, he prepares to hunt them. As he pulls up on Moses' reins, he is stricken with pain, a violent cough erupting from his chest. He covers his mouth and pushes through the attack. With it over, he finds his hand covered in blood, its dark, sickening color making it almost unrecognizable. He hurries Moses to move as the fear sets in that his illness may take him before this battle is won.

Callahan cuts the distance between himself and his prey in half quickly. Again, he trots Moses, hoping to go in for the kill, when Hornet suddenly tackles the battlecat, Callahan soaring from his back while the two mechanical beasts fly into one of the local residences. Callahan quickly gets to his feet, knowing exactly who attacked him.

"Is today the day I finally collect the debt I am owed?" Callahan flashes the singular scratch in his otherwise flawless shield as he eagerly scans the area until he finally spots him: Liam the Lighting Spear. Clouds slowly cover what little sun is left, but Liam does not move or speak. A crack of electricity striking the ground between them punctuates the silence.

"You earn my gratitude, thief," Callahan says, thrilled at the chance to battle directly. "Here, I will prove I have no equal, or I will fall to the only man who has ever bested me. Either way..." The lightning strikes intensify as Callahan's armor powers up. The two knights ignore the world around them, not once breaking from each other's gaze. And for a brief instant, all stands still. Then:

"A glorious death awaits."

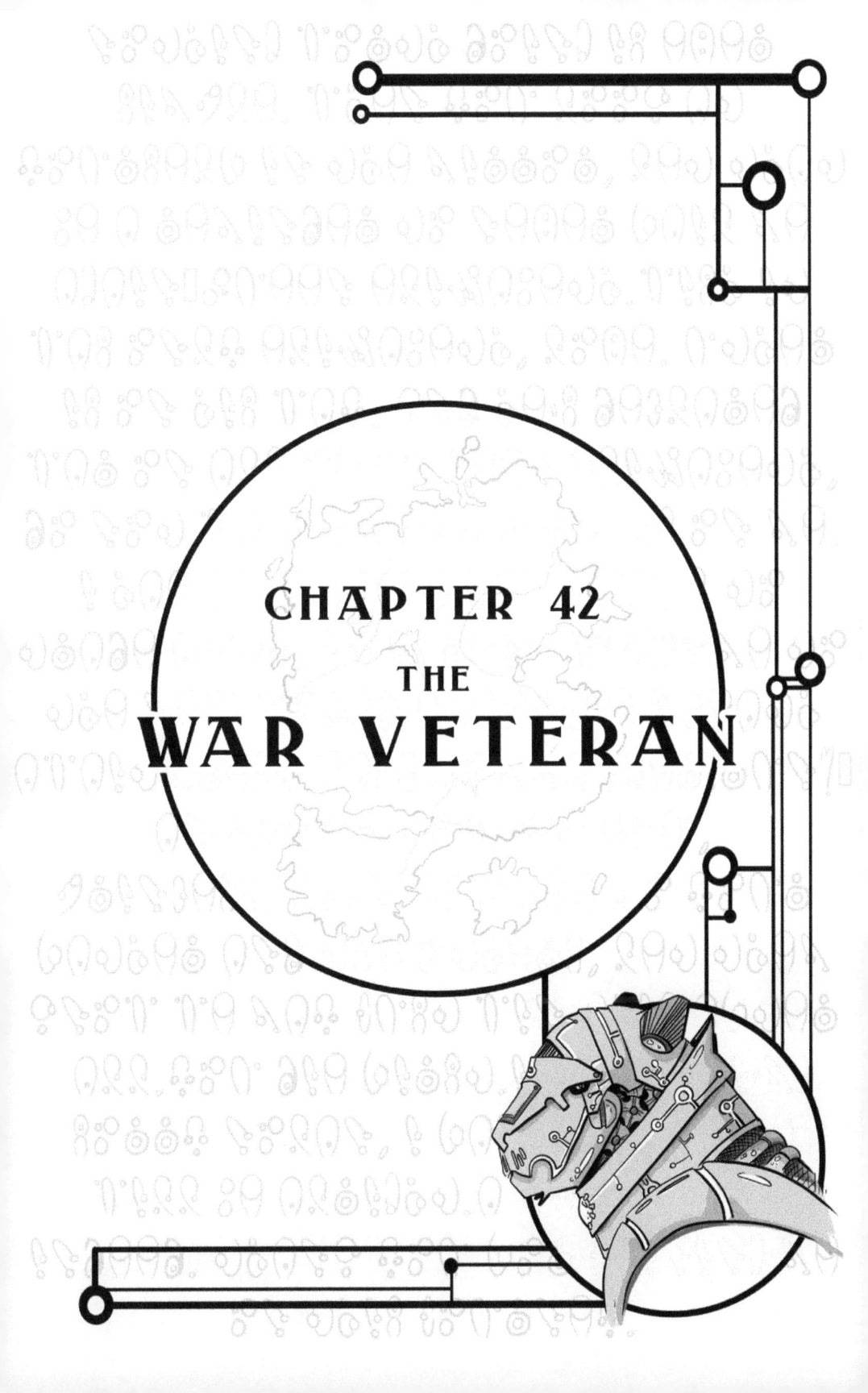

CHAPTER 42
THE
WAR VETERAN

Chapter 42

The War Veteran

Thunder reverberates through the streets of Riverhaven as Liam's spear meets Callahan's shield. The two battle-worn veterans mimic each other, blow for blow. Liam strikes rapidly, and each hit is more substantial than the last, while Callahan stands sturdy, an unmovable wall of defense. The onslaught of their engagement transforms the city around them. Glass shatters, doors fall from their hinges, and as the two find themselves in a standstill, entire buildings crumble.

Callahan uses his shield to push Liam back, creating distance between the two men. Liam quickly returns to the offensive, charging his spear before attacking. Once more, Callahan braces for the impact, this time, each of Liam's strikes is followed by a bolt of electricity. Try as he might, the fury of the assault gets the best of him. Callahan drops his guard for a mere moment, and Liam takes advantage. He spins his spear, sweeping his opponent's legs. Callahan hits the ground, and Liam goes for a killing blow. Instincts take over, and Callahan uses his Q.A.S. boosters installed in his shield to push himself away.

Escaping by the skin of his teeth, he rolls back to his feet. The time for defense is over, and he becomes the aggressor. As he charges forward, Callahan tosses his shield ahead of him. Liam can deflect the shield into the air, yet it still manages to force him backward. Using his speed, Liam is quick to steady himself just in time to dodge Callahan, who has barely jumped into the air, caught his shield, and brought it down upon him like a hammer. The impact leaves a sizable crack in the street.

Callahan's march doesn't end there; he is quick to toss the shield toward Liam again. Learning from his mistake, Liam deflects the shield to his side this time. Unfortunately, this leaves him open to a spear from Callahan. The attack drives Liam into the ground, where

Callahan thwarts him with various punches. He can defend himself enough to frustrate Callahan, who returns to a standing position before transitioning behind Liam, gripping him by the waist, and suplexing him into a nearby home.

Liam watches Callahan catch his breath as the house around him cracks and bends. The tone of the battle has intensified, leaving Liam no choice but to improvise. As Callahan reacquires his shield, Liam surveys the building for anything that may aid him. He notices this family has installed a series of connecting Q.A.S. Tech lights around the home, and the stones that power each light are the same as his spear.

Liam uses his weapon to lift himself back to his feet. Once standing, he wedges his spear into one of the lights and turns it on. As he had hoped, the spear absorbs the electricity from the building. Liam's hand trembles as the spear surges with power. Knowing it's only a matter of time before the unstable power overloads to deadly levels, he removes it from the light and aims at Callahan. With little time left, Liam twists the throttle. From outside the house, Callahan watches as a blinding light radiates from it, and an enormous lightning bolt comes charging at him.

Callahan shields himself from the blast but is still sent flying through the air before crashing into yet another home, this time crumbling around him. Liam's blast causes just as much damage to the building that houses him. Thankfully, he's able to escape before it falls on top of him. His relief is short-lived as a tremendous roar breaks out. From beneath the rubble, Callahan, atop Moses, returns to the battlefield.

Blood drips down Callahan's arm, as Liam's blast is doing notable damage. His shield is no longer pristine, now covered in blackened ash. He removes his helmet, more blood running from his right eye. Moses is also notably damaged, with many of her inner workings exposed, her right eye missing in ironic symmetry.

Callahan lifts his bloodied arm, the weight of which induces another wave of coughs. In the heat of battle, he doesn't bother covering his mouth. By the end of this medical episode, blackened blood flows down his face. The blood's discoloration does not go unnoticed by Liam, but there is no time for pity.

Determined not to allow Callahan to again gain the upper hand, Liam dashes forward. Although his attacks continue to be as fast as ever, he's unable to make contact with Callahan. When Callahan cannot defend a strike, Moses swipes away, protecting him. Not long after, the numerical advantage of the undead army gives Callahan an edge, allowing him to disarm Liam. Moses digs a nail into Liam's armor, touching the flesh underneath.

The slash may not be deadly, but it is still more profound than a flesh wound. Liam uses his agility to slide backward, leaving a streak of blood between them. His next move is an attempt to reach his spear, but before he can, his opponent tackles him into a memorial to those who lost their lives in Chief Ramon's liberation of Riverhaven. The force of his collision ruins the memorial's foundation. Unable to move, Liam prepares to be crushed, but to his surprise, he remains unharmed by the falling debris.

Hornet stands above him, protecting Liam by allowing the rubble to fall on top of her instead. His most loyal ally saved him in his greatest time of need. Hornet helps Liam mount her and howls a warning to his enemies of her intent to kill. Liam could not be more proud of Hornet's resolve, but it is apparent that Moses won their first encounter. Hornet's claws are torn or missing, and her gears creek as they move. Oil drips from most of her body. Liam's beloved friend is on his last leg.

With all she has left, Hornet charges into her final battle, her master mounted atop her. Callahan leads Moses, steering them headfirst towards their approaching opponents. Just as they are about to collide, Hornet leaps over them. This bait-and-switch surprises Callahan and, in the time it takes him to get his bearings, Liam recovers his spear.

Yet again, the two warriors stand across from one another, but this time feels different. Liam revs his spear, and Callahan tightens his shield. Hornet bares her fangs, and Moses digs her claws into the ground. Simultaneously, they charge one another. Their beasts swipe and bite at each other. Callahan's shield and Liam's spear rapidly make contact with one another. The chaos of scrimmage rivals that of a hurricane. Lightning crashes as thunder echoes around them. Then, just when they think they have come to a standstill again, Hornet tears off one of Moses' legs. As she loses her footing, Hornet bites into her neck and pins her to the ground. Callahan goes flying from her back, unable to do anything as Hornet tears out Moses' throat, leaving the creature lifeless.

This killing blow takes its toll on Hornet as well. Even after her victory, the faithful hound can barely stand. Liam dismounts and embraces his old friend. Tears fall from his eyes as he pets Hornet one last time, reassuring her that she is a good girl and can rest easy now. Hornet lays and takes her breath in the arms of her best friend. Liam turns to Callahan, who sees the rage in Liam's eyes and knows his fate is sealed.

Liam charges his spear beyond a point he ever has before. Callahan stands determined to go out fighting, even though he knows the outcome of what's to come. He turns his shield to protect himself, but it's too late. Liam strikes with such integrity that sound itself can not keep up. Callahan's shield, now split in two, falls to the ground. Liam uppercuts Callahan high into the air before catching him atop his spear. As the weapon digs into Callahan's chest, Liam twists the handle, and a bolt of electricity rips through his back and shoots into the air. It is done.

Liam gently places Callahan on his knees and removes his spears. Callahan can no longer feel his body, but the pain inside it is gone. Liam puts away his spears and kneels to be eye-to-eye with his rival.

"How do we end this?"

Callahan looks up at the Knightfall as it hovers high above.

"Unlimited bodies... yet only one mind..."

Liam looks up at the nightfall, understanding Callahan's cryptic message. He goes to find the others, but Callahan calls out to him one last time.

"Finish what you have started...knight."

In a flash, Liam uses his spear to decapitate Callahan. The head hits the ground, and Liam speaks his parting words:

"Rest easy...commander."

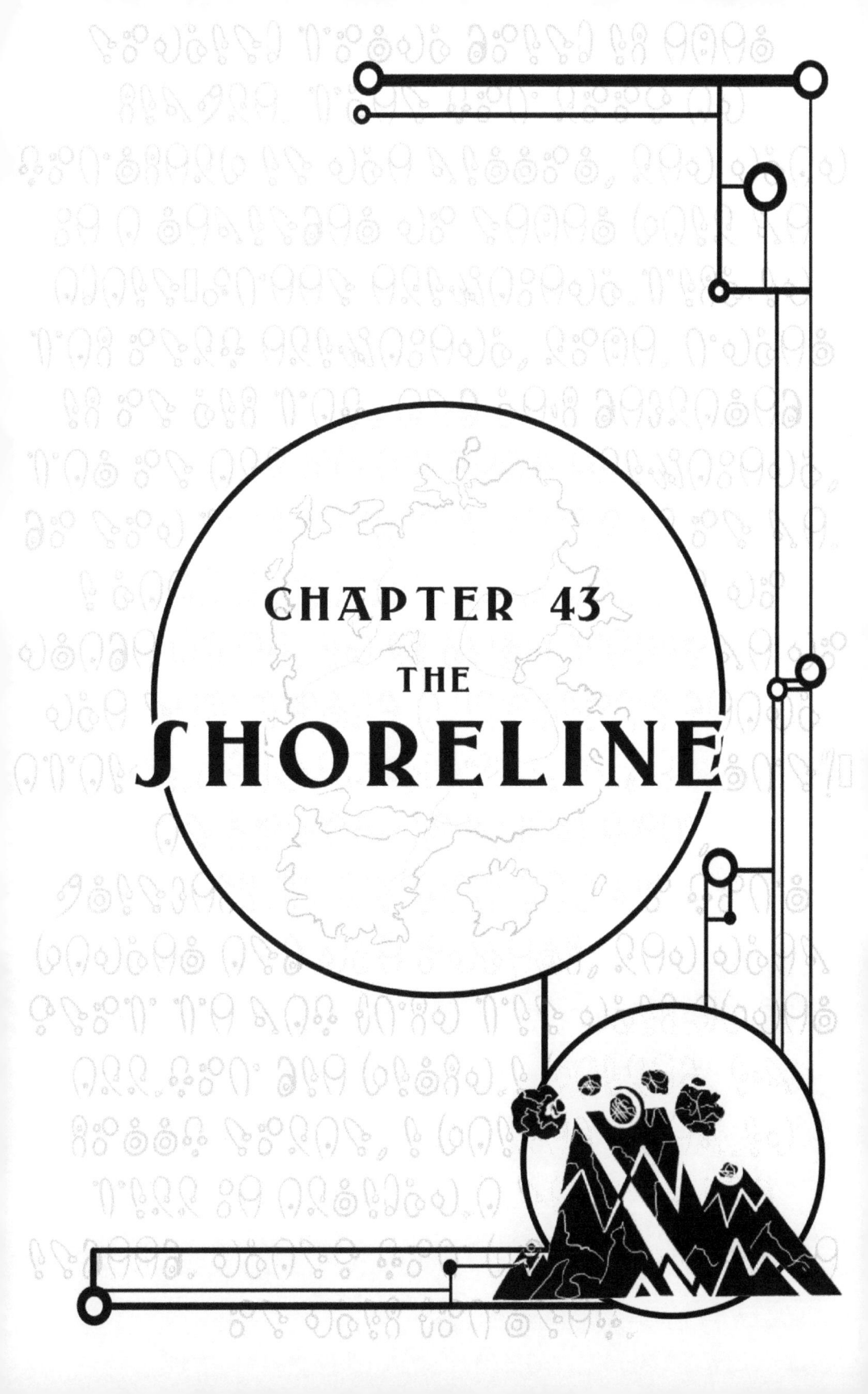

CHAPTER 43
THE
SHORELINE

Chapter 43

The Shoreline

Through the eyes of his puppets, Uther watches his prey flee towards Riverhaven's shoreline. With his will, Uther orders the undead army to chase Ramon, Helena, Luna, and Creed.

Determined to get Luna to safety, the others prioritize escaping over fighting. Uther uses this to his advantage, gathering more and more of his forces behind them. With the ocean in view, the dead grow more aggressive, increasing their speed and tossing spears and pitchforks.

With no choice, Helena tells the others to go ahead without her and turns to the horde. She fires arrow after arrow in a failed attempt to slow down their pursuers. Out of options, she again charges her bow but holds the attack longer than ever. Helena takes aim, waits for the army to get as close as possible, leaps backward, and releases her shot. The sizable frozen blast creates an ice cheval de frise, a final obstacle between her and the monsters.

Helena lands on her feet, but her bow is no longer there, its mechanics destroyed. She watches as the frontline of the undead collides with arctic spikes. Not once do they hesitate to use their bodies to create safe passage for those behind them. Ever the warrior, Helena readies herself for an unwinnable battle. Luckily, before she has to defend herself, Marcus and Zayn make their arrival. Behind them, yet another horde of undead marches.

Zayn erects a stone wall in front of Helena, but the barricade is notably less defined than his typical structures. As he and Marcus regroup with Helena, Zayn creates a second stone wall to block the horde chasing them. This second wall is even more haphazard than the one before.

"I fear the worst, Helena," Marcus confesses as he pulls Helena close. They hold each other for as long as possible, then embrace a reminder of what they are fighting for.

"Hate to be that guy," Zayn warns, exhausted, "but my walls won't last long." On cue, the undead ram their bodies into the walls. Each time, I broke the structure down more and more. "Orens haven't had to use magic this way in ages. I'm sorry, but my body wasn't prepared for this."

"No need to apologize, you have done more than enough." Helena thanks Zayn. "The others are up ahead – all but Liam. Have you seen him?"

"No, but not too long after we heard Creed, it sounded like all hell broke out downtown. I'm willing to bet he has something to do with it," Marcus tells her. Together, they decide it is best to regroup with the others, trusting their friend will return to them alive.

Helena, Zayn, and Marcus race forward and, in a short time, have eyes on Creed and Ramon fending off a few dozen assistants. To their glee, Liam also fights beside them, helping even the odds as the three of them do all they can to keep Luna safe. Seeing this as the final opportunity to strategize together before the one last push towards their escape, Zayn uses the ground to quickly carry Helena, Marcus, and himself to others. Once everyone is together, he summons a stone cage around them, protecting them inside while the dead ferociously carve at it from the outside.

"I'm afraid that's all I have left, friends," Zayn apologizes, and he falls to the ground. Liam helps him while the others decide what to do next.

Ramon is the first to speak up. "Our only option is to retreat. We are almost to my ship; it's docked just up ahead." He points down the shoreline where the ship's sails can be seen.

"But then what? We float in the ocean in hopes someone comes to save us before these things learn to swim?" Marcus questions, believing Ramon's suggestion only delays the inevitable.

"What else would you have me do? I will not have my daughter dying on this beach!" Ramon barks back. Luna will always be his priority.

"So a coffin at the bottom of the sea is a better idea?" Marcus claps back.

"Stop it! There are more than enough of them out there; no need to fight amongst each other!" Liam de-escalates the two. "Retreat may be one of the better options. This isn't a fight we can win down here."

"What do you mean 'down here?'" Creed asks. Liam points his spear to the Knightfall flying high above.

"Uther controls them all from there. If we take him down, they will all follow suit."

The others question the certainty of Liam's claim, but a simple nod from him is enough to convince them.

"Gee, if only we had wings, this would all be over." Marcus says facetiously. Although the group is not fond of him, they can't help but acknowledge his words. As they contemplate another way, Helena watches the undead knights strike away at the cell, each hit causing more cracks in the structure.

With their time running out, she turns to them with a suggestion. "I may be able to–"

Zayn interrupts, "The Orens. I may be tapped out, but I'm one of many. If I can get the Disciples to fight, this war is over. Hell, if I only get Rhea and Chili to join in, the odds move in our favor."

"But will they?" Liams doubts.

"The chances are slim, I won't lie, but they have to realize that Goldleaf is next. They won't give a damn about helping humans, but maybe I can convince them that bringing the fight here is the only way to save our home from ruin."

"Let's face facts: our chances of surviving here are slim. Zayn's plan might be the best chance we have at stopping Uther," Marcus speaks up in support. "This has to end here. Losing Riverhaven is a tragedy, but if he does this to even a handful of Orens, he'll be unstoppable."

"The boy's right," Ramon gives Marcus his approval. "Allow me to get Luna out to sea, then I'll stay behind. With the knights' help, we can hold them off as long as we can. That will give Zayn a chance to gather as many allies as he can."

"I will not leave you behind!" Luna demands.

"Don't be stupid, young lady, I should have never let you convince me to let you stay in the first place," Ramon rebukes his daughter before bringing her in for a hug. "It will be your job to let your father know what has happened, warn the others, save what's left of our people, and maybe give the rest of Grandiose the fighting chance we didn't have."

"So we have a plan." Marcus takes the lead, continuing, "Helena, Liam, and I will stand our ground here. Creed will help Chief Ramon get Luna to that ship and make it back to us as soon as possible. Zayn, do you have enough in you to tunnel away like you did in the desert?"

"I should be able to at least get to the swamp."

"That is settled. We have our orders. Knights, to my side."

Liam and Helena take their positions next to Marcus. Luna again jumps on Creed's back while Zayn takes a deep breath. Simultaneously, Creed crashes through one side of the stone cage as Zayn tunnels into the sand below. Marcus releases his sword, guiding it through the heads of a dozen corpses surrounding them.

The knights stand their ground as Ramon, Creed, and Luna make a break for the ship. Zayn's defenses finally crumble and the corpses break through the stone walls, the cage turning to dust. Liam strikes first, charging into the horde, creating an electric buzz saw by swinging his spear in front of him. Marcus cuts down the undead who make it past Liam, leaving the unarmed Helena as the last line of defense. The knights fight with all their hearts, rejuvenated by the prospect of Zayn's success. Unfortunately, they do not realize they are being watched the entire time.

Just as Uther can see through his army's eyes, he can hear through their ears. Their plan is already compromised. From Knightfall's helm, an Uther arrogantly aims his cannons at Ramon and Creed. With just a thought, he fires one directly at them. It flies to the ground at such speed that no one has time to react.

The cylinder makes contact right behind Ramon, blasting him across the sand and into the ocean. Due to his size, Creed fares better, and he only travels one or two body lengths away from the impact. He makes it back up in time to see Luna lying unconscious between him and the devices. As the cylinder primes to launch the sharpened purple quartz, Creed races towards the young girl. Luna comes just in time to watch Creed jump in front of the stone streaks flying at her. His scales do their best to deflect the assault, but he can only take so much.

What is only moments feels like ages, but soon, the stones stop coming. Luna remains unharmed, but Creed turns to her in pain. He falls to one knee, and she notices a few dozen shards deep in his chest. The stones illuminate while a teary-eyed Creed looks at Luna and begs,

"Run!"

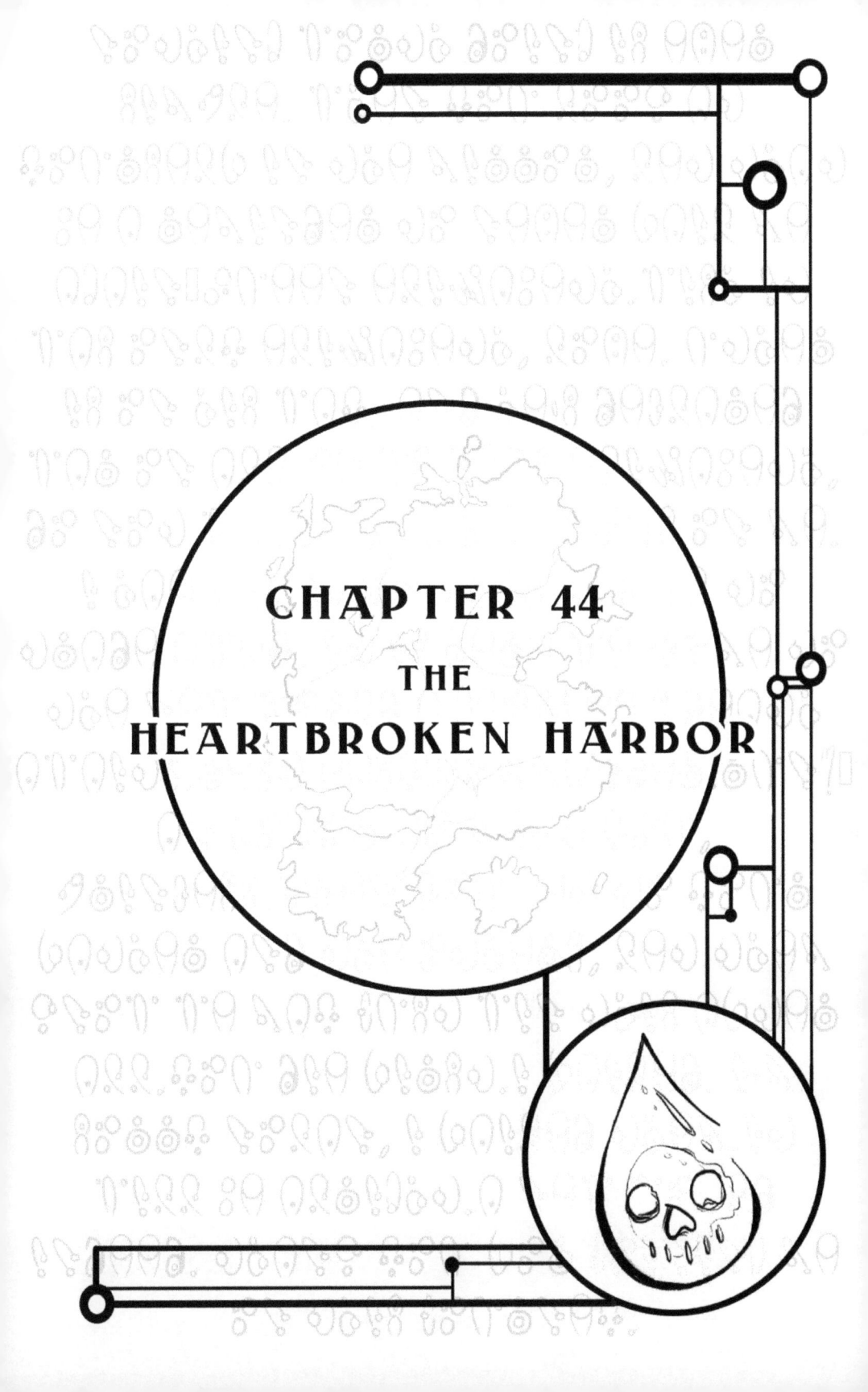

CHAPTER 44
THE
HEARTBROKEN HARBOR

Chapter 44

The Heartbroken Harbor

"Helena!"
"Marcus!"
"Liam!"

These are not war cries, but Creed's plea for help. He tries to pull the quartz from his chest, but the more he yanks at them, the deeper they seem to embed themselves. Above, Uther can feel his grasp on Creed's mind tighten, but in all his training, Uther never prepared to control a Dargone. Creed is stronger than the hordes of citizens and knights Uther has brought back, fighting Uther's control and death itself. Determined to catch this new prize, Uther loosens his grip on the horde, focusing on Creed. This brief relapse slows the horde long enough for Marcus, Helena, and Liam to answer Creed's call.

The knights find Luna attempting to walk to her father, Chief Ramon, who has washed to shore unconscious. Close by, Creed claws away at his skin, doing all he can not to lose himself. Tears flow as smoke begins to rise from underneath his scales. His tail pounds as he sinks his claws into the sand. Yet Creed is no longer in agony; he feels nothing at all. His life is fading, and Uther is taking control. Creed's heart stops, the thud of his body hitting the sand acting as a final warning of what's to come.

"We need to get Luna and Ramon to that ship, and fast," Liam urges.

"You're the only one who can carry Ramon; it has to be you, Liam," Marcus orders. "Helena and I will cover you. Just get back as soon as you can; we're going to need the help."

With everyone in agreement, Liam throws Ramon over his shoulders and moves quickly towards the ship. Alone, Marcus and Helena cautiously move closer to Creed's lifeless body.

"He's really gone...just like that." Helena mourns her friend from afar.

"Take solace in knowing that he gave his life protecting a place he could finally call home," Marcus consoles her. "But why hasn't he changed?" Keeping their distance, Marcus and Helena circle their fallen ally, both ready to attack.

"Maybe the magic doesn't work on his kind?" Helena hypothesizes.

"If only we were so lucky."

At that moment, Marcus and Helena notice the undead army again moving towards them; unlike before, the horde moves slowly and is no longer aggressive. Instead, they keep their distance from Creed's body, creating a barricade that traps everyone within the shore.

"That can't be a good sign," Marcus warns, and draws his blade

With the army in place, the Knightfall's engines roar, and the sky darkens again. The air thickens as a horrified Helena, with Marcus by her side, watches Creed's dead body rise from the sand. The Dargone's shadow looms over them, the life in his eyes gone. Marcus lunges forward and takes a hefty swing at his former friend. The slash is ineffective, and Creed does not flinch before retaliating with his tail. Creed's inaugural attack sends Marcus backward, his body digging into the sand.

With Marcus no longer a threat, Creed turns his attention to Helena. As he slowly walks toward her, his flesh melts off his skull and the purple flames underneath grow. Creed stops just shy of Helena, and for a time, they stand face-to-face. Not once does Helena seem intimidated by the flaming head of Dargone in front of her. Creed, on the other hand, seems hesitant, almost as if he recognizes her.

Nevertheless, the truce is short-lived.

Creed makes the first move, swiping directly at Helena's head. With ease, she ducks down and kicks at his legs. Creed blocks, his tail swinging at her, before clawing at her back. Helena quickly rolls forward, allowing only the tip of Creed's claw to make contact. Steel sparks jump from her armor, but Helena stays unfazed. With her next move, she pushes herself into the air, turns midair, and kicks at Creed's head. He grabs her leg before contact and slams her to the ground. As her body bounces from the impact, he uses his opposite hand to punch her back down. This attack forms a small crater at his feet, likely breaking Helena's ribs. Blood flies from her mouth, hitting Creed's skull, only for the flames to evaporate it.

Now, with a chance to end Helena's life, Creed goes for a second punch, only for Marcus's blade to hit his fist before Creed makes contact.

The blade bounces off and returns to Marcus' hand. Ineffective, but the attack is enough to draw Creed's attention. He picks Helena up from the collar of her armor and attempts to use her as a projectile. Believing her to be unconscious, he is caught off guard when she wraps her legs around his arm and twists her body to break it. Marcus does not hesitate to take advantage, charging forward and unleashing countless attacks upon Creed. Very few of the slashes do any damage, irritating Creed more than anything.

Creed wraps his tail around Helena's neck, pulls her from his broken arm, and uses her to bat away Marcus. He tosses Helena at Marcus, and together, they plummet to the ground. Quickly, the knights make it back to their feet, only to see Creed charging at them. As Creed's intensity grows, any sympathy he may have had left for the knights was gone. Mid-charge, Creed leaps into the air high above them, using his healthy arm to punch down into the earth.

Seeing the attack coming, Marcus and Helena jump to their sides, dodging the attack. With his broken arm, Creed makes a follow-up attack, snapping the bone into place and healing mid-punch. Marcus is the victim of the surprising feat, taking the punch directly to the chest. His heart skips a beat, leaving him open to a second jab to the jaw. To prevent Marcus from taking another attack, Helena runs up Creed's back, jumps up, and hammers down both fists to the back of his skull.

For the first time, Creed stumbles, he gives the knights enough time to put a little over an arm's length between them. Creed shakes off Helena's attack, bolting forward to continue his raid. Helena and Marcus do their best to block or deflect the blitz of slashes and punches, but Creed's fury is too much. A punch to the gut, followed by a tail to the back of the head, drives Helena to the ground. With her down, Creed focuses the entirety of his power on Marcus. With each punch Marcus defends, Creed pushes him further away from Helena. Aggravated by his hands continuously hitting Marcus' blade, Creed uses his tail to slap it out of his hand. An unarmed Marcus becomes a victim of Creed's most vicious combination yet. Haymaker after haymaker, followed by Creed's tail smacking Marcus off his feet, only for the Dargone to catch the knight by his head, repeatedly smashing it into the sand.

If this battle were taking place in the city street and not the beach, Marcus would already be dead, his skull plastered on the cobblestone. At least Marcus lives, if not by a thread, the sand soaking up the blood dripping from his nose. Creed's tail grips Marcus's feet, lifting him upside down before hitting him in the stomach with a fury of jabs. Sensing victory, Creed decides to toy with his victim, even in death, showing his childish side. He tosses Marcus into the air, flipping him the opposite way. Before Marcus hits the ground, Creed slaps him across the back, sending him flying for the umpteenth time. With playful malice Creed chases after the battered Marcus and leaps on him.

Finally bored with his prey, Creed decides it's time to end Marcus' life. The undead Dargone pins down the knight's arm, leaving Marcus' neck open for the killing blow. Creed bares his fangs, ready to take his life. With death in front of him, Marcus looks to the sky.

"I'm sorry Nolan, I failed."

His final words pause Creed's attack and, for an instant, Uther loses control. Marcus can again see his friend in Creed's eye for a moment. Unfortunately, the feeling doesn't last long, and after shaking his head, Creed again bares his fangs. Intent to kill, he goes for the throat, but before he makes contact with Marcus, something grabs him by the tail and, with ease, pulls him off Marcus. The Dargone finds him slammed into as if he weighs nothing more than the average man. Marcus looks up, assuming Liam has come to his rescue, but Helena has come to his aid.

Just as baffled, Creed looks over at Helena and sees an intensity in her that sends chills down his spine. Her muscles are tight, and her breathing is calmed. Her heart beating like a drum, all her previous wounds missing. Creed stands, and the scent of something familiar to him reaches his nose. Before he can make sense of it, Helena's elbow is deep in his stomach. Her movement was so fast that he didn't realize she was on the attack. Again, Helena kicks him across the face before he can move, knocking one side of his jaw off the hinge. Creed now finds himself at the end of an assault that rivals his own.

Helena whales away at Creed, each punch hurting more than before the last. Marcus watches in awe as Helena beats down Creed like a giant facing a child when he realizes she is changing. With each hit, she grows in size, her armor breaking off as she moves. Her skin is changing color as it seems to harden. Then, before his eye, the most glorious crimson wings sprout from her back. Soon, her punches are followed by a whip of her tail. And as the last armor falls to the ground, she lets out a heroic roar, embracing the beauty of her true form, a final punch sending Creed soaring across the sand.

Marcus collects himself, determined to get closer to Helena. He makes his way to her, but still in pain, he loses his footing. Marcus stumbles but instead finds himself back on the ground. He lands in the arms of a heavenly crimson-scaled Dargone. Her wings glisten in the sunset and her eyes are piercing yet inviting. Her snow-white hair drapes down her back, only broken by the tail she wraps around him. Like a love-struck teenager, Marcus looks up at her and, with a giant smile, says,

"An honor to meet you, princess."

CHAPTER 45
THE
LAST STAND

Chapter 45

The Last Stand

The earth outside Goldleaf's swamp bridge opens, and an exhausted Zayn crawls out from the underground tunnel. He can barely close it, so worn down, his magic is useless. After pulling himself up, Zayn trudges to the closest tree. Once in reach, he places his hand on its bark and thinks, *'Send help.'* Through the plant life, he knows Titus will hear his plea. Knowing it may be some time before aid can reach him, Zayn turns his back to the tree, sliding down it to a sitting position.

Deep breath after deep breath, the Oren tries to recover. Zayn closes his eyes, listening to the world around him. The ocean crashes against the sandy beach like a symphony. The breeze whistles through the tree like an operatic chorus. Even the hum from the Knightfalls engine adds to the harmony. All of these sounds he could never hear were hidden away in Goldlleaf.

Zayn finds himself at peace when his rhapsody of revelation is interrupted by a familiar sound, another's breathing. Opening his eyes, he sees a hooded figure walking towards him. He hurries to his feet, raising his fist, prepared to fight. The hooded figure stops. Expecting a fight, Zayn attempts to create a defense of stone spikes, but at last, all that rises is pebble-sized rocks. The hooded figure removes their cloak, and although hair covers half of their face, without question, he recognizes Elizabeth.

"Flew all this way back to finish the job?" A worn-out Zayn drops his guard before falling back against the tree.

"I made a mistake. No, I've made many mistakes," Elizabeth confesses as she pulls back her hair, exposing her missing eye and the scar that replaces it. "I wish to rectify at least one of them."

Elizabeth reaches out to Zayn with a vial in her hand. He takes it from her and looks it over. The color is unfamiliar to him, and after opening it, he finds the smell putrid.

"It's an antidote for the poison made from my blood. If you get it to your father, there's a chance he'll survive." Elizabeth returns the cover to her head and begins to walk away. Zayn leaps to his feet, grabbing her hand before she gets too far.

"Where are you going?" He asks her. Elizabeth turns to face him, stunned to see Zayn's concern.

"I don't know, but I refuse to go back to him."

"Then don't maybe Helena and the others... Talk to them, maybe they will forgive you."

"I don't deserve their forgiveness, I don't deserve any honesty. I am a monstrosity born to the streets who was shown the heavens only as a reminder of a life I could never have." Elizabeth pulls her hand away from Zayn.

"Don't be a fool! You and I both know no matter who comes out the victor here, you're a wanted woman. Not to mention, you are far from a horror!" The passion in Zayn's voice that is unfamiliar to Elizabeth. "Your mere existence is proof of a better future. Have you made mistakes? I'm certain, but that doesn't justify some self-proclaimed death sentence."

"What do you suggest? I fall into your arms so you can claim the praise that comes with saving me? I am not trading in one false paradise for another." Elizabeth's words are harsh, but subconsciously, she isn't opposed to the idea.

"No. I mean, if that's what you want, but no, that's not what I'm saying." Zayn removes Elizabeth's hood. " You said you want to repent, do so by standing in front of the world not hiding in its shadows. Be the beacon for a future greater than I'll present."

Zayn's words take Elizabeth back. Despite all she has done to him, he still wants more for her. He looks at her and sees something she doesn't believe exists. Most importantly, he speaks of a world with no cages.

"Why are you so certain of my redemption?" Elizabeth, still baffled by Zayn's optimism, takes a step back.

"Look around if your fall can bring all this, just imagine what can come of your rise."

Just then, a vine reaches from the swamp and wraps around Zayn's ankle. Titus has gotten his message and is ready to bring him home. With Marcus, Helena, and Liam relying on him, Zayn knows it's time for him to leave. Determined not to give up on Elizabeth, Zayn reaches his hand out to her.

"I cannot promise the road ahead will be easy but I forgive you and more importantly I believe in you."

*****

On the opposite side of the beach, Helena introduces Marcus to her secret side. As a royal Dargone, Helena – or Krisom, as she was once known – sports large red-scaled wings. She stands at an arm's length taller than Marcus, and although slender, she is almost entirely muscled. Where once was a head of crimson hair, she now dawns long diamond-white locks. Her ruby scales reflect the light, giving her silhouette a mesmerizing aura. Yet, with all these differences, her violet eyes remain the same.

"So many times I wanted to tell you, but I was so scared you'd reject me," Helena confesses as Marcus stares at her silently. "When I lost my mother, I feared it would only be a matter of time before my secret would be exposed, so I ran." Helena makes her way over to where Marcus' sword lays in the sand and picks it up. "I thought I left any chance of family in Dakuhm, but then I met Nolan, and he gave me that and more. Even knowing the truth, he gave me a home, showed me how to be a knight, and led me to you."

Helena returns to Marcus and hands him the sword, who dusts the sand off his blade before sheathing it. He takes Helena's hand and gives it a gentle kiss.

"There has yet to be a day that I find you anything but the most beautiful thing in my life, and that will never change. I look forward to getting to know Krimson the same way I have come to love Helena." Marcus' acceptance means the world to Helena. She leans down to press her head against his. As they embrace, the world melts away; together, they feel whole.

Regrettably, the moment is short-lived; Creed has returned to his feet. The undead Dargone pushes his jaw back into place. Uther wills his horde to attack again, acknowledging that the battlefield has changed. Creed takes to all fours and rushes into the fight. Helena quickly meets him halfway, the two clashing together with monstrous impact. As the two Dargones brawl, Marcus fights through his pain and dashes into the horde.

Blow for blow, Helena and Creed beat each other into the ground. The crater created by their scuffle acts as a makeshift ring. With his punches not making any headway, Creed hooks Helena's leg and rams her into the crater wall. With her pinned down, he hammers away at her ribs. To escape, Helena wraps her tail around Creed's waist and tosses him before catching and driving him to the ground with power. Without letting go, she repeatedly crashes his back into the crater's floor. Each slam causes the hole to grow inches closer to the ocean.

Sensing defeat, Creed swipes furiously at Helena's eyes. Although the attacks cannot scratch her cornea, the distraction is enough to loosen Helena's grip. Creed rolls backward to his feet and ponces forward, tackling Helena to the ground. Now, on top of her, he grabs her neck and slams her head to the ground several times; again, the crater grows. Water starts to pour into the massive hole; using this to his advantage, Creed holds down Helena's snout in an attempt to drown her.

With her head now underwater, Helena is running out of air. In a last-ditch effort to survive, she wrestles just enough to get her mouth around Creed's wrist. The water turns red as she bites Creed's hand clean off. In a panic, Creed tries to keep her down with the other hand, but he now lacks the strength to submerge Helena. With a whip of her tail, Helena pushes Creed off her, then lands a punch that breaks his orbital plate. Again, on her feet, Helena spits out Creed's hand, but once in the water, the body part swims its way back to its owner.

Creed's hand attaches while the water reaches the Dargone's waist. He looks Helena in the eye and goes on the attack. Using her wings, she floats back, dodging his advance. Helena's agility leaves Creed off balance, and she makes the most of the opening. She takes to the air, swoops down with her claws, and tears her nails into Creed's chest. With her momentum, Helena flies Creed across the crater, slamming it into its wall, and like a dam, it breaks and collapses, followed by a rush of ocean water.

The crashing wave of water causes the front end of the beach to crumble into the ocean. In an instant, Riverhaven's famous shoreline is no longer there. Even the undead horde struggles to traverse the now uneven terrain. Marcus, meanwhile, is quick to adapt, using the chaos to thin out the moving corpses, cutting out their legs from beneath them. He pushes as many as he can into the waters, watching the struggle to return to dry ground. Although Marcus seems to be winning this battle, his concern for Helena has yet to resurface.

Marcus fights his way to where he last saw Helena. He surveys the waters to no avail, panic setting in as he fears the worst. Marcus calls for her as he continues to bat away the undead. Just as all hope seems lost, Helena's wings break through the water, and she flies into the sky. In her hands was an unconscious Creed. Helena tosses the Dargone above her head and grabs his tail. Higher and higher, she flies until she is barely visible. After spinning Creed around to build momentum, Helena releases him into the horizon, and his body lands in some of the deepest oceans. Creed sinks into the navy abyss while a victorious Helena joins Marcus on dry land.

Upon landing, Helena flaps her wings, creating a gust of wind that pushes back the undead horde and relieves Marcus.

"We can't hold them off forever, Helena," Marcus vocalizes while continuing to swing away at the undead.

"I can fly us up to the war ship but we'd be leaving Liam to fend for himself."

"He'd want us to take the shot if he thought he had one," Marcus reminds her of the mission. Helena recognizes he is correct, so she grabs him by the hand and takes him off. The horde jumps at them, trying to pull them back down. Marcus defends them, cutting off the hands and arms in the way. Before long, the two are high in the air, facing what may be their greatest challenge. As they soar closer to Knightfall, Liam loads Luna and Ramon onto the escape ship. Luna is first to notice the ruby Dargone flying towards the warship. Liam looks to the sky and grins. Before he pushes Luna out to sea, he leaves her with a message for the other survivors:

"When you get to your father and the others, let them know we may just win this after all."

CHAPTER 46
THE
DEVIL AT THE HELM

Chapter 46

The Devil at the Helm

From above, Uther looks down at a battlefield no longer in his favor. His army is directionless, his general headless, and his mightiest weapon is on the ocean floor. Yet his arrogance will not let him feel fear. Instead, he brews in anger. Even as Marcus and Helena approach, he never doubts his victory. He is so confident they pose no threat he opens the stern door and welcomes their arrival. Not long before, the knight and Dargone find themselves face-to-face with Uther.

"How pathetic. When faced with a god, all this world has left to defend itself is an ant in armor and its pet lizard." Helena takes offense to his comment, growling at him while bearing down her teeth. "Do you truly believe you can win here? Why? Because you swatted down a few flies on your way to me? Their usefulness is their expandability. Callahan I'll give you; I'd hoped he'd last longer, but even he has had the taste of death on him for sometime."

"You sure talk a lot. I've come to find people tend to talk most when they're scared," Marcus taunts while drawing his katana.

"Scared! Of you?" Uther laughs. "The two of you are barely footnotes in my story. In fact the most relevance you will have in my history is as a hood mount. Because after I rip your innards from your body I will mount you at the front of this ship. That way you will be the first thing my enemies see as I approach, a final warning of what will come if they do not bow down to my future!"

The time for talking is over. Uther flexes his muscles, and tenable energy flies off him. His flaming indigo dreads wrap around his body like serpents, the head of his morningstar bursting into a matching flame as he tightens his grip on it. Now ready to fight, his eyes are no more than glowing purple orbs.

Marcus takes the initiative, seeking to make the first attack. With ease, Uther moves out of the way. He swings again, yet Uther seems floating away from the blade. Uther avoids Marcus' numerous slashes, moving side to side as if he is staking on ice. Just to mock Marcus' inability to hit him, Uther glides his way behind and strikes the knight in the back of his head with the hilt of his Morningstar. Marcus stumbles only for Uther to slide in front of him, kneeing him in the face before hitting the ground.

With Marcus outmatched, Helena joins the fight, flying at Uther with a fury of crawling attacks. Although she has some size on him, Uther can still avoid Helena's advances. Having to make slightly more effort to fend off the Dargone princess, Uther uses his weapon to deflect Helena's swipes. Needing to adjust her assault, Helena uses her tail to wipe at Uther's legs. In a haunting display of athletics, Uther cartwheels over her tail, kicking Helena across the face while avoiding the attack.

Once again, Uther toys with his opponent by putting one hand behind his back. Uther blasts Helena with a barrage of kicks before stomping down on her tail. He drags her back end towards him, landing a massive headbutt to Helena's chest, followed by running up her body and drop-kicking her in the face. Uther does all this and still manages to land on his feet, not once taking his hand from behind his back. Regrettably, Uther's arrogance is more than justified for Helena.

Uther twirls his morningstar, causing sparks each time it hits the floor below. Like a phantom, he fades from Helena's line of sight and only reappears behind her. Before she can react, Uther slams her to the ground by the hair. Laying on the floor, Helena looks up as Uther lifts his leg above his head. She soon finds his heel driven deep in her stomach, and the Knightfall shakes from the impact. Before Helena can catch her breath, Uther kicks her across the ship like a child playing with a ball.

With Helena down, Uther makes his way over to her to make the final blow. Finally, back on his feet, Marcus rushes to her aid. He fires his sword at Uther, landing a glazing blow against his cheek. Uther watches as the blade returns to Marcus. Uther laughs off Marcus' attack, wiping the blood off his cheek before a purple flame cauterizes the cut on his face. Now annoyed by Marcus' persistence, Uther removes him from the equation.

In one instance, Marcus finds himself nose-to-nose with Uther. With one hand, Uther lifts Marcus by the neck. He wedges his morningstar into the metal floor. With his now free hand, Uther pounds away at Marcus' ribs. The power of his punches alone can dent his armor. As blood drains from his mouth, Marcus is confident his ribs are broken. The pain is devastating, and in poetic irony, Marcus only finds relief when Uther tosses him into the Knightfall's armory.

An assortment of weapons fall atop a prone Marcus, among them several swords but, more importantly, a handful of bows. He scrambles to grab one. Once in hand, he tosses it at Uther with all his might. With ease, Uther moves out of its way, the weapon never having a chance to make contact.

"Did I knock what little intelligence you know of that head of yours? Or are so desperate you have forgotten how to use a bow." Uther's bass finally gets the best of him, for what he believes to have been a futile attack turns out to be a well-thought-out plan by Marcus; from behind Uther, an arctic arrow pierces his chest. To his disbelief, Helena managed to catch the bow and began a secondary assault on the king.

Arrow after arrow comes flying through Uther, leaving him in shock just long enough for Marcus to go on the offense. At the same time, Helena releases arrow after arrow as Marcus lounges in with an array of sword strikes. Without armor to keep the bow charged, it soon runs out of ammo to keep the duel attack going. Helena drops it and rushes in with a series of swipes to Uther's back. In unison, the two knights wear away at the stunned king's armor, but just as they feel they may have the upper hand, Uther summons enough strength to block both attackers.

With unbridled rage, Uther releases a wave of dark magic that pushes both Marcus and Helena away from him. His body begins to tremble as the scars etched in his skin begin to burn. A haunting fog fills the ship as the taste of death fills the air. Both Marcus and Helena fall to their knees as their beaten-down bodies heat up with pain. With the atmosphere within the Knightfall wholly changed, the ice arrows in Uther's body start to melt, but they are not all to succumb to his hell fire.

The knights watch as the heat from Uther's body melts away his armor's upper half, leaving only his blackened gauntlet. They are disgusted by Uther's self-mutilated anatomy, each part of his skin carved runes smoldering from the purple glow. Piercings made from the arrow start to heal themselves as Uther calls for his morningstar. The weapon lifts out of the ground and flies into his hand. Once rearmed, Uther's skin tears away, turning into ash as indigo flames overtake him.

No longer does a king, let alone a man, stand before Marcus and Helena. Only a fiery corpse with the sole intent to kill them. This new horror points his morningstar at Helena and warns her,

"You die first."

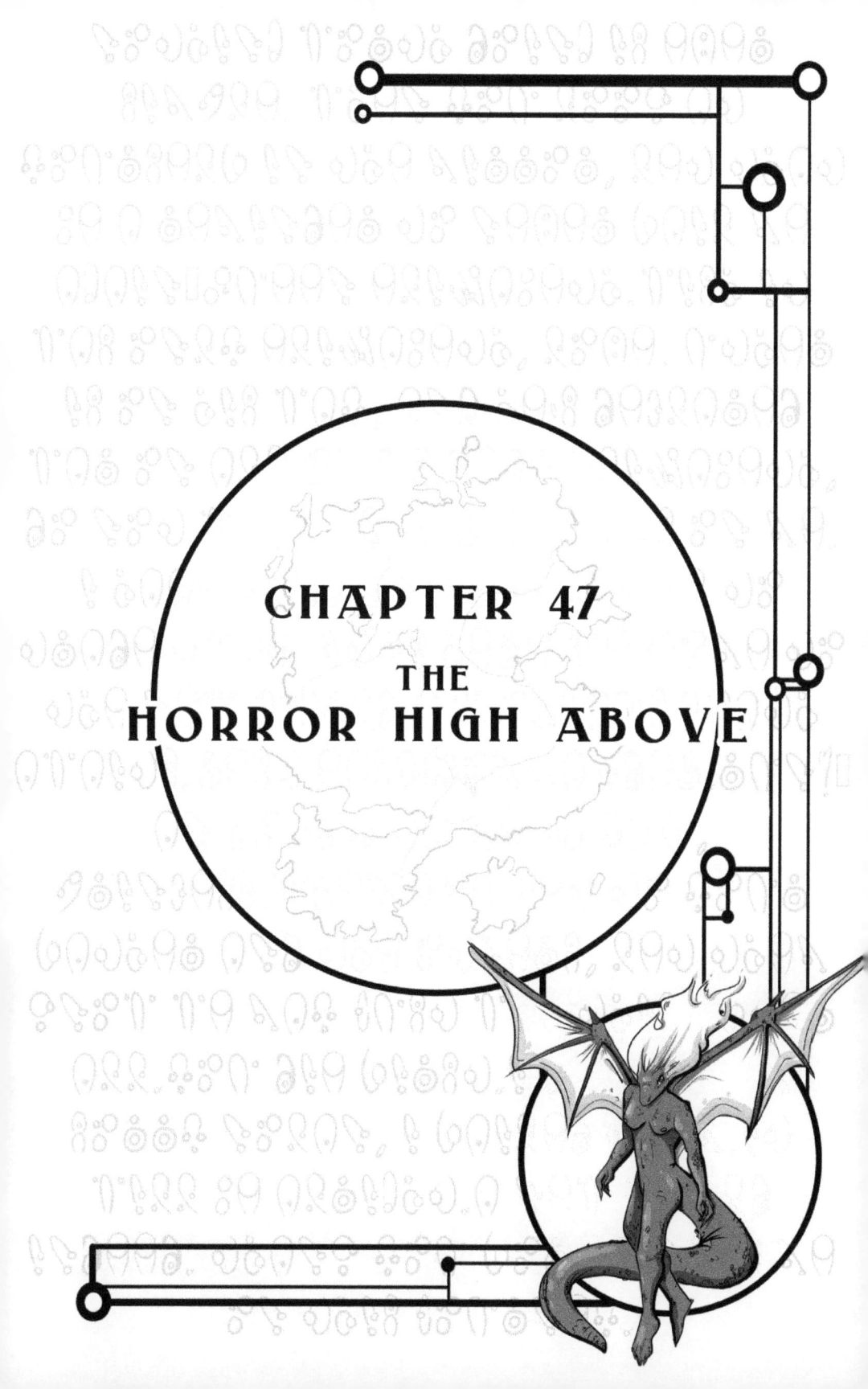

CHAPTER 47
THE HORROR HIGH ABOVE

Chapter 47

The Horror High Above

As night falls, the glow from Liam's spear continues to light up the shoreline. Under the rising moon, he cuts away at Uther's undead army, Riverhaven's last line of defense. High above him, the Knightfall hovers, but now the ship rattles, buckling under the magical pressure its captain gave. Even the horde suffers from Uther's ascent, taking longer to reassemble after Liam's attacks. Aware of the changes around him, Liam prays for the safety of his allies. Unfortunately for Marcus and Helena, his prayers have only reached deaf ears.

Within the Knightfall, the monster that Uther has become grows more powerful. Helena circles him, dodging his relentless attacks. Like shots from a cannon, Uther releases flaming orbs from the head of his Morningstar. Yet when the orbs hit the ship around, they don't damage it. Instead, it creates a burst of energy that fills the ship with unexplainable dread. Helena uses her agility to avoid impact while Marcus strives to land a blow, only to be slapped away easily by Uther.

Again, Marcus finds himself crashing into the ship's wall, the indigo haze making it ever more challenging to return to his feet. Laying on the floor, he watches Helena continue to weave in and out of Uther's relentless bombardment. He knows it is only a matter of time before Uther gets the best of her, but at the same time, Marcus knows Helena is their best chance of victory. With his body giving out on him, Marcus knows he may only have one final chance at creating an opening for her. He pulls himself up, leaving his sword on the floor. Gathering his will, Marcus detaches his sheath before shifting it to his dominant hand. With all his might, he charges at Uther and, with a roaring war cry, swings his sheath at the demonic king's head.

Without even a glance, Uther bats Marcus away like an annoying insect. Unbeknownst to him, this was part of Marcus' plan, for as the knight flies through the air, he uses the controls on his sheath to guide his sword directly towards Uther's head. In an instant, Uther finds Marcus' blade lodged where his right eye was once housed. Marcus again hits the ground but continues to drive his blade into Uther's skull. At last, the sword breaks through the back of the king's skull, and Marcus loses grip on the controls. With a sword wedged in his head, Uther finally ends his assault.

An exhausted Marcus watches through hazy eyes as Uther turns his attention towards him. In the blink of an eye, Marcus finds the king standing atop him, Uther's boot on his chest, pinning him down. He tries to punch away at the leg, but the monster never flinches. With his free hand, Uther swiftly grabs Marcus' shoulder plate and tears away all the armor on the knight's left arm. Uther stabs the tip of his Morningstar in the unprotected palm.

Marcus screams in excruciating pain as Uther digs his weapon deeper into the knight's hand. As the gash widens, the skin around it starts to burn. Marcus watches in fear as his hand slowly decays, his flesh tightening around his bones as the pigment blackens. It is not long before everything below the wrist is lost. The black magic now creeps its way up the rest of Marcus' limb, while Uther enjoys the suffering like a glutton during a holiday feast.

"Do not fret; soon, all life will be drained from your body, and your pain will end," Uther speaks as if he is doing Marcus a service, as if it wasn't he who caused the pain to begin with.

"Is this the legacy you have chosen to leave! Slowly murdering an entire race of people with sinister glee!" Marcus curses at Uther while the pain intensifies.

"Murder?" Uther looks down at Marcus, confused. "You truly believe I would do all this merely to perform genocide? How pedestrian." Uther laughs at the notion. He leans close to Marcus, pushing down on the knight's chest and hands even more. "I've promised my people a new world and tend to deliver on that promise. Humanity has grown stale, and it needs to be refreshed. Yet this process needs a jump start; that's what this is for."

"What the hell are you going on about? Refresh? Jumpstart? Sounds like the bull shit of a madman!" Even with his forearm succumbing to the decay, Marcus fights with Uther verbally.

"Such a simpleton, no foresight at all. You knight, look at all I have done with only a glimpse of Oren wisdom. Death bends to my will as I sail the sky like the sea." Even in this monstrous form, Uther's twisted passion comes through. "Yet I am no fool; I see the price this power has taken. My body, my blood, and my genetic code all limit me. But the Orens wield it with ease. Even as children, they play with fire as we do with dolls, and then, as adults, they can move mountains. Humans deserve that power." Marcus shudders at the realization of Uther's true intentions. He can barely believe what he is about to hear. "Ever since my father gave me Elizabeth, I knew what fate was in store for me. I will liberate the Orens from their mediocre existence and breed a new generation of man. Human hybrids are unshackled by our current constraints with access to all of the Orens' wisdom. A new world of perfection."

"You're crazier than I thought! The fact you think the Oren will see you as some hero and not the bastard you are is insanity," Marcus continues to bark back at Uther even as he can feel his life fading away.

"I don't need to be a hero; history will make me a revolutionary. The Orens will bend their knees over time. Their place will be clear, and their obligation to the new age will be inevitable. And if they disobey, your corpse will remind me of what I am willing to do to those in the way of change." Uther stands once more and pulls his morningstar from Marcus' hand. No longer interested in toying with him, Uther points his weapon at Marcus' head and readies his kill shot.

With Uther's morningstar directed for his head, Marcus is convinced this is the end, but he only finds relief when a fearsome Helena again saves him. The royal Dargone uses her massive claws to grab Uther's head from behind. She lifts him into the air, squeezing down on the skull and using her tail to hold down his arms. Much like glass hitting the pavement, the skull breaks into pieces. Bone fragments fall to the ground around Marcus, his sword now in two parts, an unfortunate casualty of Helena's attack.

With the rot creeping up his arm, Marcus quickly thinks of using a piece of wire as a tourniquet. He reaches for the hilt of the sword and, with what remaining blade is attached to it, cuts off the dying limb. Severing the arm just above the crawling decay seems to save the rest of Marcus' body, but stock is setting end as blood pours to the ground. Determined to survive, he turns the pommel towards himself and turns on its engine. With its flames, he cauterizes what is left of his arm. The pain is unbearable, but Marcus pushes through long enough to seal the wound but blacks out.

Helena watches as Marcus collapses; she drops Uther's headless body to the floor and rushes over to him. She never reaches him, for once again, Uther escapes death's embrace. The headless corpse pulls her back by her tail, slamming her to the ground repeatedly as if trying to drive her through the metal floor. With Helena bloodied and beaten, Uther reassembles his head again, drawing power from the ship.

This resurrection significantly affects the Knightfall, causing many of its mechanics to break or burst into flame. Unfazed by the destruction, Uther feeds off the ship's magic, growing in size while what remains of his human body melts away, leaving nothing but a blackened skeleton surrounded by indigo fire. Yet Uther's hubris finally gets the best of him, draining so much of the ship's power and causing one of its engines to blow out, the explosion causing the vessel to plummet downward.

As the Knightfall makes its impromptu descent, its inner workings fall apart. Panels fly from the walls as more and more of its electronics spark. Anything not bolted down, including the unconscious Marcus, starts to spiral towards the ship's bow. For the first time, a panicking Uther questions his next move. With more and more of the ship crumbling around him, he decides that his best option is to escape. Again, he draws from the energy from the magic around, expediting the Knightfall's collapse but molding the flames around him into wings.

With flight now at his disposal, Uther takes to the air and makes his way to the open at the back of the ship. Just as he reaches the sky outside the boat, Helena soars to place him, blocking his escape—the two brawl as the Knightfall plunges towards the sea. Not long into their fight, Helena comes to a horrifying realization: the ship's path does not lead to the sea but to the Void. Knowing Marcus still lies within the ship, she turns her attention away from Uther and dashes back into the ship.

Unaware of the situation, Uther chases Helena down, attacking her in the air again. With Marcus her priority, she tries to fight Uther off while returning to the ship. The king is relentless. They find themselves both crashing into the ground within the Knightfall. The impact of the two behemoths caused even more devastating damage to the ship, exacerbating its dive into the Void.

With no Uther in sight, Helena pulls herself out of the debris and rushes to find Marcus. After a hasty search, she sees him just outside the captain's chambers. Marcus is even more bloodied and battered than before but is again awake. The door to the chamber is broken off, and a massive hole has formed at the ship's bow; it's clear to Helena that Marcus, too, was attempting to escape. She quickly comes to his aid, helping him to his feet while assuring him they will survive. Woefully, her optimism is short-lived. As they make their way towards the opening in the bow, the Knightfall makes contact with the Void's wall.

From afar, the barrier surrounding the Void seems invisible, but now close to it, Marcus and Helena see a slight discolor in the air. The barrier ripples like the ocean as the head of the Knightfall breaks through. Merge contact with Void causes the Q.A.S Tech powering the ship to react instantly. The quartz stone bursts into shards as they seemingly lose all power. Time is now of the essence as the Void pulls the Knightfall deeper into its prison.

Ever aware that once within the Void's barrier, there's no escape, Helena and Marcus turn back to the ship's stern, hoping to outrun the Knightfalls free fall. Luckily for them, the Void's wall causes a visual distortion, warning the knights of its approach. Using her strength, Helena helps Marcus outpace the ancient magical force long enough to return to the main chamber. With each step, the Knightfall breaks apart behind them. In a short time, the moonlit sky is in front of the knight, and for a moment, hope is restored. Marcus and Helena take flight, freedom within their grasp, until they are again met with despair.

Just as Helena and Marcus reach the Knightfall's back door, Uther reemerges, confronting them, eager to continue the bloodshed. Grabbing Helena's wings, he tosses her to the floor, separating her and Marcus. She tries to crawl away, but Uther quickly mounts her back and pushes his forearm into the back of her neck. Any humanity Uther had seems to be gone; no longer a cunning king, only a demonic force lusting over death. He pulls at Helena's wings, pulling the one's bone from the socket, not letting go as it tears from her back. Helena is helpless as the ship falls apart around her. The front of the Knightfall crumbles as the island within the Void grows ever closer.

With no other choice, Marcus makes the ultimate sacrifice. Charging forward, he tackles Uther. Both of them roll forward, falling so fast that neither can stop. Finally, their momentum is halted when they crash into what little ship debris remains. Realizing what Marcus has done, Helena rushes to her feet, but is too late. Both Marcus and Uther have crossed the Void's impenetrable barricade.

Unaware of his fate, Uther returns to his attack, hands first at Helena's neck with the intent to kill. It is not Helena he makes contact with but instead the Void's invisible wall. Both of Uther's hands disintegrate, and he is quickly reminded of the pain sensation. Marcus quickly makes the most of this opportunity and rams his shoulder into Uther's back, trapping the king between himself and Void's one-wall defense. Before Marcus and Helena's eyes, the Void eats away at Uther until he is no more. The battle is over, yet this is no time for celebration.

The Knightfall is nearly wholly trapped within the Void, Marcus included.

"Helena, now is your chance to leave before the rest of this ship goes down." With his fate sealed, he begs Helena to leave while she still can.

"I'm not leaving without you!" She refuses at first, tears running down her face.

"Don't be a fool; we all know the void is a one-way trip. There is no reason we both have to die here," Marcus insists as he, too, is now crying. "There's more out there for you; I know that now more than ever." Helena backs away from the Void's mystical wall, staying one step ahead while trying to think of a way to save Marcus. "Nolan knew you were the best of us, that greatness was destined to walk side-by-side with you. If you die here, this world loses more than a knight or princess... it loses a beautiful future paved by your actions," Marcus reminds her of all the times Nolan praised them and how proud he always seemed of her accomplishments.

"Marcus... we should be paving that future together. A home... a family... Nolan wanted that for me as much, so I can't leave you here!" Helena pleads, now having to leap backward as the Knightfall descends faster.

"Helena, you can't have those things with a dead man, let alone one inside the Void. You need to escape, you need to live on! You are our legacy. I'll die a hero but you will become a legend! Now go!" Marcus's final words resonate with Helena, and she finally agrees. They whisper one last goodbye to one another, and with only moments to spare, Helena uses her one good wing to escape. Marcus watches her fly away and gives in to the enormous amount of suffering his body has endured. Lying prone on the ship's floor, he looks out the starry sky before closing his eyes.

"See you soon, Nolan..."

Upon their boats, the survivors of Riverhaven watch as the Knightfall crashes into the island surrounded by the Void. As the ship folds in on itself, flames burst from its engines upon contact with the island. On the shoreline, Liam watches as the horde of the undead ceases to move. The purple stones embedded in them fade to a milk-white color before the bodies fall dead to the ground. Not long after, a worn and nearly defeated Helena crashes into the sand, barely able to fly to land. Liam gets to her as quickly as he can, pulling her on his lap as he checks for signs of life. She is barely breathing but still alive. He holds her close before realizing she is alone. Liam looks out to the sea, and the smoke from the burning knight falls trapped within the Void's wall. He knows the worst has happened. He pulls Helena closer before bursting into tears. Few words escape his ragged breathing:

"I failed. I'm sorry Nolan, I failed them."

CHAPTER 48
THE
AFTERMATH

Chapter 48

The Aftermath

An impatient Zayn paces around his office once again back home in Goldleaf. Since his return, the other Disciples have put the Oren master on house arrest. Even after begging to see his dying father, his colleagues refused. He tries to pass the time by reading the many library books, but all he can think about is his time outside Goldleaf's wall. Zayn pulls the antidote Elizabeth gave him from one of his pockets. Staring at the vile hypnotizes him. In his hand, a cure for his father was given to him by the same person who put him on his deathbed. That is not why it fascinates him; instead, the fact that he holds a piece of her means even more. Zayn's trance is only broken when a knock comes from his door.

"I come with news, Master Zayn." Master Titus lets himself in. "Your father has requested your presence. As the elder, his wishes overrule any opinions."

"About time." Zayn quickly puts the vial back in his pocket. "It's been a day since I returned, and all they have done is treat me like I was his assassin."

"Zayn, be honest with yourself," Titus says as he escorts Zayn to his father's chambers. "To them, you brought the enemy into our home, then disappeared in the night with them."

"You were supposed to cover for that, remember?" Zayn attempts to pass the blame.

"I did; I told them the assassin returned and took you as well as the knight's hostages," Titus defends himself from the accusation that he did not fulfill his end of their agreement. "When you return only for a ship to crash into the Void shortly after, you raise too many questions."

"I told them my freedom was granted as an act of diplomatic faith after Elizabeth was taken into custody." Zayn reiterates the lie he told the other Disciples as if saying it aloud again will somehow bring truth to it." As for the ship, she honestly had nothing to do with that."

"Zayn, it is not I you need to convince. Even if there is honesty amongst your fabrications, you are on thin ice." The two Orens have reached their destination. "But this conversion can wait, your elder and more importantly your father needs to speak with you before it's too late."

Zayn reaches for the antidote in his pocket, intending to let Titus know he has a cure. Yet he doesn't; rather, he only thanks Titus for bringing him to his father.

Titus opens the chamber doors, revealing the Oren elder lying on his bed, surrounded by many flowers and gifts. Zayn approaches his bedside, and Titus closes the door to give them privacy. Zayn looks down at his dying father and is shocked by the difference he seems in such a short time. His already frail figure is now nearly nothing but skin on bone; his skin lacks all color other than the fungus-like green around his stab wound. His face was fully exposed due to all his hair falling out. The Elder opens his eyes; they, too, now lack color. He smiles at the sight of his son and reaches for Zayn's hand.

"Father save your strength, I have something that might—"

"Silence my boy, I need you to listen before I leave you."

"But father, you don't—"

"Boy, shut your mouth, or I'll use my dying breath to weld it close!"

Zayn knows his father is too stubborn to let him talk, so he gives in, hoping he'll finish his lecture in time for him to take the antidote.

"I need you to know how much I love you. My duties as an Elder left me little time to express that. Please know how much I regret that. Know that I've only pushed you as master because I know you will be a great Elder." His father's admiration makes Zayn teary-eyed. " But that time is not now."

His father's words take Zayn aback. It is well known that he is next in line to be Elder, so what could he mean by this?

"I don't understand, father. What are you saying?"

"You're rash, a symptom of your youth. Not to mention your obsession with the world outside our own is dangerous. Just look at what a handful of those vermin have done here."

"Father, it's not that black or white. There's complexities to every situation, this one included." Zayn is quick to justify his ideals.

"This is exactly what I'm saying, Zayn." Even in his weakened state, the Elder can raise his voice. "As long as you're hellbent on changing what has kept us safe for ages, you're just as much of a threat as our enemies. But I have faith you see the error in this way of thinking in time. Unfortunately, our people need a leader now." The elder points to a small desk with an ink pen and a scroll near his bed. Zayn walks over to it, picks up the scroll, and unrolls it. The words are written in the Oren tongue and are incredibly shaky. The elder worded this while in his ill state. Zayn takes a moment to review his father's intentions, piecing them together. After a few passes, though, he understands.

"My final order as Elder is to appoint Nigel as my replacement. He has always been loyal to our ways and will be a safe figurehead until you are ready." The Elder makes sure Zayn knows this is his dying wish.

"You can't seriously want this. For cycles you have been grooming me to be Elder, and now you're just gonna hand that to someone else. Is that how much you fear change?"

"What you want isn't change Zayn, it's mass suicide. The world out there doesn't want us and frankly we don't want to be a part of it. In time you'll see your childish ambitions were nothing more than a fairy tale. Now let me die in peace, with my son by my side."

Zayn returns to his father's bed, rolling up the scroll.

"Does Nigel already know?" Zayn questions as he shoves the rolled-up parchment in his pocket.

"No, I wanted you to be the first to know; it's only fair. I'd hope you'd be the one to tell them. Acceptance will go a long way to earning back the people's trust." The Elder again reaches for Zayn's hand.

Zayn holds his father's hand as he falls back to sleep. Once he rests, he kisses him on the forehead and leaves. He returns to his office, pushing a stack of books covering his fireplace. After starting a fire, he looks into the flames for ages. Zayn does what he thinks is best at a crossroads with himself and tosses the scroll with his father's dying wish into the fire. As the paper turns to ash, he reaches into his other pocket and pulls out the antidote. Once more, he looks over it before throwing it in the fire. Zayn wipes away his tears as he watches it all burn away.

"I love you father...you will be missed."

*****

On the other side of Grandiose, Liam has returned to Nolan's home. He has spent the day cleaning out the stable. Once empty, he begins digging a shallow square-shaped hole outside its opening. As dusk approaches, he removes a stone platter from his work wagon. Liam fits the stone into the hole, refilling any extra shape around it with dirt. Now done, he puts his tools away. As he does, a royal-appearing carriage pulls up. Expecting someone of authority, he wipes away his sweat and pats the dirt off his clothes.

To Liam's surprise, upon the carriage driver opening its door, none other than Helena steps out. Once again, in her human form, she stuns in a ruby red dress with the Greyscale family chest embroidered throughout. A golden tiara held up her ember hair. With nails done and done up with the finest makeup, Helena stands in front of Liam more heavenly than ever. She approaches him before reading the stone plate at the stable entrance.

"Loyal -Fierce-Heroic"
"Rest Easy Hornet"

"I am sorry we could not save her, Liam." Helena gives her condolences.

"No need to apologize, dear. Hornet lived two fulfilling lives. This stable will be more than enough to honor him." Liam goes for a hug before realizing he is dirty. "Oh, maybe that's not the best idea, I don't need to lose my head for soiling such an elegant garment." He jokes as he brushes more dirt from shirts.

"Believe me, I much rather dress like you." Helena pulls on the dress, trying to get comfortable. Together, they laugh.

"I heard the Council is sending you home," Liam inquires as he walks Helena back to the carriage.

"Unfortunately. My father is convinced the humans kidnapped me when I was young. Wouldn't even allow me to tell him the truth, but it doesn't surprise me." Helena sighs, foreseeing the upcoming aggravation. "The Council believed returning me home safely was the best way to quail his anger. Not once was I even consulted on the matter."

"Wouldn't you have time for a drink by the fire before you leave?" Liam offers, knowing how much good a little normalcy could do for them.

"You know the one perk about dawning the crown again? They pretty much let you do whatever you want." Helena gleefully accepts.

With nightfall approaching, Helena prepares the fire while Liam pours the drinks into the house. She finds solace in the warmth of the fire, but home just doesn't feel the same. Around the fire where sitting logs once laid sits three large stones, each with a rudimentary engraving.

"Nolan"
"Warrior-Leader-Brother"

"Creed" ◻
"Enigma-Savior-Free" ◻◻◻

"Marcus"
"Swordsman-Brave-Legend"

Even something as simple as the flickering light bouncing off their names gets Helena choked up. Soon, she finds a blanket draped over her shoulder and Liam handing her a drink. He sits next to her, and together, they look through the flames at their fallen friends.

"To be honest I had a hard time returning here at first. The home may be small but for the first few days it felt enormous," Liam confesses. "Carving helped clear my mind, expressing things I couldn't say out loud."

"I understand. As much as I don't want to go back to Dakuhm, I'm not sure I'd want to be here alone either."

"Well I won't be here much longer."

"No?" Helena questions.

"I've been reassigned." Liam worries Helena will be upset that he, too, is leaving where they all once called home.

"To another squad? And one not in Grandhaven?" Thankfully, Helena is more confused than upset.

"Not a new squad per se, but by request of Chief Ramon, I am to relocate to Riverhaven, where I will be a member of a group of knights there to assist with rebuilding the city." Liam takes a small sip of his drink, being notably seduced compared to his everyday drink habits. "Normally, my sentence wouldn't allow me to be part of such an endeavor, but heir apparent Regalia seems determined to please his other Council members."

"You have no idea." Helena responds with a tale of her own. "I had to sit in the Council chamber for one meeting to prove my existence to my father, and I don't think I've ever seen more brown nosing in my life."

"There is no secret when it comes to how smart Red and his brother are. Everyone knows they had a hand in Uther's attack, but they covered their tracks well." Liam takes a slightly longer drink. "Ramon says there will be a trial but, without evidence, it's only a formality. It is only a matter of time before Red is handed the crown."

"Certainly not; they must fear that their list of allies is thinning." Liam looks over with curiosity as Helena takes a sip of her drink. "Word is as reassurance of my safe return and the large sum being donated to Riverhaven's rehabilitation; President Newsome and the Regalias have proposed offering a Council seat to the Orens. Belief is that Ramon will also sign on, and upon my arrival, so will my father."

"Smart. And with Zayn now elder there's little doubt their offer will be accepted." Liam downs his drink. "After everything, it looks like Uther is getting his new world after all."

Helena and Liam sit in silence for some time. Helena stares into her drink, and a tear falls from it. "I truly tried to save him, Liam, please believe me." Helena's tears fall faster. "I was willing to jump in after him, but he insisted I get to safety. He talked about who I am, our legacy, and the world's need for me. He sounded so much like Nolan..." Liam pulls Helena in for a hug, letting her cry into his chest for as long as she needs. She continues her unnecessary plea for forgiveness through the tears. "I've let another loved one die, first my mother, then Nolan, Creed, and now Marcus. Yet everyone swore I was the final piece to some greater picture. What if they're wrong? What if I'm not a blessing but a curse?"

"No, dear, you're the one that's wrong." Liam lifts Helena's head and wipes away her tears. "You are greatness. You may not see it now, but whether it's Princess Krimson, knight Helena, or whoever you choose to be, the mark you leave on this world will be glorious."

"How can you all be so certain? I haven't done anything but run away or simply do my duty. And now I am on the way back to the same cage I fled from to begin with." Everyone's confidence in her continues to baffle Helena.

"The simple answer is that's what Nolan believed. Take from some, who had more years behind him than in front of him, who trusted Nolan. He promised me a squad and delivered. Then he told me he had found the greatest swordsman alive, and sure enough, a few cycles later, I was fighting side by side with Marcus. When he told me about you for the first time, he used one word: special. And it wasn't your skill with the bow or your immense beauty he spoke of, it was the warmth you bring." Liam turns Helena towards the fire. "Just as this flame brings us together, so will you the world. I don't know how and I doubt it will be easy. But as hard as this moment is and as dreadful as the path ahead may seem we have to believe…" Liam takes Helena and looks at the glistening moon above them together, and the wind carries the words over them:

"It will be alright."

End of Book One:
Knightfall

EPILOGUE
THE
NEXT STEP

Epilogue:

The Next Step

A tiny light flickers in a large, dark room as a familiar Elderly figure enters. He carries with him a cylinder carrying case with a blue glow shining through its seams. The man enters the room while whistling in a playful tone. Once inside, he places the case on a large desk just below the singular light. Next, he places his hand on a strange marking embedded in the desk.

The marking glows bright yellow, and suddenly, the room is filled with light. With the room fully lit, the man is revealed to be a Red Regalia. The room is a laboratory, with mechanical parts and surgical equipment hanging from every wall. Piles of assorted quartz stone fill every corner. An assortment of blood-stained maps and blueprints are scattered throughout. Most ominous is best described as a bed with a large black sheet covering it that takes up the middle of the room.

Red continues his whistle, seemingly unfazed by the concerning environment surrounding him. He pulls the cylinder case in front of himself and removes a piece of paper attached to it. Opening the note, he reads, *"Have fun. Love, your little brother."* After reading, he tosses it into a trash bin next to the desk, which instantly incinerates it. Then, he takes the case over to a wall with several levers in front of it.

Red pulls the levers peculiarly before touching another odd craving at the wall's center. Again, the carving glows, and once Red removes his hand, the wall creeps down into the floor. Behind this secret door is a large walk-in freezer filled with human body parts stored in large, liquid-filled glass containers. Red takes the case inside with him. As he walks deeper into the freezer, he passes an array of brains, hearts, lungs, eyes, and almost any other body part that one could think of, some labeled with hauntingly familiar names.

Once Red reaches an open spot on a shelf, he sets the case down on the floor. He twists the handle open the container and pulls at a glass jar with a human brain floating in it. After examining the specimen, he places the jar in the open space, locking it in a groove on the shelf. As he twists it in place, a label becomes viable, the name of which reads, "*Callahan.*"

Red leaves the freezer, the wall returning to its place as he walks out. With his brother's gift stored away, the soon-to-be king makes his way over to the bed in the middle of the room. The entire time, he was whistling the happiest of jingles. He grabs a chair and wheels it up to the bed on his way. He pulls the black covering off and, lying in the bed, is an entirely mechanical woman. Built similarly to the mechanical steed a knight would ride, the only other significant difference being a large set of metal wings attached to her back.

Red walks around the metal woman, picking up a few unrecognizable tools along the way. With all his equipment in hand, he sits before opening the woman's metal chest plate. Inside this cavity are thousands of wires, gears, and several small Q.A.S. engines. At the center of all these mechanics is a still-beating human heart. Red takes a moment to admire his work before he begins his tinkering. Sparks fly, and the sound of metal on metal echoes within the laboratory. Like a child playing with his toys, Red is devilishly gleeful. Throughout, he continues to whistle, only stopping to laugh at his internal jokes:

"A new world indeed."